THE CROWN'S SHADOW
OF FIRE AND LIES
BOOK TWO

NEENA LASKOWSKI

BELLES & OATS LLC

The Crown's Shadow

Copyright © 2023 by Neena Laskowski

All rights reserved.

This is a work of fiction. All names, places, characters, and events are fictitious. Any resemblance to actual individuals, events, or locations is entirely coincidental.

No part of this book may be reproduced in any form or by any electronic or mechanical means, including information storage and retrieval systems, without written permission from the author, except for the use of brief quotations in a book review.

First Edition published December 2023

Published by Belles & Oats LLC

Map Design and Internal Illustrations © Neena Laskowski

Cover Design © 2023 Moonpress

https://moonpress.co/

Identifiers:

ISBN: 979-8-9876368-2-4 (paperback)

ISBN: 979-8-9876368-3-1 (E-book)

THE CROWN'S SHADOW

NEENA LASKOWSKI

OF FIRE AND LIES
BOOK TWO

To the people-pleasers who are now in their reputation era.

THE SEVEN KINGDOMS OF VANERIA

THE MIST

THE WHISPERING SPRINGS

PONTIA

THE RED SEA

BORGAN

HEATHER LADIES

TETRIA

THE QUEEN'S CROWN

CONTENT WARNINGS

The Crown's Shadow includes elements that may not be suitable for all readers, such as references to alcohol consumption, mature language, characters in mourning, violence, gore, torture, manipulation, panic attacks, on-page death, and assault. If any of these topics are harmful to you, please proceed with care.

PRONUNCIATION GUIDE

Please note: these are fictional characters and places. The following pronunciations are simply the way the author pronounces them. However, if you, the reader, have a different way of pronouncing the names, please do so.

People

Cetia - *ket-EE-uh*
Domitius - *do-mi-TEE-us*
Esmeray - *es-mer-ay*
Euralys - *ur-el-ees*
Fynn - *fin*
Graeson - *grey-sin*
Danisinia - *dan-i-sin-EE-uh*
Dronias - *dro-NEE-us*
Jacquin - *ja-quin*
Kalisandre - *kal-ih-SAN-dra*
Laurince - *lore-INS*
Lothian - *loth-EE-in*
Loralaine - *lore-UH-lane*

Lysanthia - *lis-an-THI-uh*
Lystrata - LIS-chra-ta
Lucien - *lu-CEE-en*
Marsinia - *mar-sin-EE-uh*
Medenia - *muh-deen-EE-uh*
Myra - *MY-ra*
Phaia - *FAY-uh*
Rian - *RYE-in*
Sebastian - *sa-BASH-tin*
Sylvia - *sil-VEE-uh*
Terin - *TARE-rin*
Troia - *TROY-uh*
Valrys - *val-RIS*

Gods:
Barinthian - *bar-in-THI-an*
Misanthia - *mis-an-THI-uh*
Nerva - *nur-VUH*
Pontanius - *pon-TAN-EE-us*
Ryla - *RYE-la*
Sabina - *sa-BEE-na*
Tanzia - *tan-ZEE-uh*

Kingdoms:
Ardentol - *ARE-den-tall*
Borgania - *bor-GAN-EE-uh*
Frenzia - *Frenz-EE-uh*
Kadia - *Cade-EE-uh*
Pontia - *Pont-EE-uh*
Ragolo - *ra-GOL-o*
Tetria - *te-TRI-uh*

CHAPTER 1
KALLIE

Kallie gripped the railing, her weight pressing onto her wrists as she stepped across the chasm between the ship and the dock. Darkness had blanketed the sky hours ago, and the midnight breeze did little to cool her hot, sticky skin as the remnants of salt and fish lingered on it.

The boat ride from Pontia was excruciating. Without anyone to help her sleep, Kallie turned to the next best thing: whiskey. By the time the ship had docked in Frenzia, there wasn't a drop of alcohol in the decanter. The burning liquid, however, had done little to quench her nausea or dull her raging thoughts.

In truth, what Kallie needed was an outlet, a way to release her emotions.

An outlet the boat could not provide, unfortunately. Not with the prying eyes or the thin floorboards. Kallie couldn't even confide in her best friend without fearing that someone might overhear.

For the past couple of months, Kallie had tucked away any thought that might reveal her true motives to the Pontians or the man who could read her thoughts. In the months leading up to the choosing ceremony, Domitius had taught Kallie how to shield her thoughts.

Of course, Kallie no longer had to worry about the mind reader infiltrating her thoughts because Fynn was dead. Her *brother* was dead. All because of the choices she had made.

On the ship, she had yearned to lean on Myra, to seek solace in the one friend she still had. Yet she had remained silent. She would not give Domitius any reason to think she was a traitor. Blood or not, he was her father. He was the known, the familiar. The Pontians were nothing but strangers.

And yet . . .

Kallie inhaled, forcing the creeping feeling away. The smell of sea salt and fish was poison on her tongue, but at least she was on land. She needed a new distraction, a mission.

Beyond the pier, moonlight seeped through the blanket of fog. Somewhere in the castle upon the hill was her new target.

This time, she would not let her heart get in the way. She would focus on what she came here to do: capture King Rian's heart and steal his throne.

Leaning on the railing, she stumbled down the dock, yearning for the solid, unmoving ground. Kallie longed for a hot bath and a solid night of rest. Sebastian, on the other hand, had not stopped talking. Currently, he was bragging to Domitius about accomplishments Kallie could not care less about. During the voyage, the two men were often found lounging on the ship with drinks in their hands. Sebastian was not the only one reminiscing. Domitius also took advantage of the opportunity to relive past adventures.

At all hours, their voices seeped through the cracks of the old wooden beams of the cabin. Every time they rejoiced in their small victory over the enemy, nausea formed in Kallie's throat.

Did they not realize that they had started a war? Or did they not care? Perhaps they didn't. Perhaps they were too ecstatic about their victory over the unruly islanders. At first, Kallie had tried to join in on the revelry. Or at least she had pretended to until the seasickness claimed her, forcing her to crawl back to her room, drained and green. Even the pride oozing from her father's brown eyes couldn't keep her standing beside him.

But this was what she had wanted. For years, she had wanted to earn her father's respect, to be enough for him, and to celebrate their shared victory. How could she celebrate when sour guilt clogged her throat?

Kallie had betrayed the Pontians in the hopes of changing her father's opinion of her. Now, her body betrayed her in turn, and she only had herself to blame.

She had been grinning and bearing it for months. She needed a moment, one second, to let the mask fade away.

Unfortunately, now was not the time. So, with every step down the dock, Kallie buried those thoughts deep in her mind.

It was a habit of hers to let her mind wander to places it shouldn't, but she would get control over that little hiccup soon enough. Soon, she would have a queen's crown on her head and the Frenzian throne beneath her.

A hand fell atop hers, and a calmness seeped over her instantly at her friend's touch. Kallie met Myra's hazel eyes, and a soft smile graced her friend's lips as Kallie squeezed her hand. An instant rush of relief soared through her veins. While she hadn't had the time to talk to Myra openly yet, Kallie was grateful for her friend's unexpected presence nevertheless. On the ship, Myra had been a welcome companion. While Kallie was weak and tired, Myra's mere presence had quieted the raging sea that roared beneath the boat.

Peering at her handmaiden and friend, Kallie's mind cleared. She removed her hand from beneath Myra's.

She was on Frenzian soil now. It was time she stepped into her new role.

If Kallie wanted her father's respect, she would prove to him that she wasn't this fickle human who would let the sea break her. She was fire, and she would make the sea burn.

As she rocked her head in a small circle, the movement released the tension in her muscles. Her gait grew steady; her breathing became even. Then, masking her face with the indifference she had perfected long ago, she slid into the open space between the two men. It was time she stopped hiding.

Gaze forward and footsteps even, Kallie tipped her chin higher. She saw King Domitius's mouth twitch upward from the corner of her eye, approval embedded into the movement.

Beside her, Sebastian cleared his throat. "I've sent a messenger ahead of us to notify my brother of our arrival. It is later in the night than I had hoped we would return, but I am sure he will still want to greet both of you."

"Very well," Kallie said, flicking off a piece of dust from her shoulder as her heels slapped the brick road. She pushed her shoulders back. "In the morning, we shall meet and discuss our plans. You may think them naive, but sooner or later, Pontia will retaliate," Kallie said, her attention forward as she gained a slight lead in front of the men.

Sebastian's pace quickened. "King Domitius and I already—"

Kallie stopped in her tracks, extending an arm. Sebastian narrowly missed it.

Tilting her head, she cocked a brow. Sebastian believed Kallie to be a princess needing a knight, but she was so much more than a damsel in distress. "Let me make things clear, Sebastian. When I marry King Rian, I intend to make Frenzia my home. I *will* be a part of these conversations." Kallie's gift stirred beneath her skin. She was tired of the men around her keeping her in the dark. Darkness had become too close of an acquaintance for her liking, and she was determined to let the stars shine on the opportunities set before her.

She would no longer sit in the shadows. She took a step forward. "I will be heard. Is that clear?"

With murky green eyes, Sebastian uncurled his fingers. "Yes, Princess."

"Now," Kallie said, as a broad smile split across her face. "Let us meet my future husband, shall we?" She spun and continued down the winding stone path that led to the carriages.

The guard, awaiting their arrival, nodded to Kallie. When he extended a hand, Kallie placed her palm in his and stepped into the carriage, giving the men her back. As she sat, she straightened her skirt. Before docking, Kallie had changed into one of the many dresses Domitius had brought from Ardentol. The navy gown had a structured corset with tiny pearls woven throughout the embroidered design. It was simple, elegant, and designed with the fashions of Ardentol in mind. Completely different from the free-flowing dresses she had grown used to wearing the past few weeks in Pontia.

Her father followed after her and sat on the bench across from her. While Sebastian sat beside him, Domitius' gaze locked onto Kallie's. He tipped his head, a devilish smirk flashing across his face.

As the line of carriages took off, Kallie pushed back the curtain. She stared at the night sky with a smirk pushing at the corner of her lips.

Silence filled the carriage. Rocks crunched with each turn of the creaking wheels. Besides the few guards patrolling street corners and alleyways, the village was lifeless as they rode through the streets. No light streamed through the windows, and no people wandered.

Off in the distance, the silhouette of the Frenzian castle peaked through a thick layer of fog sitting atop the hill. Tall, iron fences surrounded the castle's property. Kallie's ankle burned as though the sight alone could rip open the freshly healed wound. But unlike the fence that lined the Pontian palace, even the frail body of a child could not fit through the space between the iron poles.

When they reached the front of the castle, Kallie stepped out of the carriage and took in the sight of her new home. Compared to other castles, the Frenzians favored a simplistic landscape. Clean, smooth stone led the way toward the main entrance. Neatly trimmed bushes lined the exterior walls of the black stone castle. Frenzia didn't need the extravagant gardens or luxurious fountains to appear grand. The Frenzian castle was a fortress, a stronghold. The perfect place to build an alliance and strengthen ties. Even without knowing their history, it was no wonder Domitius sought a union with the Frenzians. If a war were coming, Frenzia would be the diamond in a pile of sea glass.

Kallie should be happy that she was the key to establishing the alliance between Ardentol and Frenzia. Why, then, was there a heavy weight sitting at the bottom of her stomach as she stared upon the stone structure?

Small stones rolled over her feet as her father and Sebastian exited the carriage, pulling Kallie from her thoughts.

Domitius nodded to his guards in the carriage behind them. The Ardentolian guards began unloading Kallie's belongings from the carriages. Myra gave Kallie a meek smile before she returned her attention to the guards, directing them. The faint murmur of the guards searching the chests in the other carriages.

At the entrance, two guards pushed open the heavy iron doors, revealing the castle's interior shrouded by darkness and dust. Eager to meet her betrothed, Kallie strutted past Sebastian, who had stopped at the threshold.

Only a bare, heartless hearth greeted her. Dimly lit by a few scattered lanterns hanging on the walls and sitting on a couple of tables, the entryway of the Frenzian castle was dull, to say the least. The grey stone walls were bleak, cold, and empty of decorum. The ghosts of picture frames spotted the walls, the resemblance of any living memories stripped from them.

Kallie forced a smile as she lifted her chin. This was her new home. The blank walls only meant more space for new memories. A blank canvas to be painted with whatever her heart desired. A space to create, build upon, and form something new.

"King Domitius," said a stout woman, rushing into the room and falling into a curtsy.

Domitius made a halfhearted grunt in acknowledgment and passed the servant without a cursory glance.

The woman straightened and shrunk within herself.

Kallie, who still had not been acknowledged by the woman, cleared her throat, and the woman blinked.

While Kallie would do anything for King Domitius, a fact she had proven in Pontia, she would not be overshadowed. Her father had said Kallie would be the primary ruler over Frenzia once she married the king. That the day-to-day decisions would be hers to make. Yet here he was, greeted first by the staff while she remained no more than a second thought. Kallie didn't know if she would ever escape his shadow.

Still, she would try.

"Princess, you have finally arrived," the woman said after a moment. "I am Lystrata, the housekeeper."

Behind Lystrata, a few other members of the staff lined the hall. Sleep colored their countenances. The ends of the men's hair stuck up in odd directions. A woman's dress was ruffled with a piece of fabric bunched under her simple corset as if it was haphazardly put on. Kallie could feel her father's judgment, but she did not care if they looked as if they rolled out of bed a minute ago. She searched the line for the red hair belonging to the royal family. However, the king was nowhere to be seen.

Relaxing her features, Kallie returned her attention to the housekeeper. "As I am sure you are well aware, I was a little tied up."

The whites of the woman's eyes became more prominent. Clearing her throat, Lystrata tipped her head down. "My lady, I meant no offense. We were all worried about King Rian's bride when we heard you were kidnapped."

King Rian's bride, *not* their future queen. Another reminder of how everyone saw her. To the people, Kallie was a pawn in this political game. Little did they know that Kallie would be the one turning their king into her puppet.

"Prince Sebastian, welcome home," the woman said, curtsying as the doors clicked shut behind the captain.

"It is good to be back." Sebastian inhaled with his hands on his hips as if he could breathe the castle into his lungs. "Now, where is my brother?"

The woman rose from her bow, her fingers twitching at her sides. With a downcast gaze, she addressed Sebastian quietly, "He—"

Sebastian tossed his hands in the air. "By the gods, woman. Speak up."

Kallie gave Sebastian a sidelong glance. She couldn't help but wonder if this was what she had to look forward to, for she knew little about her betrothed. But if King Rian was anything like his brother, she had a strong inclination that she would not get along with him. She had no taste for men who silenced women, title or no title.

"Well?" Sebastian asked.

Lystrata's attention flicked to Kallie but just as quickly returned to Sebastian.

Kallie quirked a brow in question.

Eyes cast on the ground, Lystrata said, "The king is indisposed at the moment."

Kallie took a step forward, in line with Sebastian. "Indisposed?"

She had been around the lords of Ardentol long enough to know that being *indisposed* only meant one of two things. And from how Lystrata's body begged to shrink back into the shadows behind her, Kallie knew she would not like the answer.

"Yes, my lady, as I said, King Rian is indisposed," Lystrata said, repeating the word as if Kallie simply had not heard the woman. As if Kallie was a naive princess from a foreign kingdom who did not know the hidden meaning behind the word. Because the only reason a man would be indisposed was if they were preoccupied with other activities—activities a bride would not want to hear her betrothed participating in upon her arrival.

"If that is the case, please give your king a message when he is not *indisposed*," Kallie said as she lifted a hand, observing the sharp nails that needed extra maintenance after a week at sea. If her betrothed wished to treat her arrival with indifference, Kallie would also treat his absence as such. "Tell him his bride says hello."

The woman's brows knitted together in the center of her forehead. "Hello?"

Kallie nodded.

"Anything else?" Lystrata asked, waiting.

Kallie pursed her lips, tapping a finger against her chin. With a sharp glint in her blue eyes, she added. "Please tell whichever whore he is with that their time with him is short-lived and that they should make the most of it while they can."

The servant gasped, surprise flaming her cheeks. Yet Lystrata held her tongue, not bothering to convince Kallie otherwise.

"Oh, and one more thing." Kallie opened her mouth but closed it as she looked at the woman expectantly.

"Lystrata, my lady," the woman said, annoyance reddening her round cheeks.

"Lystrata," Kallie smiled softly. In truth, she had not forgotten the housekeeper's name, for she never forgot a name. Not that of a king, a long-distance relative, or a staff member. A name was everything. A name was power. Kallie had seen how her father used them as weapons, how people reacted when he addressed them directly. She had also learned from her father that forgetting a name could be just as powerful. The Frenzian staff needed to know that she was here to stay and that they would not deter her.

When Kallie spoke again, her voice was cold despite the fire brewing in the pit of her stomach. "Next time, you will do well not to insult my integrity or my intelligence."

Lystrata's eyes widened as the blood rushed from her face. "My lady, I—I—"

Kallie huffed, dismissing the woman. She turned to the rest of the staff. "Who can show me to my rooms? I am exhausted and have been looking forward to sleeping on a bed that is on solid ground."

"Princess Kalisandre," a young woman said, stepping out of line and curtsying. The handmaiden had pin-straight black hair, and, if Kallie had to guess, she was no more than Kallie's age, perhaps even younger based on her sweet, round face. "My name is Phaia, and I have been placed under your service as one of your handmaidens, courtesy of the king and Queen Mother. It would be my pleasure to show you to your rooms, Your Highness."

"Wonderful," Kallie said to the servant. She turned to Domitius. "Father, I will see you in the morning."

Domitius gave her a slight nod, and Kallie noted the small flame flickering within his gaze.

She turned on her heel and followed the young handmaiden. Her shoes clapped against the dusty floor, the sound ricocheting off the empty walls and down the dark hall as Phaia led her. With each step, Kallie reminded herself why she was doing this.

As the Princess of Ardentol, she has spent her entire life looking up at her father as he sat on his throne. While she was happy to be able to assist her father in the pursuit of unifying the seven kingdoms, she craved more. Frenzia was not only her opportunity to bring them one step closer to achieving that goal but also to grant her the freedom she desired.

For weeks, she had seduced, lied, and betrayed the people around her, her family, her blood. Pontia, however, was only the precursor for what was to come.

Now, it was time she stole the throne.

CHAPTER 2
GRAESON

GRAESON'S GAZE FELL TO THE WOODEN DECK WORN FROM DECADES OF men and women carrying their sorrows on their shoulders as they trudged down the dock toward the Black Lake. Years of grief were streaked into the scuff marks emblazoned on the oak boards.

Being here, standing at the edge of the sand, was not an unfamiliar occurrence to any of the onlookers present. Many had been in Graeson's shoes before, for carrying the dead was a tradition handed down from when the gods walked among them. People from all over Pontia had come here to send away the deceased when elders passed of old age or when missions abroad went awry. For a mortal, death was imminent. Death was inevitable. It was familiar to all. But that didn't make it any easier to deal with when a mother had to say goodbye to her son. Or when you carried your friend's body.

The weight of a lifetime of memories pressed down on Graeson's shoulders. The smooth wood dug into his calloused palms as Graeson carried the canoe with his best friend's name etched into the grain: Fynneares Andros Nadarean.

Unlike when Graeson had made the trek to the island off the coast of Pontia before, he was one of the people carrying the wooden canoe. This time, along with five others, he was the one who placed the canoe onto the deck and helped lift the small wooden structure into the lake. Who, once the canoe was set into the water, still couldn't shake its weight off his shoulders.

His body was rigid; his mind, blank. He was numb—they all were. For the past three days, they all were cold, empty, directionless shells.

Being numb was easy. It was what came afterward that Graeson feared the most.

Soon, the numbness would melt into something else, something too complicated to name. Something Graeson didn't have time for—not with the people around him falling apart. Not with the kingdom disintegrating to ash everywhere he looked.

So, instead of dealing with the complications, Graeson bottled it up. He would deal with it tomorrow. If not tomorrow, then soon.

Eventually.

When he had no other choice.

With the help of the other canoe bearers, Graeson pushed the boat away from the dock and deeper into the Black Lake.

This was the last time he would see his friend, his brother in everything that mattered but blood. After the Frenzians had attacked him, he had been nearly unrecognizable. Cotton wrappings covered Fynn's entire body, concealing the stark wounds that had been gracefully sewn closed. They all thought that Fynn was invincible. They never questioned whether he would rise to the throne. But now, Fynn would never be crowned king of Pontia, a kingdom now broken and almost burned to the ground.

Graeson ground his teeth together.

They should have been celebrating the return of their stolen princess, not grieving the loss of their future king.

As he stared at Fynn's body, Graeson felt helpless.

His hands fell from the oak, and his attention slipped to the lake. Graeson couldn't recall ever being this close to the dark waters. He had always maintained his distance, the superstition of the water ingrained into his mind. Only the dead were allowed to touch the water without consequences. That did not prevent the cursed water from calling to the living, tempting them to enter the pool.

Graeson's hand was only a couple of feet above the water, one hand out in the air and the fingers of the other curling around the end of the plank. Small ripples distorted his reflection. Even near the coast, the bottom of the lake was impossible to see, the water too dark, too clouded. Graeson knew he shouldn't touch it, yet it called to him, beckoned him, like a whisper on the breeze.

A little further, he would be able to feel the cool water touch his skin. Bliss awaited him. Just a few more inches and—

A snarl came from the back of his mind, and the sight before him fluttered in and out of focus as Graeson tried to force the dangerous thoughts away from his mind.

He couldn't think about why they were here. He *wouldn't* think about it. He could not afford to think about her, not right now. Not when she—

The tip of a bow scraped against the deck, and a flash of black leather boots appeared in his peripheral vision as Dani's sleek figure stepped toward the end of the dock, bow loose in her hand.

Graeson blinked. His jaw clenched, and pain shot through his teeth, the sharp sting clearing his mind. He wouldn't let the lake drag him down. He wouldn't let it cloud his mind. He had things to do. He had people to care for and a kingdom to help look after.

He pushed himself up, ripping himself away from the Black Lake's tug, lest Graeson wish to call upon the god of death to claim him next. He fixed his gaze on Dani. She didn't need to be the one to do this. She shouldn't be the one to set her husband's body ablaze. Graeson had tried to argue against it. They all did. But no matter what her friends and family said, no matter what they did, Dani wouldn't budge. It was her responsibility, she had said, not as his wife but as a general. If it were one of her soldiers in the boat, she would have been the one to release the flaming arrow and relieve them of their duty. Fynn deserved the best shot, and Dani was, without a doubt, the best.

When Terin squeezed her shoulder in reassurance, there was the tiniest flinch, the slight scrunch of the muscles in Dani's face as her husband's twin touched her. At the same moment, Graeson saw the dejection pass through Terin. They had been friends since they were children, yet his touch was no longer a comfort Dani wished for. To Dani, Terin's presence was an unintentional slap in the face. An ever-present reminder that her husband, her partner, was gone forever. Yet even though Fynn was dead, she would never be able to escape his face.

Terin's hand fell to his side, limp.

Dani stared at Fynn's canoe, and Graeson saw the brief moment flash across her face when she thought, why *him*? Why *hers*?

Terin took a slow, jolted step backward, adding distance between Dani and himself.

Dani's eyebrows scrunched together, shuddering at the thought that had slipped beyond her carefully crafted walls.

Since Fynn died three days ago, Dani had been no more than a ghost of her former self, barely there as she prepared for Fynn's final voyage to the Beneath. She had barely glanced at Terin. In truth, she hadn't given anyone attention. Still, her detachment was worse in Terin's presence.

Dani needed time.

At least, that's what everyone said.

Graeson, however, knew time could not heal all wounds. Time would lessen the pain. It would allow Dani to forget some of the heartache. But it was the forgetting, Graeson had learned, that hurt the worst. The moment when you couldn't remember their voice anymore or when you couldn't remember the exact shade of their irises or the lilt in their laughter.

Graeson had lived with loss his entire life, but his familiarity did not make this loss any easier. The only thing that helped, he found, was shutting down, letting the flame inside of him fade to nothing but an ember.

Dani, however, couldn't turn it off. She was not him. She was too human.

As Dani took a shaky breath, the canoe sailed away further into the Black Lake, into the thick fog that crawled over the water's surface. If Dani waited too long, she wouldn't be able to hit it, and Fynn's canoe wouldn't light up. His soul wouldn't leave his body and travel to the Beneath. Instead, it would be lost in the Between.

Still, Dani didn't release the bow.

The hairs on the back of Graeson's neck stood. She was running out of time, yet Graeson didn't move. He couldn't.

Then, Dani exhaled.

She dipped the oil-soaked bundle tied to the end of the arrow into the blazing torch perched at the end of the deck. She placed the arrow on the string of her bow and raised her arms. The tips of her fingers grazed her cheek as she pulled the arrow back.

Still, the canoe kept floating further and further away.

Still, time ticked by.

The tension in the air grew taut as the arrow remained between Dani's slim fingers and the bowstring remained stretched.

Dani closed her eyes and took a second breath. This time, however, there was no shake in her body or tremble in her hands. Her eyelids fluttered open, her chin tilted higher, and her back straightened.

Then, Dani released the bow, and Fynn's canoe went up in flames in an instant.

CHAPTER 3
KALLIE

With the door shut behind her and her new Frenzian handmaiden along with it, Kallie slipped down the length of the old oak door. The wood scratched and tugged on the fabric of her dress as she fell to the ground.

In the privacy of the queen's quarters and without the paper-thin walls of the cabin, the mask Kallie had carefully crafted disintegrated. The heaviness of the past week fell upon her, sinking into her body and forcing her to crumble onto the ground. The crash unsupported and unrelenting.

While Phaia led Kallie through the halls of the dark, foreign castle, Kallie kept her mask tight to her face as she mentally connected the path to the maps she had studied. Over the past several decades, Domitius had only been able to gather a few maps of Frenzia's castle. The maps were not all-inclusive. Corridors and sections of the castle were unlabeled on the maps, strange juts in the infrastructure depicted in the blueprints that were not normal. So Kallie took note of every side hall, every door they passed. Anything to distract herself.

By the time they had ascended several flights of stairs of one of the palace's five high towers, Kallie's legs ached. Days of being sedentary on the ship had done her no favors. Soon, she would need to return to a regular training routine. Although she did not believe she would be fighting masked assailants, she couldn't be found slacking.

Today, however, gravity pulled her down.

Beneath her, the bare wood floor stole any warmth left in her body as she sat against the queen's bedroom door. Before Phaia had left, Kallie had requested water to be delivered in the morning for a bath to scrub off the thick layer of salt and sweat sticking to her skin. Tonight, she had no strength to wash the sea away.

Reaching into the front of her corset, Kallie pulled out the folded-up painting with shaky hands. After folding and unfolding the stolen portrait a hundred times over the past week, permanent creases marked the fine parchment and started cracking. The subjects' faces, thankfully, were unmarked.

As she stared at the family portrait, her father's questions from that first night on the ship rang in her head.

Who has cared for you all this time, Kalisandre?

Who has trained you all of these years?

Who has promised you power, the power you otherwise would not have access to?

Has your time here softened you?

There was no doubt in her mind that he had heard her screams as Fynn died, no doubt that he had seen her crumble to the ground.

Had she grown sympathetic for the Pontian prince? Of course. How could she not? Fynn was her brother. But more than that, Fynn had a way of infiltrating someone's heart and making them care for the boyish, cocky prince.

A part of her would always care for the family Kallie had longed to have. She had spent years searching the Ardentolian castle for a painting of her mother, so she could put a face to the woman she did not remember. When asked, the staff would say that the king had requested all paintings of her mother destroyed. Now, Kallie knew that they had never existed at all. He had tricked an entire castle and made them all believe a lie. She once thought a portrait of her mother would give her the answers she sought, but holding the portrait in her hand now provided no clarity.

The five people in the portrait were her flesh and blood. Her family. So yes, a small part of her would always care for them, but that did not mean she had lost sight of the mission. All Kallie wanted was the truth. For her whole life, she had thought something was missing. For years, unexplained nightmares haunted her sleep. She loved her father, for he had taught her all she knew. But what was she supposed to do now when she had discovered that her father was the cause of some of those dreams? That the nightmares held some truth?

Kallie didn't have the answer.

A dull ache buzzed in her head. She pressed her palms on either side of her head, squeezing it as she took slow, deep breaths.

Birth father or not, King Domitius was the man who had raised her and cared for her all these years.

It did not matter that he did not share her blood.

It did not matter that he had lied to her. Her father had lied to her to *protect* her.

Why would he have trained her and provided her with an abundance of opportunities—opportunities she would not have been granted if she had been raised among her brothers—if he did not care about her? Domitius had given her a path and the tools she needed to achieve the power she craved. He, unlike her mother, had come for her. He had *fought* for her, unlike the people who shared her blood. Unlike her supposed *family*, he had not let a peace treaty restrict him. When a hole had been ripped into their carefully crafted plan, Domitius had done what he needed to do. Not only had he focused on what was important, but *who* was important: his daughter.

Domitius had come for Kallie because she was what mattered to him at the end of the day. Esmeray, on the other hand, had done none of that. When Kallie was taken as a child, Esmeray had stayed on her island.

Blood, Kallie realized, only dictated the color of your eyes, the texture of your hair, and the skin you bore. Not your values or priorities. Not your loyalty.

Domitius was right: she was *his* daughter.

She was not needed in Pontia, but Kallie was needed here. Her father needed her *here*. To solidify the alliance, to take the throne.

Her time with the Pontians did not soften her. If anything, it had made Kallie want the power that this arranged marriage promised that much more.

She was not angry at him. Domitius was not the one who had driven a blade through her brother's heart. He was not the one who had his men pile on top of Fynn, brutalize him, and rip him to shreds. He did not throw Fynn's body overboard. No, Sebastian was to blame for those wrongs. *Sebastian* was the one who had attacked him, the one who had given the orders to throw Fynn overboard when his body hadn't even grown cold yet. *Sebastian*, the man without a sense of humanity coursing through his bones, had done all that.

Anger rose within her, coating her blood and devouring her flesh. Her body shook against the door. Her retinas burned.

It did not matter if Sebastian was the king's brother. He would not be forgiven.

When she exhaled, Kallie released everything she had refused to feel since leaving Pontia. Anger, it seemed, was not the only emotion threatening to consume her.

Since boarding the ship, she had shoved her sorrows down and pushed away her traitorous thoughts to the wayside. After the last several months, it was practically second nature.

Kallie knew she had simply done what she had been assigned to do. However, somewhere deeper and further back in the shadows of her mind, past her loyalty for her kingdom and father, grief consumed her. Even though she knew she shouldn't because of her commitment to her father, she wept for the family she had given up.

For the first time in a week, Kallie let herself mourn, and the tears were a torrent—a flood she had prevented from falling for too many days.

She knew she had no right to mourn. Fynn may have been her family, but she had betrayed him. She had betrayed all of them.

She knew it had to be done, for there was no other way to prove herself to her father, to prove to him that she was worthy of a crown. That she could be trusted when distance separated them. That was all she had wanted. She would have done anything to earn her father's respect.

Before.

Before she had known who the Pontians were. Before she had known they were her family by blood. Before she had discovered that she had been granted the ability to manipulate minds not by the whims of a god, which is what she had once believed, but because it ran in her veins. Her ability was more than some blessing or gift granted by chance. It was *who* she was. A manipulator.

Kallie didn't know how to be anyone else. She didn't know if she could.

She might have been Pontian by blood, but she wasn't one of them. Not even close.

She was a fraud.

For weeks, she had masqueraded as someone who had believed everything the Pontians had told her. To them, she was a victim, someone lost to the darkness.

Slipping on a mask was nothing new. She had manipulated hundreds of people before. But this time, she had fallen too deep into her role. At some point, Kallie, the girl who had vowed against love, had learned to care for someone other than her father and handmaiden. She had learned to care for people who didn't even belong to her kingdom. The enemy.

Now, Kallie wasn't sure where she belonged.

At the beginning of the voyage south, Kallie had allowed Domitius' approval to consume her mind. On that first night, pride had lit Domitius' face as he clinked glasses with Sebastian during the first meal on the way back. He had cheered the soldiers for their successful rescue of the stolen bride. With Kallie's safe return, he was one step closer to uniting the seven kingdoms. Kallie should have been thrilled to be a part of it, yet a sour taste had coated her tongue.

The rescue mission had always been a part of the plan, even though it had happened sooner than Kallie had expected. Still, she had accomplished her father's assignments nevertheless. She had infiltrated the Pontian kingdom, strengthened her gift, and uncovered more about the abilities of her enemies. She had learned that her brother could force his victims unconscious, her sister-in-law had an uncanny ability to track down animals and people, and her mother could recall a person's memories. And that was only the beginning of what the Pontians could do with the blood of the gods running through their veins. However, like Kallie, each user had limitations on how far they could stretch their gifts. Strengthening one's gift was a skill, and it was tied to binding oneself to one's immortal ancestors and opening oneself up wholly and completely.

It was no wonder Kallie had struggled to strengthen her gift before. A part of Kallie—a part that was so intrinsic to the blood that ran through her veins, to her very own history—had been closed off.

Still, this victory was not sweet. It burned her throat and shook her body. As the memory of that night on the ship came rushing back, tears streamed down her face faster than she could swipe them away.

THE CROWN'S SHADOW

A FRENZIAN SOLDIER WHISTLED, and the crew's chatter halted as they turned toward the King of Ardentol. Some, Kallie noticed, rolled their eyes as the foreign king demanded their attention. Others only half listened, simply happy to have their cups full of mead. Still, Domitius lifted his cup. And by the request of a foreign king or not, the soldiers listened when someone lifted their cup with the promise of drinking and hollering.

Sitting beside Myra at one of the tables bolted to the deck's floor, Kallie silently raised her cup, her hand trembling. They had only been on the sea for a few hours, but her stomach was already churning, her body growing weak.

"A final round of toasts," Domitius began as he overlooked the crowd before him. "First, to you, the brave soldiers who fought tirelessly tonight."

Cheers erupted as the Frenzians shouted into the sea-coated air, "To us!"

Domitius lifted his glass again. "To the soldiers who were lost tonight, gone but never forgotten."

A mournful silence followed as the soldiers raised their cups to the sky and then tipped them down so splashes of mead hit the floor, commemorating their fallen comrades.

Kallie, too, poured an ounce of the alcohol onto the ground, allowing her grief to show for a single moment before she had to bottle it up again. When she lifted her head, Domitius was watching her.

She took a sip of the mead, swallowing hard as the mask of indifference returned to her face, an act that took Kallie little effort now.

Domitius held her gaze, unmoving. "And to my daughter, Kalisandre. Thank the gods you are back in our graces, safe and unharmed by those Pontian brutes."

The soldiers on the ship shouted, loudly and drunkenly, "To the princess!"

Kallie gave a small smile to the soldiers who looked her way before taking another sip of her drink.

Kallie should have been happy. She should have been rejoicing with the crew. For years, she had tried to gain her father's approval, his respect. In the past, no matter what she had done, she had struggled to achieve it. Yet when

Kallie had finally earned Domitius' approval, she struggled to celebrate it. The red stain on the ship's deck consumed her vision. Images of Fynn dead on the ground, his blood smeared on the wooden boards resurfaced. The false happiness faltered. Her lip twitched, and the backs of her eyes burned.

Beneath the table, delicate fingers wrapped around Kallie's wrist, and Kallie leaned against her friend.

Kallie was thankful Myra had managed to escape the Pontian castle and board the ship before they had departed. Her friend had surmised that something was amiss when she spotted Sebastian and his men carrying Kallie out of the Pontian castle, so she followed them.

As Kallie focused on her friend's touch, on the faint floral notes beneath the smell of old smoke, Kallie's nerves calmed.

IF ONLY A FRIEND *could mend a broken heart*, Kallie thought.

Myra had always been able to make Kallie feel somewhat put together. Unfortunately, Myra was not with her right now, so Kallie couldn't rely on her friend to help take away the pain. Perhaps it was for the best. Because when Kallie was alone at night, the thoughts always came tumbling back. Maybe it was time she succumbed to them.

When Kallie was alone in the cabin on the ship, she tried to drown out the thoughts and drink them away. She didn't want to remember the sacrifices she had made or the ultimate betrayal she had committed in order to arrive at Frenzia's doorstep. However, despite her best attempts to flood her mind with liquor and allow the darkness of sleep to be a reprieve, Kallie had been unsuccessful. Even in her dreams, the gods were merciless. They tormented her with images of her brother being beaten, Dani's screams, Graeson's unwavering stance on the sea, and the disappointment on everyone's faces when they realized Kallie had given an enemy a secret code without anyone's knowledge. And the worst part: she couldn't deny the truth this time.

She knew why she did it, yet the pain wouldn't stop. As the memories consumed her, Kallie sat helpless, paralyzed.

Her father believed her emotions made her weak. If he could see her now, he would think she wasn't strong enough to lead a kingdom.

Kallie, however, was not weak.

Even when she pretended to lose against the Pontians when they attacked or when she let them capture her time and time again. She had never been weak. But sometimes, one had to lose the battle to win the war.

There were many ways to show one's strength. Fighting was an obvious display of one's physical ability; running or riding horseback, another. But there was also strength in waiting—waiting for one's prey to relax, waiting for them to drop their guard, waiting before one let their arrow loose. Yes, there was strength in that.

Strength could be seen in knowing when to play the game versus when to put someone out of their misery, to dig the dagger deeper into the victim's heart.

And then there were the moments of private strength—the quiet strength. The moments when a person was left alone. When a person was honest with themselves, and when they finally shed the mask that they tricked themselves into believing was real. When a person was forced to reveal their true self. It was not flashy. It did not require the person to wield a heavy sword or a shining coat of armor. It would not result in some medal of honor. It required a different sort of strength. Something far more difficult.

Honesty.

And for the first time, Kallie allowed herself to be honest with herself, and the tears fell freely from her face.

Tears were not weakness, she reminded herself. Tears were a sign she was human. A sign she cared. Tears showed strength. Despite what her father thought, the ability to mourn, to shed one's skin, and to show vulnerability was true strength.

With each tear that rolled down her face came a truth that Kallie had buried within her mind. As each tear fell from her face and into her palms, Kallie allowed herself to accept the three truths she had been harboring inside:

> 1. She had a secret family which she did, in fact, care for despite knowing she shouldn't. She was the reason her family's home had been attacked and burned to the ground. Although she had not pushed the blade through Fynn's chest, her choices had led to his death.

> 2. Guilt may have plagued her thoughts, but she was unwilling to give up her quest for power.

> 3. Kallie no longer trusted anyone.

Once the truths piled into her palm, she let them slip through the spaces between her fingers and fall to the ground, where they melted into the floorboards.

She pushed herself off the floor and folded up the family portrait.

There would be no more tears.

CHAPTER 4
KALLIE

Kallie awoke sweating and disoriented as she searched for the comfort of something familiar in a foreign room. A room much too large for the limited number of belongings in it.

The walls of the queen's quarters were charcoal black, and the deep color swallowed any light that seeped through the thin white curtains. Only a large bed, a small vanity with a short stool, and the three wooden chests from the ship, nearly overflowing with custom Ardentolian dresses, occupied the room. The rest of the room was bare, cold, and lifeless.

Last night, Phaia had informed Kallie that while these were the queen's quarters, the former queen had not used them. According to the handmaiden, Tessa favored her late husband's quarters over hers. When King Lothian died and her son took his place, Tessa moved into a different section of the castle that wasn't filled with memories of her husband.

Kallie did not fault the former queen for sharing her husband's quarters. Still, the staff could have at least maintained the space and outfitted it for Kallie's arrival. But they hadn't, even with the extra time to prepare.

Kallie's brows furrowed.

Unless the staff had believed that Kallie was never going to arrive. . .

First, Rian's blatant absence last night because he was *indisposed*, and now this.

Kallie threw the blankets off her sticky skin.

"Morning, Kals!"

Kallie inhaled sharply at Myra's bright voice calling out from the closet.

Myra peered around the closet door, her smile wide and straight blond hair shining. "How are you—" Myra cut off her question as she inspected Kallie. She hurried forward, a satin sky-blue dress scrunched against her chest. "Are you all right, Kallie?"

Kallie forced a smile, but her lip twitched at the corners. "Only a nightmare."

Myra sat, her knees lightly bumping into Kallie's. She placed a hand atop Kallie's and squeezed it. "Do you want to talk about it?"

Kallie shook her head. Talking, she realized, wouldn't make the piercing screams disappear from her memory; it wouldn't prevent the next nightmare from coming. What Kallie needed was to forget, to move on.

"I just need a bath."

Myra squeezed her hand again before releasing it. "I'll go prepare it."

Myra stood, but before she could walk away, Kallie reached for her hand, tugging her back. "I appreciate your help, but I think some time alone would do me well."

Concern swam in Myra's hazel eyes. "Are you sure?"

Kallie nodded.

"All right," Myra said, shifting on her feet. She bit down on her lip. "If you need anything, though—"

Kallie dropped Myra's hand. "I'm fine, Mys. Truly."

Myra sighed but nodded and left the room, tossing a small, sad smile at Kallie before she closed the door behind her.

Kallie squeezed her eyes shut and counted to ten.

Myra's presence was usually a comfort Kallie sought out, but today, she couldn't bear to see those sweet, hazel eyes staring at her, full of sympathy.

At ten, Kallie headed into the attached bathing chambers. She found the pail of water she had requested last night already waiting for her. The coals beneath the water bucket were growing cold. She dipped a finger in the water. Still warm. Not bothering to fill the tub, Kallie let her nightdress fall to the floor and stepped into the tub. The mint and rose scent of the soap filled the air, and she scrubbed away the lingering stench of the sea from her skin. If only the water could wash away the dirt beneath her skin.

Once done, she dried off and put on the robe lying on the stool beside the tub. As she towel-dried her hair, she headed toward the chests filled with her belongings and ignored the wrinkled light blue dress Myra had picked out. The chest's hinges creaked when she pried it open, and various shades of blue spilled out. She pushed past the scratchy fabrics. Since the trunks had been packed in Ardentol at the king's request, Kallie had no say in the items inside and did not have the energy to examine them on the ship. She snatched a dark navy dress that, in the shadows, appeared black and readied herself.

She had a king to meet.

THE LATCH CLICKED BEHIND HER, and Kallie slipped into the vacant hall.

Flickering shadows danced across the dark stone walls. With only a few windows sprinkled across the palace walls, the primary light source came from scattered torches.

This was not what she expected of the military stronghold. Then again, Kallie never had time to think about her future home since she had been focused on the Pontian mission. Before, it was more important for her to learn about the island's layout than it was to know about Frenzia's. That mission posed more danger since her cover could have been blown at any minute. If Fynn had been able to break through the manipulation she had placed upon him during their dance that first night and read her thoughts, everything would have been ruined. There had been no room for mistakes.

However, as Kallie wandered through the halls alone past dawn, she regretted her negligence.

These days, regret was a shadow trailing after her. And with each passing day, the shadow only grew longer.

She did what she had to do for her people, for her crown, Kallie reminded herself. She needed to focus on that and follow the plan: win the king's heart, finalize their marriage, and steal his throne.

To do that, she needed to find King Rian.

Based on the simple blueprints of the castle she had previously studied, the queen's quarters were not too far from the king's. Kallie envisioned the map as she continued down the path.

As she walked, she surveyed the castle and drew a mental list of things she wanted to change and add, like vibrant paintings, mirrors, and perhaps a small liquor cabinet for her rooms.

When Kallie reached the end of the hall, a single window overlooked the small garden, and Kallie peered through it, her palms pressing against the window sill. Rose bushes lined the castle's exterior walls and formed a circle around a solitary bench. In the early morning hours, a thick blanket of fog crept over the ground and crawled toward the flowers, filling any nook it could find. Through the mist, Kallie spotted a few scarlet buds preparing to bloom, a blood stain on the fallen clouds.

For a moment, Kallie's gaze lingered there. When nausea

returned, she forced her attention beyond the garden. Pine trees were scattered across the property before leading to the black iron fence that encircled the palace's perimeter. All in all, the castle's landscape was muted. The colors dull, the air thick with a haze. Even outside the castle, the kingdom mourned their late king, who had passed two months ago. Death was written all over the castle's walls and lands as though there was no escaping it. As if a permanent mark of grief stained the earth.

Kallie bit down, her jaw clenching.

She went to pull away from the window but stopped when she spotted a lit candle sitting on a window sill in one of the other towers. In the flickering light, a golden crown sparkled.

Triumph twitched at her lips.

Found you.

King Rian might have refused to greet her last night, but Kallie didn't have a problem going to him first. She would be cordial, kind. She would be the good little princess her father trained her to be. Whatever it took to win the young king's heart.

Then, she would do what she was best at: she would stab it.

PORTRAITS FRAMED in gold-coated wood covered the hall of the king's wing. It was the first area of the castle Kallie had visited that had any decor on the walls.

To her left was the portrait of Lothian Dronias. It had been years since she had seen him in person. The former king stared at her with a blank expression, bringing with it a pang of guilt that Kallie immediately swallowed. The central point of his golden crown was painted with a steady hand, its point as sharp as an arrow and embellished with bright red rubies. The crown was the only object painted with such precision and detail besides the king himself. The charcoal background was blurred out, having been deemed unimportant by the artist.

Glancing down the hall, Kallie noted that the rest of the paintings were painted in a similar manner. While the brush strokes changed here and there as the artist changed over the years, the focal point remained the same throughout the portraits. Just the men and their crowns.

Based on the brilliance of the hues, the absence of cracks in the paint, and the royal's apparel, the paintings at the front were more recent. That meant...

Kallie spun around.

She approached the painting across from Lothian and brushed a finger down the gilded frame. She had never seen Rian before, not even a portrait, so she only had Lothian's and Sebastian's features to go off when creating a mental depiction of her betrothed. Based on his portrait, the image she had made hadn't been too far off, for Rian shared some similarities with the men in his family. The red hair, green eyes, and sharp chin all belonged to his father. But there were more differences than similarities. Unlike his brother and father, either because of a change in artist or the artist's choice, Rian's shade of hair was a touch brighter, a smidge deeper, bolder. In the portrait, it was more of a burned copper rather than the fiery orange belonging to Sebastian and their father. Rian's skin was also darker, not as fair as his father's and brother's. Like in a portrait of his mother that Kallie had seen, it was a light brown with a golden undertone. Rian's gaze was also softer, gentler than the hungry green glare Kallie had grown accustomed to from Sebastian. Kallie had spent over a decade studying portraits, and the brush strokes above his cheeks suggested that the painter had attempted to hide the purple bags beneath Rian's eyes. Despite their attempt, grief bled through the pigment, making the sorrow on the young king's face a permanent mark on the walls.

Rian was a king granted his crown before he was ready.

Her father always said that one's misfortune was someone else's gain. Perhaps Rian's sudden rise to the throne would make it that much easier for Kallie to steal it from him.

Kallie tilted her head. While she had never preferred redheads, she supposed Rian wasn't too bad to look at if the painter could capture his likeness accurately. One might even argue that he was handsome, dashing even—sadness and all. The combination of his features was both unique and striking.

But not as striking as the man who appeared when Kallie closed her eyes.

Kallie bit down on her tongue as thoughts of Graeson tried to surface. She refused to think about him or the rising pain in her chest. A couple of months with him was nothing. A mere blip in her life. It didn't matter if they had a history (one she could barely remember). There was no future with him. She had made sure of that.

Kallie turned on her heel.

She swept her gaze over the rest of the portraits as she marched forward. Even though Vaneria had split into the seven kingdoms only one hundred years ago, the hallway of kings would have suggested otherwise. Every few feet, a new pair of eyes followed her. Hundreds of faces stared at Kallie as her heels clicked against the floor. One after another, men wore the same sharp, gold crown until a handful of portraits down the hall where there was a change. The golden crown disappeared, replaced by a simple gold ringlet encircling the men's fiery heads. These were the lords of the Frenzian territory before the Great War and before there were kings and queens of the land.

Kallie twisted the ring around her finger. With each passing portrait, one fact became glaringly obvious: Frenzia had never been ruled by a woman. Not unlike most of the kingdoms of Vaneria— besides Pontia and Tetria, that is.

Kallie was tired of the traditions and the roles she had to play. Unfortunately, she still had a role to play to earn her seat. Winning Rian's heart was one thing, but winning the hearts of the people might prove to be another.

Nearing the end of the hall, Kallie slowed her pace as voices, muffled and unfamiliar, seeped through the crack beneath the door. Having crept closer, Kallie put her ear against the wood.

"Does it matter, Rian?" a woman asked from the other side. Her voice was mature and as solid as the stone walls of the castle.

"Of course, it matters! I made a promise," a man—Rian presumably—answered. Unlike the woman, his voice shook, not less confident than the woman but more strained.

With furrowed brows, Kallie pressed the side of her face firmly against the wood.

"*You* made no such promise," the woman shouted. "Your brother did."

Sebastian? Could Rian possibly mean—

"And whose fault was that?"

"Rian, do not start this with me. You know as well as I do that you needed to stay here. Your *kingdom* needed you here, not at some frivolous ceremony that we all know was purely for show." The woman huffed. "That man has always been obsessed with his reputation and appearance. If he has an opportunity to show off his wealth or success, he will take it. The girl will no doubt be the same."

Kallie's nails bit into her palms as she listened to the woman insult her and her father. Was Domitius boastful about his accomplishments? Sure, but for good reason.

Insult aside, Kallie now understood why the king didn't greet her last night. He didn't want to marry her. If that was the case, Domitius was not the only king interested in upholding his reputation. Why else would he have sent Sebastian to retrieve her?

Somewhere on the other side of the door, Rian sighed. "I know, Mother. I know I had to stay, but—"

"But if you had left," Tessa said, interrupting, "it could have destroyed our people's faith in you, Rian."

"I understand that, Mother. I stayed, didn't I?"

Tessa grunted in response.

Rian continued, "If I break this promise, I could lose the faith and respect of not just our people but Vaneria as a whole. You do not wish that for me, do you?"

Kallie clenched her jaw. Her suspicions had been correct. The former queen was trying to end her son's marriage before it even began. Kallie, however, would not allow that to happen. She had already risked enough for this engagement to lose her crown before acquiring it.

"Fine!" Tessa shouted. "But you need to understand that there is more at work here than it may seem. Your brother should not have made promises that were not his to give. We had thought we were in the clear, but here she is. At the end of the day, *you* are the king now. It is your problem, your choice. But I warn you, if she is anything like her father, do not let your guard down ."

Kallie took several quiet steps away from the door when heels clapped against the floor on the other side.

The door cracked open an inch before it halted. "If you must keep your word, we will find a way to work around it. No matter the cost."

Tessa pushed open the door, but when she saw Kallie approaching, the former queen took a jilted step out of the room. She slammed the door shut before Kallie could peer inside the room.

"Queen Tessa," Kallie said, curtsying and pretending she had not heard their entire conversation.

Creases formed at the corner of Tessa's eyes. "I believe it is Queen Mother now. Especially since you are to be queen soon enough, Princess Kalisandre."

Kallie offered a small smile, one meant to soothe rather than threaten, but Tessa's gaze barely softened.

Tessa was a woman about to lose her power. No doubt she would be on the defensive. While Kallie never enjoyed making herself appear smaller, especially in front of other women. She would need to tread lightly here. If Tessa were threatened by Kallie and her father, Kallie would show her just how conniving she could be.

Kallie's smile turned shy, her gaze dropped, and the lie left her lips with ease, "From what I have heard, those are tough shoes to fill, Queen Mother."

In truth, Kallie knew Tessa was beautiful, but beyond that, she had heard little about the queen. Tessa preferred to hide in the shadows of her husband. However, Kallie was not so naive to think that the woman's beauty or quiet leadership meant that the woman was not a threat to Kallie's future rule.

"You are too kind, Kalisandre," Tessa said with a tight smile.

Kallie giggled softly and then glanced behind the queen.

Tessa's hand fell from the doorknob, and she folded her hands in front of her stomach. She tipped her head to the side. "Is there something I can help you with, my dear?"

Kallie held back the eye roll and donned a look of innocence as she fiddled with her fingers. "I was hoping to speak to your son. Unfortunately, we arrived rather late last night, and he and I were unable to meet. The staff, Lysandra?"

"Lystrata," Tessa corrected.

"Yes. Lys-stra-ta said King Rian was unavailable due to the late hour."

"I see," Tessa said, glancing back at the door as Kallie waited.

Kallie cut through the growing silence, stepping forward. "Is Rian available?"

The queen's gaze flew back to Kallie as though she had forgotten

Kallie stood there at all. Tessa shook the expression from her face and pursed her lips. "Oh," Tessa cleared her throat. "No."

"No?" The ice in Kallie's throat was potent even in that one word.

Tessa shrugged. "My son is busy. He is a king, after all. He'll find you when he is available." She flicked a hand in the air. "Come. Let us find Phaia. She will show you around in the meantime." The queen glided forward and encouraged Kallie to follow with a wave.

Kallie, however, hesitated. She did not want to follow the queen. She did not want someone else to show her around. What she *needed* was to meet Rian and ensure their wedding was set. While Rian might wish to remain faithful to his word, his mother, on the other hand, was bound and determined to find a way to thwart it.

A warm hum buzzed in her stomach. Kalie could easily manipulate the woman and force her way through those doors. But her gift would only get her so far in this situation. She had to play the long game.

Perhaps what Kallie needed the most right now was to get to know the former queen. Maybe Tessa wasn't the quiet queen everyone believed her to be. After all, people far too often misjudged women, belittled their work, and dismissed their quietness for ineptitude.

With a saccharine smile, Kallie turned her back on the king's doors and followed the former queen down the hall.

Staff rushed from room to room only to pause when they saw the women walking.

Men and women whispered in each other's ears, and the spot on the back of Kallie's neck prickled as they sent pitied looks in her direction. Despite their sordid attempts to keep quiet, the wind carried their whispers to Kallie.

"Poor girl captured by those assailants," one woman mumbled.

"Helpless to even protect herself," another whispered.

"What do you think they did to her? Do you think she is still a good fit for the king?"

"Do you think she's still normal after that?"

"Bless the gods, Prince Sebastian was there to rescue her."

"I heard he killed twenty of them."

"I heard Prince Sebastian burned their castle down."

"I heard the Pontian prince tried to capture her again, that he became animalistic, feral."

They all believed that Kallie had been traumatized and brutalized when she was captured, that the Pontians were horrendous people who had dragged Kallie by her ankles across Vaneria. But in truth, she was the one who had harmed them.

However, none of them would learn about that. None of them would discover that it was all part of King Domitius' elaborate plan to get her on the throne, to align another kingdom more permanently with Ardentol. They didn't know that King Domitius had orchestrated the whole event so that Kallie could better understand her gift and learn about her enemy.

No one knew that she had sacrificed her men, her guards—her heart—in the pursuit of something greater. In the quest for power.

If they did, they would know who they should fear.

"Phaia!" Tessa's voice echoed in the barren palace, shaking Kallie from her spiraling thoughts. Stopping at the landing in the middle of the staircase, Tessa pressed her palms against the railing and looked down at the floor. After no response, Tessa shouted again, "Lystrata!"

The housekeeper popped her head out of one of the side rooms. "Yes, My Queen?" Lystrata asked.

Tessa cleared her throat, throwing a sideways glance at Kallie. "Where is Phaia? She should have been outside our guest's rooms this morning. Yet it seems that she is nowhere to be found. I should not have to go searching for her."

Lystrata shook her head in disappointment. "Of course not, My Queen. I believe I saw her assisting in the kitchens. I will find her at once."

Before the housekeeper could disappear, Tessa added, "And Lystrata, please remind Phaia of her duties."

With a quick nod, Lystrata disappeared back into the room.

Tessa groaned in exasperation, mumbling something unintelligible about the new staff.

As they waited, Kallie examined the large space. At the top of the cement walls, sunlight filtered in from several small windows and provided only enough light to illuminate the foyer. It made the ample space shrink around her, suffocating her. Everything about this castle —from the empty, blank walls to the lack of light—was strange and unfamiliar. She did not know why the Frenzians had an aversion to natural light, but it was as apparent as the darkness blanketing the floors.

To compensate for the lack of sunlight, candles littered the room: large ones, small ones, tall ones, gilded ones, half-melted ones. Most of the flames had gone out by now, but the candles that were still lit only made the air thick with smoke and wax.

"Why the lack of windows?" Kallie asked.

Tessa's foot stopped tapping. "What do you mean, my dear?"

"Well, one would think for a room of this caliber that there would be more windows, more natural light."

Tessa leaned her back against the railing, sighing. "If you are to be Queen of Frenzia, it would do you well to learn the history of our people." Tessa cocked her head to the side. "Frenzia is known as the military stronghold of Vaneria. Do you know why that is, Kalisandre?"

"Because Frenzia holds the largest military, of course."

Tessa laughed, the sound filled with annoyance and bewilderment. "Oh, my dear, that is only the tip of the iceberg."

Kallie dug her nails into her palm. If this woman called her dear one more time, Kallie's mask would surely fall. She could only be patient for so long.

Tessa, however, was oblivious to Kallie's annoyance and continued, "Frenzia is one of the oldest territories in Vaneria. The lords who governed the territory before there were kings were some of the wealthiest men in Vaneria. Unlike some men who hold on to their money as if it could grow legs and run away without a second thought, the old Frenzian lords used their money to find and pay the greatest researchers and historians in the world, beyond even Vaneria. They knew, even then, that while money was great to have, knowledge was priceless. Especially knowledge that no one else held in their possession. Knowledge is power, Kalisandre. It would do you well to remember that."

Frustrations aside, Kallie listened attentively to the former queen as she revealed insights into the Frenzian kingdom Kallie had not been privy to before. Her father and Ardentolian instructors had only ever stressed the kingdom's prized military. They had never brought up the kingdom's search for knowledge.

Although, Kallie wondered how any of this had to do with the lack of windows—a question too frivolous to ask aloud.

"How do you think improvements are made to weapons? To barricades? To armor?" Tessa asked, trailing her fingers across the banister. "Progress is made through research and experimentation. The lords of old put their heart, soul, and treasuries into funding various research programs to improve not only the people's way of life but the equipment and infrastructures that protected that life."

Tessa glided over to a nearby window. With long, red nails, she tapped on the glass. The sound was sharp in the surrounding silence. "What are windows made of, Kalisandre?"

Kallie blinked. "Glass."

"Glass is fragile, easily breakable." She tapped on the glass once more, her lips pursed to the side. "What do you think people would do to acquire knowledge?"

Kallie didn't have the chance to answer.

"A smart person would do whatever it took to gain access to knowledge." Only a few feet away from Kallie now, Tessa raised a brow. "Some might even kill, steal, or lie for it."

Kallie didn't flinch. She knew what Tessa was implying, but the former queen would not find whatever answer she sought.

Kallie would not betray her father.

With wide, innocent eyes, she asked, "So, the castle was built as a fortress to protect the knowledge it holds?"

Tessa dipped her chin in response.

Did Domitius know about this? Was this his real reason for aligning himself with Frenzia? Every kingdom had its secrets. Pontia had the abilities the people possessed. Tetria had dozens of rituals—rituals most did not understand. Ardentol had *her*.

What knowledge could Frenzia be guarding?

Smoke filled her nose as she recalled the night of the attack. A young soldier's body mutilated in unspeakable ways. Soot smeared across the cement. The shouts of Frenzian soldiers calling for an unfamiliar weapon.

Whatever knowledge Frenzia held, Kallie didn't want to be on the receiving end of it.

Kallie scanned the room. With the windows high up, attacks would be limited, but they would not prevent them entirely. The iron doors they had entered through last night were large, nearly impenetrable even. But no castle was completely unbreachable.

Men often thought the only way to achieve something was through brute force. Kallie had thought that Tessa would have been different, but perhaps not if she thought these walls would protect the information Frenzia held so dear. They would not protect the castle or the people within it from Kallie.

"After all this time, the knowledge hasn't been stolen?" Kallie asked.

"Some have tried." Tessa clicked her tongue, shrugging a shoulder. "Those people never saw daylight again."

Kallie's gaze narrowed in question. "If the knowledge Frenzia holds is so important, wouldn't it benefit all of Vaneria if that knowledge was shared?"

The queen's nail scraped against the glass, producing a loud, horrid screech that had Kallie's ears ringing and her skin crawling. "Have you not been listening, Kalisandre? Knowledge equals power. And knowledge in the wrong hands can be fatal, catastrophic even. A balance must be maintained."

Kallie supposed Tessa had a point. If people, for instance, were to know what she could do—or what any of the Pontians could do—she would be hunted. She would be used and studied because of her ability. She would never be safe if the world knew what she could do. No wonder the existence of their abilities had been wiped from the memory of the other kingdoms after the Great War.

Tessa, oblivious to Kallie's thoughts, continued, "Kadia deals in oil and ore, Borgania deals in building materials and food, and Ragolo deals in fish. To the public, we deal in troops and armor. However, in truth, it is our knowledge that our enemies and allies are after." Tessa's tone shifted as she gave Kallie a pointed stare. "And as rulers, it is our job to protect that knowledge."

Kallie took a steady step forward. "Is there something you wish to ask me, Tessa?"

If Kallie's forwardness was a shock, the former queen hid it well, for Tessa did not flinch. "Dear, I am not foolish. I know what the other kingdoms say about me, what the men of our world say about me." Tessa folded her hands in her lap. "But do not be deceived by the judgments they have passed. I am no figurehead."

Kallie tasted the threat hanging in the air between them. Her gift, previously asleep, awoke, now a rolling fire in her stomach. "Ask me what you wish to know, Tessa," Kallie commanded.

A slim, milky haze swirled in Tessa's green-brown eyes. "Why are you here? What do you want?"

If the Frenzians held knowledge—information important enough to protect—there was no way Domitius was ignorant of it. But what was so important that he would want access to it? Kallie had not been tasked with uncovering Frenzia's secrets but solidifying an alliance. An alliance that would grant him access to that information.

Perhaps it was time Kallie chose her own mission.

"I want everything," Kallie whispered, her knuckles turning white around the railing. "What knowledge are you hiding?"

Tessa's mouth fell open, the answer on the tip of her tongue.

Pairs of footsteps echoed in the near distance, and Kallie straightened, releasing the command as Lystrata and Phaia entered the room. Tessa's clouded light hazel eyes shifted, her attention flicking to the people approaching and her mouth snapping shut.

The Frenzians hid something within the castle, and Kalie would find out.

No matter the cost.

CHAPTER 5
GRAESON

BURNED LUMBER, SHATTERED GLASS, AND RUBBLE COVERED THE streets. And ash. So much ash had settled on the destroyed buildings and layered the piles of charcoal and timber. As the villagers and soldiers trudged through the remains of the rubble, ash floated in the air. It coated their hair, attached to their clothes, and stuck in their lungs and noses.

Destruction was all around, but for once, Graeson wasn't to blame.

At least, that's what the others kept reminding him. It wasn't Graeson's fault, his friends had said, that the Frenzians had brought foreign weapons to their shore and destroyed their homes. It wasn't Graeson's fault that the person he was fated to be with had betrayed them without a second glance. It wasn't his fault that Kalisandre had led the enemy to their shore.

But it was.

He should have known. He shouldn't have let himself become blind by her return.

Ten days had passed since the fire burned down the seaside

village, yet the smell of smoke remained potent. It covered everything it touched like a thick blanket.

Seven days had passed since Fynn's funeral, yet grief still soaked the soil.

Every day, Graeson tried to bury himself in all the work that had to be done, including cleaning up the mess left behind.

The days were easy. During the day, there was plenty to do: rubble to remove, houses to build. By focusing on the reconstruction, his emotions fell to the wayside easily.

The nights, however, were haunted by his thoughts, nightmares, and desires. Once he stopped moving and was alone, Graeson couldn't prevent the onslaught of thoughts. Everything he had run away from when the sun was out came rushing back.

Usually, Graeson thrived underneath the moon, when the stars lit the sky, when the sun rested. Now, Graeson dreaded the night because he could no longer distinguish between the facts and the falsehoods. At night, everything was gray.

Not a night had passed since she came back into his life when Graeson did not think about Kalisandre. How she stood on the Frenzian ship and watched her brother get thrown overboard. How she turned her back on her family without looking back.

Those thoughts weren't the ones that kept Graeson up in the middle of the night. It was her carefree smile as she danced alongside Myra, the soft press of her lips that quickly turned hungry, the unbridled laughter as they ran through the hallways to the cavern's roof. Were those moments together false?

Kalisandre had kept her motives hidden from them all.

In the days leading up to the fire, Dani had questioned Graeson and the twins about Kalisandre's reserved tendencies. Graeson and Fynn, however, had defended her. Kalisandre needed time, Graeson had said —time to acclimate, time to get to know them and *trust* them again.

Now, Graeson couldn't help but wonder if Kalisandre even tried.

Although, if Fynn was right about his suspicions, she couldn't. According to Fynn's assessment, something was preventing her. But if Fynn had truly believed that was the case, why had he only confided in Graeson? Why hadn't he trusted anyone else with the information?

"Because Dani and Terin need proof," Fynn had said. "They all will."

If the others knew something was off from the beginning, they wouldn't have let her in. They wouldn't have given Kalisandre a chance until they knew what was preventing Fynn from accessing her mind.

At the time, Graeson understood where his friend had been coming from. Before, there was no point in worrying the others, not when Kalisandre was finally acclimating. Or so it seemed.

If only they had trusted the others. If only Graeson and Fynn had listened to them.

It did Graeson no good to dwell on the past because when he tried to sift through the events leading up to the attack, he only grew more confused, more conflicted.

Still, he couldn't stop his mind from trying to find a way to fix everything. Every night, he tried to form a plan that would solve everything. But every night, he came up empty-handed.

Everyone was grieving, everyone was angry, and everyone was tired. A plan could not fix that.

Sensing his thoughts about to spiral, Graeson reached within and closed off that section of his mind. He knew he shouldn't. He knew what shutting off his emotions did to him, how it made him feel less . . . human. *Other*.

Turning it off for a moment wouldn't hurt, though.

Graeson tossed a piece of charred lumber into the bin and focused back on the task at hand.

Today, Graeson and a few others had started clearing the houses on the third block in the village. Fortunately, these houses were not as badly destroyed as those closer to the pier. Some parts of the houses, they believed, could be restored. No more tearing through everything with reckless abandonment—something Graeson had enjoyed doing the past few days. They had to dig through the wreck and remove the unusable pieces while salvaging as much as possible.

With his emotions locked away, nothing seemed worth saving.

"Graeson, some help over here?"

Graeson groaned because, even more unfortunately, he was working with Armen today. His emotions weren't tucked far enough away to hide his revulsion.

On the other side of the pile of rubble, Armen stared at Graeson as he struggled to pick up a large piece of wall that had collapsed.

Graeson rolled his eyes. *Imbecile.*

When Graeson was young, he had surpassed his own age group's training early on. He joined the next age group to learn more advanced techniques before Graeson surpassed them, too. Armen, a few years older, had been jealous of Graeson's natural affinity for fighting. Graeson hadn't liked Armen then, and he didn't now either. He never cared for those who would rather criticize their peers' success than celebrate it.

Graeson's distaste for the man had only grown with age. After several years of living in Ardentol under the guise of Kalisandre's guard, Armen had become more arrogant. How the man had managed to rise in the ranks of the royal guard and become the captain of Kalisandre's guard was beyond Graeson. His enhanced hearing could have only gotten him so far.

When Armen returned from Pontia, he traveled north to see his family after not seeing them for several years. On horseback, the ride took several days. By the time the news of the attack had arrived in

Armen's home village, Linthon, Fynn's funeral had already passed. Armen returned only a few days ago to help with the reparations.

As much as Graeson didn't want to help Armen, Queen Esmeray's words earlier that week echoed in his mind: "Now is not the time to fight with one another. It is the time to show a united front. We are all hurting. We are all grieving. But we will get through this together. We will rebuild together. We will be stronger. Together."

So, Graeson held his tongue.

Heading to the other side of the rubble, Graeson picked up the other end of the fractured wall. Dormant debris fell onto the ground. Together, the two men heaved it onto the large cart.

Armen sighed heavily. He brushed his hands together, rubbing off the dust sticking to his palms. "Thanks, man. I appreciate it."

The muscles in Graeson's jaw tightened, but he merely nodded and turned around to head back to his area of the destruction.

Armen, of course, kept talking, "I wish I could have been there."

Graeson halted. He tried to propel his feet forward, but his body wouldn't move. His tongue did. "And what would you have done, Armen?"

"I could have helped," Armen said, kicking at a piece of debris. "I hate seeing all of this. I hate that I wasn't here to help. I should have been *here* instead of in Linthon. As much as I missed my family, I should have stayed here. I should have known something like this would have happened."

Graeson's jaw clenched. "How would you have known?"

Armen spat on the ground. "She was one of them. She wasn't one of us anymore, you know?"

Graeson tilted his head an inch, an eyebrow arching. "No, I don't know."

Wrinkles creased Armen's forehead. "What do you mean?"

"Tell me," Graeson said through gritted teeth, "how Kalisandre, our queen's daughter, isn't one of us." His body vibrated. Anger was the only thing he saw when the rest of his emotions were locked away. The only emotion that seeped through the cracks, making it harder to control the monster within.

Armen huffed as if Graeson's question was funny. Graeson, however, wasn't laughing.

When Graeson continued to stare at him in silence, Armen scratched the back of his head, shifting on his feet. "I mean, she was raised by the Ardentolian king. Kallie believed Ardentol was her home, Gray. She's always been reckless and careless about others. Since I was there, I only knew her to care about three things: her father, her title, and that handmaiden of hers. In that order. She doesn't care about anyone or anything else. Is she as cruel as Domitius? No. But even though they do not share the same blood, she is his daughter."

Graeson's lip curled. "But she's not."

"Not what?" Armen asked.

"Domitius' daughter." Graeson cracked his knuckles, his gaze locked on the rings on his fingers.

His control was slipping. He should have turned away and kept walking. If he were a good man, he would have. Graeson, however, wasn't *good*.

"Sure, not technically." Armen rubbed the back of his neck. "Not by blood, anyway. But does that matter? I mean, take you, for instance, Esmeray is practically your mother. After all, she did raise you after—" Armen's mouth snapped shut as Graeson's head jerked up.

Graeson didn't need to say anything, though. This might have been his home, but everyone was afraid of him. They tried not to be. They tried to pretend that Graeson was normal, that he wasn't a monster. Because they needed him. He was *useful*. He was a tool they would need for the coming war. Because for years, they had known war was coming, ever since Domitius' first attack on their homeland.

Before, it was only a matter of time, but now it was closer than ever. So, even though they didn't know *when* it would happen, they knew that Graeson—no, the monster living inside of him—would be vital for their victory.

When Armen spoke again, his words were hurried as he stumbled to clean up the mess he had made. "M-my point is that I wish I could have stopped. That's all."

Wrong answer.

The blood beneath Graeson's skin buzzed. A frigid river begging to break through the slab of ice on top. It took every ounce of willpower not to act on the rising anger. Every ounce to stay put as Armen kept on talking.

"If I would have been here, maybe I could have caught a conversation between her and Myra. Kalisandre and the handmaiden were very close, you know." Armen chuckled awkwardly. But despite the daggers Graeson was sending through his icy glare, Armen continued, "After all, that was why *I* was sent to Ardentol in the first place. My hearing is beyond exceptional. I could have—"

Crack.

The brittle wall shook as Armen's back pounded into it, sending a burst of dust into the air. Graeson's fingers dug into the front of Armen's shirt. The fabric scrunched inside his palm. A crack spread across the wall.

No matter. They would have to demolish this wall anyway due to the damage from the fire.

Armen coughed.

As Graeson watched Armen wiggle beneath his hold, the beast inside him smiled. Graeson still owed Armen a fist in the face for insulting Kalisandre's character after the carriage attack. While Kalisandre didn't need anyone fighting her battles, Graeson would not listen to Armen spew insult after insult. He would not listen to Armen's claim that Kalisandre wasn't worth it.

Little did he know, she was worth *everything*. Because even though the situation was complicated, the bond that pulled Graeson toward her was still there, humming in the pit of his stomach. And he would not give up on that.

Graeson tightened his grip, his elbow digging into Armen's shoulder. His face was only inches away from Armen's, his breath hot in the space between them. "And what would your special *hearing* have done, Armen? How would it have helped us when our people were dying and their homes were burning down?"

Armen swallowed.

"Go on, tell me." Graeson slammed him against the wall again, and the crack spiderwebbed. "How would it have helped when Fynn was dying? He was one of our *best* fighters. How would *you* have helped?"

Armen's lips parted, but Graeson slammed him against the wall again. Graeson sensed the presence of a crowd growing around them, but he didn't care. No one would stop him. No one could.

Graeson's gaze flitted over Armen's face. Armen's skin had gone pale, fear emblazoned on his face.

What are you waiting for? A voice said in the back of Graeson's mind. *Give him what he deserves.*

Graeson's nose twitched.

Do it.

Graeson's nail dug in. Red shaded the corners of his vision.

Then his shoulders dropped.

I am not a monster, Graeson told the voice. His fingers unclenched, but a wrinkled ball remained above Armen's heart. "For once in your life, Armen, make yourself useful."

As Graeson walked away, the monster inside of him roared.

CHAPTER 6
KALLIE

After Phaia had given Kallie a tour of the grounds, which included everything from the staff housing to the castle's private hospital wards in the west wing, Phaia left Kallie in the queen's wing.

While the handmaiden was nice, Kallie was thankful for a moment of reprieve after having been dragged around the castle for several hours. She could only handle so much nodding, so many fake smiles. She needed time alone to process everything. Noon was approaching, which meant she still had time to sneak away before meeting her father and Rian to discuss the next steps.

She reached for the doorknob, but her hand froze, an eerie prickle scaling up her arms as whispers seeped through the door.

Tossing a wary glance over her shoulder, Kallie reached underneath her skirt and unclasped the dagger attached to the holster strapped around her thigh. The loud thump of her heart echoed in her ears.

Adjusting her grip around the dagger's hilt, she cracked open the door. Through the tiny slit, she spotted a pair of polished black shoes. Dragging her gaze up the person's leg, Kallie exhaled in relief.

Domitius sat at a new small maple wood table one of the servants must have brought to her room while she was gone. His gaze was directed away from the door while he talked to someone hidden from view.

Kallie loosened her grip around the dagger and quickly returned it to its holster. After fixing her skirts, she pushed the door open. Domitius was quick to snap his head toward her. His expression, previously austere, softened ever-so-slightly—as soft as his sharp features would allow anyway.

"Father," Kallie said as she strolled into the room, her stride now steady. "I was just about to come find you."

The corner of Domitius' lips twitched. A near smile formed, but it was too fleeting to reach his eyes before his normal flat expression returned. "Kalisandre, we were just talking about you."

Myra stepped out of the spacious closet with a dress folded over her arms. From the days traveling on the ship, Myra's pale complexion had reddened from the sun. Somehow, though, her cheeks managed to appear even redder despite the sun's kiss. Something akin to embarrassment and concern flushed her countenance.

Kallie's stomach dropped.

She hadn't seen Myra since arriving last night. But if her handmaiden was in the king's presence alone, Kallie could only imagine the ridicule she had been enduring before she arrived.

"Is that so?" Kallie asked, glancing at Myra. Domitius never enjoyed being in the presence of the servants, especially Kallie's handmaidens. He was constantly throwing them out of the room when he visited Kallie.

"Mhm," Domitius hummed. "The Frenzians have several servants and handmaidens that they will undoubtedly put in your employ once you and Rian marry. After all, they have already placed that one girl—what was her name?" He snapped his fingers in the air. "Flora?"

"Phaia," Kallie corrected.

Domitius shrugged and continued as if Kallie hadn't said anything, "Unfortunately, bringing your old handmaidens with us to Pontia was out of the question due to the potential dangers and the nature of the trip. When I return, I will bring the others with me. In the meantime, this handmaiden must suffice."

"I'm sure I will be fine, Father. Myra has never let me down before." Kallie smiled at her friend, whose gaze was directed at the floor.

"Is there something else I should know?" Kallie asked as she sat across from the king. The availability of handmaidens could not have been the main reason her father had visited her rooms.

The light patter of Myra's footsteps sounded behind her, and Domitius' gaze flicked to the handmaiden. Bouncing a foot in the air, he brushed his fingers against his graying beard. "Myra, you are dismissed."

"Yes, My King," Myra said. She folded the dress over the vanity chair. As she passed, she brushed a light hand across Kallie's shoulder, then hurried out the door without glancing back at either of them.

Kallie shrunk back into her seat, her chance to confide in her friend following the handmaiden out the door. Beneath the table, she twisted the ring around her finger. Despite the connection to the people she had betrayed linked to the gold metal band, she had not taken it off. After wearing it for as long as she could remember, the ring was a part of her. A part she was not ready to be rid of yet.

"Kalisandre."

Kallie's gaze snapped to her father sitting across from her. Disdain coated his countenance.

"Yes, My King?"

"Have you met with Rian yet?"

Kallie looked down. "No, but . . ."

"Enough with the mumbling. You are to be *queen*. Enunciate," he spat.

Kallie pushed her shoulders back, steadying her gaze. "This morning, I overheard a conversation between Rian and his mother that I believe you may find interesting."

Domitius yawned, but when he didn't interrupt, Kallie quickly continued. "It seems the former queen does not support my marriage to her son. She wishes to persuade Rian to break it off."

"You are surprised?" he asked, brows drawing together. "Once you marry her son, the old queen will have no place in the castle. Right now, she has access to her son's ear. When you marry the boy, that will change." He sighed and rubbed a finger across his temple. "Kalisandre, I cannot emphasize this enough. You need to ensure this marriage happens. I do not care what you have overheard. Tessa is a figurehead, nothing more. Do not let her get in your way."

A *figurehead*—that was what Tessa had said the men called her. Tessa, however, seemed to be more aware of the happenings around her than Domitius gave her credit for.

Kallie blinked, her finger freezing around the metal band as she realized the second meaning of his words. He still believed she would fail, even after her success in Pontia. Kallie straightened in her seat. "I would never let her get in my way of the throne, Father."

"Whatever means necessary," Domitius said.

Kallie nodded. Then the corner of her lip tipped upward as she recalled her previous conversation with the queen. "Although the former queen could be of use to us."

"Oh?" Domitius mumbled noncommittally.

"She suggested that Frenzia holds some hidden knowledge that is even more priceless."

"Hmm." His brown eyes lit with hunger, and that look alone confirmed Kallie's suspicions. Her father already knew about the hidden knowledge. He straightened his collar, and his gaze bore into her. "You *cannot* make the same mistakes you made last time, Kalisandre."

"I—" Kallie paused, her head cocked to the side. "What mistakes?"

Even when they sat at the same level at the table, Domitius was able to cast a downward glance in Kallie's direction that had her tensing beneath it.

"You allowed your heart to get the best of you. You sympathized for that boy."

Kallie's jaw clenched. "What boy?"

"The Pontian boy." Domitius flicked his hand in the air. "The one on the ship."

Kallie's mouth grew dry, and the words refused to leave her lips.

Fynn was not *some* boy. He was her brother—a brother Domitius had neglected to mention to Kallie before the start of her mission. The Pontians were supposed to be strangers, a rogue group acting out against Domitius' mission to restore Vaneria to their former glory under one ruler. They were supposed to be people who simply knew how to strengthen her gift. While they had been strangers, the Pontians were also her blood.

And one of them had died because of their plan.

Domitius, however, did not want to hear that.

Looking back at her father, her anger simmered, although a dull pain pierced her temples. He was not to blame for Fynn's death; Sebastian was.

She tipped up her chin. "Blood is only as thick as one makes it."

He scoffed. "Do not preach my own words to me. I know them better than anyone. I have treated you like a daughter all these years, Kalisandre. If blood mattered to me, would I be handing *you* a throne?"

A throne you *still would oversee*, a small part of her thought.

A throne was still a throne, and a throne meant power. Power Domitius was granting her.

Domitius flicked off a piece of invisible lint from his lapel. "Be that as it may, women often let their hearts guide them too far. Your mother is guilty of this. Always has been."

Kallie's heart stopped.

Before Kallie had discovered that her mother was alive and the queen of Pontia, Kallie had been led to believe that she had died during childbirth. This was the first time Domitius had brought up Kallie's mother on his own accord.

A log cracked, embers popping from the low fire. Yet despite the heat in the room, Kallie's hands were cold as she stared at her father.

"You knew her?"

Clicking his tongue, he said with a toss of his hand, "That is neither here nor there." Before Kallie could question him further, Domitius returned to their previous conversation. "Do not let your emotions get the better of you. You need to have a clear head while I am gone. Our goal must stay at the forefront of your mind."

Kallie nodded as she ground her teeth together. Not only was he once again avoiding the conversation about her family, but he was also questioning her ability to focus on the task at hand. She knew what she had to do. She didn't need him telling her like she was an insolent child. Would he ever view her as more than a child, though?

"I will," she said.

"Begin planting the seeds in the king's mind."

"I will start when we meet with him and Sebastian this afternoon, Father."

Domitius leaned back in his chair. "We will not be meeting today."

Her mouth fell open. "I thought—"

Domitius held up a hand, and Kallie snapped her mouth shut. "I am leaving earlier than I thought, so there is no time. Plus, Rian and Sebastian are meeting with some locals today in a nearby village."

"But—"

"Enough. There is something far more important that we must discuss, Kalisandre."

Domitius pushed a vial forward, and a heaviness filled her chest. A clear liquid filled the small container enclosed with a cork. Even without a label, Kallie knew what was inside, for Domitius had presented Kallie with similar vials before. When tricking the mind was not good enough, other precautions had to be taken.

She stripped away any emotion from her countenance.

"Who is it this time?" she asked as she inspected her nails, freshly sharpened and painted. In the reflection of the low fire, flames danced within the pale pink coat of paint.

King Domitius shrugged. "A servant in the castle."

"A servant?"

She had expected someone of stature, someone with a title. Someone who was making too much noise. Not a staff member. Her father had never deemed the staff worthy of his attention before. Firing them had always been his preferred form of punishment, cutting off their supply of income and making them unemployable. She detested it, but she had no say in the matter.

"You question me?"

"No, My King, of course not." Kallie tipped her head in repentance. With a gentle tone, she said, "I only wonder what the servant could have done."

He rolled the small glass vial between his thumb and forefinger. "You always did have a soft spot for the staff." After a moment, he placed the vial back on the table between them and leaned back in his chair. "There have been rumblings."

"Rumblings?" Kallie asked.

"Yes, an investigation of sorts." He flicked his hand in the air. "Apparently, some Frenzians, Tessa specifically, do not believe Lothian died of natural causes."

Kallie folded her hands on her lap beneath the table, twisting the ring.

Was this why Tessa was suspicious of Kallie's intentions?

Thankfully, Kallie's gift had strengthened, so she wasn't concerned about Tessa recalling their previous conversation. Still, from now on, Kallie would have to be careful and ensure there were no traces left behind, no cracks in her manipulations.

Domitius scooted closer to the table and leaned across it. A stray blond curl fell from his slick-backed hair. His palm pressed flat on the oak tabletop. "We cannot have people questioning Lothian's death right now, Kalisandre."

Kallie's head pounded harder as his brown eyes bore into her. Heat soaked her skin, and the fresh air from the opened window was thick with humidity.

Still, she asked, "What do you need me to do?"

"Make them believe." He pulled out a folded piece of parchment and slid it across the table.

Unfolding it, she scanned the page, her eyes bouncing across the wrinkled parchment as she flipped it over and over. "It's empty," she said, looking up at him.

"Get a servant to confess."

"But—"

"Have the servant write the confession down. Then . . ." Domitius pushed the vial forward. He didn't bother saying the next step of his plan. He didn't need to.

King Domitius wanted this servant to take the fall for King Lothian's death. To take the blame for it so that any suspicions leading to Ardentol were dealt with before they latched onto anything concrete. Anything that would put the blame on them.

Kallie glanced at the vial, and her heart thumped in her throat as she reached for the poison. From a young age, Kallie had been trained to seduce, disarm, and kill. Yet she had never driven a blade through her targets' hearts. Poison was always Domitius' preferred method. Easy to conceal, unsuspecting, and silent. Kallie had never stayed around to see the aftermath of the poison. But when news of the victim's death reached the castle's doorsteps, guilt always stained her hands. Sickness claimed her every time.

Yet, as her father sat across from her in the foreign castle, the power still in his hands, she did not flinch. She did not react. Instead, with a straight face, Kallie asked the question he expected, "Who's the lucky winner?"

She would not disappoint him today.

Domitius leaned back in his chair, resting his elbows on its arms and folding his hands beneath his chin. He smirked, and Kallie's skin itched. "Player's choice."

Her hand froze, hovering over the vial. "My choice?"

"Don't you think you've earned it?" Domitius asked, tilting his head slightly.

Kallie swallowed, but her mouth was dry.

"Yet you hesitate, Kalisandre." He clicked his tongue, shaking his head in dismay. "I thought you would be overjoyed to have this responsibility, to have my trust. To have the choice of who gets to take the blame."

"I am, Father." Kallie sat up straighter, and beneath the table, she ran a shaking hand along the top of her skirt. "I'm only surprised."

She picked up the vial, eyeing it.

To choose who was to die and who was to live had never been the kind of decision she wished to make. Although, was it that much different from if her father had given her a name himself? Either way, she would have had to deliver the poison. Either way, someone would die. Still, how would she decide who lived and who died? She was not a god.

From the corner of her eye, she saw Domitius studying her. A satisfied glint sparking in his eyes. At that moment, she saw this for what it was: a test. A test to see if Kallie was still loyal to him.

She had learned early in her life that backing down was not an option when her father gave her an assignment.

So, with a flourish and a feigned smirk, Kallie pocketed the vial inside the front of her corset. "I am thankful for the opportunity, Father." Her voice was steady, yet her head ached.

"There is no room for hesitation when one is in a position of power. And this," his gaze fell to where Kallie had hidden the vial, "is only your first taste of it." Standing, Domitius brushed the new wrinkles from his trousers and strode toward the door.

Kallie sunk back into her chair, the tension in her body releasing an inch. She exhaled a quiet sigh.

When Domitius reached the door, he braced a firm hand on the doorframe, stopping. "And Kalisandre?"

"Yes, Father?" Kallie asked, squinting against the ringing in her ear.

"While I may be returning to Ardentol, I have eyes and ears everywhere."

Kallie had always known that he had spies throughout Vaneria. During advisory meetings, she had heard the various pieces of information the spies had sent to him, the findings they had discovered—sometimes trivial, other times monumental, such as the Pontians' plan to abduct Kallie. They spied on lords raising a fuss, nearby kingdoms, and their allies to ensure they were not planning against them. But never her. Never Kallie.

Not until now.

Domitius dropped his hand to the doorknob and cocked his head to the side. He brushed the fallen curl away from his face. "Do not give me a reason to doubt you again."

She had no intentions of betraying him, yet his words still struck a chord.

"I would never betray you, Father."

"Yet I have reminded you, nevertheless." His knuckles blanched as he gripped the handle. "Be careful who you trust in this palace. No one knows about your gift." He swept a critical gaze over her. "Best keep it that way."

Domitius turned the doorknob and pushed the door open, disappearing into the dimly lit hall before Kallie had a chance to respond.

In his wake, the scent of whiskey coated the air as the cold vial of poison lay against her sternum.

Maybe her father was right; perhaps she was too soft-hearted. This decision would have been easier if she cared less about the lives of innocents. Kings had killed for worse before. But did she want to be the kind of ruler who killed without reason?

Still, didn't Tessa say that it was a ruler's job to protect a kingdom's secrets? If the Frenzians were getting too close to discovering the truth about Lothian's death, that Domitius played a part, shouldn't Kallie be willing to do anything to protect him? Protect her kingdom?

Did she have a choice?

CHAPTER 7
KALLIE

Lystrata looked pointedly at Kallie, waiting for a response. Kallie, however, had not heard a word the housekeeper had said, for her mind was elsewhere.

Domitius had left two days ago, yet Kallie couldn't shake the feeling that someone was watching her.

To make matters worse, Kallie hadn't had any time to figure out how she would accomplish her father's new assignment. Since her father had left, the housekeeper had kept Kallie busy. Apparently, Myra's doing, for according to her friend, the Frenzians were behind on wedding arrangements—something Lystrata had blamed on the efforts to rescue Kallie. Kallie wondered if Tessa's apparent disinterest in the wedding was a factor. Even still, when Myra set her mind to something, there was no stopping her. The staff raced about, inside and outside the castle, to ensure that the wedding went smoothly. Still, how was Kallie supposed to plan a wedding representing her and Rian's relationship when she didn't even know the man?

Busy or not, one would think a new king would make his presence known in the castle. Since arriving, Kallie had met dozens of staff members, guards, and prominent men and women who visited. There were so many new faces, yet the one she wished to see remained hidden. If Kallie didn't know better, she would have guessed the Frenzian castle was larger than it was. How could a king remain unseen for days?

She had commanded servants to retrieve him. Yet every time they returned, they came back alone, providing some excuse on behalf of the king. Her ability was useless if she couldn't access the source. Other than late in the night, Kallie didn't have time to hunt him down. Based on how Rian had spent his evening when she had arrived, Kallie wasn't too eager to meet her betrothed when he was in bed with someone else. And despite her efforts, she had no luck finding the person who occupied his nights.

During the day, Kallie was too preoccupied with wedding arrangements. Today's planning session was no more than a trivial reason to keep Kallie busy. Did they think Kallie would not see through their tricks? Their tactics? Tessa could not keep Kallie separated from Rian forever. One way or another, Kallie would find a way to win his heart.

She always did.

Lystrata cleared her throat, dragging Kallie's attention back to the housekeeper. "The flowers, Princess Kalisandre. Do you have a preference?" Lystrata asked, repeating her question.

Picking flowers. This was how she was to spend her time? Kallie wanted to laugh. Were the flowers that important? They would wither away a few days after the ceremony, only to be tossed outside somewhere to wilt. Back in Ardentol, they had never needed to cover the place with flowers or other adornments, for the castle's grandeur spoke for itself.

Kallie looked around the Frenzian grand hall and sighed.

Kallie glanced at Phaia. At this point, Kallie should have let the handmaiden oversee the decisions. She knew Rian's favorite appetizers (a supposedly delicious crab-filled pastry customary of the Ragolian kingdom), his favorite wine (a hearty red from Borgania that he had tasted when he had visited there over a year ago). The handmaiden probably knew the answer to this as well. But alas, Kallie needed to pretend she cared about her wedding, even if it was some frivolous display.

"May I suggest red roses, Your Highness?" Phaia said.

An amused grin nudged at Kallie's lips.

Of course, Rian's favorite flower would be the kingdom's signature flower, the one that peppered the streets and the castle's garden. It was traditional, safe. A perfect representation of the young king who was trying to prove something to his people. Kallie, meanwhile, would have preferred peonies or something unique.

Kallie nodded, "That's a great suggestion, Phaia." She pointed up at the wooden beams that ran from the middle of the wall and over to the above foyer that overlooked the hall. Whether the flowers withered away or not, the castle needed to be perfect. "Let's add greenery everywhere. Something that doesn't take away from the stone but still adds some warmth to the palace. Be sure that there are enough candles to light each table. The grand hall does get rather dark once the sun sets."

With a tepid hum of acknowledgment, Lystrata scratched her quill across the parchment. Flipping through the pages, she nodded. "All right, almost all the details on today's docket are done. Do you remember the schedule, Princess Kalisandre?"

Quill still in hand, Lystrata pointed to the three nearly identical napkins on the table, only differing in hue and slight texture.

Kallie nodded passively as she ran a finger across the fabric of one of the napkins laid out in front of her. She held up the bright white cloth, and Lystrata marked it on the parchment.

Kallie recited the schedule, "On the first day, we will host a grand dinner to welcome our guests, followed by a ball. The next day, the women will gather for tea and pastries in the queen's garden. Then the traditional Frenzian hunt will take place on the third night."

Kallie did not understand why a hunt occurred in the middle of the wedding festivities. But when Kallie had asked Lystrata about it before, the housekeeper had flicked her hand in response, saying there was no need to worry about it. Kallie had dropped it after that. Tradition was tradition, she supposed. If the men needed to hunt some wild creature, so be it.

Looking up from the papers, Lystrata arched a grey brow.

"The ceremony will take place two days after," Kallie added.

Lystrata nodded, brushing back a strand of hair.

Sharp steps clapped against the wooden floor.

"These next four weeks will be gone before you know it, Kalisandre," Tessa said, wearing a simple burgundy dress. As she walked toward them, she straightened a flower arrangement as she strolled past it. "It will be the largest wedding that Vaneria has seen in centuries. Everything must be perfect."

Tessa's reminder was pointless.

The list of people invited was lengthy, and for a good reason. The more people who attended the wedding and acknowledged Kallie as queen of Frenzia, the more weight her crown held.

Lystrata walked around the table, pointing to the silverware options.

Kallie pointed to the simple silver set laid out. "I mean no offense, Your Highness, but I know the importance of my own wedding."

Tessa scoffed, shaking her head and pointing to the gold set. Without glancing at Kallie, Lystrata crossed off Kallie's choice and replaced it with Tessa's.

Kallie arched a brow. Tessa seemed to care a lot for a woman who did not even want this wedding to occur. Perhaps Domitius was not the only one who cared about his reputation.

"That may be so, Kalisandre." Kallie's name on Tessa's lips

sounded as if she was eating each syllable, awkward and uncomfortable. "But if I may be frank, you have been deemed 'the diamond of Ardentol.' What good does that title do for you once you marry my son?"

Iron coated Kallie's tongue.

"Vaneria, however, has not seen you as the Queen of Frenzia." Tessa picked up the gold cake cutter Kallie had picked out, flipped it in her hands, and then set it back down with a halfhearted shrug.

"Yet," Kallie mumbled.

"Yet," Tessa repeated with a soft smile, folding her hands below her stomach. "Everyone will be watching. When your father returns, will you stand beside him?" Tessa paused as she walked around the table, the toe of her heels nearly touching Kallie's. "Or will you stand beside your husband?" Tessa tilted her head. "Who will you bow down to, Kalisandre?"

The rage within Kallie grew taught beneath her skin. Kallie folded her hands behind her back, cocking her head to the side as her brows drew together in false confusion. "Are you suggesting that Frenzia and Ardentol are not of one mind, Queen Mother?"

"The tide of the people is ever-changing. One can never know what to expect or what someone's intentions are, my dear. I believe it is important to know exactly who my son is marrying and if she will be loyal to *him*." Tessa lifted a single brow. "Or someone else."

Kallie met Tessa's cold glare with her own. "Your words suggest I only have two options: be loyal to my betrothed or my father."

"Is there a third option that I am not aware of?" Tessa asked.

Kallie lifted her chin and looked down her nose at the former queen. "My loyalties have and will always lie with myself. I will always do what is best for me and my people."

While Kallie had ties in Ardentol, Frenzia would become her home. Everyone would expect her interests to align with those of her husband, but she would not ignore the needs of the people of

Ardentol. The purpose of this alliance was to join the kingdoms, not further separate them.

"And who are your people, my dear?"

Kallie stood her ground as Tessa raised her chin in challenge. "Unlike those before me, I will not have my reign defined by the lines men have drawn."

Tessa huffed a quiet chuckle. "Be careful, Princess."

Kallie blinked, her eyelashes fluttering. "Of what, Queen Mother?"

"Of reaching too far beyond your reach. The gods do not look kindly on those who step out of line."

Kallie smirked. "Good thing I was never on the line to begin with." She turned on her heel and strolled out of the grand hall, leaving Tessa with her jaw on the floor and her two handmaidens rushing after her.

THE NEXT SEVERAL days blurred together. More wedding planning, more unfamiliar faces, and more questions about Rian's absence. Every day was the same. And with every day that passed, the small vial pressed against her chest grew colder.

While Myra and Phaia exchanged ideas for Kallie's wedding apparel during their late morning stroll through the gardens, Kallie's thoughts were on the letter stuffed in her pocket.

Kalisandre,

I have returned to Ardentol. I'll be back before you know it, daughter.

- K.D.

Two sentences. Two sentences in his handwriting were all it took to remind Kallie of her place. Domitius may have been gone, but he was not in the dark. Somewhere in the castle, his spies lurked around the corners, watching Kallie's every move.

His message was clear: choose a victim.

Over the years, the two of them had developed a code of sorts to discuss Kallie's assignments without worrying about who could be listening. Hidden messages within casual conversations. It was how Kallie had delivered the message to the soldier when she had run into them in Borgania. The message that had changed everything and lit the match that sparked the fire.

Domitius' message was unsurprising. Kallie had been dragging her feet, whether or not she wanted to admit it. For the past few days, she had observed the staff in an attempt to pinpoint a person she would feel less guilty about choosing.

It should have been easy to choose since she didn't know these people. They weren't *her* people. But with each passing day, the question of *who* became much more complicated.

Kallie had been taught from a young age that her kingdom should be her priority. Everything her father did, he did for the betterment of Ardentol. Domitius wanted his people to reap the rewards of his accomplishments. If Kallie was to become Queen of Frenzia, shouldn't she also seek to protect Frenzia's people? She had always valued the staff in Ardentol, for they were vital to the kingdom's success, even if her father did not see it that way.

In the past, her victims had deserved their punishments. This time, no one had wronged Domitius. On the contrary, her father had asked her to manipulate someone because the consequences of his actions were rising to the surface. The Frenzians were right to be suspicious of King Lothian's death. Domitius, after all, had orchestrated it. Kallie had no choice but to make the problem disappear. If it was discovered that he had poisoned King Lothian so that Rian would take the throne, what would happen to the wedding? What would happen to Kallie?

Her father was beyond the mountain, safe in his marble castle. If the truth were unveiled, the Frenzians would undoubtedly think Kallie was a part of the scheme. While Kallie had not been the one to kill King Lothian, she had known about her father's involvement. Or had assumed, anyway. Domitius had never outright confessed—he was too smart to do that. All it took was one look from him months ago for Kallie to know the truth.

She had always known that her father would do whatever it took in order to achieve his goals. After all, she had heard the myths about him, the whispers that skittered down the halls outside her room in Ardentol as servants passed. Inflated or not, myths stood on some foundation of truth.

Therefore, it did not matter if Kallie shoved the poison down King Lothian's throat herself or if she had known about the plans beforehand or not. She was an accomplice. Because either way, Kallie stood to benefit from Lothian's death.

The kingdom's crown was just beyond her reach. If they didn't deal with this problem, everything Kallie had sacrificed would be for naught.

As they walked, a swift breeze brushed across her skin. The summer heat she was accustomed to in Ardentol seemed to have skipped over Frenzia's land. Goosebumps scattered across her arms, and Kallie pulled the shawl tighter around her as they made a sharp turn down the path that weaved between the pine trees.

At first, she had thought about manipulating a prisoner, but that would be too easy. Domitius would discover the truth. This letter was proof enough that someone was watching her.

Kallie tilted her head as Phaia laughed. Her black hair fell down her back, straight and unknotted, almost reaching her hip. She had a careless sway to her gait.

She would be an easy target. She was accessible, slightly naive. Over the past few days, the woman was almost always in Kallie's company. She would be easy to manipulate without anyone noticing. But as the handmaiden threw back another boisterous laugh, Kallie's stomach turned. She hated to admit it because it would only prove that her father was right, but Kallie liked the woman too much.

As they strolled through the garden, Kallie thought of the alternatives.

The way the housekeeper's gaze swept over Kallie as if she was nothing more than a guest in the castle and not the future queen did irk Kallie. Tessa was also particularly fond of the housekeeper, it seemed, which was indeed a welcome bonus. Yet Lystrata hadn't done anything to warrant death.

While Kallie may not have liked the woman, she was not heartless.

Was this what it was like to be in the seat of power?

Her father never struggled to make these decisions. He wore a look of indifference as if it was a badge of honor. And Kallie should have aspired to do the same, for rulers needed to make hard decisions daily. Domitius wasn't the only leader to make decisions that Kallie questioned. Esmeray also had decided to put Pontia's safety first when it came to Kallie's own life. Sacrifices had to be made. Was Kallie willing to sacrifice an innocent's life to protect her father? Was she willing to sacrifice her morality? Did she even have any morality left? If she had asked Terin or the others, they would claim she had none.

Maybe it would be easier to become the monster they all believed her to be.

Kallie brushed her palms across the sides of her skirt. Her fingers ran over the dagger strapped around her thigh beneath the soft fabric. Since arriving in Frenzia, she had not gone a day without it. It was ironic, wasn't it? A princess who carried a dagger afraid to kill by poison? Myra had not given Kallie the dagger to kill but to remind her that she was not defenseless. That even without a crown on her head, she still had power. And, most importantly, that there was always a choice.

"Princess?"

"Hmm?" Kallie looked up in time to stop herself from running into Phaia.

Having stopped walking at some point, the two handmaidens stared at Kallie.

Phaia tilted her head to the side, her eyebrows furrowed. "I asked if you were missing your family. It is unfortunate your father couldn't stay longer."

Myra wrapped her arm around Kallie's, pulling her between them as they started walking again. Myra's fingers brushed over Kallie's bicep, a soothing touch.

Kallie nodded haphazardly. "Oh, well, my father does have his own responsibilities back home." A soft smile slipped onto Kallie's face as she looked at the Frenzian woman.

"But it is always good to have a familiar face around, is it not?"

"I do. I have Myra," Kallie said, squeezing her friend's hand.

"Always, my lady." Myra patted Kallie's arm,

Phaia offered a small smile. "And I suppose you and King Rian will have your own family soon enough."

Kallie coughed, choking on the air that wrapped around her lungs. Phaia sent her a wary look, and Kallie shook it off, claiming she had swallowed a bug.

Children might have been an obvious next step for most young couples; however, Kallie hadn't even given them a single thought. Marrying Rian was a farce already. No need to add children to the mix.

As if she could sense Kallie's discomfort, Myra turned to the other handmaiden. "Phaia, I have been meaning to ask you something."

None the wiser, Phaia leaned forward. "Ask away."

"Is there a reason why the castle seems understaffed? For such a large castle, I would have assumed more staff would be on hand, especially with a wedding near."

Phaia hummed in agreement as she bent over a nearby rose bush. "You are correct. The staff is currently undergoing a rather dramatic transition." Her fingers danced across the red flowers, like a pianist finding their starting key. With a flick, she plucked a bright red rose, all of its petals pristine. Instead of holding onto it, Phaia began picking at each perfect petal, dropping them onto the ground behind them one by one. "I'm afraid to say that the undertaking is taking longer than planned since King Rian has decided to hand-pick the staff."

"A noble endeavor," Myra said.

Phaia nodded, and another petal drifted to the ground.

"That seems like a strange use of the king's time. Shouldn't he have someone else do that for him?" Kallie asked.

"Indeed," Myra mumbled in agreement.

"I am sure the king has his reasons." Dropping the now petalless rose onto the ground, Phaia swept her hair behind her ear, a faint blush coloring her cheeks. "I'm sorry, Princess. I shouldn't be bothering you two with this. You are our guests. It is nothing for you to worry about."

Kallie halted, tugging Phaia and Myra to a stop with her. "Phaia, this is my home now. I am betrothed to your king." She peered down her nose at the handmaiden. "The king's concerns are *my* concerns."

Phaia's eyes grew wide, and her mouth fell open.

Kallie's features softened as the corner of her lips tipped into a small smile. "I want this kingdom to flourish." She reached for Phaia's hand. "I want our people to thrive. I can only do that if I know what is going on."

Phaia raised a hand to her chest. "Of course. I meant no offense, Princess."

In the distance, bells chimed.

"I apologize, Kallie," Myra said, interrupting. "I promised the seamstress I would help her with your wedding dress. As you know, we are on a tight timeline and—"

"By all means, Myra, go on your way," Kallie interrupted.

Myra squeezed Kallie's hand once, and with a small smile at Phaia, she headed back up the path to the castle.

"Shall we continue, Princess?" Phaia asked, twisting her hands behind her back.

The sun peaked out from the heavy clouds above them. It was midday, yet the temperature had barely warmed up. Still, Kallie would rather spend her time in the fog than in the darkness of the castle.

Kallie locked her arm around Phaia's, pulling her closer. With their arms entwined, Kallie led them forward. "Now, Phaia, is there something I should know about?"

Phaia bit her lip, and Kallie sighed. She pulled at her gift with ease. She no longer wished to entertain secrets. "Phaia, tell me why King Rian is hiring new servants."

Instantly, the words flowed from the servant's mouth. "King Rian and Queen Mother believe there was a traitor among the staff."

"A traitor?" Kallie asked, her ability still lacing her words.

"Yes, Princess. King Lothian's death was unexpected. In the weeks leading up to his death, he was fine, healthy. Then, all of a sudden, he grew immensely ill, not just a cough or some other casual sickness but rather violently ill. He had been around no one who had demonstrated similar symptoms—or any symptoms for that matter. It was a complete shock, even to the healers."

So, her father was correct. Rian and Tessa were investigating Lothian's death.

"Do you mean to suggest that they believe the late king—may his soul rest in the Beneath—was poisoned?"

Phaia nodded. "And that one—or more—of the servants helped."

"Hence, the staff changes," Kallie mumbled.

And hence why Father wants me to choose a servant.

Phaia sighed. "Unfortunately, Your Highness."

"Are you concerned about your position, Phaia?"

Phaia's clouded eyes enlarged. "Me? Oh, no. I am one of King Rian's new hires. He would not have put me in charge of your care if he did not trust me."

Kallie nodded, smiling. Phaia was not one of Domitius' spies then. But she could be one of Rian's.

"Tell me about the king," Kallie said.

An instant blush ran across Phaia's face. "The king is very handsome, more handsome than the former king or his brother."

Kallie held in her chuckle. The girl had a crush on the king. How *cute*. No wonder she knew his likes and dislikes. It wasn't from careful observation but rather infatuation.

"And?" Kallie prompted.

"He has a strong chin, gorgeous eyes." Phaia's gaze grew distant, her tone airy. "Hair the color of a burning sunrise over the horizon."

This time, Kallie didn't bother muffling her chuckle as she released the pull on her gift. While Kallie had strengthened her connection to her gift when she had visited the Whispering Springs in Pontia, she would rather not overuse it so carelessly, especially when Phaia seemed more than willing to discuss Rian without it.

"And besides his appearance?"

Phaia's brows bunched together in confusion. "What do you mean?"

Kallie huffed. The servant was oblivious.

"What is his *mind* like, Phaia?" Kallie asked.

Phaia pulled at her lip as she thought. "Well . . . he's kind."

"Kind?" Kallie pulled Phaia closer to her, nodding. "We can work with that."

Phaia cast Kallie a cursory glance, and Kallie pushed forward. "What else?"

"He's loyal. King Rian is always thinking about his family and his people first. King Lothian was a good ruler, but sometimes he got caught up in all the politics. If I am to be honest, Prince—I mean *Captain* Sebastian inherited that trait, but King Rian did not. He truly cares."

At that, Kallie was thankful Sebastian had been born second and not given the throne. To marry him was a thought that made her stomach churn. Yet the king was not as *good* as Phaia believed, Kallie thought as she recalled that first night.

After a moment of silence, Phaia asked, "Have you not met King Rian yet, Princess?"

Kallie bit down on her cheek before saying, voice terse, "Unfortunately, our schedules have not aligned."

Phaia shrugged. "Ah. That's not surprising. He's a very busy man."

"So I've been told," Kallie said under her breath.

Phaia continued, "And private. He likes his space and the quiet. He's often in the family's library if he's not stuck in a meeting with one of his advisors."

"And his advisors—were they too changed after King Lothian's passing?"

"I do not believe so. The Queen Mother remains one of his closest advisors, alongside Jacquin, Harold, Florence, Draxin, and others, most of whom were chosen by the former king, I believe."

"Most? But not all?" Kallie asked. It was strange that Rian would be more suspicious of the servants than of the advisors. Kallie's initial thought would have been to question those closest to the king, not the servants.

Phaia nodded. "Yes, King Rian chose his right hand, a friend he grew up with. Lorince trained with the king when they were both young boys, I believe."

Kallie glanced up at the king's tower. Perhaps it was time she finally met her betrothed.

"As one of King Rian's chosen staff members, do you see him frequently?"

Phaia tipped her head up in thought. "I would not say frequently, but at least once a day."

Kallie nodded. "Can you deliver a message to him?"

"Of course, Your Highness."

Kallie smiled. "Tell King Rian his bride requests his presence at dinner tomorrow night."

CHAPTER 8
KALLIE

The glass bottle was a stone against her bosom, frigid and piercing despite its smooth surface.

She had no more time to lose.

In the cover of darkness, she crept through the halls and willed confidence in her quiet steps as her heart thumped in her chest.

Any guards she passed as she traveled through the halls, she commanded them to turn a blind eye.

The door creaked open, and she halted, peering into the shadows of the room. Swallowing, she entered when no one stirred.

The air inside the room was cold, stiff. She tiptoed into the room, her slippers quiet on the floor.

Despite the temperature, her palms were slick with sweat as she pulled back the curtain.

At the sound, the man turned in his bed, creases denting his forehead. He blinked.

In the dim moonlight that seeped through a small window nearby, the servant's eyes were streaked with red. As she hovered over him, he stared up at her.

"Ryla?" the servant whispered. "Please, Ryla."

The back of her eyes burned as the man called upon the goddess of healing and begged her for mercy. Still, she did not correct him even though there would be no mercy to be found tonight. She had sealed his fate.

She pulled a piece of parchment from her corset. With a silent prayer to Sabina, Kallie whispered the command.

Her target had been chosen.

CHAPTER 9
GRAESON

Graeson leaned back, his right foot braced against the wall and his shoulder against the window.

At high noon, the sun cast shattered rainbows across the pine floor of the royal meeting room. No additional lighting was necessary, for the ceiling-high windows supplied enough natural light to fill the space. Long vines of spring green leaves from the pothos plants hanging from the ceiling cascaded down the length of the glass. Decades ago, the royal meeting room was one of the many sitting areas in the castle. It wasn't until Queen Esmeray's grandfather, King Esile, decided to move the council meetings here. The former meeting place was in an old room in the back of the castle, hidden from the sun, with a breezy draft from the island's coast. Graeson, however, would have preferred that room. There, he would have been able to sink into the shadows.

Here, on the other hand, the sunlight poured into the room. The light only made the large room more suffocating today. Grief was meant to live in the darkness, unseen, not illuminated by large windows.

It was the first council meeting without Fynn, and his absence loomed large over the advisors at the table. You could see it in the grieving gaze of the queen, the purple bags carved beneath Dani's eyes, Terin's lost stare as he sat in Fynn's former seat.

Terin was never meant to sit in the inheritor's seat. Their roles had been decided from a young age, their abilities and personalities dictating their future. Terin's place had always been across from Fynn during these meetings, where he listened attentively and provided an opinion when asked. Terin was supposed to be Fynn's right-hand man, not occupying the inheritor's seat. Still, the seat had to be filled. Now, Terin was supposed to provide answers, not suggestions like he had been trained to do for years.

The prince, however, had no answers to offer in response to the queen's previous question about what to do about the attack.

None of the advisors at the table did. Not Airos, the Captain of the Queen's Guard; not Theenah, the Head of Medicine; not Harmonia, the overseer of Port Clareis; not Menides, the Head of Strategy. None of the other older advisors sitting around the grand table had an answer.

No one, that is, except for Dani.

"We need to strike back," Dani said, pounding her fist against the table.

"We cannot strike back," Esmeray argued, rubbing her temple. Exhaustion soaked her tongue. Almost two weeks had passed since Fynn's death, yet none had time to mourn. Meetings went on, reparations continued. It was as if Esmeray thought the kingdom would crumble if she stopped to mourn. But what happened when everyone was falling apart, nevertheless?

Esmeray continued, "The treaty—"

"Fuck the treaty!" Dani spat, slapping a palm against the table.

Silence filled the room as the advisors' attention flicked between the two women.

Despite Dani's disrespectful tone, Graeson knew no one would punish her for it.

Since Fynn's passing, Dani had been off-kilter, and for good reason. Her other half was gone, now walking in the Beneath. No one dared to confront her, to tell her to let Fynn go. Dani would never be able to let him go, and Graeson couldn't blame her. None of them could.

Even Esmeray, who had her partner ripped away from her by Domitius decades ago, was hesitant to broach the topic. The queen was the only one at the table who had lost their other half and knew what it felt like to have a broken soul bond. Unlike Dani, whose ring remained snug on her finger, the queen's thin gold band hung on a chain that disappeared down the front of her dress. Dani should have removed the ring when Fynn passed, or at least after his funeral. According to the stories, a bond ring without its connection to its other half could drive the wearer insane. The loss of the connection had been compared to drowning beneath the frozen glaciers—cold and suffocating with nowhere to go but down. Even knowing this, Dani had made no move to remove the ring.

Was this the madness the others had spoken of? Or just the grief that plagued Dani?

Usually, Graeson would step up to the challenge, but not this time. He couldn't lest he wished to be called a hypocrite. He knew better than to tell someone grieving to calm down, especially when he was grieving and angry, too. After all, he still wore the gold band his mother and Esmeray forged from the rare metal blessed by the god Pontanius. Graeson had never taken it off, even when everyone told him Kalisandre was gone. Even when they said she was a lost cause. He, however, was more attuned to the metal's rhythms than the others, and the ring still hummed. The connection, although faint, was still there. If he couldn't let go of Kalisandre, how could Dani let go of her husband, the man who had wanted to save everyone?

So instead of saying anything, Graeson stood silent in the far corner of the room while the other advisors shifted in their seats uncomfortably.

At last, Menides brushed a light hand over his daughter's shoulder.

Dani shrugged off his unwelcome hand and continued to press her fist into the wood. Assessing the others at the table, she slowly pulled her fist back and sat down.

Wary glances were passed around the advisors, and Graeson instinctively looked toward the inheritor's seat. Only to remember that Fynn wasn't there. Fynn who would normally be reading everyone's thoughts and putting their concerns to rest. Instead, Terin looked to his mother.

In time, the prince would get used to his new role.

Or at least Graeson hoped Terin would.

Menides raised a disappointed brow at his daughter.

Dani ignored him. "We've been holding back for years," she said, pressing onward. "We've been standing by for years, hiding on this godsforsaken island, waiting. And for what? When will we stop waiting?" Dani stood again, her words fueling her. "Domitius has come to our kingdom, burned our land, and killed our people *twice*."

"And kidnapped one of our own twice," Graeson mumbled.

Not having heard him, Dani continued, "And we are not going to retaliate? What does that say about our kingdom? About our people?"

Menides sighed as he rubbed a hand across his forehead. "Danisinia, this is more complicated than you think."

Dani snarled at her father. "Do not belittle me, Father. I may be young, but that does not mean I am ignorant. I have earned my spot at this table just as you have."

"I never said your youth was the cause of your ignorance. Your *youth*, Daughter, is why you are here. Why the three of you are here." Menides looked at Dani, Terin, and Graeson.

Foreigners would have thought it strange how many of the royal advisors were a part of the younger generation—like Terin, Dani, and Graeson—but it was Pontian tradition. A way to make transitions smoother. It ensured the new advisors for the new leaders would have experience sitting at the table and have a chance to learn from their predecessors.

Menides continued, "While we are old and are more experienced than you, we are often blinded by the past, by tradition. Your youth is a gift. An advantage."

Dani laughed, but the laughter didn't reach her green eyes. "If that is the case, if you truly value my opinion, listen to it rather than blindly dismiss it, Father."

Menides sighed again. Quieter, he said, "While it may not be your youth that I am weary of, Dani, your grief, on the other hand, is a cause for my concern."

Dani stepped back as if she had been slapped in the face. The pearl beads wrapped around her braids smacked against each other, clattering. "What is *that* supposed to mean?"

"You have never been a fool; do not play one now. You are grieving. You are in pain. Your husband, our prince, has passed. And we are all grieving and upset. Fynn—" Menides pursed his lips, fixing his gaze upon the ceiling for a moment before returning his attention to his daughter. "Fynn was one of the good ones." Straightening, Menides looked at the rest of the advisors sitting at the table. "If we let our anger blind us and our desire for revenge guide our path, then we will fail in whatever we do."

Dani huffed a soft, icy laugh. "Then what, Father, do you suggest we do? Because from where I stand, we are doing nothing." She stepped toward her father, but Menides held his ground as the two stood head-to-head. "How is that any better?"

The two warriors were mirror images of each other. Their dark brown braids hung down their backs, their arms crossed over their chests, and their innate stubbornness painted their countenances. Dani's mother was a petite woman, only an inch or two over five feet tall. Meanwhile, Menides was all muscle and height. Dani was just barely shorter, and from a short distance, they were nearly eye-to-eye.

Menides had only himself to blame for his daughter's brazenness. She, like her father, was a born strategist.

When Dani, Graeson, and the twins were growing up, they all shared a tutor. Although younger than the three boys, Dani had surpassed all of them in their academic studies. She took additional lessons with her father outside their regular study hours as a child. And she took to those lessons like a moth to a flame. Dani learned from her father with eager eyes and an open mind.

Later on, those extra lessons paid off. Dani had climbed the ranks in the Pontian military quickly—faster than anyone had before her. Despite this, when she was first named general, some soldiers gave her wary gazes. It was neither her gender nor her age that had made them question her position. Unlike kingdoms like Ardentol and Kadia, Pontia had never restricted their ranks to men. The soldiers also understood that there was strength in youth. The future generation would carry the burdens they left behind. Therefore, Dani's age was a sign of hope. It indicated to the kingdom that the future would be strong, sturdy, and lethal.

Instead, the soldiers' hesitation and suspicions resulted from her lineage. The soldiers had thought that Dani had been handed her title of general with neither merit nor experience but rather because of *who* she was: a Ferrios. Not only was her father the Head of Strategy and the Commander of Pontia's military, but her brothers were also prominent figures. Her older brother, Sawyer, was a master of any weapon he touched. Xander, her younger brother, had become Pontia's lead blacksmith at nineteen, his gift in metallurgy and craftsmanship aiding him in his career. Strategy and swordplay were in Dani's blood.

However, the Pontians prided themselves in being able to choose their leaders. Unlike other kingdoms, anyone could rise in the ranks. Only the royal titles were passed down by blood, and even that title sometimes floated to another family depending on the history, reputation, and the gift the ruler bore. When Menides announced Dani's promotion to general, Esmeray simultaneously announced the decision to pass down Menides' role as Head of Strategy to his daughter when the time arose. To some, this was a shock. What the people did not realize, however, was that the advisors and small council of lords and ladies all unanimously supported both decisions weeks before the announcement. Some soldiers remained suspicious.

Then, they saw Dani fight.

They saw her command.

They saw her lead and put her soldiers first, her *people* first.

They watched Dani fight alongside the experienced soldiers and train the new ones. They witnessed her acquire improved housing for the soldiers, increased pay, and better benefits for their families. Respect was earned in Pontia, and Dani had earned it without question.

Therefore, when the unsurprising news came that Dani and Fynn were engaged and, shortly after, married, the people went to the streets with shouts of happiness. Music, laughter, and cheer blanketed the nights across Pontia for weeks after the wedding; even in the villages far north of the palace, the people celebrated the union. Everyone was overjoyed to celebrate their future royals, for Dani and Fynn promised a bright future. A future where the people's voices were uplifted and heard. A future of unbridled strength.

Then the Dark Night came. The night everything had gone to shit when the people's hopes burned to ash alongside the crumbling houses on the outskirts of the village.

Not even a week had passed before some people began to spread rumors that Dani was to marry Terin to secure her place in the royal family. The people, it seemed, were eager to grab onto something to hope for. But those closest to Dani and Terin knew that would never happen. Not only did Dani not care about a crown, but Dani and Terin's love for one another was strictly platonic, one similar to a pair of siblings. Both of them knew Fynn would want them to be happy, would want them to be loved. They would never be able to provide what a true romantic relationship did—what Dani and Fynn had once upon a time: a bond between soulmates.

The ancient blood of the gods had created the bonds. When a person found their soul bond, their gifts flourished. Their relationship balanced them, enhanced them. Soul bonds were two people whose gifts sang to each other. And Dani and Fynn's connection could have filled a concert hall.

A person had one soul bond. One other half that made a person whole. The rings helped solidify that connection, for the metal of the gods strengthened the thread between the two souls.

Dani's person was gone. Yet her love for Fynn continued to burn inside her, and it called for revenge.

Graeson knew that kind of love all too well.

He stepped forward.

"Dani has a point." Everyone's attention turned to Graeson. After standing in the corner for so long, many advisors had forgotten his presence.

Dani and Menides hesitated, unwilling to let the other win. But after a silent debate, they met an understanding and simultaneously took their seats.

Graeson continued, "The treaty states that no kingdom may attack another kingdom without just cause. Ardentol and Frenzia both broke the treaty."

Esmeray sighed. "Yes, and from our perspective, they did not have the right to attack our lands."

Graeson heard the *but* on her tongue, and his shoulders sank.

Esmeray met the eyes of each of her advisors as she observed the room filled with her closest friends, allies, and confidants. "As many of you know, my daughter was taken from me when she was three. Kalisandre has lived in the enemy's castle for years, unknowingly pretending to be someone she was not. The night of the attack, she sacrificed herself to save not only myself but Terin, Airos, and several others as well. In exchange for our safety, she was taken once again."

The advisors nodded. They all knew this story already. Even still, some advisors found it hard to empathize with Kalisandre's poor fate. Theena bit her cheek, and the northern lord's jaw ticked at the mention of Kalisandre's sacrifice. It didn't matter that Kalisandre was the daughter of their queen. She was a traitor.

But not everything is black and white in the game of politics.

"Everyone believes Kalisandre is the daughter of Ardentol, that she is his blood and the daughter of his late wife. However, only we know the truth. Only our kingdom knows that the Princess of Ardentol does not exist. And the three of you," Esmeray's gaze fell to Graeson, Dani, and Terin, "witnessed most of those kingdoms vow to protect her if someone tried to get in the way of the marriage between her and her chosen suitor. King Rian was chosen. Frenzia attacked in the name of the vow they promised. To the rest of the kingdom, *we* are the ones in the wrong. To them, we were unjust."

"Then tell them the truth." Graeson crossed his arms in front of his chest, holding back the rising anger. He would not break now. His ire would do no good here.

Esmeray rubbed the side of her temple. "Kalisandre is in the hands of Domitius. From your account, Domitius was on that ship. We do not know if Domitius knows that Kalisandre knows the truth. It could endanger her life if we announce it to the world."

"Her life?" Dani spat, her fists crashing down on the table as she leaned forward in her chair. "What about Fynn's life? Because of her, *he* is dead."

Esmeray arched a brow, the only visible sign that Dani's words pressed a nerve. "Danisinia, heed your father's words. Grief and a thirst for revenge will only get you so far."

"It's not about revenge! Can't any of you see it?" Dani swept a hand in the air, nearly smacking her father. "*She* is the reason they came here in the first place! She brought them here, led them to our home. Kallie does not care about any of us. Why should we care about—"

Dani did not finish her sentence as she slumped back into her chair.

Menides' jaw dropped as he stared at his unconscious daughter.

Graeson snapped his attention to Terin. Sadness tainted Terin's countenance. While Terin's gift was not as potent when he was not in contact with someone, it was still strong enough to knock them out cold.

The queen straightened in her seat, folding her hands on the table. "I hope that you all will forgive me. I do not enjoy silencing any of you." Graeson did not miss how Esmeray's gaze stayed on him longer than any of the others. They both knew her threat was futile in his case, for Terin's ability did not work on him. None of their mental abilities did, not unless he let it.

"But I believe it is best for everyone. Menides, I will apologize to Dani after today's meeting. To the rest of you, I will say this once and only once: I do not take my son's death lightly. Like many of you, I am enraged. I not only lost my son but my daughter as well. *Again.* King Domitius has taken too much from our kingdom and myself over the past two decades. But if we do as Dani suggests, we *will* start a war. A war we are gravely unprepared for. We need time, we need a strategy in place, and, most importantly, we need the reparations to be completed. Our people here must come first."

The queen's blue eyes darkened as though a sea storm lived within her irises. "I promise you all, Domitius will pay in due time."

A knock sounded at the door, and Harmonia jumped in her chair.

Wiping the building storm from her face, Esmeray waved at Airos, who stood near the door.

When he opened the doors, Gia, one of the queen's servants, hurried in with a letter.

"Your Majesty," Gia said as she fell into a deep curtsy. "A messenger delivered this, and based on the sigil, I believe it is of great importance."

Airos took the letter from the servant. Peeling off the golden wax stamped onto the red envelope, he scanned the letter before passing it to the queen. Her face revealed nothing as she read it.

Then her jaw ticked.

When she looked up, Graeson's heart dropped.

"Kalisandre and Rian are to be married in a month."

No one spoke. At least, if they did, Graeson didn't hear them. The blood rushed from Graeson's body as he processed the queen's words.

He thought someone said his name, but he didn't stay to find out. His rising anger propelled him forward as he stormed out of the room. He barely sensed the stares of the advisors fixed on his back as he disappeared around the corner.

When he passed the staff in the halls, a couple attempted to wave, but their hands fell limp at their side once they took in Graeson's expression, his blazing silver eyes. With their heads down, they scurried past him. They knew better than to gain Graeson's attention in this state. Whether they had seen him in action or not, they knew what he could do—or at least thought they did. Everyone in the castle had heard the story about what had happened when Graeson was a child, and that was reason enough to strike fear in their hearts.

Many of the people wondered who he was, *what* he was. Some had their guesses based on the myths that traveled the streets, but none of them truly knew. Only those who needed to know knew the truth about his *gifts*.

Still, even Graeson didn't understand the full extent of his abilities. He never let himself get that far. And he would not let his anger win now, would not allow it to unravel everything he worked so hard to protect as he tried to block out Esmeray's words. But he was quickly losing that battle. The words cycled in his mind on a continuous loop.

King Rian and Kalisandre were to be married.

And Graeson only had a month to stop it.

CHAPTER 10
KALLIE

At the great doors to the royal dining room, Kallie stopped in her tracks. Voices from inside the room seeped out into the hall, and she recognized Tessa's voice instantly.

"She may look sweet, but do not forget who her father is, Son."

Kallie's nails bit into her palms. Would she always live in his shadow?

Maybe Tessa was right, for the vial of poison no longer sat against her chest. It's victim now chosen.

"She is brazen, Rian. If she is to live here in our kingdom, she must respect our traditions, our way of life."

Tradition, Kallie scoffed. *More like hiding beneath a king.*

Tessa might have been wise, but at the end of the day, she would be remembered for being the wife of a king and the mother of another. Nothing more because she followed that tradition. Because Tessa had stayed within the lines drawn in the sand by the men in power. It didn't matter if Tessa held knowledge. She would not be remembered for it. That was how the cards fell when a woman played by a man's rules.

Kallie, however, would not be confined to such rules. While Kallie may have been following King Domitius' plan by marrying Rian, she would not be an obedient princess. Her goal was to rule, and rule she would.

Kallie ran a hand down the side of the elegant floor-length dress, smoothing the fabric. Tonight was more than a meeting with her betrothed. It was about facing all the choices she had made in recent months and taking the next step to claim her throne.

Kallie only hoped she had made the right choice.

"Princess?"

Kallie looked at the guard beside her, and Argon straightened. He took a step back, clearing his throat. "Is everything all right?"

Either Argon had not heard the conversation between Rian and Tessa, or he was pretending not to. Whatever the truth was, Kallie did not care. Tessa's words would not affect her. Kallie knew who she was and knew what she fought for.

Pushing her shoulders back, she strutted forward, the guard's question left unanswered in the hallway.

When Kallie entered the royal dining room, Rian snapped his mouth shut and swallowed whatever words had been on his tongue. The crystal glasses on the table rattled when his thighs hit the edge of the table. A blush rose to his cheeks as he steadied his glass.

Introductions were not necessary. Kallie had studied his portrait countless times over the past week. As the painting in the king's hall suggested, Rian's hair was indeed a dark copper, filled with warmth. His deep brown eyes were softer than Sebastian's piercing green ones. Although his quiet, bashful demeanor suggested otherwise, Rian's appearance demanded the room's attention. He was strikingly handsome, and the painting had not revealed his height. His sharp jawline, his height, his broad shoulders that seemed to say he could carry the weight of the kingdom on them—it all demanded to be looked at, to be admired and fawned after. His suit, paired with a dark red wine jacket with simple black pants, was well-tailored, hugging his lean, muscular build. A gold watch wrapped snugly around his wrist. He wore no crown, yet his hair wore the mark of one, his amber curls indented.

Phaia was right. The king was undoubtedly attractive. But more than that, Rian was someone who would either rise on the throne or crumble beneath it.

While Kallie observed him, Rian notedly observed her as well. And Kallie knew what he saw. Her appearance tonight had been crafted with care and precision.

The new black silk dress, carefully chosen, clung to her body as if it were water rolling over her skin. Unlike her standard dresses, this dress was meant to lay everything bare, to entice. Kallie had been stripped of the layers of tulle and chiffon customary of the Ardentolian dresses. Kallie's dress bore a simple heart-shaped neckline, drawing attention to the glittering diamonds dripping from her necklace. And it indeed drew Rian's attention. His gaze caught on the sparkling stones laying on her collarbone, then dipped to the silt that stopped mid-thigh.

Kallie was keenly aware of the vial's absence as he inched his way down her body. For a week, the small vial of poison sat hidden behind her corsets, a constant reminder of the task she had to complete. But now, it was gone.

Willing her stomach to settle, Kallie forced a small smile to her lips and strolled forward.

In the hearth sitting along the back wall, a small fire crackled. Beneath the smell of coals, Kallie identified the faint rosemary and sage from the venison sitting in the center of the large oak table—a table too large for today's attendants. After all, this was a dinner for two. And yet . . .

In the seat to the right of Rian, Tessa sat, wearing a high-collared maroon dress with her hair pulled back in a loose bun, tendrils of auburn curls framing her face. The flicking flames of the candles cast a gold hue across her light brown skin.

Offering Kallie a small smile, Rian tipped his head. "Princess Kalisandre, it is an honor to make your acquaintance."

An honor to make my acquaintance?

A laughable jest after she had to request his presence after a week of living in the castle. As king, Rian should have been one of the first to greet his guests, especially if the person in question was the individual whom he was to marry. But no, he was *indisposed*. But instead of letting his words visibly irritate her, Kallie shook them off and lightened her tone when she spoke. "My King, I assure you, the pleasure is all mine."

"Please, sit," Rian said, pointing to the table.

Three extravagant place settings were laid out. The only available seat was on the opposite end of the table. In normal circumstances, the queen would sit at the opposite end of the king. However, these were not normal circumstances, and Kallie saw Tessa's presence for what it was: a way to put distance between Kallie and the king.

I'll have to fix that, now won't I?

Kallie shifted out of Tessa's sight and closer to Rian.

She smirked, the heat of her gift warming her body as she reached out a hand as if brushing off a piece of lint from Rian's shoulder. "You will ask your mother to leave us," Kallie whispered in his ear. She felt the release of her gift as it left her body to weave its limbs around Rian's mind, forcing his hand and changing his will.

"Mother, leave us." The command rolled off Rian's tongue as if it were his own wish.

In Kallie's peripheral, Tessa's jaw dropped open. Kallie smirked behind him, pleased.

Rian would be an easy target, indeed.

Wiping away her smugness, Kallie turned toward Tessa, a hand on her chest. "Oh, Queen Mother, I didn't see you down there."

Tessa's attention flicked to Kallie, eyes narrowing.

"Mother." Rian pointed toward the door. "I would like to spend some time with my bride."

"But, Rian, that's not—"

"*Mother.*"

Tessa clenched her fists as she walked over to Rian. She tried to shift her body in a way that would put distance between Kallie and her son. As she did, Kallie saw the opportunity to try a new tactic.

"Oh no, have you grown ill?" Kallie asked, her gift lacing her words. She had never tried to command through questioning, but she had seen her father do it to his commanders when they questioned his orders. If Kallie incorporated her gift with it, it could work even better.

Intention. Confidence. Execution. Those were the three things her gift required.

The fire crackled.

Then, the familiar haze slipped over Tessa's brown eyes, and her hand fell to her stomach. "Yes, actually. I am feeling ill."

"You should go lay down and rest," Kallie said, the feigned concern poisoned with command.

"Yes . . . yes, I think I need to lie down." Tessa's hand fell from Rian's shoulder.

"Oh, Queen Mother!" Kallie called after Tessa.

Tessa stumbled as she glanced over her shoulder.

Kallie smirked. "Do feel better soon."

Tessa only offered a tense grimace before taking her leave with her shoulders hunched as she gripped her stomach.

Kallie's manipulations were only a trick of the mind. Once the common passed, Tessa would feel better.

Although, hopefully, not too quickly.

Kallie turned back to Rian. "Since it is just us, do you mind if I sit here instead?" She pointed to the newly vacated seat.

Rian smiled and gestured with his hand to the chair. "Please, Princess." He moved around the table and pulled the chair out, the legs of the chair barely scratching against the floor.

As Kallie claimed the seat, he pushed it in, and Kallie picked up Tessa's wine glass with two fingers. "Would it—"

Rian signaled the servant waiting by the doors to the kitchen. The servant, a man who appeared to be younger than Kallie, probably eighteen, hurried forward and removed the used glass.

"Thank you . . ." Kallie hesitated.

The servant froze, his fingers still on the new glass. "Parker, my lady."

"Parker." Kallie smiled sweetly at the man, and a blush rose to his cheeks.

He cleared his throat and bowed, then rushed out of the room.

The silence had barely settled before Parker and Trina, another servant Kallie recognized from an earlier encounter, began serving them. Trina piled venison and an assortment of vegetables onto Kallie's plate. Then, with a nod from Rian, the two servants left the room.

Cutting the venison, Rian asked, "How are you finding the palace, Princess?"

"It is quite—" Kallie took a sip of wine as she searched for a way to describe the barren castle—"spacious."

Rian's lips twitched, and he glanced at her through dark lashes. "No need to sugarcoat it, Princess."

Clamping her lips together, Kallie ducked her head. "Very well, then." She brushed her hair behind her ear and observed the room. "The castle, I admit, does have good bones, but it needs a little . . . life, don't you think?"

The bump in the middle of his throat dipped. "I suppose you are right. I haven't had much time to redecorate. The council keeps me busy these days."

"So it seems," Kallie said. She ran a finger up the stem of her wine glass. "Although I must say, I did wonder if you were avoiding me."

With a downturned mouth, Rian cut off another bite of meat. "I apologize if it appeared that way, for that was not my intent. I've had little time to myself."

"Understandably so." She popped a potato into her mouth, chewed it, and swallowed. "But I do hope we can find some time to get to know each other better. After all, we are to marry in what? Three weeks, is it?"

Rian pushed a hand through his hair and lightly pulled at the strands. A boyish chuckle left his mouth, a small dimple appearing on the right side. "Is it in three weeks already?"

"Don't worry," Kallie said, reaching a hand across the table and laying it atop his. With Rian's hair out of his face, the purple beneath his eyes was prominent. This was the face of a king who had placed too much on his shoulders too fast. But that was why Kallie was here. To take that burden away from him.

She squeezed his hand. "I have it taken care of. Like you, the staff have been keeping me busy this past week. Invitations were sent out a week ago. Arrangements have been made, and orders have been placed. All you have to remember is show up." Kallie raised a brow, a soft smirk splaying across her face. "Think you can manage that?"

Rian laughed, an amused glint in his irises. "I think I can convince my advisors to clear my schedule that week."

At least he has some sense of humor, Kallie thought, smiling.

Rian flipped his hand over, holding her palm, the touch awkward and strange. "I do sincerely apologize for my absence, Princess."

Kallie slipped her hand out of his, reaching for her fork. "No apologies necessary, but I hope you will learn to share those burdens that weigh so heavily on you in time. Your rule will only be as strong as you are. And if you don't mind me saying—you, King Rian, look exhausted. You should rest more."

He sighed and mumbled, "A wishful thought."

"What do you mean?"

Rian shook his head, but the smile that tugged at the corner of his lips did not reach his eyes. "Nothing for you to worry about."

Clearly, the king was the type of person who kept things close to his chest but wore his heart on his sleeve. If Kallie could get him to trust her, he would crack right open like an egg.

She could not force that trust, however. She needed to nurture it first. A long-term manipulation would only work if it had a foundation to attach itself to.

Kallie leaned toward him. "Someone needs to worry about the king who worries about everyone else. Isn't that what a queen is for?" Kallie smiled sheepishly, forcing a blush on her face. Let him think his presence affected her. Let him believe that she was here only for him.

"Oh, and please do call me Kallie. Kalisandre and Princess are much too formal for two people who are to spend the rest of their lives together."

"Very well then, *Kallie*." He chuckled to himself, rubbing the back of his neck with a hand, then added. "I would offer a nickname to you as well, but there's not much one can do with a name like Rian."

"Ry?"

"Like rye bread?" Amusement mixed with disgust forced his brow to raise.

Eyes lit with a twinkle of mischief, she cocked a brow. "I suppose I will just have to get creative, won't I?"

"I suppose so."

The trap was laid, now to reel him in.

CHAPTER 11
GRAESON

Graeson drew his arm back before letting it fly through the air. His knuckles smashed into the training dummy. Straw poked through the top of its head from the force of the blow. He pulled his hand back and jabbed it with his other fist. He struck again.

And again.

And again.

He would continue to strike until all his anger had run through his veins and flown out of his hands. Until all the straw pieces had been forced out.

The announcement shouldn't have come as a surprise to him, yet hearing the words spoken out loud sent him storming out of the castle. Before he realized it, he was at the training grounds. An icy fire in his gaze and a knot in his stomach. If he didn't release his anger in some productive way, it would come out in the worst way possible. And he didn't want those around him to hurt more than they already did.

With each punch, Graeson let out a small piece of himself, a piece he usually kept closed off and under close guard. Ever since he was a child, he made sure to keep that monstrous part of him on a tight chain. He pulled it tight against the morals and hid it beneath everything that made sense.

When Graeson was younger, he had feared the thing that lay inside him. Had feared *this* side of him. The monster was a reminder of the father who had abandoned him. It was because of that man that Graeson lived with it. Perhaps if his father had stayed, Graeson would not have feared that side of him growing up, but Graeson hadn't been that lucky.

Graeson didn't know he was not like the others until he had lost his temper and then quickly his control. That day, he had lost almost everyone.

Only a week had passed since Domitius had found his way onto their land. When he had surpassed the kraken and the cliffs, past their defenses, and burned down the summer home they had been staying at for the month. Graeson couldn't remember what had set him off—he was too young at the time to remember. Graeson only remembered the red coating his vision, the icy anger coursing through his veins. He had been trying to hold himself back all week, but one day, he had finally combusted. And when he did, he had blacked out.

No one told Graeson exactly what had happened. They even tried to hide it from him. After all, how do you tell a child that he had killed two grown adults and injured a dozen?

It didn't take Gaeson long to discover the truth. He had seen the destroyed room, the blood on the floors, the way the servants cowered away from him. Then, when he had heard the piercing cries from the infirmary and asked what had happened to the patients, no one could look him in the eye.

Since that day, Graeson ensured that the monster living within him—his cursed *gift*—remained locked away. Over the years, he learned to contain the beast residing within him. He learned to dampen it, control it.

He never rereleased the beast. Not entirely, anyway.

Even now, when the monster's rage fueled him, Graeson kept a tight hold on the beast. Only a faint crimson haze blurred the edges of his vision. He needed to release that anger before it consumed him. Or else that control would falter, and there would be no going back. And lately, his control was built on a shaky foundation. One wrong move, one wrong step, and the floorboards would fall through.

"Graeson," someone nearby said, but he ignored it, his name flying away in the breeze. Whoever it was could wait. Right now, Graeson wanted to do anything besides talk.

Graeson slammed his fist into the training dummy.

In this state, he was dangerous. He could sense his grasp on it slipping. Still, he couldn't bring himself to rein it in. It felt too good, too freeing to let the beast out and put his emotions behind a locked door. He didn't want to feel; he didn't want to think.

He wanted to fight.

He wanted revenge.

And he wanted the world to drown as his vision became coated in a violent red hue.

"Graeson," the person repeated.

He faintly recognized the voice, but he couldn't pinpoint it. Everything in this state was hazy, blurry. Gray.

All Graeson could manage was a garbled grunt, unable to form words as his breathing became labored with each successive hit. He adjusted his stance and circled the training dummy, searching for a new target to attack. Finding it, he reared his elbow back again.

A hand gripped his arm, stunting his movement. *"Graeson."*

He snarled, a feral sound originating from the pit of his stomach. A sound not wholly his but something other.

No one should be ordering him around.

No one honestly could, though, could they? He wasn't one of them. It was only because of his upbringing that Graeson allowed the others to command him. In truth, those commands were beneath him.

Remind them who you are, the beast hummed inside of him.

"*Gray.*"

Graeson blinked, snapping his head in the direction of the voice.

Dani jerked back, her eyes widening. Then, she steeled her gaze, her shoulders pushing back and the muscles in her arm straining as she struggled to maintain her firm grip around his arm.

Of all people, she should have known better than to step in his way when he was in this state. Dani, however, no longer cared about her well-being.

Her stare was solid, firm, her grip even tighter. "She's gone. Let her go."

Dani's words struck a chord inside of him.

Kalisandre wasn't gone; Fynn was. Graeson could still help her; he could still save her. There was still time. Time he hadn't had to save Fynn.

He knew what Dani wanted him to do—what he *should* do. However, what he *should* do versus what he *needed* to do were two vastly different things.

The wedding was coming, and Graeson shouldn't have been surprised. After all, Kalisandre had warned him, hadn't she? She had told him what mattered to her: power. A throne he could not give her, but Graeson could give her so much more.

"If it was Fynn, would you let him go?"

Dani's cold green eyes narrowed as she pointed at him, her lip curling into a snarl. "Don't—don't do that."

His heart ricocheted against his rib cage as they stared at each other. He knew he shouldn't have said it. He didn't need to see her flinch at the sound of her husband's name to know that it hurt her.

But *he* was hurt, too.

Every day that went by, Graeson felt lost. Before Kalisandre had come back into his life, he had a goal. He had a purpose: to find her, to save her.

But to see her walk away? To see her give herself up so easily to them—to the enemy? Graeson didn't know what to make of that.

All he knew was that when he saw the fire reflected in Kalisandre's eyes and the darkness hidden beneath the flames, he knew the woman who stared back wasn't the same woman he saw at the cavern. The same woman who shook beneath the stone feet of the gods. Or the woman whose body trembled as she met her mother for the second time. Or when she collapsed against him as Esmeray showed her the truth. Those vulnerable moments were not the reason why he cared for her. They weren't why his whole being was electrified around her. She was his, and he was hers. And he would do whatever it took to get her back. He had made a promise long ago, even if he had to pry her from Domitius' cold body.

Graeson looked at his old friend, and an iciness coated his skin, dulling the anger. "Dani," he whispered.

Dani refused to look at him. She sucked her teeth, holding back the tears that were beginning to fill the corners of her eyes.

Graeson wanted to shake the sadness out of her. Instead, he approached her like he would approach one of his horses. Slowly and with careful movements. "Dani, it wasn't her. You need to understand that."

She scrubbed her face with her palm, a red hue tinting her brown skin. When her hand dropped, her green eyes finally met his, and there was no life left inside of them, only an endless coldness that was all-consuming. "Are you truly that lovesick? She *brought* them here, Gray."

His blood heated, melting the ice coating his body. He brought his fist back and slammed it into the training dummy. Hay exploded from its head.

So many had told him it was Kalisandre's fault. No one believed him, no matter what he said or how he tried to defend Kalisandre. No one understood why Graeson still wanted to help her. Why he thought she was worth saving at all.

"That wasn't her, and you know it," he said, marking each word with a punch.

"Graeson, she was a *child* when we knew her. People change. Kallie isn't the person we thought she was." Dani sighed, gathering her braids into a ponytail. "She's not one of us anymore."

With no hay left in the dummy, Graeson's hands hung at his side. His entire body trembled with anger. "There's something wrong with her. When—"

"Graeson," Dani said, interrupting as she untied the dummy from the pole and let the disheveled fabric fall to the ground.

Graeson shook his head, pressing his hands against the sides of his head. "*Listen* to me."

Pity filled Dani's gaze.

Graeson tried to blink away the pain, but he couldn't. He needed Dani to hear him, to believe him.

"Please," he begged.

Rubbing her face, Dani spun away from him, and his heart sank. Dani was one of his best friends. She was one of the few people in this world Graeson thought would have understood where he was coming from, but even she appeared to have given up on him.

Graeson wanted to save Kalisandre, but he couldn't do it alone. He had hoped that if he could convince Dani to help him, he could convince the others.

She was the one hope he had, and now it walked away with her.

"When we were at the cavern, she was . . . different," Graeson whispered, afraid to speak too loudly lest he scare Dani away. "I know it sounds strange or that I'm looking into something that isn't there, but her . . . her aura was different. She was lighter, like a fog was being lifted from her mind."

Dani mumbled something unintelligible, and Graeson froze, unsure if he heard her correctly. Then, Dani spun around and said one word that gave him an ounce of hope: "Fine."

And Graeson latched onto it—as abysmal as the line of hope was, he would grab onto it as if his life depended on it because it did.

And so did Kalisandre's.

Dani squinted, her head tilting to the side as she leaned against the pole. "Maybe you're right, but maybe you're wrong. I mean this with love, Gray, but you sound crazy." The corner of her mouth twitched. "And I know crazy."

"I'm not crazy!" Graeson shouted.

Dani placed her hand on her hip, her head hung to the side as she peered at him.

"I'm not. You didn't—" Graeson groaned, digging his fingers into his hair. "You didn't see her, Dani. Something is wrong with her."

Dani pointed to her head. "Yeah, her mind."

His hands flew into the air, a smile stretching across his face. "Exactly!"

"And that's a good thing?"

He squeezed a ball of air in his hands as if the action could force Dani to understand. "Don't you get it? It's her *mind*, Dani. She's not in control of it!" The words tumbled out of his mouth in a rush.

"Graeson." And suddenly, he hated the sound of his name. Dani took a wary step toward him. "Think about what you're saying."

"I *have* thought about it! It's the only thing I have thought about since . . ." Graeson hesitated. The truth had to come out. Now or never. He took a deep breath in, then exhaled. "Since Fynn told me he had sensed something was off."

Dani, having begun to reach for him, froze. Her hand hung in the air as if something was pushing against it. "What do you mean?"

Graeson started to pace in the middle of the training field. Fynn wasn't here to help. It was only Graeson's word Dani had to go off. As crazy as Graeson was about to sound, hopefully, his friend could still find the strength to trust him.

He took a deep breath, preparing himself for the ridicule he was about to face. "Fynn told me that when he would try to read Kalisandre's mind, there was a wall stopping him from reading her thoughts. As if something—or *someone*—was pushing back against him. A barrier. He could only pick up certain thoughts as if he was being spoon-fed them."

Dani huffed, shaking her head. "Come on, Gray, that's ridiculous."

Graeson scoffed, spinning on his heel to face Dani head-on. "Then why didn't Fynn know she was a traitor? Fynn should have been able to read her mind. Haven't you wondered why he couldn't see it coming?"

"He's not a seer, Graeson! He's—" Dani hissed. Her shoulders dropped. "He *was* only a mind reader. There were limitations to his gift."

Sneering, Graeson shook his head.

A breeze brushed over him, and Graeson welcomed the cool air's kiss on his sweat-slicked skin.

Dani tilted her head up to the sky. "Okay, fine. Fynn's strength over his gift was beyond exceptional. However, maybe Kallie's a fast learner. Maybe her ability to manipulate minds has given her a stronger handle on her own mind."

"Seriously?" Graeson pushed a hand through his hair. "You know it's not as simple as that!"

Dani's face contorted as she thought of any other possible explanation. Any reason that *wouldn't* suggest Fynn wasn't as strong as everyone had believed him to be.

But she wouldn't find another reason.

Graeson approached Dani, placing a hand on her shoulder. "That's why Fynn didn't know that Kalisandre had given a message to the soldier in Borgania. He couldn't read her thoughts, Dani. Not all of them."

"But that's—"

"Impossible?" Graeson suggested, his hand falling to his side. "Is it really?"

Dani said nothing as her gaze dropped to the ground once again. Then she grabbed his shoulders. "Look, Gray. I want to believe you. I know how hard it is to lose someone you care about, but are you sure you're not reading into this too much?"

"There has only been one other person he couldn't read, Dani." Graeson shook off her hands. "Me."

Dani's natural warm hue drained from her face. She was undoubtedly thinking of the ramifications of having two people who were more like monsters than humans. But that wasn't what Graeson was suggesting. He knew where Kalisandre came from.

She wasn't like him. No one was.

However, before he could say that, Dani responded. "We both know you're different, Gray. Fynn probably just let his feelings get in the way. You know how hopeful he was about having his sister back."

That may have been true, but as hopeful as the twins were to rescue their sister, Dani was the first to say she would save Kalisandre the first time. However, the fire that had once burned bright within Dani had been extinguished.

"That's not true," Graeson countered. "As your father said, there's more at work here than we think. Someone is manipulating her. Someone has tangled her mind and warped it into something that is not hers anymore."

Dani shook her head. "She's not your problem. If that letter is proof of anything, she is not yours, Graeson."

His feet stopped propelling him. Body immobile, Graeson closed his eyes as Dani twisted the knife deeper into his heart. His voice was ice on his tongue. "She wears my mother's ring, Dani. She is more mine than she is his."

"Graeson," Dani warned, and in that one word, Graeson could sense the pity that filled every letter of his name.

He hated it.

"I have heard Esmeray talk about your mother's vision many times, and you no doubt have heard Esmeray repeat it more than I have. So, you know as well as I do then that there is one path here that does not unite the two of you. One path that will cut that thread."

The muscles in his jaw ticked. Through clenched teeth, he gritted out, "This is *not* that path, Dani. I have felt it. I sensed the connection between us."

"Soul bonds or not, there is always a choice." Dani sighed, taking a step forward. "Even if you can save her, she might choose not to accept the bond."

Dani made it sound simple, but it wasn't. Soul bonds were gifts given by a force far greater than the gods, a force so ancient that even the gods themselves rarely understood how the bond worked. Among a pair of soul bonds, at least one of the individuals bore a gift, sometimes both, like with Dani and Fynn or Esmeray and her late husband. When Pontanius first found his wife, Alisynth, he did not understand the connection that pulled them together. It was a connection that promised something great, something extraordinary, something nature willed to happen. Few ignored that pull. And those who did . . . Well, the majority of those stories have been buried in the past, long since forgotten.

After hearing how his gift sang when Kalisandre was around him, when his lips touched hers, when she finally began to open up to him —Graeson would never be able to let that feeling go.

He refused to be one of those stories.

Not without trying first.

"I will not stop fighting for her," Graeson said, voice pained. "I can't."

"She has made her choice, Graeson."

Graeson willed the anger to settle within him as Dani said out loud what he refused to admit.

"And she didn't choose you."

"I will believe that when we free her mind," Graeson whispered.

"What do you mean?" Dani asked, her tone skeptical.

He met her gaze. Ice ran through his veins, the monster's anger seeping out from the closet that it resided in inside Graeson's mind.

"Graeson... What are you going to do?"

A smirk crept onto his face. "I have a wedding to attend."

"Does the queen know?" Dani asked, following after him.

Graeson laughed as he stalked forward. "We both know Esmeray does not control me."

"Graeson, wait," Dani's footsteps quickened behind him. She reached for his shoulder. "You can't."

Graeson shook her hand off. His mind was already set.

"Be honest with yourself, Dani." Graeson faced his friend one last time. "Esmeray will not allow you to have the revenge you crave, but I will." Graeson paused, but Dani didn't deny it. "At the end of the day, it is *your* choice what you wish to do. You can stay on this island, waiting for Esmeray and her advisors to decide. But all you will be waiting for is for our enemies to attack again. Because you know as well as I do that a war is coming." Graeson looked down his nose at her. "What will your role be in that war, Dani?"

Dani stared at him, and for a moment, Graeson thought he saw the flash of the fire she once possessed. But then, she said nothing. Her green gaze cold.

"You blame Kallie for Fynn's death, and I can understand why you think it is her fault. But, in truth, she is not the one to blame. And I will do whatever it takes to prove that to you. With or without you, I am going to save her. Fynn deserves justice. Do not forget who else will be at this wedding."

Kalisandre was a victim here, too. Somehow, Domitius had wrapped his claws around her mind. He had manipulated the manipulator. Graeson only needed to prove it and free Kalisandre from his grasp. Then, he would show Kalisandre once and for all that he could give her more than a crown or a throne. He would give her the seven seas and the stars above. He would give her everything.

If Kalisandre still did not want any part of him at that point, Graeson would let her go. It would kill him to do so, but at that point, it would be her choice and her choice alone.

That's all he wanted for her. No matter if her choice broke him. At least it was hers.

"Graeson," Dani whispered behind him.

A smile tugged at his lips, but he didn't turn back. "I have a few pieces of business I need to take care of," he said, continuing down the path to the castle.

Graeson knew Dani had already made up her mind. In truth, she had probably made her choice when she decided to find him. Revenge was Dani's second calling, the flower she couldn't help pick in the garden. She only needed a little push.

Over his shoulder, Graeson said, "We leave in three days."

CHAPTER 12
KALLIE

Glass shattered on the dark oak table, now stained red, as a scream rang through the hall outside the dining room.

Rian stood, the white shirt beneath his tailored jacket now stained red.

Hurried footsteps echoed outside the royal dining room.

It was time.

Blood rushed from Kallie's face. Moisture licked the back of her neck. On trembling legs, she stood, joining Rian and grabbing a hold of his arm.

At her touch, he straightened, covering her hand with one of his own.

"What—what was that?" Kallie asked, pressing a hand against her chest as if she could prevent her heart from bursting out of it.

A Frenzian guard burst through the doors, sword unsheathed. Eyes blazing until they landed on Rian. "My King, are you all right?"

"Fine, but what's going on, Laurince?"

Another guard rounded the corner, shouting, "Your Majesty! There's been a—" The newly arrived guard chopped off his words once he spotted Kallie. He cleared his throat. "We uhm . . . we have a situation, My King."

"Out with it then, Syrus," Rian demanded.

"One of the servants has . . ." Syrus swallowed. "One of the servants has taken his life."

Rian froze. "Are you sure?"

"Yes, Your Majesty."

"Show me." Rian stepped forward but stopped when Kallie stepped with him. He squeezed her hand. "Kallie, please. This is not something I wish for you to see."

Kallie pushed her shoulders back. "As I said earlier, your problems are my problems, My King. If there is an issue with our people, within our *home*, I want to know about it."

Rian glanced at Laurince, who shrugged, before returning his attention to Kallie. "All right. But if it gets too much, we will leave instantly."

She gave a small nod.

Despite what Rian may have thought, Kallie did not need to prepare herself. She already knew what she would see. Her target was dead, and Domitius' assignment was complete.

Now, she needed to ensure its success.

When they finally reached the storage closet in the servant's quarters, a hand flew to Kallie's mouth, and she gripped Rian's arm tighter.

"Are you all right, Princess?" Rian asked, moving to shield her from the body on the ground. He brushed a stray hair away from her face, the small act causing his cheeks to flush slightly.

Kallie nodded. "I'm fine."

Her feigned shock was only half false. While Kallie had known whom she would see lying dead on the floor, she had not expected it to smack her in the gut to such a degree.

Behind Rian, the healer rose from a crouch. "My King, perhaps the lady would do better if she was brought to her rooms?"

Rian looked at Kallie, and she shook her head. She needed to see this through.

"If the Princess says she is fine, she's fine. Now, please, tell me what happened."

The healer scratched the top of his head with a quill, "I cannot be too sure. No one was around when it happened."

"Who found him?" Rian asked.

Trina, the servant from dinner, stepped forward, eyes now bloodshot and face tinted green. "I did, Your Majesty. I was returning from the washroom, and—" The woman choked on her tears, cutting off her words.

Knots formed in Kallie's stomach as a wretched noise escaped Trina's lips.

"Are you sure there was no foul play?" Rian asked the healer.

Kallie tried to avoid looking at the servant who lay supine on the floor, but her attention kept wandering down, the guilt dragging her attention to the body. The little dinner Kallie had managed to eat threatened to come up.

"Yes, My King. The vial in the servant's hand is without a doubt poison, and there was a note." The healer held out a piece of wrinkled parchment.

Rian reached for it, but Laurince grabbed it first, crinkling the paper in his hand. He sniffed the piece of parchment, held it toward the candle, and inspected it. When he unfolded the paper, Laurince's face paled.

"Laurince," Rian demanded, with his hand outstretched.

Laurince brows quivered. "But we should have this—"

"Hand it over," Rian ordered.

Lips in a flat line, Laurince held out the paper.

As Rian read, his shoulders sank, and he gripped the paper tighter.

"What is it?" Kallie whispered.

Shaking his head, Rian turned the paper in her direction. Kallie scanned the note but couldn't read it as her vision blurred, making the words swim across the page. Kallie, however, didn't need to read the words to know what the note said, not when she was the one who had commanded them to be written.

> I cannot live with this weight any longer. I am a traitor to my family and my kingdom. My family had suffered for so long. We were barely making ends meet each month. I had asked for a raise, and he said no. In my anger, I poisoned King Lothian. But now my guilt eats away at me. My family deserves better.

Rian shook his head again. "I had vetted them all, I thought that I had already—"

Kallie stumbled, her body going limp.

"Kallie!" Rian shouted. He shoved the note back at the healer as he pulled Kallie up. "I think we've seen enough." With a gentle hand, Rian led Kallie by the elbow, and she leaned into his side.

"Wait, My King!" the healer shouted as they turned away from the servant's cold body.

Rian glared at the healer, who grew silent beneath the king's stare.

The back of Kallie's neck grew damp, and her body shook. The faux concern becoming all too real.

"What is it, Winston?" Rian snapped.

Winston cleared his throat. "Would you mind if I studied the body?" The healer's gaze flicked to Kallie before landing back on Rian. "For scientific purposes, of course."

"He has confessed to being a traitor. Do with him what you will," Rian said in a rush.

Winston bowed. "Thank you, Your Majesty."

Rian led them forward and called for his guard over his shoulder.

Armor rattled behind them. "Yes, My King?"

"Send reparations to the family. He may be a traitor, but his family should not suffer because of his wrongdoings."

"But what if they're—"

Rian interrupted, shaking his head. "It does not matter. Let this kindness show them that I am not my father."

Laurince nodded.

Rian pulled Kallie closer to his side, but even with his warmth, Kallie's skin grew cold as if a layer of ice coated her flesh. She stumbled, her ankles weak. Reaching out, she tried to grab onto something. Her hand wrapped around someone's wrist as she fell.

As darkness swept over her vision, two golden brown eyes stared back at her, and Kallie fell into them.

CHAPTER 13
KALLIE

The ground trembled beneath Kallie. A roar, guttural and earth-shattering, pierced her ears.

She fell to her knees as the ground vibrated, ripping apart. A crack split across the pavement, dozens of tiny cracks splintering off it. Large chunks of concrete fell away into the chasm, the ground around Kallie quickly deteriorating.

A shout sounded from the other side, and Kallie dragged her gaze off the ground.

Frightened golden brown eyes stared back at her. A boy sat on an island of broken concrete, tears filling his eyes as pebbles tumbled down the sides of the island.

Kallie hurried forward, her nails scraping against the ground. She peered over the edge. Nothing but blackness greeted her. The chasm between her and the boy was growing and fast.

She gnawed on her lip.

The ground shook again, and Kallie fell onto her stomach as she gripped the edge of the concrete, hoping that it wouldn't collapse beneath her.

"Kalisandre!"

Kallie jerked up and fell back onto her palms. Her heart thumping in her chest.

She couldn't move.

She couldn't speak.

The boy previously seen sitting on the island had changed, aged. Her breath lodged in her throat as she stared at the man before her.

"F-Fynn?"

Her brother gave her a small smile. The cockiness long gone. "Kalisandre, you have to fight it," Fynn said.

"Fight what?" Kallie asked.

Fynn opened his mouth to speak, but his attention was dragged to his right as a large chunk of pavement plummeted into the black void.

Dust plumed and filled Kallie's lungs. She keeled over, coughing. Her eyes burned, dust and water blinding her.

"Find it, Kalisandre," Fynn shouted.

The island rocked, a rumble loud and deafening.

"Fynn!" Kallie threw out a hand. But she was too late, too slow. Her fingers brushed Fynn's, and she couldn't find her grip on his hand before the pavement collapsed beneath him.

As Fynn fell, his shout echoed down the black void, "Fight it, Kallie!"

Kallie awoke, suffocating as her heart thundered in her chest. Sweat caked her skin as a warm liquid spread across her forehead. Red laced her vision.

She tried to inhale, but the air was a ball in her lungs as she tried to figure out whose blood it was.

Had she blacked out? She tried to recall what had happened, but her memory was hazy. In the back of her mind, she heard the echo of a scream and the flash of brown eyes.

She tried to count, to hold her breath. She tried to steady her racing heart, but she couldn't. None of her strategies worked to alleviate her panic. It wrapped around her throat, strangling her.

When she opened her eyes, darkness engulfed her.

Was this what death felt like? An endless, impenetrable darkness so deep that she couldn't see where she started and where it ended. But she could hear the sound of her heart beating. Surely, if she were dead, that wouldn't be the case.

Then, her body was overtaken by a constant shaking that she couldn't stop.

Hands squeezed her shoulders, and Kallie screamed. She struggled against them, but her body was too weak. A flame burst to life in the corner of the room.

Light.

Nearby, someone whispered, "That took a toll on her, didn't it?"

Kallie tried to see who spoke, but tears blurred her vision, tears she didn't even know she had shed.

Lavender filled the air, and a soft, light hand brushed her cheek. Their knuckles featherlight as they ran over her skin. As Kallie focused on the person's gentle touch, she ever-so-slowly regained control over her breathing.

Then the hand was gone, and cold air kissed her forehead.

Vision clearing, Kallie spotted a moist towel in Myra's hands, and realization struck.

There had never been blood, and yet her hands were stained red.

"Myra?" Kallie tried to swallow, but her throat was raw. Voice hoarse, she asked, "What happened? Where am I?"

Kallie tried to push herself onto her elbows but fell back onto the mattress with a thud.

Myra grimaced. "You fainted. King Rian had one of his guards bring you back to your rooms. By the time I had heard what happened, you were fast asleep. I left only for a moment so that you could rest." Myra's voice was gentle, but she didn't bother to hide the truth from Kallie. "You must have had a nightmare. You started screaming."

Kallie shivered beneath the thin blanket. She didn't remember being carried back. When she tried to recall the moment before she blacked out, all she saw was golden brown eyes staring back at her. Kallie would recognize those eyes anywhere. For the past couple of weeks, she had stared at the boy's face for hours when she couldn't fall asleep.

Fynn.

But Fynn wasn't the one who had died tonight, who had fallen victim to Kallie's actions. The servant was.

But it could have been worse, couldn't it?

Domitius had told Kallie to choose a servant to take the fall for Lothian's death. However, her father had not specified whether the servant needed to be alive.

On that first tour of the castle, Phaia had shown Kallie the small hospital ward on the castle grounds.

When Kallie was debating how to complete her father's assignment without taking an innocent's life, she accidentally wandered to the hospital ward. Two servants occupied the otherwise vacant beds. One dying and one recovering from a broken ankle after an incident in the kitchen. Winston, the healer, had said the servant, Jericho, had only a few days left—weeks if he was lucky.

After manipulating Winston to inform her discreetly when the servant passed, Kallie planned to deliver the poison before word of his death spread. Because even though it was unnecessary with his state, she needed the people to believe that Jericho poisoned himself. She didn't wish for her father to figure out the truth. If it worked, an innocent servant would not have to suffer, and Domitius would never know.

Day by day, Jericho's health waned. Too slowly, though. As the days passed, Kallie grew more impatient.

With the arrival of her father's letter, she had to act quickly before the Frenzians found evidence that would link Lothian's death to Ardentol.

The night before the dinner, Kallie crept into the hospital ward and commanded Jericho to scribble down the confession. Before leaving, she commanded the healer to give the servant the poison in secret once the man passed. Then, she had given one last command to two guards to stage the body in the servant's quarters during her dinner with Rian.

The next day, the victims of her manipulations were quiet, their recollection of Kallie's commands nonexistent. Yet throughout dinner, Kallie's gut churned. While Kallie had not killed him, she had destroyed Jericho's name, his legacy. It didn't matter that he was a servant or held no position of power. He still had a family.

A family Rian had mercy on, even though he believed the man to be a traitor and to have killed his father.

Kallie's throat burned.

At dinner, she recalled thinking that Rian would be an easy target. And while the young king would indeed be easy to manipulate, Kallie couldn't prevent the shame that rose in her throat. Rian was *good*— too good for the world and role he had been born into.

Myra squeezed her hand, the familiar touch a small comfort. "You're all right, Kallie," Myra whispered gently.

Kallie wasn't sure if it was a statement, question, or reassurance, but she nodded.

"Do you want me to stay with you?" Myra asked.

Kallie's small smile wavered. She didn't know if it would be any better with Myra here. Myra didn't know what Kallie had just done. If Myra knew, her friend would not be sympathetic to her woes.

Kallie looked up at Myra. She, too, was too good for Kallie. Kallie didn't deserve her friend's sympathies; she didn't deserve her friend's careful hands and comfort.

Kallie shook her head, and Myra, although hesitant, left.

Kallie didn't want to be in her friend's vicinity, not when she looked at her with such pity.

The princess who couldn't stand the sight of a dead body, that's what they would say. Not the princess who had ruined a man's name.

CHAPTER 14
GRAESON

"It's done," Terin said.

Graeson dragged his gaze from the waterfall and looked back at Terin, kneeling before Sabina's statue.

The last time Graeson had visited the Whispering Springs, he had been with Kalisandre to help strengthen her gift.

Little did they know she would turn around and betray them.

He should have known then that there was something wrong. Meeting the gods was always draining, but being forced unconscious was rare when a gift-user opened themselves up to the gods. Few would pass out from it, but most could bear it if they were honest with themselves. That day, Kalisandre's body had grown cold, heavy. Graeson had been foolish to ignore it, but he had thought it was because of her age. Most came to the springs when they were children. Even when Kalisandre had confessed to what the goddess had told her, Graeson had ignored the concerns it raised.

Now, he understood those words too well.

If the truth within is not found, then one may not find what one seeks. Find it and destroy it.

Before, he hadn't been able to put two and two together. But now he couldn't help but think that Sabina's warning was connected to why Fynn couldn't read her thoughts.

"You know, if my mother finds out you are doing this—"

"Esmeray doesn't need to know everything," Graeson said, cutting Terin off before he could finish, eyes blazing.

"She's the queen, Graeson."

"I am well aware of her title, but that does not mean she must know my whereabouts day in and day out, nor do I need her permission. She is my queen, not my controller. I am doing this for Pontia. That is all that matters."

After casting Graeson an incredulous look, Terin stood, stretching his limbs after sitting hunched for nearly an hour in front of the goddess. He reached his arms over his head, the muscles straining beneath the tension.

Esmeray would be told that they had all gone to the summer house to help in their grieving process. After Domitius had destroyed the first home, they had not visited it for years. But a decade ago, the home was rebuilt. The four of them, Graeson, Dani, and the twins, had visited the house at least twice a year to get away from the noise of the castle. It was a plausible excuse, at least until someone came looking for them.

For Graeson's plan to work, Terin needed to ensure that his connection to the goddess and his bloodline was firm. Unbreakable. And the best way to do that was to go to the source. The springs' waters were infused with the gods' spirit. It could boost a user's abilities—if Pontanius or Sabina willed it.

But now, Terin appeared even more drained than he had before.

Despite the question on the tip of his tongue, Graeson refrained from asking Terin how he was doing. They hadn't discussed the events of the past few weeks, for there hadn't been time. But as Graeson took the time to inspect Terin, he saw the face of a man who was barely holding on.

Terin's hair, which was normally shaved close to his head, had grown longer in the past few weeks, making him look more restless and unruly. A deep purple coloring tinted the skin beneath his eyes. And with Terin's gift, sleep had always been challenging to acquire. But the heavy bags beneath his eyes suggested the cause was more than the effects of his gift.

Graeson had not wanted to ask Terin to join him, but he had no choice. He needed the prince. His gift was bound to be helpful, especially if Kallie's mind was as warped as Graeson believed. Still, the guilt ate at him. Esmeray had already lost one son; she did not need to lose another. If something happened to Terin and Kalisandre's mind was too far gone, the Nadarean line would end with the queen. As much as she thought of Graeson as a son, they both knew that Graeson would never be able to replace the twins. No one could.

When Graeson moved to take a step forward, Terin turned around, his head tilting up to the ceiling of the cave, crossing his arms over his chest.

Facing the other way, Graeson gave Terin a moment of privacy. He stared at the water rushing down from the cliff above them as the smell of salt and moss hung in the air.

He hated that he was putting Terin in a position where he was forced to keep secrets from his mother, something Terin never enjoyed doing. As a child, Terin was always the first to tattle on them when they would sneak out or get into the royal liquor cabinets as teenagers. Secrets were not his forte. Yet, Terin had always followed after them. To Terin, he believed it was his duty to be by Fynn's side, to be wherever his twin was. But now his twin was gone, and they were no longer children.

Still, Terin followed. Part of him would always feel the pull to protect those he cared for. Terin had always protected those he loved in ways the rest could not. Dani could handle herself. She was a born warrior, a fighter, a leader. Graeson, of course, could protect them all from an attack. But Terin? Terin had always offered them something that was ingrained within his very soul: hope.

Although when Graeson turned back around and stared at his friend, Terin looked like he was one step from following his brother to the Beneath. Right now, what Terin needed was hope.

Hope that things would be okay.

Hope that they would get his sister back.

Hope that the brewing war was won before it ever began.

And maybe Graeson could give him that.

In the distance, the faint song of the Red Spirit sounded beyond the rushing water of the waterfall. A red bird flew through the stream of water. Landing atop Pontanius' head, the bird shook off its feathers. Then, the bird started its song again.

Graeson grasped Terin's shoulder and squeezed it once. "Come on. It's time."

CHAPTER 15
KALLIE

Tapping her foot, Kallie stared at the bed. Myra and Phaia had left hours ago, but the last thing Kallie wanted to do was wait for the nightmares to creep in.

What she needed was a break, a break from those golden brown eyes. She needed control—to control something, someone. And she needed a drink.

Tomorrow, she would see the healer and ensure he believed that Jericho poisoned himself. But right now, she needed a distraction.

Didn't Tessa say that Kallie should get to know the kingdom and the people who lived within it?

Going to the closet, she flicked through the hangers. Deep inside, she found a simple beige cotton skirt. She paired it with a white blouse and a maroon corset that was laced in the front so she didn't have to request the help of one of the handmaidens. Her fingers, however, hovered over the wool cloak, hesitating.

Only a few Frenzians knew what she looked like, but Kallie couldn't take the risk. She threw on the cloak without a second thought, and smoke wafted off the thick material. She coughed, batting it away. Even though the handmaidens had washed the garment, it still reeked of smoke. Perhaps this was how the gods wished to punish her. A reminder that she couldn't run from her choices but had to live with them.

Swallowing the lump in her throat, Kallie sprayed perfume on the cloak before grabbing a piece of parchment. She jotted down one sentence, folded it, addressed it, and slipped it into an envelope. With the envelope in hand, Kallie opened the hall door.

An unfamiliar guard stood outside her door and turned toward her as the door creaked.

"Princess," the guard said, bowing. "Are you feeling better?"

Kallie tossed a smile at him, ignoring his question. "I don't believe we have met."

"Sansil, Your Highness."

"Sansil," Kallie said, dusting off his shoulder.

The guard straightened beneath her touch, his cheeks reddening.

"Is there—" His voice cracked. "Is there something you need help with, Princess?"

Her hand fell from his shoulder, and she held out the letter. "I need you to give this letter to the postmaster."

Sansil took the letter from her hand and flipped it in his hand. "Your father, Princess?"

"Mhm." Her gift hummed in her veins as she stared at him.

Sansil nodded and was about to leave when Kallie called after him. He halted.

There was no room for mistakes.

With Sabina's gift lacing her voice, Kallie commanded, "No one is to enter my room. If someone asks about me, tell them I am still not feeling well and do not wish to be disturbed. You will not tell anyone you saw me."

The guard straightened, a slight glaze spreading across his stare as his expression went blank.

Satisfied, Kallie hustled down the hall in the opposite direction.

THE CROWN'S SHADOW

Calling upon her ability caused an intoxicating buzz to course through her, powering her footsteps as she strolled toward a temporary moment of freedom. A buzz powerful enough that, for a moment, she could shove aside the other thoughts and focus on that freedom.

She weaved through the halls, taking a less common route that Kallie had discovered during one of the trips to the hospital ward.

Since she had arrived in Frenzia, the castle had slowly transformed. The once-blank walls were now decorated with various paintings and relics. It was finally taking the shape of a home. Even though it was her touch on the newly decorated walls, Kallie still felt like a guest in the castle. With time, that would change.

She hoped.

Peering around a corner, Kallie spotted another guard patrolling the halls. While the staff may have been lacking in numbers, the guards were not.

As she approached him, Kallie didn't bother to silence her steps. When the guard spun around, she offered him a saccharine smile, and his expression relaxed.

"Princess," he said, tipping his head in greeting, "is there something I can do for you?"

The pit of her stomach heated. Her gift purring, begging her to unleash it. For weeks, she had been losing control, playing the pawn for her father. But tonight, she would claim an ounce of that control back.

"You didn't see me," Kallie said, the command wrapping around her voice.

The guard stood paralyzed momentarily as the spell weaved into his mind, and then the fog seeped in.

For a kingdom praised for their military's strength, their guards' minds, however, were weak.

She continued through the castle and found two other guards, each exactly where she suspected. With every command, she grew more eager, more hungry to leave the castle.

She had often snuck out of her father's castle, but she had only ever been able to use her gift once or twice before she was drained. Now, it seemed like her gift was an endless well.

And to use it because she wished to rather than to complete an assignment? That was a freedom she had never experienced before. Her body buzzed with excitement, eager and ready for the night ahead.

Outside the castle, a nearby guard spotted her immediately. "Prin—"

Kallie cut him off, caressing his face. "Grab a carriage. We're going for a ride."

Then she was off. The politics, the scheming, and the false bravados behind her as the castle faded into the fog.

One glass of wine.

That was how many glasses Kallie had said she would have at the tavern. Yet here she was, two and a half glasses deep and a warm buzz forming. The drink wasn't her first choice, for she would have preferred something more potent with a little more kick. But when her only choices were wine or piss-poor ale, she opted for the former. And she had to give the Frenzians credit, for they made a decent wine. The white wine was crisp with a pleasant tartness that didn't linger too long on her tongue.

Sitting at the bar, she tapped her foot to the beat of the fiddler's song. Like the taverns she frequented in Ardentol, this one was just as crowded with the same grimy surfaces. When Kallie arrived, a large crowd was already at the back of the tavern, their bodies sashaying as the band played one tune to the next. Now, a group of women twirled together, taking turns spinning one another. Nearby, several men slunk over a high-top table, drinks in hand, and gazes half cast. One man tipped his jug of ale up, chugging it. Slamming it down on the table, he pushed himself up and stalked toward the women.

The woman with sandy brown hair saw him coming, and she turned to her friend, giggling. The man approached her and said something Kallie could not hear. Hand on her hip, the woman declined him and turned back to her friends.

The man sulked back to his table of men, his head hanging low. Meanwhile, the woman was smiling brightly as she continued dancing with her friends. What Kallie would do to be able to dance so carefree. With no more guards to command, the energy humming inside had nowhere to go and begged her to move. But despite her body wanting to dance, her mind kept her planted firmly in the seat.

On the other side of the bar, the bartender took an order from a patron sitting a couple of stools down. As he polished the glass in his hand with a rag, he sent Kallie a cursory glance accompanied by cocked eyebrows and a wide smile. After placing a jug of ale in front of the guest, he threw another look in her direction.

Kallie turned her back to him and scanned the crowd, even though she had already scoped out the tavern for any familiar faces.

As the wine warmed her body, Kallie questioned why she had come here. All taverns, no matter the location, were the same. They were all occupied by people who had one too many drinks. Strangers engrossed in loud conversations. There was nothing here for her—nothing but self-pity.

But at least there was music that was unrestricted and untethered by politics and etiquette. It breathed and lived in the humid, sticky building. Its rhythm called to her. Her foot continued to tap in the air, her body swayed.

The point of coming to the tavern was not to restrict herself even more. The point was to let loose, to forget her title and her responsibilities. Forget the deaths that weighed heavily on her shoulders. Even if that was an impossible task, it was worth the shot.

Perhaps it was time she answered the music's call.

Her fingers ran over the loose change in her pocket. She tossed the change on the counter and let the music guide her to the floor.

"Join us!" one of the women shouted, pulling Kallie into their circle.

A timid smile crept onto her face as she twirled, swayed, and spun with them, her movements loose from the wine.

This, *this* was what she needed. Music to drown her thoughts and alcohol to sweep her inhibitions away. Laughter filled the room, and Kallie almost jumped at the sound that came from her lips. She couldn't recall the last time she had laughed, and the noise sounded foreign on her tongue. It filled her with a sort of bliss she never wanted to forget. A moment when she didn't need to plot or scheme. When she could be a young woman who didn't care about what was happening around her for a night.

Cigar smoke and whiskey floated around her.

"Care for another, my lady?" a husky voice whispered in her ear.

Kallie tilted her head toward the stranger, eyeing him. And for a moment, her heart flipped, but then her vision adjusted. His hair was not black but the darkest shade of brown she had ever seen, with deep brown eyes to match.

She should say no. This man was a stranger. He wasn't—

She mentally shook herself from her wandering thoughts and arched a brow at the stranger. Maybe this was what she needed. Yes, she was engaged to the king, but if the king could have his fun, so could she. Maybe this man was just the distraction she needed. A way to forget more than one thing, more than one man.

"And who's to say I'm *your* lady?"

The stranger ran a hand along his sharp jawline. "A man can hope, can't he?"

"Hopeful or wishful thinking?" Tilting her head, she brushed a finger over her lip.

The stranger's gaze tracked the movement, gaze darkening. His voice lowered as he took a step closer. "I suppose that depends."

"On?"

His hand slipped along her waist. For a second, she wanted to push his hand away, but she didn't. Instead swayed to the music.

Fun, this is supposed to be fun.

"You."

Little did he know, Kallie would swallow him up and spit him out once she was done with him.

He pointed to her drink.

She swirled the last droplet of wine in her glass and threw her arm over his shoulder, her glass loose in her hand. With a finger, she drew a line from his collar down to the center of his shirt. She scraped a nail across the face of the button. "I have a better idea."

"Oh?" The stranger leaned down, his head hovering near hers, his breath heavy on her neck. "And what's that?"

She wrapped her hands behind his neck, her gaze sliding over him. And unless she was seeing things, Kallie could have sworn he puffed his chest out as she did. He was not the smoothest man nor the most handsome man she had ever seen or been with, but she refused to think about who owned that title.

Standing on her toes, Kallie pressed a palm against his chest and whispered in his ear.

When she fell back onto her heels, it was impossible to miss the man's reddened cheeks or the grin flashing across his face.

He peered down at her through a half-cast gaze. "Don't you want to know my name first?"

Kallie shrugged. *Who* he was didn't matter. Only what he could provide her right now.

"Can I know yours?"

Kallie sighed. It never was easy, was it?

"You can call me Kal—" She snapped her mouth shut, her intention of giving him a false name having slipped away with the wine.

"Kal?" the man asked.

"Mhm."

Kal could be short for anything, she reminded herself.

"Well, *Kal*, lead the way." He ushered a hand forward, grinning and wiggling his brows.

Shaking her head, she grabbed his hand and dragged him behind her.

Pulling him with her, she slid into the washroom. Kallie faced the door, away from the man, as her fingers grazed the metal lock and slid the lock into place.

When she faced the stranger, her gift hummed in the pit of her stomach, but she stuffed it back down. She didn't need her gift right now. Not when the man stepped forward, gaze saturated with a blazing heat.

His fingers slid across the side of her face and twisted into her hair. The skin on his palm was smooth, with no callouses to be felt.

It was almost sweet, but Kallie didn't want *sweet*.

She fisted his shirt and tugged him closer, eliminating the space between them. Her lips met his, and she focused on their softness. When his tongue poked at her lips, she parted them. Whiskey and tobacco coated his tongue. And she let herself fall into it.

The music outside continued. The dancing and laughter only getting louder.

She pulled him closer, smashing their mouths together.

Still, it wasn't enough.

"More," Kallie demanded, and she sensed the unexpected release of her gift. It was too late to call it back. The command was out there, and the stranger eagerly obeyed.

His hand moved to the back of her neck. His kiss became fiercer. He dug his fingers digging into her waist. Her heart pounded. And even though his body was pressed against hers, she could still feel the prickle of guilt on her tongue.

Not enough.

She broke their kiss, her hands flying to his shirt. She unbuttoned it as fast as her fingers would allow. At the last button, she tugged his shirt down, freeing one arm.

"*More,*" she growled.

He slammed her against the door, and the doorknob dug into her back. His cotton shirt hung off his arm as the command bid his will to hers. The man's warm breath against her skin was a reminder of just how small the space was.

She squeezed her eyes shut.

She forced her body to relax against the door as his hand found its way down her body. She focused on the movements of his hands, the way his hand skated over the side of her torso while the other weaved into her hair. She focused on how his fingers bunched her skirt together at the side. How the faint breeze that brushed against her ankles did little to cool her down as the air grew thicker, their combined breaths heating the room.

He began trailing kisses along the side of her face, and she leaned into it.

Sweat beaded at the back of her neck. She was too hot, too crowded.

Fabric rustled, and the faint smell of ash wafted toward her as he unlatched the button of her cloak. "Too warm for a cloak, don't you think, Kal?"

Kallie's eyes sprung open as if her head had been dunked into cold water. She gaped at the man before her.

Panic rose in her chest. She tried to shove it down, tried to ignore it. But she couldn't. Not as it rose within her like a tidal wave, unstoppable and all-consuming.

The stranger's head tilted, his eyebrows raising in question. "Are you—"

Kallie didn't hear the rest of the man's question before her fingers flew to the lock, unhooking it. She threw the door open and slammed it behind her.

Her chest rose with each breath as she leaned back against the door. A few nearby patrons glanced at her with wary gazes. An older gentleman shook his head as he took in her disheveled appearance, the untied ribbon of her corset, the tousled hair, the wrinkled dress.

With one hand, Kallie straightened her skirt and reached for her hood. Her hand brushed the back of her blouse. She groaned, cursing herself.

Kallie had forgotten to grab it in her haste.

Behind her, the door handle jiggled.

Before Kallie thought better of it, she hurried forward. With her head down, she passed the patrons and whispered a command for them not to say a word about her presence.

Her blood grew cold, the weight of her gift heavy in her stomach as it slumped down. The impact of using her gift on so many people at once drained her. When she glanced at a couple of patrons from underneath her lashes, hazy and confused eyes turned away from her.

Somewhere behind her, there was a rustling, and she picked up her pace, fleeing through the tavern door.

Once outside, she dipped down a side street. Covered by the shadows, she pressed her back against a brick wall of one of the buildings. Her palms scraped against the coarse brick wall in an attempt to steady herself, hoping the cool stone would ground her.

When she took a deep breath, everything she had tried running away from rushed into her lungs, filling them. It was too much. The smoke, the name, the memories were all too much.

Her stomach twisted, and she threw up the wine.

Since arriving in Frenzia, Kallie had done her best to lock those thoughts away—the moments with her family, moments laughing with Fynn. The looks she had secretly seen Graeson give her when he thought she wouldn't notice. Kallie, however, had always been looking, watching. Spying. Because that was who she had been—a spy. From the moment she had left Ardentol, she had chosen her allegiance. She had vowed to use the people who were deemed her enemy.

If she had known . . . if she had been aware of who they were from the beginning, would it have been any different? Would it have changed things?

Would Fynn still be alive?

Kallie didn't know. At the end of the day, the Pontians still had allowed her to grow up away from her true home. They had allowed her to be raised by a man who did not share her blood.

It did not lessen the guilt she felt or soften the pain coursing through her body. Because Kallie no longer knew the truth. She did not know where her heart lay.

She needed a new home, a place she could call her own.

Kallie wiped her mouth with the back of her hand.

Frenzia could be that. Kallie could make it be that. The marriage would make it permanent, something that couldn't be easily taken away.

She pushed herself off the wall and tipped her chin up.

Frenzia would become her home. She would be sure of it.

That night, Kallie dreamed of the man she had tried to forget.

CHAPTER 16
GRAESON

Pontanius' storms were meant to keep enemies away, not prevent the Pontians from leaving. But this one had hit them hard. One minute, the skies were clear, bright blues for miles. Then the clouds rolled in as if the storm had been hiding behind the sun, waiting for its moment to strike. And strike it did.

While Graeson's crew bunkered down beneath the deck, the captain's crew hurried about the ship, taking in the mainsail and locking the chains around loose furniture. They did everything they could to prepare for the change in weather. Still, the weather was beating them. Graeson, however, would not let the raging seas thwart his pursuit.

He didn't care if some thought it a warning, a sign from Pontanius himself that Graeson should not be chasing after Kalisandre.

Graeson had always been bad at listening to the gods.

He ran from post to post, doing whatever he could to help out Squires' crew. Graeson's rain-soaked hair stuck to his forehead and the sides of his face, but Graeson didn't bother to push it back. In this weather, it was pointless. As he tightened down the mainsail, one arm hooked around the pole to keep him steady as the boat rocked from a wave, a shout cut through the thunder.

"Get out of here, Graeson!"

Graeson snapped his head toward Captain Squires who stood at the helm.

"What! Are you crazy?" Graeson shouted back. "You need all the help you can get!"

Squires said something, but the lightning struck, and the thunder soaked up his words.

Graeson ignored him and finished the knot. Then spotting Seelie, one of the crew members, struggling to tighten down a cannon, Graeson sprinted to him and shoved him aside.

"Can none of you tie a knot properly?" Graeson spat.

"What are you even doing up here? You should be down below with the others," Seelie said.

"That's one way to say thank you," Graeson said, securing the rope.

"I didn't ask for your help," Seelie shouted through the rain.

Seelie shook his head, mumbling some insult as he hurried to another cannon. Graeson couldn't quite catch the entire insult, but he had heard enough for his anger to spike. He charged forward.

Graeson's momentum was cut off, and he was forced back, back smacking against the railing and forcing out a grunt.

"What the—" Graeson flinched once he spotted the captain staring at him, nostrils flaring and only inches away from his face. "Squires! What's your problem?"

"*You!*" Squires spat. "You are my problem, Graeson!"

"*Me?*"

Rain poured onto the deck, soaking it. Beyond Squires, Graeson could barely make out the others who raced around the deck as the storm picked up. Waves crashed against the side of the boat, rocking it.

"You are not the captain here. Stop telling my crew what to do and get out of their way."

"But—"

"No." Squires shook his head, and water flew off the rim of his hat. "Either go below deck with *your* crew or swim with the kraken. Perhaps you'll be more of use to her."

"Are you fucking serious right now?"

"Your choice, Son." Squires stared at him, unmoving. Even as the rain poured down on them, the captain didn't flinch.

Snarling, Graeson looked over his shoulder at the raging sea. Waves smacked against the side of the ship. For a second, he debated jumping since he would rather jump in the waters than sit idly beneath the deck with the others. At least struggling to stay afloat would give him something to do, something to distract his mind.

When Graeson still hadn't responded, Squires shouted, "Lucky!"

A large man appeared behind Squires, arms crossed over his bulging chest. Rain poured down upon him, smacking his bald head. Lucky took a step forward.

Graeson moved out of his reach. "Fine, I'll go."

"Thank the gods," Squires mumbled.

"Go fuck yourself, Squires."

"Gladly," Squires said, teeth shining. With a tip of his hat and an apology on his face, Squires turned his back as Graeson opened up the hatch to the lower deck.

Behind him, he heard Squires shout to one of the crew members to feed the kraken for good measure. Graeson, however, doubted the offering would do them any good. Once ignited, the wrath of a god was hard to extinguish.

Graeson stepped onto the ladder. He should have been pissed at the Captain, but he didn't have any fight left in him. When Graeson was a teenager, Squires had taken him under his sail. With Squires mentoring him, Graeson learned how to tie the perfect knot, read the stars, and hold his rum on the rocky waves. And for a time, the sea helped channel his anger.

Until it didn't.

The hatch slammed down above Graeson as his feet hit the ground. Laughter filled the air beneath the deck, and the muscles in his jaw twitched. He took in the sight before him, lips pressed in a firm line and arms folded over his chest.

In the center of the open space, Armen and Moris were in a full-out brawl. And now, Graeson was truly regretting recruiting them.

While Armen had not been Graeson's first choice as a member of his small crew, Graeson was not a fool. Armen's time in Ardentol gave him vital knowledge of Domitius that Graeson and the others did not possess. His knowledge of both the Ardentolian guards and Domitius' behavior was essential for retrieving Kalisandre and ridding them of Domitius, once and for all. Armen's weakness, however, was his blatant arrogance.

Did the man truly think he could beat Moris? There was a reason Moris, one of the majors under Dani's command, was highly sought after for missions. Within a moment's notice, Moris could paralyze his victims without even touching them.

Apparently, Armen didn't care, for he came flying forward with little disregard for the repercussions.

Moris, however, didn't need to rely on his gift to stop Armen's momentum. The ship tilted, a rough wave crashing into its side, and everyone slid across the floor.

Everyone except Graeson, Dani, and Sylvia, who each held onto one of the many wooden poles scattered about the ship's barracks.

Like Moris, Sylvia had joined them on their first voyage south a few months ago. The two of them had been a part of the group that had taken the shorter route back to Pontia. As one of Dani's soldiers, they trusted them. Both were solid fighters and useful gift users. However, Sylvia was a little more aware of their surroundings than

Moris. In addition to their keen observational skills, Sylvia was lethal when it came to fire. Sylvia's gift, which Graeson still didn't quite understand despite their explanation about chemicals, made them a skilled arsonist. Graeson, thankfully, didn't need to understand Sylvia's skill to know they had great potential.

Sylvia shook their head at the rest of the crew, who had their limbs entangled with one another.

Imbeciles, the monster caged in the back of Graeson's mind whispered. As much as he agreed with the monster, Graeson shut the voice out.

Shaking his head at his mess of a crew, Graeson watched them disentangle themselves from each other.

Terin reached out a hand to Emmett, who had been the last member to join their group. Terin yanked him up, and Emmett's tall, lanky body went flying. When Emmett landed less than gracefully, he burst into laughter, bending over at the waist.

Emmett had been difficult to convince to join their group at first. Emmett was not a soldier. He wasn't even remotely a fighter.

"I'm only the doorman," Emmett had said when Graeson had initially requested his help. But in truth, Emmett was so much more than the doorman of the Cavern of Catius. When Kalisandre had discovered what Emmett could do when they visited the cavern that fatal night and the doorman had hidden their identities from everyone else, she quickly saw the benefits of Emmett's skill. Emmett's ability to mask people's identities would prove pivotal to sneaking into the wedding without attracting too much attention. However, because Esmeray believed that the people should not be forced to use their gifts a certain way, Emmett had not been trained to fight. While the belief was admirable, Graeson unfortunately believed that sacrifices would have to be made soon enough whether people wanted to or not.

Fortunately, after some groveling, Emmett's price was simple: a single barrel of Frenzian wine.

When Graeson questioned the request, Emmett shrugged and said, "The imported shit sucks."

Graeson would have given him more than that, but he wouldn't argue with the man. There was no need to raise the man's price if a single barrel was sufficient.

Now, Graeson was thankful Emmett only requested one barrel. The man was already half drunk, and they hadn't yet traversed half of the Red Sea.

"What in the gods above are you all doing?" Graeson shouted as the rain continued to beat on the dock above them.

Dani's gaze snapped to him, and her smile fell flat.

"We're just messing around," Moris said as he pushed himself off the ground.

"Messing around? Is this really the time to be doing that?" Graeson asked, the anger hot on his tongue.

Armen scratched the back of his neck. "Come on, man. We're just—"

Graeson stormed forward, but Dani slid between them before Graeson could wrap his hand around Armen's neck.

"Move, Dani," Graeson growled.

"Or what, Gray?"

"Graeson," Terin said, the one word a soft lullaby on his tongue.

"Don't," Graeson barked, pointing a finger at the prince. "Don't you even dare try that on me, Terin."

Terin rubbed the side of his face and walked toward him. "Let them be, Gray. It's going to be a rough few weeks. Let them have their fun while they still can."

Nose twitching, Graeson snarled and looked around the room at his makeshift crew. Most were hesitant to meet his gaze.

Good, Graeson thought. *It's best if they fear me. Fear makes people listen.*

Terin grabbed Graeson by the shoulder and squeezed.

"Is that an order, Your Highness?" Graeson hissed.

Terin snorted, and the sound was so . . . Fynn. All Terin needed to do was tack on a *fuck off,* and he would sound like him too. Terin shook his head, sadness lacing his brown eyes, and let his hand fall. He shoved his hands into the pocket of his pants.

"Fine, if you all wish to fuck around while a storm rages on outside, be my guest." Graeson glanced at Terin. "Come see me when the storm passes."

THE HAMMOCK ROCKED as the ship rode over the waves. Graeson didn't know how long he had been trying to sleep. To avoid attracting any unwanted attention, the ship had left the pier at dusk, and the sun had set hours ago. By now, the storm had calmed down, and Terin left him a couple of hours ago. Graeson wanted to ensure their trip to the Whispering Springs was not for naught. According to Terin, his gift was as strong as ever. He only needed more sleep, Terin claimed.

Before Terin left, Graeson tried apologizing, but Terin only waved him off.

However, Graeson saw the silent question written across Terin's face.

If the stress was already getting to Graeson now, what would happen in a few weeks? What would happen if their plan didn't work?

Graeson didn't want to find out.

He rolled over to his side, using his arms to bulk up the pillow. The rough rope rubbed against him, his shirt scratching against his skin.

A few yards away, Armen snored, half of his limbs hanging out of the hammock. Graeson had half of the mind to walk over to him and flip him over, but he restrained himself.

Better Armen was asleep than bothering him, he reasoned.

The muffled sound of laughter and simultaneous groans came from the other cabin room where Emmett, Terin, Sylvia, and Moris played cards.

Thunk.

Thunk. Thunk.

He groaned and shifted in the hammock. At one of the nearby tables, Dani stabbed the wooden table with a worn blade. The metal drove into the wood. It struck again and again, slowly driving him insane.

"Dani," He groaned, rubbing his face.

Another stab.

"What?" she spat.

"You are driving me insane."

"Then perhaps you shouldn't have brought me here." *Thunk.* "I didn't want to come, remember?" *Thunk.*

"No one forced you to be here, Dani."

"If that's what makes you sleep at night, Gray"

Thunk.

With a groan, Graeson climbed out of the hammock, slamming his feet on the ground. Armen turned, mumbling something unintelligible, but Graeson ignored him as he marched over to Dani. Reaching the table, he smacked his palms onto the table across from Dani.

Unflinching, Dani sat back in the chair bolted down to the floorboards. She tilted her head to the side as she flipped her braids over her shoulder. "You know as well I do that I had no choice but to follow you."

"We would have been fine without you," Graeson countered.

Dani was like a sister to Graeson. She was one of his best friends. Even still, ever since they were children, Dani had been a narcissistic thorn in his side. But Fynn had always balanced her out—or at least, he had taken the brunt of her comments himself. And the man had done it in stride, too. There was something to be said about a man attracted to a woman with sharp teeth.

But Fynn was no longer here.

"Don't make me laugh, Gray." Dani stood, knife still in hand, as she glared at him. She waved the blade in the air, pointing to herself and then to the room where the others played cards. "Does anyone besides Terin and I even know the truth about your *abilities*?" She stabbed the table again. The handle bounced in place, vibrating.

Gaze narrowed, she leaned over the table, lowering her voice so none of the others could hear. "Do they even know what you are?"

"It is of no consequence," he bit out, his muscles growing tense. It didn't matter if they knew the full extent of his abilities or not. Graeson was in control.

Dani surveyed him. Shaking her head, she reached forward. Before she could wrap her fingers around the handle, Graeson snatched the blade. She glared at him through her eyebrows, and annoyance burned within her light green eyes.

Snarling, she thrust her chair back, and the chain bolting it down to the floor rattled. With a disgruntled groan, she stomped to her hammock, throwing herself onto the netted fabric without another word. However, the mobility of the hammock made her movements shaky, lessening the dramatics she tried to display.

Shaking his head, Graeson returned to his hammock, the blade still in hand.

After climbing into the swinging net only marginally more gracefully than Dani, Graeson inspected the blade. It was smaller than a dagger and had a simple pommel with a mud-brown leather grip. Graeson preferred his curved blades that offered quick, clean maneuvers that lay on the floor in his bag beneath him. His scimitars weren't as easily concealed, though. To sneak into a wedding hosted by the famed military capital of the seven kingdoms, they would all need to be stealthier than they had been in Ardentol.

Last time, they knew Kalisandre would be traveling after the ceremony. They knew the schedule and had someone inside the castle to assist them. This time, however, they had no one. Nor had they heard of any rumors suggesting Kalisandre would be traveling.

Graeson was not surprised. Their enemy would not be that thoughtless again.

According to the servant who had delivered the letter to the queen, Graeson and his makeshift crew would have several opportunities to snatch Kalisandre since Frenzian weddings were a week-long endeavor. So, they had less than a month to finalize their plans, arrive in Frenzia, and make their move.

Thankfully, that left just enough time to make one more stop to improve their odds.

It was time Graeson visited an old friend.

CHAPTER 17
KALLIE

THE SUN KISSED HER SKIN AS KALLIE WALKED THROUGH THE PEONY GARDEN. A breeze swept by, ruffling her hair and carrying the smell of sea salt and citrus. Hidden among the leaves, small birds chirped in a nearby fig tree, and Kallie could scarcely make out the bright yellow tails peeping out.

Smiling, she sighed and looked toward the east. From the top of the hill, she could spot the white peaks of the ocean as the waves danced across the sea. Large hawks flew down, their talons scraping the top layer of the surface. Further out, a dark spot grew on the surface. A shadow of some sort.

Kallie squinted. Unsure if her eyes were playing tricks on her.

She gasped.

There it was again.

A giant tentacle broke the sea's surface, sending a nearby bird hurrying away. However, one hawk wasn't as lucky when a tentacle wrapped around it, pulling it under the surface of the Red Sea.

"Did you see that?" she shrieked, spinning around.

An amused smirk slid across Graeson's face. "See what, Kal?"

"That!" Kallie pointed at the sea.

Graeson leaned down as if shrinking his height and looking from her *viewpoint would help him see what she did. But when she looked back, there was nothing there, and she groaned.*

"I swear I saw it."

"You'll have to be more precise than that," Graeson said with a slight lilt in his voice.

"I thought I saw—" Kallie huffed, brushing a hand through her knotted curls. "Nothing. Forget it."

"You mean to tell me that you"—his breath kissed her neck, and she shivered—"the disbeliever of myths, believe you saw the kraken?"

"Hush." Kallie laughed, knocking her elbow into his side. "You don't need to mock me. I know, it's ridiculous."

Graeson's fingers brushed beneath her chin, and he turned her head toward him. His eyes danced across her face, and not a hint of amusement sparkled in his grey irises. "Kalisandre, it is not ridiculous. If you say you saw it, you saw it."

Her brows furrowed. "Just like that?" she whispered.

"Just like that, little mouse."

"But—"

He put a finger to her lips. "No, buts, Kal. You've been around too many people who have questioned you and your word. It is time you surround yourself with people you can trust."

Kallie quirked a brow. "And I suppose you're one of those people?"

"I could be." With a gentle touch, Graeson swiped a loose strand of hair that the wind had blown free from Kallie's intricate braid. The corner of his lip twitched. "If you let me."

Her brows knitted together as she stared at him. "And what if I don't know if I can?"

"Meaning you still do not know if you can trust me?"

"Or if I can let myself trust you," Kallie whispered, her gaze falling.

"And why would you not be able to?"

Kallie shrugged, turning away. "Everything is so . . ."

"Complicated?"

She exhaled a heavy sigh. "Graeson, I can barely tell what is up from down right now. Sabina's words keep circling in my head. What does she want me to find? What am I supposed to destroy? I don't understand it. I don't understand any of it."

Kallie had tried to decipher the goddess's words countless times over the past couple of weeks, but she couldn't make sense of them. Whenever she thought she was getting somewhere, she would lose the thread. These days, her thoughts were a knotted ball. Whenever she believed she had unraveled the correct thread, it turned out to be another tangled knot.

When Graeson didn't respond, Kallie faced him.

He stood staring at the sea, his face contorted with something Kallie couldn't quite parse.

"About that . . ." he began, but the words fell off and onto the breeze as he glanced down at her.

Kallie snatched his arm. "Did you figure it out?"

"I—" Graeson hesitated, eyes flitting across her face.

"Are you guys coming or what?" Fynn shouted.

Kallie broke their locked gaze. Down the hill, Fynn stood beside Dani with his arm wrapped around her shoulders. Both wore giant, satisfied smiles on their faces.

Kallie looked back at Graeson.

Graeson pursed his lips as he looked at her, an apology written in his gaze.

"Graeson?" she asked.

Fynn yelled up at them again, "If we don't hurry, we're going to be late for dinner!"

Graeson squeezed her shoulder. "We'll talk about it later."

Kallie nodded, yet a strange feeling filled the air between them as if a bubble had formed and they couldn't pop it. However, neither acknowledged it as they made their way down the hill where they joined Dani and Fynn in the field of lavender.

Dani and Fynn's clothes were ruffled, and grass stains marked Dani's knees. Kallie plucked a leaf stuck in Dani's hair, and she couldn't help but smile as Dani winked at her.

At the same time, a tinge of regret filled Kallie's stomach. Her brother and his wife were always so happy when they were in each other's presence. Even though Kallie knew they had their disagreements, it was clear that the two were in love with each other. They lit up from within whenever they were together as if their very souls were singing to one another.

Kallie had never desired that kind of relationship before. Once upon a time, she had vowed never to love. She was made to believe that love only ever destroyed. She had never thought it could grant someone so much happiness. She had only seen love break the people around her. But seeing the two of them made Kallie question everything she knew.

Everything she learned about the Pontians was making her question something—whether it was the story of the gods, the origin of their gifts, or Kallie's own identity. She had thought everything was black and white. That they were the enemies. To them, Domitius was the clear enemy. But Kallie had seen how the king could be caring. He had never treated her poorly. Only like an overbearing father. And Esmeray wasn't all good either.

Now, Kallie wasn't sure who the enemy was.

Kallie rubbed her head as a sharp ache rose.

They started walking back to the castle. Before they made it too far, Graeson stopped and turned around.

Kallie turned, but Graeson waved her onward. "I'll be right behind you," he said.

Kallie shrugged but kept walking.

Fynn threw an arm over her shoulders, pulling her closer. Their steps became wonky as they teetered down the path. Kallie slapped him lightly in the chest, ducking from underneath his arm. "Eww, Fynn. You're all sweaty."

Fynn chuckled, squeezing Dani closer to his other side. "What can I say? Dani knows how to put a man to work."

"Oh, you loudmouth," Dani said, but a smile pushed at her cheeks.

"What?" Fynn asked, ogling his wife. "Nothing to be embarrassed about."

Dani scoffed. "I'm not embarrassed, but sometimes you can let people's minds do the assuming."

"And where's the fun in that?"

Footsteps pounded against the ground behind them, and Kallie glanced over her shoulder.

Graeson was jogging back, a bundle of lavender gathered in his hands. He held them out to her.

"What are these for?" Kallie asked.

Graeson pointed to his head. "For the headache."

Taking the lavender, she raised the bundle to her nose and inhaled the sweet, calming aroma of the flowers. As they walked, she kept the bundle close to her face, hiding the unwelcome blush heating her cheeks and the rising smile.

THE NEXT MORNING, Kallie awoke to tears wetting her cheeks and the faint smell of lavender on her nose.

CHAPTER 18
GRAESON

As Graeson bowed, black strands of hair fell in front of his face, blocking his view of the women who sat at the front of the large room.

"Rise," Cetia, the queen of Tetria, commanded.

Graeson and the rest of the Pontians straightened. A step in front of the rest of the group, Graeson tipped his chin up.

The queen of Tetria sat on a throne unlike any other Graeson had seen. Even though he had visited Tetria a few years ago when the Tetrian tournament took place, the throne's grandeur had not worn off. The seat was carved out of an enormous oak tree that the grand room of the castle had been built around centuries ago. According to the stories, the tree marked the birthplace of Tetria. To the Tetrians, the tree was more than a simple symbol of the territory's birth. It was their livelihood. The heart of their homeland. Before the seven kingdoms existed and before the castle had been built, the people who had occupied the land had gathered before this tree. The ancient oak tree, which was thought to be the oldest living thing in all of Vaneria, quickly became a meeting place. This was where they decided how to govern, how to settle disputes that had risen among the people, and who would lead. The Tetrians prayed before it and placed offerings upon its roots that now weaved beneath the thick glass titles.

When the need for a more permanent place with a roof arose, there was no question where the castle should be built. The old oak tree had become the focal point for so long that the people couldn't imagine it any other way. When the builders began, none thought to tear down the tree. They simply built around it, making it a part of the castle.

Roots sprouted beneath the transparent floors and weaved down the center and sides of the room. The grand hall wasn't simply built on top of the roots but arranged around it. The roots had created a natural aisle in the center of the room as if beckoning the people to approach the oak tree.

From ceiling to floor, windows covered the walls. Some were made from simple glass, while others were covered with broken pieces of iridescent glass laid out in abstract patterns. Stories that Graeson had tried and failed to decipher countless times when he had visited the first time. As the sun beamed behind the queen on the throne built into the bark, its golden rays hit the glass, and splotches of color poured across the floor. A golden halo bloomed around the queen, making her features indistinguishable and shrouding her in darkness.

On each side of the queen, Tetrian warriors lined the wall wearing worn leather, their weapons sheathed but within reach. Some foreigners thought the Tetrians were naive due to their lack of armor. Graeson knew better. When the Tetrians fought, they danced with deadly grace, their blades slicing through the air in an eerie silence. Armor would only inhibit their movements.

As Graeson dragged his gaze back to the queen, the warrior nearest Cetia flexed her fingers above her long sword, catching

Graeson's attention. The shadows made it hard to be certain, but Graeson swore he saw the warrior's lips twitch.

Graeson smirked. "It's been a while, Ellie."

The warrior beside the queen stepped forward, the shadows cast by the sun dissipating the moment she stepped closer.

Her hair was stark white but not from age. The top half of her hair was pulled back into a messy bun, and several small braids hung near her face. Black and silver ringlets wrapped around the ends of the braids, holding each plait together. On one braid, a single red feather had been tied with string. Black and white markings were painted on her forehead, over the bridge of her nose, and across her cheeks. Black leather straps wrapped around her torso where several blades had been tucked between thin straps. Her ribcage was covered with the all-black throwing knives favored by the Tetrian warriors.

Three years had passed since Graeson had last seen Ellie. Back then, Ellie wasn't standing beside Cetia as the Queen's first warrior, a title not easily earned.

Ellie's heeled boots clapped against the floor, her steps echoing in the surrounding silence. With her hand still on the leather-wrapped hilt, Ellie tilted her head. "A while?" Her near-black eyes were cold as she glared at him. "It's been almost *three* years, Graeson."

Graeson nodded.

"A lot can happen in three years," Ellie said, tapping a finger against the sword at her hip.

"More can happen in even less."

Only a foot separated them. Although Ellie was a few inches shorter than Graeson, she managed to somehow look down on him, her gaze narrowing.

Even though they were friends, the last time Graeson saw Ellie, they had argued—loudly and without holding anything back. Yet here he was, standing before her and seeking her queen's help. Anger and pain flashed across her face.

Then, Ellie's hand flew out, and Graeson tensed.

But when Ellie squeezed his shoulder, he exhaled, and the muscles in his back loosened.

"Let it not be so long next time," she whispered, pulling him into a hug and shoving her face against his shoulder. Sage and smoke wafted from her hair.

He smirked. Some things never changed.

She finally pulled back and gripped Graeson's shoulders with both hands. As Ellie stared at him, she observed him as if she could find the answers to why he was here after three years hidden beneath his countenance.

She inhaled sharply.

Graeson jerked back, and Ellie's hands fell to her sides, a knowing smile creeping onto her face. He knew that look all too well. Sometimes, Ellie could read him too well.

"You found her, didn't you?" Ellie whispered.

When Kalisandre had disappeared over fifteen years ago, the details about her disappearance were closely guarded. With the kingdom shrouded in secrets, outsiders would not have suspected anything amiss. Esmeray did not want the rest of the seven kingdoms to believe that Pontia was weak (a fact that was currently biting them in the ass). She didn't want news spreading that someone had found a way to break through Pontia's defenses. An island once impenetrable but no longer. Their enemies—which the Pontians had plenty of after living a life of secrecy—would have quickly attacked them if they discovered that Pontia had been invaded. Rulers did not like secrets. And the rulers of Pontia always kept their secrets close to home, a habit the other kingdoms did not appreciate.

Still, Pontia continued to maintain their relationships with one-half of the divided Borganian kingdom and with Tetria for the past one-hundred years.

When the Tetrian tournament occurred years ago, Esmeray sent a select few Pontians to represent the island kingdom and nurture the kingdom's relationship with Tetria. The twin princes had been sent as a sign of respect and trust. Predictably, Graeson and Dani tagged along—with the stipulation that they didn't do anything stupid or reckless. Like running off to Ardentol and starting a war, a thought that indeed crossed Graeson's mind once or twice at the time.

Although their time in Tetria was short, strong friendships were built. Ellie and Graeson became fast friends. However, their friendship came with a price Graeson hadn't realized he had paid. For when Ellie set her mind to something, there was no stopping her from achieving it.

The Pontians' secrets were easily extracted. At least some of their secrets, anyway.

They soon discovered that the queen of Tetria, the princess, and Ellie knew of Kalisandre's disappearance. The Tetrian women didn't know where Kalisandre was or who had taken her, but they did know about the kidnapping on a basic level. And the three women knew that Graeson and the others were planning to rescue her.

Even a decade later, Graeson and the others couldn't figure out how the Tetrians acquired their knowledge. Only that they always found a way.

"It's . . . complicated," Graeson grumbled in response.

Ellie surveyed the other Pontians standing before her. Both familiar and unfamiliar faces looked back at her.

Shaking her head, she released a strained laugh. "The runaway bride, of course."

Graeson had said nothing, but Ellie was quick to unravel his secrets. Too quick for her own good. One day, it would get her killed.

"Euralys," the queen snapped from her throne.

Ellie straightened. Turning slowly, Ellie dropped her head.

The queen tipped her head to the side, ordering Ellie to return to her post. "Let our guests speak."

"Of course, My Queen." She returned to her spot beside the queen, folding her hands behind her back.

The sun's rays were now only half-cast, the golden light fading, and some of the colors from the reflection of the stained glass on the ground disintegrating. Dusk was fast approaching.

Cetia laid her hand out in front of her. "Please, proceed."

Terin stepped forward. Although he was a prince in his own right, he bowed. "Queen Cetia, we come before you for two reasons. First, to bring you the unfortunate news that my brother, Fynneares, now walks with those in the Beneath."

In Graeson's peripheral, he saw Dani shift on her feet, her hand clenched in a tight fist at her side as gasps echoed in the grand room.

Unsurprisingly so, the Tetrian women had adored Fynn during their visit. Fynn always had a way with women, especially before he and Dani finally got their heads out of their asses.

"I had heard rumors, but I did not want to believe them to be true," the queen said solemnly. "Fynneares was a kind soul. He would have led your people well after your mother." She tilted her head to the side in Terin's direction as if she was wondering how the second son would lead in his twin's place.

Terin remained steady beneath her scrutiny. "Yes, he would have," he said.

She hummed in agreement. "While this is certainly grave news, and all of Tetria gives you our condolences, I suspect this is not the only reason you have traveled here. As you said, there is a second reason for your presence."

Terin's lip parted, but Cetia lifted a hand, silencing him. "If it is whether we have kept your secret, know that we do not go against our word once spoken."

"No, Your Majesty, that is not quite why we are here," Terin said. He folded his hands behind his back, and his knuckles grew white as he tightened his grip.

It's now or never.

Graeson stepped beside Terin. "The queen's daughter has been found."

Gasps slithered down the line of warriors. With one flick of a hand from their queen, silence fell upon the room.

"Is that so?" Cetia asked with a slight rise in her pitch.

"Yes, Your Majesty," Graeson said. "Esmeray's Kalisandre is the same as the Kalisandre of Ardentol."

Graeson's blood rushed from his face as Cetia huffed in disbelief.

"You must be mistaken. Kalisandre of Ardentol is King Domitius' daughter." The queen leaned forward on her throne, her hand wrapping around the arms of her twisted throne. "You must know this is a grave allegation you are making."

He cocked a brow. "Yet it does not make it false, Your Majesty."

Leaning back, Cetia scraped a long, pointed nail across the side of her cheek. "How? Domitius' daughter has been with him since she was born."

"Has she though?" Graeson asked.

"Yes, since his late wife . . ." Cetia snapped her fingers. "What was her name?"

Her question was met with silence.

Another story manipulated and misconstrued, no doubt. No one ever remembered the name of Domitius' wife. Not even Kalisandre knew it, which Graeson had discovered during their journey to Pontia.

Somewhere in the room, someone cleared their throat. At the sound of footsteps approaching, Graeson turned around and saw an older woman hobbling forward. A warrior walked on either side of the woman—to protect the woman or to aid her, Graeson couldn't tell. Her white hair hung past her lower back. Black beads wrapped around dozens of thin braids that clattered against each other as she approached. A wrinkled hand gripped the head of a twisted wooden cane. The woman's dark brown skin was thin enough that Graeson could see every vein not covered by fabric.

"I believe the former queen's name was Troia, was it not, Your Majesty?" The woman's voice was sandpaper, yet Graeson could hear the power that once belonged to it.

"Troia?" Cetia repeated the woman's name as if the taste of it would recall the forgotten knowledge. "She died in childbirth, did she not, Loralaine?"

Loralaine. The older woman's name was familiar. And by the way the Tetrian warriors straightened and the queen's voice lightened, Graeson knew who stood before him: the former queen of Tetria, the oldest living ruler in all of Vaneria. Loralaine had been one of the first queens in the divided world.

"Mhm," Loralaine mumbled. Then, having said what she wished to say, she sat in one of the nearby chairs. Sleep found her soon enough.

At least Graeson hoped the former queen was sleeping.

Long black nails tapped along the winding roots of the throne. "Explain. How do you know this Kalisandre is *your* missing princess?"

Graeson sighed. This had always been the fear. None of the Pontians knew how the Ardentolian king had convinced the world that Kalisandre was his daughter. Since the Pontians were separated from the rest of Vaneria, whatever mind trick Domitius had used to convince the rest of the kingdoms had not infiltrated the Pontian borders. Now, not only did they have to save Kalisandre, but they also had to convince the people, who had been told a lie that spanned decades, to believe the truth. And for that to happen, Graeson would need to divulge secrets that were not his own.

"Queen Esmeray and Domitius have a long, complicated background," he said.

"Don't we all have complicated backgrounds?" Cetia mused with a lilt in her voice.

A few warriors snorted, the single break in the women's otherwise blank expressions.

Graeson nodded in agreement. "Without a doubt, Your Majesty."

"You hesitate, Graeson." A statement, not a question.

"I do, but not lightly," Graeson explained. "You see, Your Majesty, it is not my story to tell."

"If you wish for my people's help, which I assume is the true reason you are here, I must know all the facts. Do you not agree?"

"Of course, Your Majesty." Graeson's gaze flicked to the dozens of women lining the wall.

"Leave us," Cetia said with a flick of her hand.

On command, the women snapped their feet together in unison. They turned to their queen, bowing low, and formed two lines as they left the room. The last to leave shut the doors behind them.

Ellie, another warrior, and Loralaine—who was still asleep—were the only Tetrians remaining alongside their queen.

Graeson nodded at the queen in gratitude. "We appreciate you respecting our privacy. As you know, we Pontians are protective of our kingdom's information."

"Understandably so." Leaning back on her throne, Cetia scraped a nail along the bark of the oak tree. "Although, know this: we often keep secrets to protect, but more often than not, secrets tend to hurt those we are trying to keep safe. Be wary of whose secrets you carry, Graeson."

His lips twitched. While there may have been some truth to the queen's words, some secrets would do more harm than good if they became common knowledge.

As lonely as it might have been for Graeson to keep them.

Still, Graeson pressed onward, revealing Esmeray's truth, for there was no other way. "Years ago, before my time and before the queen took her title, Esmeray was more adventurous. Before she took her crown, she wanted to travel and see the seven kingdoms of

Vaneria. If she wished to rule justly and fairly, she believed that one must see the world and see how others govern their people.

"During one of her trips across the sea, Esmeray met Domitius for the first time. Young, unmarried, and not yet tethered to the throne, both were full of hopes, dreams, and promises of brighter days. They spent months together, and soon, they fell in love. However, there came a time when Esmeray had to make a choice: stay with Domitius and leave her people behind, or leave the man she thought was the one her soul longed for. In the end, they parted ways. According to Esmeray, Domitius did not take their separation easily. When she left, he believed that Esmeray had lied to him, that she had tricked him." Graeson gritted his teeth. "Over a decade later, Pontia was attacked, her husband killed, and her daughter stolen."

"Esmeray believes it was Domitius who attacked before?" Cetia asked.

Graeson nodded.

"Because of a broken heart?" Cetia questioned, the disbelief apparent in her voice.

"We do not fully understand why he attacked us or why he took my sister," Terin interjected. "All we know is that he did."

"While the *why* is indeed important, what I wish to know, children, is how you know it was him? What *proof* do you have?"

Graeson stepped forward, and silver flashed in the last of the golden light as the two warriors unsheathed their swords.

So much for being old friends, Graeson thought, gawking at Ellie.

Ellie tipped her chin at him.

He shook his head in dismay, but he didn't back down. "He wore the helmet of the bull."

"You mean to tell me the king of Ardentol wore *his* helmet, a piece of armor unique to him and only him in an attack that breaks the one-hundred-year-old treaty?" Cetia sat forward. "Why would he do that? Although stubborn, crude, and most definitely egotistical, the man is not imprudent. You must be mistaken. You were young, an easy mistake," she said with a flick of her hand.

Graeson gritted his teeth. "He did it, Your Majesty, because he wanted us to know it was him. He wanted Esmeray to know who had attacked her kingdom, whom she had made an enemy of. Domitius wanted her to know that even though she did not choose him all those years ago, she was still his to take, his to hurt. That he had not forgotten their past even if she had."

Cetia scoffed. "This is why I never understood the customs of the other kingdoms. Marriage, whether for alliance or love, is still a social construct that is, in fact, meaningless. Why subject yourself to one partner when your heart changes as you grow? It only complicates things and creates a mess for you to clean up later." She lifted her head, staring at the windows across the room.

It was not news to him that Cetia did not believe in marriage. Many Tetrians were polyamorous. The queen had several consorts, and all three of her daughters had been born to different men.

Graeson touched the oldest ring on his hand. While polygamy worked for many, it would not work for him. His heart would not change. It never had, and it never would.

After a moment passed, Cetia snapped her head in their direction. "So you all have known where the missing princess has been this entire time?"

Terin cleared his throat. "Yes, Your Majesty."

"The *entire* time?" Cetia asked, ire tingeing her tone.

They all nodded. Although Graeson did so reluctantly. He still had not forgiven Esmeray for delaying Kalisandre's rescue. But now *he* was done waiting, done listening to the commands of kings and queens who preferred to play with politics than protect their people. If Cetia denied his request, he would find another way to save Kalisandre.

Cetia stood, throwing her hands in the air. "Then why have you let it go on for so long? Why have you allowed her to remain in Domitius' hands?"

The muscles in Graeson's jaw flexed. With some strain, he relaxed his shoulders and forced his words to sound neutral and calm. Despite his irritation with the situation, he would not betray his queen's decision in front of another ruler. "Not by choice, Your Majesty, but by necessity. As you know, the treaty—"

"The *treaty?*" Cetia scoffed. "She is one of your *own*. The treaty should not matter! Not when someone's very life is at stake."

"That is why we are here today," Graeson countered, straightening.

At the same time, he heard Dani mumble behind him, too quiet for the queen to hear, "At least she gets it."

Graeson ignored her and pressed on, "We are done being on the defensive. We are done waiting. We are here to take back what is ours." Graeson glanced back at Dani, her fist still clenched at her side, gaze cold and blank. He returned his focus to the queen. "And to give justice to those who have taken from us, who have robbed us of not only our princess but our future king."

"Fynneares' death is a part of this?" Ellie asked.

Apparently, the Tetrians didn't know everything.

"Fynn died in the pursuit of rescuing Kalisandre," Graeson said.

"By whose hand?" Cetia asked.

Dani stepped forward, rage fueling her. "Well, we—"

Cetia held up a firm hand, stopping her. "The facts."

Cetia stepped forward. The older warrior reached for the queen's hand, but Cetia swatted the warrior's hand away. Still, Ellie and the warrior remained close behind their queen, their swords in their hands but loose at their sides.

"We deal in only facts right now, child," Cetia said.

"Frenzian soldiers," Graeson said.

"Multiple?"

"Yes, Your Majesty. When we"—Graeson pointed to Dani beside him—"reached the Frenzian ship the night of the attack, we saw Frenzian soldiers throw him overboard. We were too late to save him. When we retrieved his body, Fynn had been slaughtered."

Cetia hummed in thought. "And what do you expect me to do?"

Terin took a deep breath. "We believe you saw the wedding invitation?"

Ellie's head fell, and heat flooded Terin's cheeks. Graeson smirked as the prince looked at the queen and nearly white irises stared back. Terin had forgotten that the queen was blind, and he rushed to cover his mistake, saying, "I apologize, Your Majesty. I meant no offense—"

An amused smile formed on the queen's face. "I may be blind, Terin," Cetia tipped her chin up, raising one brow as she looked at the rest of them, "but I see more than you all do. Now, tell me, what do you need from us?"

CHAPTER 19
KALLIE

Kallie slammed the door shut, startling Sansil, who stood on guard outside her rooms.

Since the dinner with the king three days ago, Rian had reverted to being his aloof self. Busy or not, his blatant absence was quickly becoming a nuisance. It didn't matter how easy the man was to manipulate if she never saw him.

Kallie had thought that the night at the tavern would help clear her mind, but the reverse happened. Her anger hadn't been sedated; her unwanted thoughts hadn't quieted. Instead, they increased tenfold. At night, her dreams were filled with Graeson's face—a face even whiskey apparently couldn't drown out. If a night out would not quiet her mind, it was time she focused on her assignment and weaved her way into Rian's heart. No more delaying the inevitable.

"Princess? Is there something—"

"No," Kallie said, cutting Sansil off. Whiskey warmed her stomach, propelling her forward. Was it her most brilliant idea to go hunting the king when alcohol most likely stained her breath? Probably not. But that's what the mints in her pocket were for.

Footsteps echoed behind her, and with a groan, Kallie skirted to a stop. "What is it, Sansil?"

The guard's cheeks reddened. He shuffled on his feet as he repeatedly gripped the hilt of his sword. "You are to be guarded at all times, Princess. If you are walking the ground, I shall follow—"

"I am *fine*, Sansil," Kallie said with a disgruntled sigh as she turned around.

While the guard's presence was not unexpected, it was unwelcome today.

Every day, she was closely guarded, and her day was filled with random, meaningless tasks and tours around the castle. To pass the time during her walks, she started counting anything she could. She counted how many benches were scattered around the property (23), the external doors (14), the sections of rose bushes in the gardens (140), the windows in the stone castle (238). Soon enough, Kallie ran out of things to count, and the thoughts came tumbling back.

Sansil was one of the few guards in the rotation whom Kallie liked. He was kind, quiet, and polite. Unlike the other guards, he wasn't afraid to show that he was more than a guard, that he was human. But right now, his morality was unneeded.

"But I must insist. If you are headed outside—"

Kallie spun around, facing him. "You do not need to worry, for I do not plan on walking the grounds. I will remain within the confinements of this castle."

"Then where are you headed?"

"To the king."

"But, the king is—"

"Indisposed?" Kallie asked with an arched brow. Huffing, she shook her head, but it only made her head hurt and her vision blurry.

Sansil continued to stare at her, brows furrowed. His gaze bounced back and forth down the hall. "Are you sure that's a good idea?"

Kallie stumbled forward but quickly recovered. "May I remind you, Sansil, that I am your future queen. I may do whatever I please."

The guard's eyes widened before he folded into a bow. "Yes, Your Highness," he said, any emotion drained from his tone.

"Do not follow me," Kallie commanded.

Kallie didn't wait to see if the command slithered into his mind before she stormed down the hallway. She pulled the metal flask hidden inside her corset. Unplugging the stopper, she chugged half of its content before returning it to its spot. With the back of her hand, she wiped her mouth.

Today was not about smart choices. Today was about getting shit done.

Who had Kallie been trying to fool? She was in no state to see Rian.

Kallie stared up at the portraits of the kings as she sucked on a mint and began to question her choice in coming here. While her anger had simmered on the walk to the king's wing, the whiskey still burned her throat and warmed her head.

She told herself that her rash behavior was a result of the wedding, only a normal consequence of the constant stress. Her future was dependent upon this marriage, and she couldn't afford any more mistakes.

Of course, she should have thought about that before she had stormed through the halls like a mad woman. She should have thought about that before she had drank most of the contents within the flask. Before her steps became shaky. Before her thoughts were consumed with regret.

Now, she stood in front of Lothian's portrait, and guilt stirred in her stomach. Guilt and whiskey were not a good combination, either.

She *should* turn around and return to her quarters, sleep off the rest of the alcohol that swam through her veins. Yet she couldn't move away from the late king's portrait.

She couldn't stop the raging thoughts, the regrets that crept in. The names that surfaced as she stared at the painted crown.

Lothian.

Polin.

Orean.

Kyen.

Fiel.

Jericho.

Fynn.

So many had died because of her choices. Or, as Domitius would say, so many had been sacrificed for a greater cause. Yet, was this crown worth this much death? This much regret?

And maybe it was because of the alcohol or the thoughts clouding her senses that she had not heard the footsteps snap against the floor down the hall. Or perhaps it was her desire for some sort of torment that she hadn't noticed the shift in the air until his voice crept over her skin. Until it was too late to head in the other direction.

"What are you doing here, Princess?"

Sharp needles pricked the back of Kallie's neck at the sound of Sebastian's gravelly voice. The heat of the whiskey coating her throat and stomach did little to sedate the ice crawling over her skin.

She hadn't seen Sebastian since they had arrived over a week ago. Apparently, hiding within the confinements of one's castle was an inherited trait for the Dronias men.

Unfortunately for Kallie, Sebastian had come out of hiding.

"Sebastian," Kallie said, his name harsh on her tongue. She turned around, her steps wavering slightly.

Sebastian stood only a few feet away, and the prince didn't bother to disguise his gaze dipping down her body, lingering for far too long.

He arched a brow, silently repeating his questions.

Kallie's fingers twitched at her side, and she willed her legs to remain steady. "I was on my way to see your brother."

The corner of Sebastian's lip twitched. "Was but not anymore?"

Kallie blinked, but she was too slow to cover up her hesitation. She tripped over her words. "Oh, I forgot something back in my room that I was going to give him."

Sebastian stepped forward, and Kallie stepped back. She stumbled. Reaching out, she tried to catch herself on the wall, but Sebastian was quicker. He grabbed her waist, and her entire body turned frigid at the contact.

"Steady, Princess," Sebastian whispered, leaning forward, his nostrils flaring. "Wouldn't want my brother to see you stumbling, now would we?"

Sebastian tilted his head, his gaze dropping to her chest. Kallie's jaw popped from the pressure of her teeth grinding against each other as he invaded her space. Panic rose in her throat. She tried to move back, but his grip remained firm on her arms, locking her in place.

She scrambled to reach for her gift, but it was a sluggish weight in the pit of her stomach. The whiskey weighing it down.

With a finger, he lifted her chin. Kallie tried to pull away, but his grip only tightened around her.

His gaze fell to her bosom, and the smirk he wore made Kallie's skin itch. He released her chin and pulled out the flask that was peeking out of her corset.

Shit.

"A little early for a drink, don't you think, Princess?"

Sebastian popped open the flask with one hand and sent the stopper bouncing across the floor. He poured the rest of the contents into his mouth. He pocketed the flask inside of his jacket. And his green gaze never left her face. His eyes darkened, a hunger simmering beneath them.

When he raised his hand, Kallie at last shook herself from her stupor.

She snatched his wrist, twisting it behind his back with a quick, smooth maneuver.

"What the—"

Kallie pulled, and Sebastian hissed. "I do not think the *king* will take kindly to you touching his wife."

"*Future* wife, Kalisandre. Do not forget yourself."

Sebastian tried to laugh, but the noise came out strangled when Kallie twisted his arm back further.

"My brother is no more a king than you will be a queen, Princess," he hissed.

Kallie's grip tightened around Sebastian's wrist. Her buzz disappeared, her anger snuffing it out.

Sebastian chuckled. "Oh, did you think it was a secret that your little daddy was the one who was actually pulling the strings?"

Kallie didn't move.

In her silence, Sebastian studied her from the corner of his eye. "You did, didn't you? You are more naive than I first thought then."

Kallie opened her mouth to speak but snapped it shut when footsteps echoed down the hall. She pulled Sebastian close, her gift buzzing beneath her flesh. "You will not speak of this."

She shoved Sebastian and quickly curtsied as Tessa appeared around the corner.

"Queen Mother," Kallie said, curtsying.

Tessa's gaze bounced between Kallie and Sebastian standing in the hall. "Kalisandre, I did not expect to see you here. I thought you were still recovering from your fainting spell?"

Kallie relaxed her jaw and offered Tessa a saccharine smile. "I'm much better now, actually. Thank you for your concern. I was on my way to the king. I wanted to thank him for taking care of me."

"Oh, Laurince was the one who took you back to your rooms. My son had better things to do than carry a woman's weight through the castle."

Kallie's hand curled into a fist at her side, and Tessa's gaze dropped to it.

"Let me save you the hassle then," Tessa continued with a triumphant smile, "The king is currently occupied."

"So it may seem," Kallie said, her gaze sliding to Sebastian.

Tessa looked at Sebastian again, noting the distance between Kallie and him—or lack thereof, for only a couple of feet separated them. Sebastian's face was flush, yet his lips remained sealed. As Tessa surveyed the hall, Kallie straightened when Tessa's eyes fell to the floor where the flask's stopper lay discarded.

Tessa arched a brow. "Perhaps that it is for the best."

Kallie's lips parted, but she didn't have time to explain before Tessa directed her attention to Sebastian.

"Your brother requires your presence in the advisors' room," the former queen said.

Sebastian cleared his throat as though he struggled to speak. "I will head there now."

"Good." Tessa nodded. As Sebastian made to slip past his mother, Tessa grabbed his arm, tugging him to a stop. "And about that issue? Have your men found anything?"

Sebastian shook his head. "Nothing yet, Mother."

Kallie's gaze bounced between the two, and the back of her neck grew cold. She noted how Tessa's grip tightened around Sebastian's arm before she released him.

"Let me know when they do," Tessa said.

Sebastian nodded before disappearing down the hall.

Tessa glanced at Kallie. "Kalisandre."

"Queen Mother," Kallie said with a sweet smile plastered on her face. "If you don't mind, I should be going now." She arched a brow, waiting for Tessa to move.

After studying Kallie for a moment longer, Tessa stepped to the side. Kallie tipped her head in feigned gratitude. As she stepped beside Tessa, Kallie stopped. "Oh, and I do hope you are feeling better as well. Must have been a nasty bug that you had at dinner."

With Tessa's countenance twisting, Kallie gave the woman her back, her steps steady and straight. Yet Kallie's stomach twisted with anxiety as she returned to her quarters.

"Phaia?" Kallie asked as she slipped her arms into the nightgown. Myra had dismissed herself earlier, stating that she needed to check on a few wedding details, which left Phaia to assist Kallie before she headed for bed.

"Yes, Your Highness?"

"Have you seen the king as of late?"

Phaia pursed her lip to the side, her brows drawing together. She shook her head.

Kallie tapped her foot.

Her gift stirred in her stomach. She needed answers. Letting her gift rise to the surface, Kallie turned to look at Phaia head-on. "Does the king have a habit of allowing visitors at night?"

"Visitors, Your Highness? I've known of several people visiting the king late at night."

Kallie chewed on her cheek as she took a step closer. Her gift hummed, begging for a release. "Like?"

Phaia blinked. "Sir Laurince and Prince Sebastian visit him frequently."

"Any women?"

Phaia tilted her head. "His mother, too, yes."

Kallie huffed, her nails biting into her palms. "And what about lovers?"

"Lovers?" Phaia asked. She shifted on her feet, clearly uncomfortable where this conversation had turned.

"Yes," Kallie said. "Lovers. Whom does the king invite into his bed?"

Phaia blanched. "No one, Your Highness. The king is a good—"

Kallie's gift poured out. "Tell me the truth, Phaia."

"The king does not share his bed with anyone," Phaia said, the emotion gone from her words as the command forced them out.

"Then who was he with on the night I arrived?"

"No one, Your Highness."

"Do you think I am a fool, Phaia?" Kallie snapped.

"No, Your Highness."

Kallie stood only a few inches before the handmaiden. With Kallie's gift still swirling in Phaia's eyes, Phaia did not balk at Kallie's approach. "Then why did Lystrata claim that he was indisposed the night I arrived? Why did he not greet me?"

"Rian did not greet you that night, Your Highness, because the Queen Mother had prevented the staff from informing him of your presence."

Kallie narrowed her gaze. "You speak the truth?"

Phaia nodded. "It was not his fault he had not been alerted. The king is a kind man. If he had known about your arrival, he would have been there to greet you without a doubt."

Kallie took a step back. Her hand unclenching.

She had labeled Rian as the type of man who would prefer to have mistresses in his bed rather than his wife, that he was the kind of man to sneak around and use his title to gain the attention of the opposite sex.

However, that was not the case, for Tessa had been pulling the strings all along. The former queen had wanted Kallie to believe the worst.

"Leave me," Kallie ordered.

As the door shut and Phaia disappeared behind it, Kallie grabbed the whiskey decanter and swallowed three large gulps.

She was a bigger fool than she thought.

CHAPTER 20
KALLIE

After sleeping off the whiskey and being poked and prodded by the royal Frenzian seamstress, Kallie made her way to the library. She recalled Phaia mentioning that Rian often visited it, so she thought it was worth a shot. However, Rian was not in the library that day.

Nor was he there the second day.

Or the third.

Or the fifth.

Each time she visited, Kallie stayed as long as she could. At first, she stayed in the hopes of seeing Rian, but she quickly grew fond of the library. It was the one room in the entire stone castle that was filled with life and warmth. During the day, sunlight poured down from the large skylights covering the library's ceiling, casting a warm light on the assortment of books littering the shelves. When the sun slipped away at dusk, candles encased in glass lit the room. Above, darkness blanketed the sky. A few stars shone bright, but most were hidden behind the ever-present thick clouds. Even the moon struggled to shine through the Frenzian fog, only able to cast a fuzzy halo of light through the mist.

Most of all, though, Kallie enjoyed the company of the books.

More and more, she could barely look at Myra without a pang of guilt spiking within her stomach. The fictional characters, at least, did not look at Kallie with pity. Nor did they judge her like the lords and ladies who wandered the grounds did. The characters in the books were too consumed with their own tragedies to care about hers.

She reminded herself that she was there to see Rian. But even she found that hard to believe when the king had yet to grace the library with his presence.

Still, the retreat to the library quickly became a part of her routine.

After a day of having quiet meals in her quarters and walking the grounds with the handmaidens and a pair of guards, Kallie would escape to the library, where she would lose herself in the books. Only after the flames went out, the candle wax melted, and the darkness settled in did Kallie throw off the dark wool blanket and get up from the brown leather couch to return to her room.

Sometimes, the words on the page consumed her mind until she fell asleep, her dreams only recreations of the stories she read. Other nights, she wasn't so lucky. On those nights, no matter how many chapters she read, her wayward thoughts came spiraling back to the surface. The stress of manipulating a king she could not get close to. The inability to forget the faces that haunted her nightmares, the ones in the portrait beneath her pillow that she didn't have the strength to throw away.

Her hope of making any progress toward her task was diminishing as the days passed and the wedding approached.

Still, she latched onto the strand of hope that hummed in her body.

ONE MORNING, Kallie awoke before dawn after dreaming of the faceless man at the springs. She did not want to think about the man or whatever possible reason there could be for him to appear in her dreams. Therefore, sweating and restless, Kallie slipped out of her room before the herd of handmaidens barged into her room. Manipulating Sansil as she left, she made the familiar journey to the library.

At this hour, the halls were nearly empty; most of the staff were still asleep. Unguarded and unfollowed, Kallie let her shoulders drop. For once, there were no whispering voices, no questions about her mental state or health, and no silent, judgmental stares.

Yet what should have been a peaceful stroll turned into an angry march down the hall.

The former queen wasn't even doing anything, yet she was winning, beating Kallie at her own game.

It couldn't have been a coincidence that Kallie had not seen Rian in over a week. Even her requests for dinner had been denied. Did they think one dinner with the king would sedate her? Was Tessa the reason Kallie hadn't happened upon him? Had she known when Kallie would go searching for him?

Before she knew it, she was storming through the library doors. As her vision adjusted to the darkness, she halted, catching the door before it slammed shut.

A faint glow flickered in the farthest corner of the room. No one was ever here.

Her heart thumped.

She grabbed a nearby candle and struck a match, lighting the wick. She took a moment to search a nearby bookshelf, which housed a few of her favorite authors. Her fingers trailed along the spines of the books running across the shelves. With a small grin, Kallie plucked the book with the gold foil on the worn black spine she had started the day before off the shelf. She flipped through the pages, scanning for where she had stopped.

Then she weaved through the tall shelves, slowly making her way toward the illuminated corner. Her footsteps were light on the dark oak floors.

With the last bookshelf at her back, she paused as she turned a page. The old paper coarse between her fingers. A loose strand of hair fell in front of her face, and with a finger, Kallie brushed the loose hair away from her face. When she looked up, she jolted back a step, book pressed flat against her heart, eyelashes fluttering. "Oh! I didn't know anyone else was in here."

Rian, who had been hunched over a desk with one hand on his head while he read a hefty tome, straightened in his chair, startled. His gaze dazed and unfocused. His pupils were dilated as if they had been glued to the pages for hours. Slamming his book shut, he shoved it underneath his arm, shaking the table as he stood. He detangled his fingers buried in his hair, and the ends stuck up in a wild pattern, making him appear more boyish than kingly.

He cleared his throat as though he had not talked for hours and could not remember how. "Kalisandre, what are you—" He stopped mid-sentence as his attention dropped to the book in Kallie's hands. "Is that Everling?"

Kallie flipped to the cover where J.S. Everling's name shimmered in gold foil and smiled. "It is. She's one of my favorites. Her syntax is . . ." Kallie searched for a word to describe the author's writing. A term that could encompass how the writer strung sentences together or how she could make Kallie sit back and reread the ink on the page a dozen times while her heart broke. Sometimes, Kallie would come across a passage and feel like the words on the page were written just for her and no one else.

"Simply superb," Rian suggested.

Kallie hugged the book against her chest, blushing slightly. "Indeed."

"She's one of my favorites, too," Rian said as he rubbed the back of his neck.

"That would explain why the Everling collection is as massive as it is. I expected to see one, maybe two books of hers. But all of them? Color me impressed."

"What can I say?" Rian shrugged bashfully. "I like to have my library well-stocked."

Kallie tipped her chin, smiling. "An understatement. It's an absolutely splendid collection, Your Majesty."

Despite their conversation's familiarity, Rian visibly shrunk within himself at the mention of his title, and a wall rose between them once again. And Kallie remembered why she had come here. She wasn't here to discuss books or their favorite authors, as easy as it was to do for a moment. This was the man she was to marry, whom she was to manipulate and steal from. Pleasantries were one thing, but finding a connection between one another? Foolish, impudent, dangerous.

Connections had blinded Kallie once before. She wouldn't go down that path again.

Kallie leaned against the bookshelf behind her, her hip popping out to the side. "Are you sure you're not avoiding me?"

Rian set the book on the table. "Despite what it may look like, Princess, I promise I am not intentionally avoiding you."

"Oh, but we're back to titles?"

"I—" He blinked, but then his gaze narrowed. "You did it first."

Kallie chuckled. "What if you had forgotten who I was? After all, we have only met—what? Once?"

"I do not believe one is capable of forgetting you, Kallie," Rian said, voice airy and light.

Kallie looked away, pretending to hide a rising blush as she curled a piece of hair around her ear. "I am not one to presume such things."

"Well, perhaps you should. You are . . ." Rian laughed nervously.

Kallie lifted her gaze as the rest of Rian's thought remained unspoken.

The little king's embarrassed. How cute.

Kallie stepped forward, holding the book tighter to her chest and tilting her head to the side. "I am . . . ?"

The candle's flame flickered, and shadows danced across Rian's face.

"Rather attractive," he mumbled.

"Oh?"

Only a table separated them now.

"Mhm." Rian rubbed that spot at the back of his head again as he avoided Kallie's gaze.

"You're not too bad to look at either, My King," Kallie said.

"Back to titles, are we?" he asked mockingly.

"No." Kallie laughed. "Just claiming what is mine."

His hand fell to his side. Something akin to shock flashed across his face as he squinted at her. "You're different from what I expected," Rian mumbled after a moment.

"Different, how?"

Rian coughed and dropped his gaze. "You must know that you have a reputation."

"A reputation?" Kallie swallowed the paranoia beginning to build. She held the book in front of her lap, her knuckles blanching. "And what, pray tell, is my reputation?"

Had he learned of her excursions to the village? Had someone seen her with the stranger at the tavern?

The smell of old paper and leather grew thick in the air. Once a comfort, now quickly becoming suffocating without a window to crack open. Her heart pounded in her chest, sweat beaded at the back of her neck.

"That you . . ." Rian struggled to clear his throat. "That you are a prim and proper woman . . ."

Kallie didn't move. There was more. There had to be. He would not bring it up otherwise. He would not hesitate if that were it.

The queen's suspicions. Kallie saw how Tessa looked at her, accusatory and wary, the other day in the hall.

Had her gift betrayed her?

She forced her face to remain neutral, keeping it all hidden beneath the facade she had mastered ages ago. She raised a brow. "Am I not a proper lady, Rian?"

"No, no." He shook his head.

Her gift hummed beneath her skin. If somehow word had spread about her . . . less than lady-like endeavors, the crown would slip through her fingers. This was just the fuel Tessa needed to burn Kallie's quest for the throne to ash.

"No?" Kallie prompted.

Rian's cheeks reddened even more. "I mean, you are by far proper. And, eh-hem, prim."

Kallie's lip twitched, the strain in her muscles lessening. "Then how am I different from what you expected?"

"Others also say that you are . . ." Rian shifted on his feet, and he looked everywhere but at her. "May I remind you, my lady, that these are not my views but rather the words of others?"

"I know what gossip is, Rian. Now, out with it." Without calling upon it, her gift seeped out, wrapping its poison around her words.

Rian stopped fidgeting with one of the books on the table, the effect of Kallie's command taking over. "They say that you are dull and daft. A parrot of your father."

Her grasp tightened around the book in her hands. "A parrot of my father?"

"Yes, a parrot." Rian rattled on, her command still guiding the truth to come out. "Although, what they say about your appearance is true. You are quite beautiful. Breathtaking, really. Your beauty truly does rival the gods. However, they were wrong about you being dull. Or daft, for that matter. I mean, you read Everling. Nor are you dull. Every conversation with you is . . . intriguing. It is as if you were crafted from the gods themselves. Now, whether you are a parrot of your father . . ." Rian's onslaught of words slowed, for even with the command wrapped around his will, he had a hard time finding the truth. "I'm still trying to figure that part out."

Kallie pursed her lips. Tessa had not completely warped her son's opinion of Kallie then, which meant there was still room for Kallie to morph it.

"You think I'm beautiful?"

"Undoubtedly so," Rian said plainly, the effect of her gift still compelling him.

Despite herself, Kallie blushed.

In the silence that followed, the strains of her gift disappeared from Rian's gaze. When the traces of her gift had vanished entirely from his deep eyes, Rian looked up at her, blinking. "Care to sit, Kallie? I believe there's still some time before Laurince comes and forces me to attend some meeting."

Kallie chuckled. She buried the anger from the parrot comment beneath her gift to deal with at another time. One day, the people of Vaneria would no longer see her as Domitius' daughter, his *parrot*.

"I don't want to impose."

Rian waved her off. "Please. You are not an imposition by far. Sit, I insist."

"Well, if the *king* commands it, then who am to deny him?"

Rian's mouth fell open as if he intended to argue. But when he saw the amused smirk on her face, he narrowed his eyes. "A princess *and* a jokester? Gods, how did I get so lucky?"

"You had the best offer, of course," Kallie said, winking and taking a seat.

Rian laughed, loud and boisterous. Kallie, however, wasn't joking. Not that he needed to know that.

Pulling one of the books from the table, Rian opened to a page he had flagged with a piece of parchment.

"Research or pleasure?" Kallie asked, brow raised at the book with a title she could not identify.

Rian shrugged. "Unfortunately, research as per usual these days."

Kallie hummed in acknowledgment. "Your mother did mention that Frenzia prides itself in its research."

Rian arched his brows. "Did she?"

At his tone, Kallie's skin prickled at the back of the neck. "Frenzia is, after all, the military stronghold of Vaneria. Everyone knows that. There must be a lot of research into strategy, material durability, and so forth to hold that title."

Rian shrugged, the concern brushing away from his countenance. "And you? Research or pleasure?"

Kallie smiled, opening her book and leaning back in the chair. She shrugged. "A mix of both."

"Hmm," Rian mumbled, an amused smirk playing on his face.

And then, they fell into an unexpectedly comfortable silence as they both turned to their books. Throughout the hour, Rian would offer Kallie a small smile. She would reciprocate, anticipating a conversation, yet Rian would return to his research, but Kallie didn't mind. She didn't even mind when Laurince, as Rian predicted, came to retrieve the king. Because it was in these quiet moments that Kallie would win the king's heart. Not through witty banter or light-hearted jabs but rather from the shy glances, the exchange of Everling quotes, and the soft, quick touches when they said goodbye.

CHAPTER 21
KALLIE

DAYS PASSED, AND KALLIE AND RIAN FELL INTO A NATURAL RHYTHM.
Before her handmaidens came to prepare her for the day, Kallie would head to the library, where Rian would already be hunched over a table, either reading one of the giant tomes or furiously jotting down notes. On the third day, Rian had anticipated Kallie's presence, and a chaise had been waiting for her near his preferred table.

Upon inquiry, Rian had shrugged it off, mumbling about Kallie needing something more suitable for leisurely reading than the straight-back chair. Yet, even though the gesture had Kallie involuntarily grinning, she could still not get a read on him. Some days, they talked; others, Rian barely lifted his head in greeting, too absorbed in his research.

It should have been infuriating, but somehow it wasn't.

Rian was a curiosity Kallie wanted to unfold. It became a game, one Rian didn't even know he was playing. As he read with an intense focus, Kallie watched, taking note of the way his face transformed as he read something intriguing or perplexing. The way his brow curled, wrinkles creasing his forehead. Or how his hand was constantly buried in his hair.

In truth, she enjoyed this time. She enjoyed not using her gift.

After a few days, Myra caught on to Kallie's absence when Kallie was running late. Upon hearing that Kallie had been sneaking off to a library of all places to meet with her betrothed, Myra burst into unrestrained laughter.

"Oh, hush," Kallie had said, pushing Myra's shoulder playfully. "What did you expect me to do?"

"You're seriously just *reading*?"

"We talk too," Kallie countered. "A little. Rian is ... different."

"And how is he different, exactly?" Myra asked, raising a brow.

Kallie sighed. "He's ... simple." It was the truth. Rian was a simple mind. Simple values, simple behaviors. But nothing about their circumstances was simple.

Myra pursed her lips. Then her gaze dropped to the simple dress Kallie wore. "Hold on—you mean to tell me you are having secret meetings with your betrothed, the *king*, like *that*?"

"Yes, why?"

"Now that just won't do, Kals." Then Myra morphed into a tornado, riffling through the collection of dresses and jewels and pulling at Kallie's hair.

Since their conversation, Myra had ensured that Kallie was well-suited for her "secret" meetings with the king. If Rian noticed Kallie's change in appearance—the perfectly braided hair, the elegant dresses which were, in Kallie's opinion, unsuitable for lounging about with a book—he did not make it known.

Sitting on the chaise, Kallie closed her book and sauntered to Rian's table.

The pile of books in varying languages gathered in front of him only ever seemed to grow. Tomes were never removed but instead stacked on top of each other. A precarious tower balancing atop the dark oak table. Some books lay half open, with another sitting in the middle, flattening the pages. The question wasn't *if* the stack would fall but rather *when*.

Kallie picked up one of the books written in an unfamiliar ancient script. The pages were thin and fragile, the text fading from wear. "You can read all of these?" Kallie asked.

Rian looked up with wide eyes. Shaking the shock from his face, he shrugged. "For the most part," he mumbled, returning his gaze to the text on the table.

Kallie studied the script. "Is this one about Frenzia?" The book's title included a word etymologically similar to Frenzia, but she couldn't make out the rest.

Rian tapped his quill on the table. "That one in particular is about ancient myths."

"Myths?" With a hand braced against the table, she leaned forward, the strap of her corset slipping down her shoulder. She peered at Rian's notes. His penmanship was dismal at best. Scratchy lines scattered the pages, and random lines struck through phrases. From afar, there seemed to be some organization system for the ideas Rian had pulled from the various texts, but Kallie couldn't decipher it before Rian covered the notes up with an arm.

The bump on his throat dipped as his gaze caught on her collarbone.

Kallie pressed her weight on her hand, blinking.

A blush rose to Rian's cheeks. He dropped his gaze, coughing. "The myths of old are extensive." He tugged at his collar. "While some of the myths have survived today and can be found in our tales and religions, there used to be more. More stories, more reasons why our world is the way it is." He pointed at a book with his quill. "That book goes over myths that predate our own."

"Such as?"

Rian leaned back in his chair, rolling the quill between two fingers. "Are you familiar with the story of the gods? When they first visited us?"

Kallie nodded but said nothing more. Since becoming acquainted with the Pontians, Kallie now knew of two different stories about the gods. The story that made Pontanius appear to be a villain and the story that made Pontanius a victim. She was curious as to which one Rian knew.

"Do you recall how they came to walk on our lands?"

"From the stars?" That was what the stories Kallie had learned growing up had said, at least. Now, she knew better than to believe everything she had been taught.

"Not quite," Rian said, his lip twitching. "The gods ripped apart the sky, disintegrating the veil that separates their world from ours. This is where some of our stars come from. Holes in the veil. According to these books, the gods had help though."

Kallie asked. "By whom?"

"Not by whom but rather by what," Rian said. Rifling through the books spread across the desk, he grabbed one of the old, brown leather-bound books where the paper was thin and frail. With a gentle hand, he flipped through the pages until landing on an image. He pushed the book forward, pointing at it. "The gods rode down on dragons. According to this, the dragons' fire was hot enough to melt the veil separating the gods' world from the mortal world. When the gods ripped apart the sky, they rode down on never-before-seen beasts that were at least six times the size of the average human. Their wingspan was said to have spanned over forty feet."

"Where are they now?" Kallie asked. Outside of the Frenzian crest, Kallie had never seen a dragon. Most believed dragons were extinct—if they believed in their existence at all.

Rian shrugged. "That is what I'm trying to figure out. When the gods disappeared, so did the dragons."

"But you do not believe that to be true?"

Rian scratched the scruff lining his jaw. "I'm not sure what I believe."

Kallie pulled the book closer and observed the faded drawing of the winged beast. Apparently, the Pontians were not the only ones who believed in mythical beasts. The ancient script beneath the image danced on the page. It almost looked familiar, but Kallie couldn't figure out why.

"And all of this," she said, referring to the books on the desk, "pertains to your research?"

"Some." The tapping continued.

"But not all?"

Rian took the book from Kallie and shut it. "My interests are vast, you could say. This is only a small portion."

Her brows drew together. "But why? Why put this much effort into it?"

Rian sighed. "I wish to make my mark on this world."

"And this"—Kallie pointed to the chaos that covered the table — "This will help?"

"I believe it will help me become a better leader, yes. To know the old stories, to understand where we came from and what is out there."

A chill swept over her skin, but Kallie ignored it and reached across the table. With a finger, she tipped Rian's chin up. The clean scruff scratched against the tip of her finger, sharp and rough. When Rian locked eyes with her, Kallie had half a mind to pull back, grab a different book instead, and ask another question. When they were together, they rarely touched, never broached the space that divided them. But with the exhaustion plaguing his countenance, she couldn't help it. Her hand reached out on instinct. "You will be a great leader, Rian."

The words left her mouth before she could pull them back, and Kallie regretted them immediately. She didn't know *why* she had said it when she was here to ruin his reign. Once they were wed, Rian's lifeline would only be as long as it took for Kallie to gain the people's hearts. When she could wrap her hands around them and command the kingdom at will, he would no longer serve a purpose. But the look across his face—the determination, fear, doubt, and disappointment—Kallie knew that look all too well.

Rian reached up, hesitating, before he finally wrapped his fingers around her wrist. His grip was light, almost nonexistent. He looked down at their hands, now entwined. "Thank you, Kallie. I wish—I wish it were as simple as that, but unfortunately, it is not. Sometimes, I wish the weight of the kingdom did not rest solely on my shoulders."

Kallie's brows furrowed. "It doesn't have to."

Rian chuckled, letting go of her hand. "Of course, it does. I am the king. Who else would bear the responsibility?" His attention was fixed on the notes before him as he gathered them into a disorderly pile.

"Me," Kallie said, her hand falling atop his.

"You?" He froze, staring at her, brows furrowed. "Kalisandre, I appreciate you wanting to help, but this is not your responsibility to bear. Frenzia is my kingdom. These are my people, my responsibility."

Since they had begun meeting in the library, Kallie had never felt disrespected by Rian. She had even started to think that he was different from the other men she knew, from her father, from the Ardentolian advisors. But maybe... maybe she was wrong.

Maybe all men in power were the same.

She should have left it at that. She should have nodded politely like she had been trained. Yet, the words spilled from her mouth before she could stop them. "But your brother said that you wished to have a queen to share the throne with, someone to share the burdens of the kingdom with."

"Do not think my words false. I do wish for that." Rian's shoulders dropped as he grabbed the pile of notes. He shook his head. "But wishing is different from doing. You must understand that, don't you?"

A tightness in her chest formed. When she spoke next, her voice shook. "So that promise was what? A lie?"

Rian shook his head again, but no matter how much he shook his head, Kallie didn't believe him.

"Of course not. I promise to do what I can. I only mean to say that certain responsibilities are mine and mine alone. You will have your own responsibilities to attend to when you are queen."

"Like what?" Kallie spat. "Tending to the gardens?" Kallie couldn't believe this. Had she really thought that Rian could be different?

"Of course not," Rian said with a gentle laugh as he stood. "The gardeners handle that."

"Oh, so planning events?" Kallie asked, crossing her arms over her chest.

"Among other things, no doubt. My mother will teach you."

"I see." Kallie's jaw flexed. Every second that ticked by only proved that Rian did not know who Kallie was or what she could do. And why would he? She was only a trophy he had won. He was the victor, the chosen one. She was nothing more than a pawn to be passed around to the highest bidder.

"Is there something else you wish to do?" he asked, his words careful.

Kallie scoffed and turned in a circle, arms thrusting out. "Who do you think I am, Rian? I am not some frivolous woman who only wishes to sew and plan charity events!"

"Kalisandre," Rian sighed, brushing his hand across his face. He braced his hands against the table. "Frenzia is very traditional, and the old ways are sewn into the threads of its fabric. While I am doing my best to unravel some of those threads, it is not as easy as one may think. It takes time. My responsibilities are my own, and neither my advisors nor my people will take kindly to a queen who oversteps her boundaries."

"Since we are making promises, Rian," Kallie said, raising her gaze to meet his. "I promise never to tread lightly when it comes to what I want. And I always keep my promises."

She raised a brow, daring him to counter her, to see if he would put up a fight. But as Rian looked back at her with a pitying gaze, she knew he wouldn't. He would not fight fire with fire.

He was not *him*.

And Rian never would be. Rian would rather put out the fire than let it burn everything down. But Rian didn't understand that sometimes things had to burn to the ground before one could rebuild.

"The game of politics is ruthless, Kalisandre. Sometimes people get hurt; sometimes we have to hurt people." The corner of his lip flicked upward, and he picked up his notes. "It is not for the faint of heart."

As Rian stepped past her, Kallie stood frozen, jaw agape.

If only he knew the truth, then perhaps he would think differently.

Rian hesitated at the end of the stacks and peered back at Kallie. The corners of his lips curled into a small, polite smile, a splash of pink tinting his cheeks. An awkwardness that hadn't existed before soaked the air, and the peace that had grown between them over the past several days extinguished.

With a single nod, he left Kallie alone without another word.

THE NEXT DAY, Rian was not in the library.

CHAPTER 22
GRAESON

For a week, Graeson paced in the guest room the Tetrians had provided him. With every passing day with no answer from the Tetrians, the floorboards grew increasingly worn. He spent a week worrying that Cetia would change her mind, that her daughter would say no once she was informed about their plan. And each day, the beast within him grew more impatient.

Time was not on their side. They needed to get moving if they wanted to arrive before the wedding.

While Graeson and the others waited, they planned, they trained, they worried.

Everything, however, rode on whether Medenia would attend the wedding and have them join her party. It didn't matter if Emmett could hide their identities if they didn't have an invitation to the wedding.

On the sixth day, Medenia finally approached them. The Tetrian princess would accept their plan on one condition: Ellie and Ophelia would accompany her.

Their party was already large enough with seven people. Adding two more people in addition to the princess would no doubt slow down their pace. But he had no choice. If that was the princess' price, it was a sacrifice Graeson was willing to make. It wasn't as if Graeson needed Medenia or her guards to assist them beyond getting them in the door. As long as the Tetrian women stayed out of his way, the additional members would not pose a threat.

Eager to get on the road and unwilling to waste any more time, they set off.

Between the ten of them, there were two carriages. Moris drove the first horse-drawn carriage, which carried Medenia and Ophelia, while Emmett drove the second, which housed Armen, Terin, and Sylvia. Since Ellie, Dani, and Graeson were the best riders, they rode on horseback.

As the Tetrian castle disappeared behind them and the swamp swallowed them, Graeson took a deep breath in and exhaled.

In a week, they would be at the doorstep of the Frenzian castle.

In eight days, the wedding festivities would begin.

In fourteen days, the wedding ceremony would take place.

Only fourteen days to rescue Kalisandre, once and for all. If Graeson couldn't stop this wedding within the next fourteen days, all hope would be lost, and his fate sealed.

WITH ELLIE LEADING THE PACK, Dani made continuous rounds, ensuring that the path ahead was clear and that they were not being followed from behind. A silly endeavor, according to Ellie, since they were in friendly territory. But Dani was not going to risk it.

Meanwhile, Graeson observed everything, Dani especially. While she hadn't done anything to warrant his wariness, Graeson wasn't sure when she would snap. Because with Dani, it wasn't a question of if but when.

As they rode through Tetria, Graeson missed his horse, Calamity. His Pontian steed had an uncanny ability to predict his movements, and he could read her moods easily. It was as if they spoke a language only the two could understand. Before they left Pontia, however, he had discovered that Calamity was pregnant. Although a loyal rider, Graeson had to leave her behind. Once he ensured she was in the best hands before leaving.

Although he had to admit, Darling, the Tetrian horse he rode now, was beautiful, even if she had a silly name. She was strong and knew the land well. Unlike the land between Ardentol and the port in Borgania, the terrain in northern Tetria was covered with swamps. The Tetrian castle sat in the center of three large lakes, the Three Ladies. Cypress trees sprouted near the lakes and rivers that snaked their way across the land saturated with water. Dry land was far and few between.

Because of their environment, the Tetrians lived in smaller groups scattered across the terrain. Most gathered around the drier spots. However, there were some who built atop the lakes through the use of raised platforms.

Ellie led them down designated trails that did not disturb the surrounding ecosystem. Even the horses were hesitant to take the path less traveled. Whenever Dani attempted to survey the surrounding area, she returned every time more irritated than she had left. Apparently, the Tetrian horse she rode, Winter, was a stubborn creature, downright refusing to travel down any path that was not one of the identified trails.

But at least Dani's anger wasn't directed at Graeson. Yet anyway.

As they rode east, Ellie turned to Graeson. "So, am I going to have to ask what happened?"

Graeson groaned. "Go away, Ellie."

Darling neighed, shaking her head as if the horse took offense to

Graeson dismissing one of her riders. Graeson tightened his hold on the reins.

Traitor.

Ellie clicked her tongue. "Come on, now. Is that how you treat an old friend?"

"You would be surprised how he treats old friends, Ellie," Dani said, joining them. She flicked her head to the left. "I'm going to do a quick round."

Ellie raised a brow. "You do realize we aren't even close to the border yet? There are no enemies out here."

Dani shrugged. "Can never be too safe," she said, then rode off. Mud kicked up, pushing the scent of fresh moss and dirt into the air.

A heron, which squatted on a broken log, flew deeper into the woods as Dani and Winter sprinted past it.

Ellie leaned over slightly, whispering, "A bit paranoid, isn't she?"

Graeson shook his head. "I don't think it's paranoia."

"Then what is it?"

"Dani hasn't been right since . . ." Graeson swallowed his words.

"Ah," Ellie mumbled in understanding. She raised a shoulder, then dropped it. "I get it."

Graeson nodded. "Death is hard."

"Yet living is even harder," Ellie said solemnly.

Silence saturated the air as Graeson and Ellie continued their trek through the Tetrian swamps. The wheels creaked behind them as the carriages rode over the loose pebbles covering the path.

Graeson was unused to the stench of sulfur hanging in the air, and his head throbbed. He pushed through the pain, focusing on the dull hum of the ring on his finger.

The silence hadn't even settled between them before Ellie pestered him with more questions. Graeson tried to shake her off, but she was persistent.

"Don't try brushing me off, Graeson. It won't work."

"I don't know what you are talking about," Graeson said, keeping his attention on the road ahead.

"You have been searching for Kalisandre for nearly two decades. Do you mean to tell me you aren't a bit excited to get her back?"

Graeson sent her a wary glance. "Excited?"

"Yes, *excited*. The last time I saw you, you were so eager to go and find her. I recall having to stop you more than once from running off and doing just that."

Graeson's jaw flexed. "Things have gotten somewhat more complicated since."

"How so?"

"Must you be so nosy about everything?" Graeson asked, glaring at her.

Ellie grinned, her black eyes alit with amusement. "I'll shut up about it once you tell me," she said, wiggling her brows.

Graeson shook his head in exasperation. But in the end, he relented and told Ellie everything. How they snuck into Ardentol, attacked Kalisandre's carriage, told Kallie the truth about her lineage, and even how she stabbed Fynn. And then how they had all been fooled by her.

When the words all but spilled from his mouth, Ellie finally spoke. "All right, so let me see if I understand this," Ellie said, readjusting herself on her stallion. "You abducted the girl whom you believe you're destined to be with because of something your mother had said before you were born. Kalisandre discovers that her whole identity has been a lie in the middle of a fight. Then, while she is trying to figure out who she is, her father and fiancé's brother attack and re-capture her." Ellie raised a single brow. "Is that about the sum of it?"

"I mean, there's a little more to it," Graeson mumbled. "But yes."

"Hmm," Ellie mumbled, nodding and returning her attention to the path.

When she said nothing else, Graeson sighed. "What is it?"

Ellie shrugged. "Nothing."

"*Ellie.*"

"It's just . . ." Ellie released an exasperated sigh. She glanced at him, her hair flying in the wind with the movement. "After all of *that*, are you really surprised by everything that happened?"

"What do you mean?"

"Come on!" Ellie shouted. "When did you become so daft, Gray?"

Graeson blinked, unsure how to respond.

Shaking her head, she continued, "The girl has practically been to the Beneath and back, experiencing one traumatic event after another. Of course, she would do something stupid, such as betray you! She barely *knew* any of you! What did you expect her to do when you all kidnapped her?"

Graeson opened his mouth to speak, but nothing came out.

Ellie had a point. Did they genuinely expect Kalisandre to trust them after practically abducting her? None of them had viewed it that way. Graeson and the others had considered it more as a rescue mission. After all, what would one call abducting someone who was already kidnapped, even if there were good intentions involved? Especially when Kalisandre belonged in Pontia.

But that was not how Kalisandre had seen it.

They shouldn't have been surprised. After all, they had tied her up. But he had thought—they had *all* thought—that they were helping her. She needed to be seen as a captive if someone had seen her with them. It was for her protection. But even so, it might not have been the right approach (even if Graeson got some enjoyment from bickering with her about it).

Still, what other option did they have? Would Kalisandre have put her faith in a group of strangers? While that was what Graeson and the others had wanted to happen, they had been naive to believe it would happen how they wanted it to.

He looked at the river nearby. Through the blanket of duckweed covering the river's surface, he could see a small turtle peep its head out of the cloudy, brown water. As the horses neared, it popped its head back beneath the surface, hiding from view.

"You're right," Graeson finally said.

Ellie gasped, a hand flying to her chest.

"What?" Graeson snapped.

"*You* admitting that *I* am right?" Ellie looked over her shoulders. "Where's my journal when I need it? I have to write this down, or no one will believe me!"

Ellie laughed. Then, the laughter died after a moment, and her expression turned somber. "So, why are you going after her if she betrayed you?"

Without revealing the whole truth, Graeson explained his and Fynn's theory.

Once finished, he ran his hand through his hair. "I can't sit by knowing she is not in control of her life. I am not foolish, Ellie. I know that there is a chance—a big chance, mind you—that Kalisandre will still not choose me even when I break whatever hold Domitius has on her."

"But?"

Graeson released a heavy sigh. "But I've been where she is. I've fought for control over my life. Some days . . . some days I still feel that pull, as if I'm losing that fight. I want her to experience freedom. It's what she deserves." Graeson stared at the sky. Branches spread across it. Through the leaves, he could see the sun breaking through. "It's what we all deserve."

A moment of silence passed between them as they continued riding. The horses kept trotting forward at an even pace, their hooves smacking the ground. Behind them, the wheels of the carriages creaked with every rotation. Then, a hoard of birds flew out of the trees nearby, scattering across the sky.

"It's a plan then."

"What's a plan?" Graeson asked.

"We destroy whatever hold Domitius has on your Kalisandre," Ellie said.

Graeson looked back at Ellie. He was almost taken aback by what he saw—or rather, what he didn't. There was no pitying look, no downcast gaze, no skepticism or hesitation painting her countenance. Just acceptance.

"You believe me?" Graeson asked.

"Gray, while you are stupid at times, your instincts are usually spot on." Ellie turned to him, her gaze steady, firm. "I trust you."

It wasn't until he had heard someone say them that Graeson realized how much he needed to hear those three words. Everyone had doubted him and questioned his sanity. But Ellie? A friend whom he hadn't seen in years? She still had faith in him.

Leaves crinkled somewhere behind them in the woods.

Ellie smirked, her black eyes widening with sinful delight. "Plus, I never liked Domitius, anyway. It'll be fun to kill him if given the chance."

"Domitius is mine," Dani shouted from the west as she weaved through the cypress trees.

"You already claimed his death?" Ellie asked, looking over her shoulder.

Graeson didn't hear Dani's response, though, for he was too distracted by her disheveled appearance. Her clothes were soaked, duckweed peaked out of her light armor, and mud was smeared across her face and clothes. There was a leaf buried in her hair. In blatant terms, she was as much of a mess on the outside as she was on the inside now.

Yet her horse was fine, the saddle merely damp from where Dani sat.

Dani pointed a stern finger at him. "Don't. Say. A. Word."

Graeson snapped his mouth shut, stifling a laugh as he turned around.

Beside him, Ellie wore a similar closed-lip smirk on her face. She raised a finger to her lips. "You might want to get the snake out of your hair, at least."

"What!" Dani shouted.

A loud *thud* followed.

When Graeson peered over his shoulder, Dani hung off the side of her horse, one hand wrapped firmly around the pommel.

"Oh, sorry. I think that was just a leaf," Ellie said with a shrug.

Dani narrowed her eyes at the Tetrian warrior, her lip curling into a snarl. She heaved herself back up and onto her horse with a grunt. "Have I mentioned how much I hate you, Ellie?"

"Missed you too, Danisinia," Ellie blew Dani a kiss, then faced forward again, the smile wide on her face.

"One laugh from you, Graeson," Dani spat behind them, "And I will throw this knife into your back."

"You wouldn't be the first to do so," Graeson said.

Ellie snorted, and then silence once again cocooned them.

A BREEZE SWEPT BY, and the smell of moss and rotten eggs covered Graeson's clothes, dripping from his sweat. He wrinkled his nose.

In the distance, a silhouette appeared through the trees and was walking beside what looked to be a horse.

Graeson's hand fell to the dagger in the leather strap wrapped around his torso. Friendly territory or not, he would not be caught off guard.

Ellie leaned forward, squinting. Then, within seconds, she took off in a flurry, her horse galloping at her command. Dirt sprayed across the ground in her wake.

Dagger in hand, Graeson clicked his heels against Darling's sides, spurring his horse to follow. He leaned forward as the horse picked up speed.

His brows furrowed. His ears must have been playing a trick on him. Was Ellie *laughing*?

Graeson tugged Darling to a skittering stop as Ellie jumped off her horse and crashed into the stranger. Her arms folded around the cloaked woman's body.

Following him, Dani sent a wary glance in Graeson's direction.

The woman was an inch or so taller than Ellie. When the two women pulled apart, the stranger pushed her hood back, revealing cherry red hair and freckled pale skin. She wore a lightweight gray cloak over leather trousers and a vest. Various crystals were pinned across the top pockets of her vest, including amethyst, jadeite, and moonstone. Most of the Tetrians had crystals on their person, whether adorning their clothes or hidden within their pockets. They believed each one had their purpose. Graeson wasn't sure how much a rock could impact one's day, but he tried to refrain from judging their practice. After all, he, too, believed in the magic of the world, the fates and powers the world had to offer.

"Graeson and Dani, this is my friend, Tyla," Ellie said. "She has graciously opened her home up to us tonight."

"Tyla!"

The carriage door opened, and Medenia's head popped around it. The princess waved her hand frantically as a broad smile split her face in two.

"Princess!" Tyla shouted as Medenia jumped out of the carriage, and Ophelia followed after her.

"Princess, you really should—" Moris began, but he shut his mouth when Medenia waved him off.

Moris had been over-cautious about Medenia's well-being since they had left Tetria. Medenia, however, didn't need another bodyguard. She didn't even need the two she had. Graeson had seen her fight in the Tetrian tournament. She was murderous with a blade in her hand.

With her skirts pulled up to her knees, Medenia trampled through the ferns and mud, running over to them. She threw herself at Tyla. The stranger met the princess with equal excitement, wrapping her arms around the princess and smiling.

"It is so good to see you, Ty." Medenia released the woman. "You didn't have to offer your home to us, though."

With a gentle push at her shoulder, Tyla huffed. "The Princess of Tetria will not be seen making camp somewhere on the forest ground of her own kingdom. You will sleep in a bed. It is a duty I am happy to perform." Tyla then raised her gaze to the rest of the group who had gathered outside of the carriages. "And so will the rest of you. You are our guests, and you will be treated as such."

Graeson tipped his head in gratitude as Dani shuffled over, plucking a twig from her hair.

"Could we bother you for a warm bath as well?" Dani asked.

Tyla quickly scanned Dani's person and then her horse before she laughed, shaking her head. "You tried to take the path untraveled, didn't you?"

Dani's mouth fell open. "How did you—"

"Winter is known for throwing off her rider if they even try to veer off the designated paths," Tyla interrupted with an amused smirk. She pointed a thumb at Ellie. "I'm surprised Ellie didn't warn you."

"Hmm." Ellie scratched her head. "I swore I did."

"You did not," Dani said, arms crossing over her chest and her hip popping out.

Ellie shrugged. "Must have slipped my mind then."

"Mhm," Dani mumbled, rolling her head. She then redirected her attention to Tyla. "About that bath?"

"And the beds?" Armen piped in.

"And perhaps . . . food?" Moris asked, rubbing his stomach.

"And a drink?" Emmett added.

Graeson couldn't help but roll his eyes at his group. For a bunch of trained soldiers with otherworldly skills, they knew how to appear . . . normal.

Terin stepped forward, bowing low and offering a small smile. "If it is not too much of a bother."

"Of course not." Tyla turned around, waving at them to follow. "It's just a short distance from here."

THE ACCOMMODATIONS WERE MORE than they could have hoped for after a day of travel. No one, not even Armen, complained. Even Emmett was content, for the man had been smiling ear-to-ear ever since Tyla placed a liquor bottle in the center of the table during dinner. Moris fawned after Medenia, his eyes rarely leaving her, even as he inhaled Tyla's stew.

As night fell over the lands, the chatter among the Pontians and Tetrians grew light and easy.

After they ate, Tyla showed everyone where they could find the bathing chambers and their beds for the night. Tyla's home wasn't large enough for each one of them to have their own room. But when they were traveling with ten people, no one expected as much. A roof over their head was more than they could have asked for. Ellie offered to room with Tyla, which left three rooms remaining.

Medenia and Ophelia took one; Dani and Sylvia took the other. The room was split between the five men. Graeson left the two beds for the others to fight over.

Even knowing this was probably the last night a bed would be available for the next week, Graeson found himself wandering outside to the stables. He spent the night brushing the horses' manes, unknotting and braiding Darling's hair, until sleep found him.

The following day, he woke up with hay stuck to his face and a mind riddled with puzzles he couldn't solve.

CHAPTER 23
KALLIE

Kallie gasped as her book smacked into her chest, the pages crumbling against her bosom. With a groan and an annoyed step backward, she peeled the book away from her body. Her brows knitted together as she spread her fingers against the pages in a dismal attempt to flatten them.

"By the gods! Watch where you're—" Kallie stopped mid-sentence as a pair of warm brown eyes stared back at her. Her shoulders dropped, and she brushed her hair behind her ear. "Oh, Rian. It's you."

"Last time I checked," Rian said with an awkward grin while he rubbed a hand against his chest where the book had smacked him.

Kallie tilted her head to the side. "Was that a joke, Your Majesty?"

"If you have to ask, it wasn't a very good one."

Rian's sleeves were rolled up, highlighting the muscles in his biceps that Kallie hadn't known existed. She couldn't help but admire the veins in his forearms that were on full display. His tailored suits always hid his body. She knew he was lean, but she didn't know muscles hid beneath the expensive fabric. In his other hand, his black suit jacket had been thrown neatly over his arm. But that was the only clean piece of clothing on the king. Scuff marks stained his shirt; dirt was smeared across his face. His hair was pointing in different directions and was coated in mud. The sight made Kallie's face contort with concern.

Kallie reached out, her fingers brushing the faint tint of red at the collar. Was that blood?

"Who did this to you?"

Rian offered her a shaky smile. "Are you worried about me, Kalisandre?"

Kallie brushed off a patch of dirt on his shirt and ignored the sharp inhale he took when she touched him. "You are my betrothed. Of course, I am worried about you. I can't have you dying on me before we even get a chance to say our vows," she said playfully.

"Ah, so the truth comes out then? You truly are just marrying me for my crown," Rian said with an amused grin.

<u>Is that what Tessa has told him?</u>

Kallie chuckled, shaking off the paranoia. "Of course not."

"Oh?"

She leaned toward him. "I'm marrying you for that library of yours."

Rian burst into laughter. And just like that, the tension from a couple of days ago dissipated along with the pang of paranoia.

She joined in the laughter.

Rian would believe anything Kallie said.

Her laughter died when she returned her attention to the patch of blood on his collar. "What happened, Rian?

He huffed, lightly swatting her hand away. "It was just a little training practice."

"*This*"—Kallie straightened his collar—"was from training?"

Rian shrugged.

Kallie gritted her teeth and began to turn around, saying, "When I see Laurince—"

But Rian grabbed her hand and stopped her before she was able to get away. "It wasn't Laurince."

A pair of servants walked by, their footsteps light and hurried. They sent cursory glances in Kallie and Rian's direction. Rian gave them a polite nod, and Kallie offered a small smile.

They bowed as they passed, then disappeared down the hall.

"Then who?" Kallie asked, staring up at him.

Rian looked down the hall behind Kallie and took a step back. "Sebastian."

"Your *brother* did this to you?" Kallie asked.

Rian shrugged again. This time, he couldn't hide the hiss that escaped as the muscles tightened from the slight movement. "Just because I am the king does not mean he should go easy on me."

"Go easy on you?" Kallie reached out a hand.

Rian leaned away, and her hand fell to her side.

Kallie's brows furrowed. "You're hurt, Rian."

"It's nothing," he said. Pain, however, laced each word.

"Fine," Kallie said, taking the hint that Rian did not wish to talk about this matter publicly. She smoothed a hand down the silk fabric of her dress, straightening it. "Where are you off to now?"

Rain sighed. "My rooms. I need to clean up before my next meeting with some of my advisors."

Kallie nodded. "I'll walk with you."

"I don't need—"

"Nonsense," Kallie said with a smile as she wrapped her arm around his. "I know you are more than capable of walking to your room by yourself. Is it a crime if your betrothed wishes to steal a few minutes with you alone before your advisors take you away from me again?"

Rian chuckled, but Kallie could still hear the hesitancy in the sound.

"And, if I am honest, I still get turned around when walking the castle. So, in truth, you would be doing me a favor," Kallie added, squeezing his arm.

Rian offered a small smile, some of the tension releasing from his muscles. "If you insist, my lady."

Gods be damned if someone saw the king needing help, Kallie thought with an inward roll of her eyes. *Men and their egos.*

And although his words suggested otherwise, Kallie knew the king was thankful for her assistance as he leaned into her.

They strolled through the halls, discussing various topics, such as the weather, Rian's past travels, and the status of the wedding. As they walked, Kallie kept peering at the growing bruises on his skin and the dirt on his clothes. And even though she knew better, she couldn't help the rising concern. She did not like Sebastian. Every encounter with the prince only made her detest him even more. The recent conversation with Sebastian echoed in her mind. She had heard the jealousy in his voice, the anger.

My brother is no more a king than you will be a queen.

While Sebastian put on a good act in front of the others, there was animosity between the brothers. Even if it was merely one-sided.

Either way, she didn't trust him.

Once Kallie and Rian reached the king's door, Rian released Kallie's arm and opened the door to his room.

Kallie didn't hesitate, and she entered the room behind him.

With a confused look, Rian paused just past the threshold, hesitating with his hand wrapped around the edge of the door.

"Rian," Kallie said, arching a brow. She placed a hand over his chest where the tip of a blade had sliced his shirt open. "Let me help you."

"But—" Rian's brows furrowed, confliction a deep wrinkle in the center of his forehead. His eyes closed, his shoulders dropped, and he released a soft, strained breath. "All right."

Rian stepped away, and Kallie walked into the king's private quarters. The door clicked shut behind them.

Similar to her own accommodations, the king's quarters opened up to a grand sitting room. On the southern wall, there was a beautiful hearth, and a black mantel was nailed to the cobblestone wall. Various items sat atop the mantel, including a small globe and a golden sculpture of a dragon. Across from the fireplace sat a black leather couch with cushions that were unwrinkled as if they had never been sat on.

On the opposite wall, a large mahogany desk occupied the majority of the space with an extravagant rug beneath it. Two twin chairs sat on one side of the desk, which were made from the same wood and adorned with velvet wine-red cushions and black jeweled buttons lining the edges. The top of Rian's desk was covered with maps, loose parchment, and books that overflowed onto the floors. It was so unlike her father's study, which was kept meticulously clean, not a single item out of place. Only once had Kallie seen pages scattered across Domitius' desk.

Rian cleared his throat.

Kallie looked over to him with a sweet smile. "Where's the washing room?"

Rian arched a brow in question.

"So I can grab a rag and a pail of water," she said.

Rian waved her off. "You don't need to do that."

"Enough of that, Rian. It's just the two of us."

Rian chewed on the inside of his cheek, then nodded. "Through there and to the right." Rian pointed to a door that was cracked open.

Kallie headed that way while Rian unbuttoned the leather strap around his waist holding his sword. Metal clanged behind her as he tossed it onto the floor. But Kallie didn't look back and instead pushed the door Rian had specified open.

Rian's bedchambers were empty of personal items besides a small stack of books on the nightstand. Around the bed, a black velvet curtain with red embroidery hid the bed. Kallie walked past it and headed for the bathing chambers.

She stopped in her tracks.

In front of the single window in the room, a gold crown sat atop a cabinet. Before Kallie realized it, she was walking toward it as if pulled by it. She had only ever seen the crown from afar or in the portraits decorating the hall since neither Rian nor his father had ever worn it in her presence. And up close, it was even more magnificent than she had imagined. The rubies adorning the golden points were brilliant, and little fires burned inside them.

Her hand reached out.

This, this piece of metal, was what she was fighting for. Her purpose.

"Kalisandre?" Rian called from the other room. "Everything all right?"

Kallie cleared her throat, her hand falling and the crown's spell vanishing in the air. "Yes, just looking for a towel," she shouted as she rushed into the bathing chambers.

"There should be some sitting near the sink. That's where Bernard usually sets them."

Kallie snatched a couple of towels from the counter and grabbed the pail of water sitting next to it.

"Found them!"

When she returned to the sitting room, Kallie had to tighten her grip around the pail of water once she found Rian. Her mouth fell slightly ajar.

Before her, Rian leaned against his desk. His white button-up hung over the back of a chair alongside his jacket, leaving him in nothing but his trousers that hung low on his hips. His gaze met hers, and a flush rose to his cheeks. He reached for the shirt. "Sorry, I can—"

"It's all right," Kallie said, shaking her head. "I can attend to your cuts better this way."

Kallie swallowed as she dropped her head.

She didn't know if his shirt on or off was worse, though, if she was being honest with herself. Part of her admired the view—a compelling part. Another part wanted him to throw his shirt back on and perhaps a bag over his head, too, for good measure. Seeing Rian like this was making it even harder not to make those personal connections she had been trying to avoid. And it definitely was not making it any easier not to have some sort of feeling about him. Even if they were superficial.

Kallie placed the bucket of water on the table beside him. He reached for the towel, but Kallie moved it away, dipping it into the water.

When she raised it to his face, he grabbed her wrist, his grip soft. "You don't need to do that, Kallie. What I said the other day . . ."

"This isn't about my role or my duty, Rian. This is simply one friend wanting to help another."

Rian smiled. "We're friends now?"

Kallie chuckled and shrugged. "I'd like to think so."

He nodded, grinning ear-to-ear as he released her hand and rested it on the desk.

With a gentle hand, Kallie washed the dirt off his face. "How could Sebastian do this?" she asked, the question no more than a whisper on her breath.

Rian cleared his throat. "It's my fault. I'm rusty. I haven't—I haven't had that much time to keep up with my training since inheriting the throne." He winced as Kallie brushed the rag across his ribs. "Sebastian did me a favor by reminding me, truthfully."

Kallie glared at him.

His features softened. "Truly, I am fine."

The stains on his shirt and the bruises already forming on his skin only seemed to suggest that Sebastian wasn't merely helping the king show him where his weaknesses lay.

Growing up, Kallie had a strict training regime, which often left her battered and bruised. But her father had always ensured that the bruises never showed and were easily hidden beneath the dresses. If one of the guards she had manipulated to assist in her training got carried away, Kallie would wake up to a new dress that covered the fresh bruises the next day. If she had not hidden them, those in the castle would have questioned what the princess was doing in her free time. And questions always led to suspicions, which never led to anything good. She was thankful for her father's precautions.

But Sebastian had not been careful. He had been ruthless.

Did Rian even realize that his brother had intentionally roughed him up, that Sebastian was jealous of Rian's title?

She reached down and pulled her gift up to the surface. "Tell me the truth, Rian. Did Sebastian intentionally harm you?"

Rian shook his head. "No. Sebastian wouldn't do that."

The haze of her gift swam in his brown eyes, yet she didn't believe a single word he said.

Was the king truly that ignorant?

She let her gift sink back to the bottom of her stomach and finished washing the rest of the dirt off Rian's face.

"I didn't even realize Sebastian was still here," she said as she dipped the rag in the murky water. She hadn't seen Sebastian since their conversation days ago. She had assumed he was gone, but apparently, he still lurked somewhere within the castle.

Her stomach sank.

Rian brushed a hand across his face, his jaw flexing. "My brother was with the troops this past week. He only just returned last night."

"Hmm," Kallie hummed. She dried off her hands and stared at the pail of water.

Rian's hand wrapped around hers, and he tugged, beckoning her to look at him. "Kallie, I have only known you for a couple of weeks now, but I know you well enough at this point to know that you always have something to say."

Kallie gnawed on her lip.

His gaze danced across her face, and he raised a hand, caressing her cheek. His voice softened. "I meant what I said before. While I respect tradition, that does not mean I wish the traditions to remain the same. Speak your mind."

Kallie blinked at him, her brows furrowing. Didn't he know that he couldn't have it both ways?

His thumb brushed across her cheek. "Please."

Kallie sighed, leaning into his touch. "If Sebastian is one of your advisors, should he not be more concerned with your reputation?"

Rian's hand fell. "I full-heartedly believe that Sebastian has my best interest in mind."

"But what if someone saw you in such shape as you were today?"

"Then they would think that their king takes his training seriously."

"And an enemy?" Kallie arched a brow.

"I have personally vetted everyone here." He grabbed Kallie's hand, pulling her closer. "If you are worried about your safety, let me reassure you now. You are safe here with me."

Kallie said nothing, only offering him a soft smile.

His gaze dipped down to her mouth, and Kallie stiffened as he leaned in.

Bells rung in the clock tower, echoing throughout the castle.

Kallie took a step back. "I should be going. I don't want Laurince chopping my head off for making you any later than you already are to your meeting."

Rian straightened, tipping his head. Yet even though he said goodbye to her with a grin, sadness leaked from his irises. But Kallie could not provide him any more comfort.

Rian believed that no enemies wandered these halls. Yet he did not see that one of his enemies stood before him, that he invited his enemy into his private quarters. And if he could not see that, how many others could be harboring ill thoughts about their king?

Sometimes, it was those closest to you that you needed to watch out for.

CHAPTER 24
KALLIE

Kallie awoke to the sound of paper sliding beneath her door. Heart pounding, she picked up the two letters. One was sealed with the Ardentolian crest, the other with a sigil of a dragon.

She opened her father's letter first:

Kalisandre,

My return to the castle has been delayed.

K.D.

Kallie didn't know if her father's absence was a good or bad thing, for he gave no evidence to suggest either. She searched the contents of his letter for some hidden message but found none.

Had something happened back home? Was he safe? Wouldn't he tell her if something was wrong? They had a code for that, and his letter did not mention bad weather. Nothing to suggest any danger had fallen upon him. Yet Kallie couldn't shake the chill that swept over her skin.

Setting her father's letter down on the vanity, she opened the second letter. Kallie immediately recognized the scratchy handwriting scrawled across the thick piece of parchment.

Dearest Kalisandre,

My presence has been requested on the outskirts of Frenzia. I will be back in five days.

Yours, Rian

"Five days?" Kallie asked out loud. That was only a day before the wedding week began. What could require the king's attention days before his own wedding?

CHAPTER 25
GRAESON

Their pace was slow as they trudged through the wetland. Usually, Graeson enjoyed riding, for there was a sense of freedom in it. This time, however, Graeson only felt trapped, locked in by time. He wished he could do something other than ride. He wanted to fight, to slaughter. And for once, the beast within his mind agreed with him.

Ellie continued to try to make small talk with him. Once he had filled her in with the details of what she had missed since they had last seen each other, the frivolous questions began.

At first, her questions were simple and ridiculous: "If you could eat anything in the world, what would it be?"

Then they turned philosophical: "Do you think the grass feels pain when we ride across it?"

And then, they were utterly outlandish: "If a kelpie jumped out of the water, sliced your horse's heels off, and brought you beneath the waters, what would you do?"

When she had asked, Graeson had glared at her. "I would die, Ellie."

"You wouldn't fight it?"

Graeson had groaned and rode further ahead of her.

Just beyond the border of Tetria and Borgania, they set up camp, and Graeson finally put an end to her questions.

Ellie tossed the remnants of her dinner into the fire, then wiped her hands along the sides of her pants. "You wish to sit in silence? Fine," she said, frowning as she leaned back on her palms.

"Thank the gods," Dani mumbled beside her.

When Ellie gave Dani a cold stare, she lifted her head propped up on the arm resting on her knee. "What? Everyone's thinking it. You talk a lot, Ellie. That cannot come as a surprise to you."

Ellie arched a brow. "I liked it better when you were across the sea."

"At least we agree on something," Dani said with a wink.

Ellie shoved Dani with her leg, their knees knocking together, and Dani smirked.

The log split, and embers shot through the air. The others had already escaped to their tents to sleep.

Ellie pushed herself up from the dirt. "We have a lot of ground to cover in the morning if we want to reach the Frenzian border in two days' time. Get some rest while you can."

Leaves rustled nearby, and Dani's gaze snapped to it. Squinting, she stared past the oak trees surrounding them. After a moment, she shook her head and stirred the fire. Borgania's forests were filled with creatures of the night. Bears, wolves, and elk were often seen wandering through the woods.

"I'll take the first watch tonight," Graeson said.

Dani nodded. "I'll go do a quick round and then head to bed," Dani said. She grabbed her bow and arrows that were sitting beside her and headed past the tent before Graeson could argue. Away from the fire's glow, the forest's shadows swallowed her.

Neither of them would be getting any sleep tonight.

Their journey through the Borganian lands proved uneventful. Graeson should have been happy about that, for they didn't need any complications. They had plenty of those already. Yet here he was, hoping for some sort of run-in—as crazy as that sounded.

Maybe it was the restless nights, the long rides, or the constant yammering around him. No matter what it was, he was bored, restless, and angry.

They had been traveling for three and a half days, and nothing had happened. They hadn't even run into any of the predators that lurked within the forest. The only animals they saw were birds flying through the foliage of maple trees and deer roaming through the brush in the woods.

Nothing was ever this easy, though.

At one point, his paranoia had risen so high that when Dani had burst through the trees after scouting, Graeson had pulled out a throwing knife, ready to strike.

He was on edge.

All of them were. Even if the others did not admit it. He saw it in the way Ellie's words grew more clipped, in the way Ophelia kept nagging Medenia about her sore neck. Moris' jokes increased with a shaky jolt. With every hour that ticked by, Armen grew more quiet. Dani's rides around their camps grew more frequent. They all had their way of distracting themselves. A way to pass the time and avoid thinking about their growing anxieties.

They would infiltrate the kingdom with the largest army in less than a week and steal Kalisandre from their enemy's grasp. One week until Domitius would have a blade driven through his heart.

If everything went to plan, that is.

And perhaps it was because of that growing paranoia and because Graeson had all but wished for a fight, that the gods gave him one.

CHAPTER 26
KALLIE

"This cannot be right!" Marsinia, the royal seamstress, shouted, snapping the measuring tape at her side.

She was a small, older woman who could strike fear in anyone with her needles and measuring tape. Myra had been working closely with the seamstress for the past couple of weeks to ensure everything was perfect.

"Lux!"

A young girl, no more than sixteen years old, stepped forward. "Yes, Miss Marsi?"

"This measuring tape is all wrong," Marsinia tossed it at Lux, and the young woman stumbled to catch it.

"Wrong, Miss Marsi?"

"Yes, *wrong*."

Stretching the measuring tape between her arms, Lux surveyed it.

In the mirror, Kallie saw Myra release a silent sigh before turning around. A moment later, she returned, a new measuring tape in hand. "Here, Marsinia. Try this one."

The seamstress snatched the measuring tape from Myra's hands and flung it open. Mumbling nonsensical words, Marsinia wrapped the tape around Kallie's waist once more.

Once it was lined up, she bellowed in frustration and threw the measuring tape onto the ground. "This one is wrong too!" Marsinia shouted with a sewing needle between her teeth.

Kallie cleared her throat and ran her hands down the fabric of the silk dress. "Excuse me, Marsinia, but may I ask what the problem is?"

Marsinia pulled the needle out of her mouth and shook it at Kallie. "*You.* This is your fault!"

Lux and the group of handmaidens gasped. Kallie, however, just stared blankly at the woman.

Marsinia shoved the needle closer. "Are you eating?"

"Excuse me?" Kallie asked, giving a wary look at the needle, then the seamstress.

The seamstress fixed her searing gaze on Myra and Phaia, pointing the needle at the handmaidens next. "How much is she eating?"

Phaia's gaze dropped to the ground as though the floors were suddenly captivating. Beside her, Myra wrung her hands together at her waist while the other handmaidens fidgeted uncomfortably.

"Well?" Marsinia waved her hand in the air.

Pursing her lips to the side, Myra mumbled. "I suppose I have noticed that the Princess' appetite has decreased since arriving in Frenzia." Myra's knuckles grew white, her fingers twisting together. "Somewhat, anyway."

"Somewhat?" Marsinia tossed her hands in the air. She pointed a firm finger in Kallie's direction. "She has lost over an inch around her waist, if not more, since the last time I measured her only four weeks ago!"

"But that can't be," Myra said, coming to take a look at the measuring tape. "The measuring tape must be—"

"Wrong? That's what I thought. But there is no way. I mean . . .

look at her! She was already small-chested to begin with, and now . . . ." Marsinia clicked her tongue. "Now I have to take in all the dresses, or else they will sag in all the wrong places! This is my reputation on the line! Do you know how much work that is going to be? How much time that is going to take? These dresses are incredibly intricate and delicate. These things take time to adjust. Time and patience, both of which are quickly dwindling."

Kallie looked down at the dress. An inch around could not have made that much of a difference. The seamstress had to be exaggerating.

Kallie turned to her reflection in the mirror.

She looked the same as she did every day, yet her brows furrowed as she studied her reflection more closely.

She fixed the thin strap of the red silk dress that had fallen down her shoulders. The dress for the welcome dinner was loose in the middle. While Kallie did not oppose loose-fitting clothing, Marsinia had designed this one to hug her curves. The mockup she had tried on a couple of weeks ago had accentuated her femininity, embracing her wide hips while complimenting her less-than-average bosom. But today, it sagged around her curves. Her collarbone was more prominent, and the tops of her breasts were less plump.

How had she not noticed that she was losing weight?

Kallie sucked the inside of her cheek, biting down on the flesh.

"This will cost the crown extra," Marsinia groaned.

With the faint taste of iron on her tongue, Kallie said, "We will cover it."

She wagged a finger in Kallie's face, the needle close to Kallie's eye once again. "You need to eat, child. If it's the Frenzian cuisine that you do not favor, have one of your handmaidens ask the cook to prepare something"—she waved the needle in the air—"more suitable to your taste buds. Whatever it is, I do not care."

Marsinia bit down on the needle as she grabbed a pin from the cushion tied to her wrist and began pinning the fabric.

As the seamstress pinched the fabric and marked where the adjustments needed to be made, Kallie peered in the mirror again. Even her face looked thinner, narrower. She had not been trying to lose weight. On the contrary, she had given little thought to her weight. Like many young girls, Kallie was often self-conscious about her appearance as a child. When she started training, she had a new focus: to be strong. She learned that she needed to provide her body with the proper nutrients in order to build the muscle mass she wanted. Over the years, she had grown to love her body. Even when it changed—and it changed frequently. As her menstrual cycle took its course, naturally, her weight shifted. But it had never been a problem, at least not for her.

But now, Kallie couldn't help but notice how she had changed since she arrived. Not just in her weight but her overall appearance. The cloud-covered skies of Frenzia had done little to warm up her complexion. Her skin, which not too long ago bore the kiss of the sun, had dulled. The freckles the sun had once brought months ago from riding horseback had nearly vanished. The sun's touch did little for her skin, even with the numerous strolls around the grounds.

Once the seamstress finished, Marsinia told Kallie that she was on strict orders to maintain her diet, making Kallie promise to eat more. But at the mere mention of food, Kallie's stomach flipped. These days, she had a hard time keeping anything down. No wonder she had lost weight.

When the seamstress and her assistant Lux left, taking the scattered notes for the alterations, Kallie dismissed the group of handmaidens. Myra was the only one to remain behind.

In the reflection of the mirror, Kallie looked at Myra. "You see it, too. Don't you, Myra?" Kallie asked as she put on the simple dress she had been wearing before the fitting.

Myra shook her head, and concern and disappointment drew her brows together. "I don't know how I missed it."

"You've been busy, Mys. I do not expect you to take note of everything I eat. Especially not when there are more pressing matters to take care of, such as the wedding."

"That is not an excuse," Myra said.

Kallie sighed. It was not Myra's fault, yet Kallie knew her friend would still bear the weight of it. "Myra, I am my own person."

Myra bit her lip. "I know, but you're hurting, Kals. It's my job to—"

"What are you talking about?" Kallie interrupted, peering over her shoulder.

Myra motioned to Kallie with a tip of her head. With a heavy sigh, Kallie turned around and inhaled. Myra secured the corset with a neat bow before walking around to face Kallie. She grabbed Kallie's hands, and a flood of emotion swept over Myra's countenance. So many emotions and so fast that Kallie could only recognize one: remorse.

"Kals, we haven't talked about what happened."

Kallie's hand slipped from Myra's grasp as she stepped down from the pedestal. Myra followed her.

"What is there to talk about?" Kallie asked.

Myra released a disbelieving chuckle. Sadness peppered her sweet hazel eyes. "You are allowed to grieve, Kals. You are allowed to miss them."

Even at the mere thought of the Pontian family whom Kallie had barely gotten to know, water burned behind Kallie's eyes. She turned away, her finger running along the rim of the crystal water glass.

She didn't want to shed the tears. She couldn't.

Grieving was one thing, but missing them? Missing the Pontians was a betrayal to her father, and she could not afford for her father to question her loyalty right now.

Myra spun her around. "Kals."

Kallie bit down on her tongue, wishing for the tears to evaporate. With a strained voice, Kallie whispered, "If my father finds out..."

Biting the bottom of her lip, Myra shook their joined hands. "It's just you and me, Kals. You can trust me."

Kallie sighed, and her head dropped. "I know." Kallie trusted Myra with her whole heart. Her friend had never betrayed her, misled her, or told Domitius about any of her midnight rendezvous outside the marble castle walls. Myra was faithful, loyal. She was the one person Kallie could always count on.

So, through tear-filled eyes, Kallie finally admitted the truth that she had been harboring inside for too long. "I'm so confused, Myra."

Myra squeezed her hands. "Confused about what?"

Staring up at the ceiling, Kallie tried to force the tears away. But no matter how long she studied the ceiling, the tears refused to roll back inside her head. "Part of me knows that my father is not to blame, that he didn't kill Fynn..." Kallie bit down on her tongue.

Myra's brows furrowed. "But?"

Kallie took a deep breath in. "But I cannot help but feel shameful because it was his actions that brought Sebastian there."

To herself, Kallie thought, *and it was by my command that the soldier had stepped in and that the other soldiers felt the need to join in.*

Myra offered her a sad smile. With her thumb, she wiped away the tear that had slipped free.

For once, her friend's touch provided Kallie with no comfort.

"I know my father did what he had to do to ensure that I was safe. But how am I supposed to live here, Mys? How am I supposed to dine with Sebastian when he was the one who killed Fynn?" With every word, her voice shook even more. "He killed Fynn, and I can't even —"

"Shh, it's going to be all right, Kals." Myra dropped Kallie's hands and wrapped her arms around her.

The two women stood like that for several minutes. Neither one of them spoke. Myra didn't draw attention to Kallie's quiet sobs, nor did Kallie point out how Myra was shaking.

Or was that Kallie who was shaking Myra?

The embrace was meant to be a comfort, yet it only forced the guilt to swallow Kallie whole. And then, before she could stop them, the rest of the tears streamed down her face. Because what Kallie wanted to say, what she finally let herself admit to herself, was that she, too, was to blame for her brother's death. It was by Kallie's command, her actions, her betrayal that Fynn had met his death.

An overwhelming sense of remorse and regret coated Kallie's tongue. And the only way to release it was through the truth. Yet she couldn't bring herself to say it out loud, for so many secrets lived between Kallie and Myra now.

Kallie opened her eyes and stared at the back of her friend's head in the mirror, watching Myra's soft hand rub the back of Kallie's head.

Before, Kallie never bore the weight of her missions for too long, and the secrets Kallie held growing up never felt this large. They never forced Kallie to keep Myra at arm's length, but now Kallie felt suffocated by Myra's perfume. The sweet scent of lavender and mint in Myra's hair was a noose around Kallie's neck.

A good friend would confess.

A good friend wouldn't keep so many secrets.

A good friend would be *better.*

Was Kallie a terrible friend then for keeping her gift a secret, too? If Kallie told Myra, wouldn't she worry that Kallie was manipulating her too? How would Myra know truth from fiction?

Even if Kallie had promised herself long ago that she would never use her gift on Myra, that didn't mean Myra would believe that to be true.

So, despite the growing divide between them, Kallie kept her mouth shut.

CHAPTER 27
GRAESON

"What is that?" Moris asked, his words barely audible as he crouched beside Graeson.

They hid behind a thick, overgrown bush in the darkness of the Thornwood Forest just past the Frenzian border, watching a group of men in light hunting armor and cloaks.

They were two days away from the castle. While Graeson and the others had been looking for a place to camp for the night, Dani spotted a small encampment a couple of miles away. Unwilling to take the risk, Graeson, Armen, Moris, and Dani went to check it out while the others remained at their campsite.

The men were gathered in front of an iron crate. Graeson tried to see what was hidden in the crate, but a tarp covered it. Something growled as a chain scraped against the floor.

Graeson looked at Dani and then Armen. Both shook their heads, unable to identify it.

One man stepped toward the crate and opened the front of the tarp. As he did, nails clawed the metal floor of the crate. Fear tainted the night air—the soldiers' or the creature's, Graeson couldn't be too sure.

With narrowed eyes, Graeson leaned forward, peering beyond the trees and foliage. Even with exceptional vision, he struggled to identify the creature before them. All he could see in the shadows of the crate were large, glowing red eyes peering out, wide and alert. Whatever creature cowered in the back of the large metal cage, only one man was brave enough to step close. The others gave the cage a wide berth.

The man closest to the stranger, the wrangler Graeson presumed based on his confident gait, reached for the bundle of locks on the cage.

Were the thick iron bars not enough to keep the animal caged? Were the twisted chains truly a necessity?

Graeson's teeth ground against each other. At the edge of his vision, red began to seep in. The leather-wrapped hilt bit into the flesh of his palm as his knuckles turned white around it.

The cage's final lock landed on the ground with a thud, and the creature hissed.

The wrangler fiddled with something at his side, but Graeson couldn't identify the object in the darkness. The creature, however, could.

Metal screeched, and chains rattled as the man pried the heavy door open, his heels digging into the ground. The man shifted, and then a *crack* ripped through the air. Graeson jerked back as the snap of the wrangler's whip rang in his ears.

The wrangler took a step forward, whip in hand. The creature crawled further back into the shadows of its cage, its eyes no longer visible in the dim light of the flickering torches.

The wrangler only took one step, only far enough inside to squat down, lean forward, and pick up a chain lying on the ground. The chain rattled and scraped against the metal flooring, followed by a piercing screech from the animal. A noise so sharp that Armen almost fell to the floor, his head falling into his lap.

As Graeson tightened his grip around his throwing knife, a hand fell on his shoulder. When he looked over his shoulder, Dani stared at him, shaking her head no.

Lip curling, Graeson forced his attention away from her.

As the tension in the air grew strained, so did Graeson's hold on the beast within him.

Nothing good ever came from men standing around a caged, scared animal.

Yet even though every bone in his body told him otherwise, he only watched, his body eerily still as he bit down on his tongue.

The wrangler pulled at the chain. When the animal still didn't walk forward, the man pulled harder. Nearby, the horses tethered to the trees shuffled, their hooves a nervous patter on the ground. After two tugs, the creature finally relented. It stepped out from beneath the tarp. The flames licked its skin, casting flickering shadows across its body. With its large head hanging low, the animal exited its cage.

At its approach, the men's hands went to the hilts of their swords, their jaws falling slightly agape. The surrounding men took several slow steps back, and Graeson couldn't blame them. In Graeson's twenty-five years, he had seen many things, so it took a lot to surprise him. But this . . . he couldn't even begin to comprehend what he saw standing before him.

"What is that?" Dani asked, leaning forward.

"It looks like a . . . dragon-puppy?" Moris said, his tone questioning.

"There's no such thing," Armen whispered.

"Are you sure about that?" Moris asked. "Because that's what whatever *that* looks like."

Graeson, however, wasn't so sure. Puppies were cute; puppies were sweet. The animal in front of them was anything but. The creature's head appeared kin to either a wolf or a large herding dog, with a medium-sized snout and wet nose. Not the slitted nose depicted in the books he had read about as a child, which described the legendary dragons. Irises, the color of rubies, glowed in the flickering flames of the torches that lined the makeshift campsite. Four large legs, with paws three times the size of Graeson's fists, supported its massive body. Its hind legs were ripe with muscles. The wrangler led the animal around in a circle, whip in one hand and chain in the other, and the creature's side came into view. Scales covered the animal's sharp shoulders that then trailed down its spine. But what caught Graeson's attention the most were the giant wings protruding out of its shoulder blades.

Inches from the beast's long, yellowed claws, the wrangler cracked the whip against the ground. At the sound, the beast tried to retreat. The chain went taut as it pulled away from its handler.

Crack.

Another loud, painful screech erupted from the animal's mouth as the wrangler cracked the whip, hitting one of the animal's paws.

A sharp white pain seared through Graeson's right arm as the hilt of the throwing knife bit into the flesh of his palm. No animal deserved this.

When the wrangler cracked the whip again, Graeson jerked forward, but Dani and Moris forced him back, their fingers digging into his shoulders.

Upon the snapping of the thick rope, the animal spread its wings out wide. Whereas the creature's legs, chest, and stomach were covered with fur, its wings appeared webbed, and the torches' flames bled through its opaque skin. An amber glow flickering within its wings.

The handler pulled something else from his belt. From their hiding spot, it looked to be a pelt of some sort. A skinned squirrel or rabbit, perhaps. When the man held it in the air, the beast lowered its head, its shoulders sagging, wings still spread out. When the wrangler tossed the pelt high in the air, the animal tried to jump, but the chain pulled it back down.

Laughter erupted from some of the men in the circle as the beast was tugged back to the ground.

The creature whimpered, yet it still managed to catch the carcass in its mouth. In a matter of seconds, the beast devoured it whole. Then it dragged its snout across the dirt, looking for more food. When the creature found none, the men chuckled nervously.

Meanwhile, the wrangler hooked the animal's chain to a post sticking out of the ground and turned to the men.

"What are they saying?" Dani asked Armen.

Armen shook his head. "That with time, the creature will only grow more fierce, more deadly. They're working on producing more of its kind as they speak."

Graeson blanched.

This creature had not been merely born but created. The testing alone that the animal must have gone through was unfathomable. Let alone the confinement the animal had to endure. To be chained your entire life, stuck in a cage, never knowing that there were open skies above your head where you could soar until your wings gave out, was not a life. It was a prison. This creature did not know freedom. It didn't even know freedom existed. All it knew was pain and suffering.

Graeson spat on the ground. "They're all dead."

"What do you mean? They're not—" Moris snapped his mouth shut, Graeson's threat finally hitting him.

"Graeson," Dani hissed. "What are you doing?"

"What I should have done the moment we got here," Graeson said, shoving Dani's hands off him.

Then, without thinking anymore, he hurled not one, not two, but three knives into the backs of the closest soldiers, one after another. As the blades met their marks, three men slunk to the floor.

One of the remaining soldiers snapped his head in the direction of his fallen comrades. "We are under attack!"

The torchbearers drove the bottom of the torches into the dirt and, in one fell swoop, unsheathed their blades, their Frenzian sigils flashing in the flames.

"Go!" the soldier closest to Graeson's group shouted over his shoulder.

Two men sprinted, mounting two of the nearby horses. They disappeared into the forest in a flash, their horses galloping into the darkness.

"Moris! Armen!" Dani shouted. "Follow them!"

Moris nodded, pulling Armen with him as he took off.

"Dani?" Graeson asked, his fingers wrapping around his scimitars hanging on his back. His gaze bounced from the soldiers to the beast and then to the man slithering away.

The swish of metal sliding out of leather cut through the air. "It might not be Domitius, but at least I get to kill someone," Dani said.

The beast within him smiled, its craving for vengeance palpable on Graeson's tongue.

He slid his scimitars out of their holsters and stood in one smooth movement. Without another word, they moved.

The first two men couldn't even raise their swords as Dani and Graeson's blades sliced through the air.

Graeson drove his blade through the next soldier's rib cage.

Every individual Graeson's scimitar sliced through was marked in his memory. There was a reason for each death that he caused. Every victim who fell prey to his wrath was doomed to die from the moment they decided to harm an animal, belittle a woman, or get in his way. And there was one man in particular whose blood his blade craved even more than the rest. But where had the wrangler snuck off to?

A flicker of movement flashed in the corner of his eyes.

Graeson called out, "Dani!"

She hissed, kicking a man in the gut and knocking him to the ground as she spun and sliced her dagger through another's neck. "I got this. After all—" grunt, kick, "I'm used to cleaning up after you."

With a roll of his eyes, Graeson tumbled forward.

In his haste, he hadn't seen the animal cowering beside the cage. The animal roared, standing on its hind legs with its wings spread out. But Graeson's bloody blade was not meant for the creature. He ducked, then dove.

Pushing himself off the ground, he rounded the corner of the cage. His head swiveled, and his gaze swept the area, searching for the wrangler.

An object on the ground caught his attention. Smirking, he swiped it just as he saw a shadow moving in the forest. He struck, the whip snapping in the air.

A hiss followed, then a crash.

Graeson sprinted forward, whip in one hand, scimitar in the other. At the edge of the tree line, the wrangler tried to get up.

Again, the monster in the back of Graeson's mind demanded, and Graeson's hand twitched around the whip's handle.

Again!

The whip fell from Graeson's hand.

He stormed forward, and his foot fell atop the man's ankle. Graeson dug in, twisting it into the dirt.

Within Graeson's mind, the monster's door cracked open an inch, and its anger and rage slipped out. Red flooded his vision. He pulled at the back of the wrangler's collar, yanking him up.

The man yelled out in pain, and the sound reverberated through Graeson's body.

Graeson snickered. "How does it feel?" He asked as he wrapped his other arm around the handler's neck and tugged. "To be whipped? To be struck? To have your life's fate in someone else's hands?"

The man opened his mouth to speak, but he choked on air as Graeson tightened his grip around his throat.

"Oh, I'm sorry. Did you think I cared?"

And whether it was the monster within his mind fueling him or his own anger, Graeson didn't know or care. His scimitar slid across his throat, and the wrangler's body hit the ground.

DANI WIPED her blade on the side of her cotton trousers. Sheathing it, she stretched her arms above her head as Armen and Moris returned through the forest. Their breaths were heavy, and their clothes clean of blood.

"Well?" she asked.

Moris shook his head. "They're long gone."

Graeson nodded, his jaw straining.

A problem for another day.

Bodies lie around them, dead. But beyond the blood on Dani and Graeson's clothes, they had managed to come out unscathed. They were lucky. Whatever weapon the Frenzians had used during their attack in Pontia was nowhere to be seen tonight. If they had been equipped with that weapon, even Graeson would have had trouble defeating them.

Next time, they might not be as lucky.

Jaw clenched, Graeson pulled a black handkerchief from his pocket and wiped his blades clean.

The animal's chain rattled, and a whimper followed. Graeson redirected his attention to the creature.

"Gray," Dani whispered, her arms frozen above her head. "What do we do with it?"

Graeson looked at the creature and then at the others. "Why are you all looking at me?"

"I mean," Moris said, rubbing the back of his head with a hand, "we are in this predicament because of you."

Graeson sighed. Moris wasn't wrong. If Graeson hadn't moved, if he hadn't made the first throw, they could have easily let things proceed as they may. But he hadn't. He had acted. He would always fight to protect those who couldn't defend themselves.

Graeson looked at each one of them. "Fine. Just don't move, all right?"

The others nodded, and he stepped forward, hands low, head slightly dipped. While Graeson did not know what this creature was, he knew enough about wild animals to know that he did not want to appear threatening.

The moment the animal's muscles went rigid, Graeson froze.

The animal's wings were drawn tight to its sides. The creature had moved in the fight, and now the post that the chain was hooked to was between its two hind legs. Even if Graeson did manage to unhook the chain from the base without being trampled—which was a long shot—the creature would still have a chain hanging from its neck.

So, there was no other choice. He had to get up close if he wanted to set it free. Graeson took a careful step forward, and the animal's lips rolled back, baring sharp, yellow teeth. Hot breath seeped from its throat.

Slowly, Graeson reached out a hand. Then, he waited.

Its nostrils twitched, and the animal sunk its head low. Its shoulders raised like a wolf would as it crept toward its prey.

Then, the creature straightened its wings. A warning.

Graeson remained steady, his hand out. He wasn't easily threatened—although he couldn't say the same for the other three Pontians if the rushed footsteps and twigs snapping were any indication. From the corner of his eye, he could have sworn that he saw Armen fall backward, hissing out a curse.

Graeson lowered his gaze and waited. He would let the animal come to him. His legs became tree trunks rooted in the dirt. He peered through his brows as his arm muscles strained, and he kept his hand steady.

The dragon-wolf slunk forward, its steps slow and calculated. One shoulder dropped as the other moved forward.

With even breaths, Graeson watched the animal approach. He knew the length of the chain after watching the wrangler show the creature off and noting the distance the man had maintained between him and the beast.

The beast was just out of reach now.

One more step.

The animal's nostrils flared as it inhaled Graeson's scent. Its lip curled, and its rancid breath hit Graeson in the face.

Still, he did not budge.

The creature's ruby red glare slipped to Graeson's scar on his face. Graeson had worn the scar all his life. He knew when people—or creatures, in this case—stared at the mark by the passing judgment and pity that flashed in their gazes. Many thought scars were a sign of weakness. But they weren't to Graeson. The scar that ran from above his eyebrow down to his cheekbone was a reminder of where he came from and what he had survived.

His gaze flicked down and caught on the scratches embedded into the animal's skin, the bald patches in its fur.

Graeson relaxed his muscles. Animals, he knew, could sense fear and hesitation. Monsters knew when someone approached them with hate. And Graeson knew all too well how fear had its way of sinking into its victim's skin, flowing into its bloodstream and tainting it. Feeding it—fueling it with more fear and hate. Once fear had a hold of you, there was no going back.

Graeson was a monster, though, too. He feared no man, no beast.

He was something someone had created and birthed for war, then abandoned.

He feared something far greater than an individual or death. He feared losing hope.

All this creature knew was fear.

Perhaps this animal, whatever it was, was more similar to Graeson than he first thought. It just needed someone to reach out a hand.

The creature inched closer. Its snout pressed against the skin of Graeson's hand, and Graeson exhaled. His hand stroked the top of the creature's nose, and instead of retreating, the animal leaned into Graeson's touch. With his other hand, Graeson scratched beneath the dragon-wolf's chin, and the animal turned its head slightly. As he did, someone gasped behind him.

The corner of Graeson's lip twitched into the faint mark of a smile.

"Do you have a name, little monster?" Graeson asked, continuing to scratch its chin.

Bright blood red irises blinked at him.

"A name?" Armen asked, shock coloring his voice.

Graeson shrugged. "Everyone deserves a name."

"What? Do you plan on keeping it?" Armen asked.

Graeson rolled his eyes. Like that was Graeson's choice to make. The animal hadn't even tasted freedom yet. Graeson would not take that away from it before it even had a chance to feel the wind beneath its wings.

"I believe the question actually is, do you plan on keeping *her*," Moris corrected.

"What?" Armen asked, taking a careful step toward Moris. Now that Graeson was distracting the animal, the others seemed more comfortable moving around again.

"Look," Moris said. "It's a female."

"Congratulations," Armen mused, and Graeson shook his head, feeling the eye roll boring into the back of his head.

Faint footsteps sounded behind him, and Graeson knew who it was before she even spoke.

"Graeson," Dani warned.

"What?"

"Release it."

Graeson dropped a hand and peered at the collar. He reached forward, and the animal stared at him, questioning his movement. That, or questioning why he had stopped scratching her jaw.

He petted the jaw once more. "Don't worry," Graeson whispered. "I'm here to help."

The beast huffed, but she shifted, giving Graeson clear access to the collar.

After inspecting the metal, Graeson reached for one of the throwing knives he had retrieved from a Frenzian's body.

A sorrow-filled noise escaped the animal's lips at the sight of the blade.

"Helping," Graeson reminded the animal. He held the dagger near its nose, blade flat in his palm.

The animal sniffed it, then huffed again.

Taking that as much of a sign of approval as he was going to get, Graeson reached for the lock. He unlocked the mechanism with some maneuvering, and the chain fell to the ground with a clang. Graeson stepped back.

With the weight gone, the animal stretched its neck toward the sky. The hybrid dragon-wolf stretched its wings. She batted them in the air as if testing their durability. Then, with what looked to be a nod in Graeson's direction, she sprinted and jumped. As she launched herself into the air, Graeson caught sight of more scars lacing her back, and the anger returned.

At least she was free now.

"What the hell was that?" Dani asked, voice shaking from both terror and awe as she watched the beast take flight.

"I have no fucking clue," Graeson said at the same time as Moris said, "A dragon-puppy."

Dani and Armen burst into laughter, releasing the tension.

Graeson, however, didn't laugh. His brows knitted together as he watched the animal's silhouette fade into the night sky. All jokes aside, the animal was not natural. It shouldn't exist, yet here it was in the flesh. If the others hadn't seen it, too, Graeson would have questioned if the lack of sleep over the past week had made him delusional.

That left only one question: what the hell were the Frenzians doing?

CHAPTER 28
KALLIE

With one day left before the wedding festivities started, Rian's absence lingered uncomfortably in the air. He was supposed to be back by now, yet there had been no word from anyone about his return. A fact no one dared speak about in Kallie's presence, yet it soaked every conversation.

Kallie's nerves rose as she stood on the balcony overlooking the large courtyard, watching the staff finish the preparations for the welcome dinner. Lystrata shouted command after command from the front of the room as though she was the director of an orchestra and the servants were her musicians. As the staff raced around the room, they knocked into the corners of tables and the chairs set up.

Guests had been arriving at the castle every hour. While Kallie had not seen the new guests, their presence was made known by the way the castle shifted. An influx of servants and guards flooded the castle. Kallie's walks became confined to the castle's halls, the guards too nervous for her to be outside so close to the wedding. They were not willing to take any risks. Where Kallie walked, no less than four guards followed. Even her nights in the library were closely guarded.

Upon arrival, the staff directed the visitors to the guest houses surrounding the castle. People from all over Vaneria had arrived, including Ragolo, Kadia, and Borgania. Kallie had heard nothing about Tetria or Ardentol's arrival yet.

A thin layer of guilt coated her stomach, and a burning sensation rose in her throat.

Delayed or not, her father would be here soon. Once he arrived, there would no doubt be questions about her assignments. While she had covered her tracks, there was still a sinking feeling that he would somehow discover that she had not killed the servant herself. And she had made little headway in learning what knowledge the Frenzians were keeping secret. With Rian's absence, she hadn't been able to pry it from him as she planned to do.

Her finger tapped anxiously on the railing.

Below, two male servants were hanging the drapes across the beams. One stood atop a ladder, draping the thin black chiffon fabric across the wooden beams, while the other held the ladder's base steady on the ground. The nearly transparent material was stark yet delicate against the solid oak beams. The addition of the chiffon made the room look enchanting and ethereal. But the man putting it up couldn't be less so. Even from her position, Kallie could see the man's sweat-soaked shirt and ruffled hair. The man on the ladder tossed the fabric, aiming for the beam.

He missed, and the fabric floated in the air before falling out of his reach.

The servant tossed his head back in exasperation, reaching for it and extending his arm as far as possible. His fingers brushed against the fabric, but he was still too far away to grab it. He tried again, and after struggling for a moment, he managed to grab it.

Meanwhile, the man holding the ladder struck up a conversation with a female servant carrying a bundle of eucalyptus. The man glanced at his comrade on the ladder and then back at the woman. He took a step toward her, a loose hand on the ladder.

The man atop the ladder tossed the fabric over the beam again. As he shifted his weight, the ladder wobbled.

Kallie's heart pitched in her stomach. She began to call out, but someone beat her to it, stealing the words from her lips. "Phil! The ladder!"

Kallie straightened at the voice.

Beside her, Rian pressed himself against the railing, his dark features tinted with panic and his fingers digging into red wine hair.

Continuing to stare, Kallie's forehead creased, but then a noise from below forced her attention back to the man on the ladder.

Phil, who had been talking to the woman, panicked and grabbed the ladder, steadying it. Above him, the servant on the ladder pressed a clenched fist against his chest as he held onto the ladder with a white-knuckled grip.

"Whoever idea it was to hang fabric from the ceiling is an imbecile," Rian muttered, shaking his head.

Kallie leaned her hip against the banister, arms crossed over her chest, and arched a brow as she gave Rian a pointed look. "That imbecile would be me."

Gaze still forward, Rian turned bright red. He turned, clearing his throat. "Did I say imbecile? What I meant to say was . . ." He ran a hand through his hair, tugging at the short strands. His face twisted. "Was that they had an impossibly imaginative mind and a foresight for design?"

Chuckling, Kallie uncrossed her arms and eliminated the space separating them. She ignored the twist in her gut and the way the air between them stiffened. All the progress Kallie had made over the past month seemed to have vanished when Rian had left. And although the king had returned, their easy comfort hadn't.

"I had thought it would help spruce up the place a bit, but I couldn't have predicted that it would result in someone nearly falling to their death," Kallie said.

As he looked back at the fabric, Rian asked, "And you chose black of all colors because?"

Kallie glanced at him, her brows scrunching together. "Because of Frenzia's house colors, of course. Black, gold, and red."

"Ah." Rian nodded.

She tilted her head. "You act as though that is a strange choice."

Rian shrugged. "I suppose it is not. But if you wanted to, as you say, 'spruce up' the place, should you not have chosen a brighter color? Something more . . . lively, perhaps?"

The corner of Kallie's mouth tipped upward. "Perhaps, but it'll be effervescent once the candles are lit and the greenery is everywhere. You'll see."

Below them, servants had already begun placing thousands of candles encased in glass cylinders on the tables. A few servants were currently scattering eucalyptus leaves atop the dark oak tables. Even these tiny touches had dramatically impacted the cold, stone palace. It was moody, warm, perfect.

She smiled. "'Even in the darkness, there is life,' after all."

"Everling?"

Kallie nodded, smiling faintly. Despite the thickening awkwardness, she had never had someone to talk to about her favorite books. It was a comfort that she had not known she had been missing until she had met Rian. And yet . . .

The king grew quiet, and Kallie glanced up at him. Rian stared at her with a look she could not entirely read. It was almost as if he was trying to see through her, see within her, but he couldn't.

She dropped her gaze.

She needed to be careful with him. Rian may have been quiet, but he was not a fool. He always seemed to be silently watching. He never said too much, never gave too much away about what he was thinking.

Kallie brushed a stray piece of hair behind her ear. "How was the trip?"

Rian sighed, his shoulders sinking with the weight of it. "Complicated."

Kallie's brows furrowed. "How so?"

He shook his head. Apparently, he was still reluctant to share the ongoings of his kingdom with her.

"What happened, Rian?" Kallie asked, the command seeping into her words, her gift rising to meet her irritation.

"Our men were slaughtered."

Kallie inhaled. "There was an attack?"

Rian nodded, his fingers wrapping around the railing.

"Why would they have called their king out then? Wouldn't that put you in a precarious situation?"

"The location had already been secured. How the assailants knew our men would be there remains a mystery."

"Hmm." The hairs at the back of her neck stood.

"Do you know who was behind it?"

"No. Sebastian and I had to flee before we could identify them."

"That's—"

Kallie jumped.

Glass shattered down below, shards skittering across the floor. Lystrata shouted at the servant who had dropped the glass.

When she looked over her shoulder, Rian was already walking away with Laurince beside him and hushed words passing between them.

Kallie sank back against the railing. The gold ring pressed into her finger as she tightened her grip around the banister.

CHAPTER 29
GRAESON

"War is coming," Graeson whispered as the fire popped.

A breeze brushed by, and glowing sparks twisted up into the air. The scent of pine needles and burned lumber tickled Graeson's nose.

The days that followed freeing the animal (now permanently deemed the dragon-puppy by all but Graeson) were filled with speculation and trepidation. Everyone had their own theory about what they saw and why they saw it. At first, those who had stayed back were reluctant to believe Graeson and the others, skeptical of their eyesight and sanity. The only one who seemed unfazed was Emmett, but that was most likely a result of the liquor he had been suckling on from a flask he kept hidden in his sleeve. Still, whether they believed it entirely or not, one thing was clear: the Frenzians were preparing for a war.

They had all been tiptoeing around it as they made the last trek across Frenzia. Graeson had learned early on what could happen when people were too afraid to speak the truth. So, finally, as they sat around their last fire before arriving at the castle's doorstep tomorrow, he said the three words on everyone's mind: *War is coming.*

And a cold silence met him.

For weeks, they had said it in passing, but now it finally felt real. The truth was always hard to hear, but avoiding it wouldn't help anyone.

"I just . . . I don't understand," Medenia whispered, hugging her shawl tighter around her shoulders.

Summer was in full swing, yet the Frenzian air was cool on their skin as they sat huddled around the fire. Ophelia added another log to the fire and sat closer to the princess on their shared log.

"Why else would they have a creature like that, though?" Dani asked. "They're preparing for something—something big."

"Princess, you didn't see the beast. It was . . ." Moris' gaze dropped to the fire, a long, unfocused look spreading across his face. "It was otherworldly. That creature should not exist."

"Whether the animal should exist is not up for you to decide," Ellie said over the fire, her features masked in shadows as the flames flickered. "That is up to the goddess."

"And which goddess would that be?" Armen asked, his elbow digging into his knee as he leaned forward. "Misanthia or Ryla? Because either way, neither the goddess of war nor the goddess of fate has ever created something for the betterment of humanity."

"Has any god?"

"Pontanius has," Armen said.

Ellie spat into the fire. "Impudent man. The gods do not care whether we live or die—"

Medenia raised a hand, and Ellie sat back down, snapping her mouth shut with a sneer in Armen's direction.

"It is not that I do not believe you all. I do," Medenia said. "What I do not understand is *how* it is possible. I realize we have been down this road already, but it still does not sit right with me. The dragons have not walked this earth for centuries. Since the gods themselves disappeared."

Ellie mumbled something unintelligible, and Armen's brows quivered, snarling. Graeson ignored them.

Graeson had thought about the dragon's disappearance. He knew the stories and myths that swept over Vaneria. He also knew that not everything was always as it seemed.

"Maybe . . . maybe this is the reason," Armen said under his breath.

"The reason for what?" Dani asked.

"Kallie marrying the Frenzian king was not some chance event," Armen explained.

"What do you mean?" Ophelia asked, leaning forward.

"I was stationed in Ardentol for over five years. You can learn a lot when you listen."

"Care to elaborate?" Ellie asked with an impatient lilt in her voice.

A cocky smirk pushed at the corner of Armen's lip as he leaned onto his arm, getting closer to the fire. Armen was purposely dragging this out, for the man liked the attention the Tetrian women gave him. He liked feeling like he had knowledge that the others did not.

The flames lit Armen's face, painting shadows across it. "Domitius never does anything by accident. He was always going on and on about the knowledge that Frenzia had, knowledge which he wanted. Perhaps this dragon-puppy thing is what he wanted access to."

"If that's the case . . ." Dani began, but her words fell off.

She didn't need to finish her sentence, though. Everyone already knew what she was going to say: if that was the case, the wedding was only the beginning.

When the Frenzian castle became open to Domitius, all the information he wanted would be his for the taking. If the wrangler was right, the Frenzians were already creating more of those creatures. And as gentle as the creature had been with him, Graeson was not naive enough to believe that the dragon-puppy wasn't a natural-born predator. If it truly was a mutation of a dragon and a wolf, he knew they hadn't seen the full extent of the creature's wrath. Wolves played the long game, testing their prey, waiting for the perfect time to strike. They could sense any weakness or vulnerability. Dragons were no different based on the myths Graeson had heard as a child. They could smell the fear that poured out of their prey's skin. They thrived off it.

According to the stories, dragons had once owned the skies. They were on the top of the food chain, but the dragons had disappeared with the gods. Now, they were little more than legends.

With the existence of the kraken in the Red Sea, Graeson knew better than to doubt the truth in those stories.

Still, with no one having seen dragons for centuries, it prompted the question: how did the Frenzians create the creature? Because there was no doubt in Graeson's mind that the Frenzians had made it.

Moris was right; the creature was otherworldly. Too unique to be a natural occurrence.

As Graeson stared at the fire, thinking about the consequences of the Frenzians' creation, the fire breathed, and the charcoals burned bright. In their presence, the dragon-puppy hadn't breathed out fire like its predecessors, and Graeson hoped they would never find out if the creature could.

"So, now that we are only days away and know that Frenzians are keeping plenty of secrets," Ellie said as she ripped off a bite of the cooked rabbit, "are you finally going to tell us how exactly you will accomplish this?"

Eyes bounced across the circle, but no one moved to speak.

Graeson cracked his neck. They had avoided the specifics of their plan for a while. Graeson was aware that they couldn't avoid it forever, but he still wasn't ready for the question. The Tetrians knew plenty, but they didn't know everything.

"The less you know, the better," Graeson said.

Ellie pointed the meat at Graeson. "Enough of the bullshit, Gray. Do you think we are that daft?"

"What are you talking about?"

"You may have the other kingdoms fooled, but some of us remember."

"Ellie," Medenia snapped, but Ellie pressed on.

"No, we are not pretending anymore. If a war is coming, we need to be honest with one another. We need to know who our allies are. They need to know."

"Know what?" Dani asked, leaning forward.

Ellie rolled her eyes. "We know."

"Know *what?*"

Medenia groaned but didn't stop Ellie from continuing; she only shook her head softly, her gaze falling to the dancing flames.

"About your gifts."

No one moved, no one spoke. A breeze swept through the campsite, and an eerie chill grazed Graeson's cheek and ruffled the few fallen leaves.

Sylvia broke the silence. "Excuse me? What did you just—"

"I *said* we know about the gifts you have been granted."

Dani snorted, leaning back on her palms. "I mean, we are gifted warriors, but that is no secret. Although it is kind of you to admit it finally."

Ellie quirked a brow and chucked a piece of meat at Dani. Dani caught it in her hand, and with a wink, she tossed it into her mouth.

Ellie groaned. "That is not what I mean, and you know it. You may have the other kingdoms fooled, but some of us remember."

Dani leaned over to Graeson and whispered so only he could hear. "They're bluffing. Queen Marina wiped their memories."

Graeson's gaze bounced between the Tetrian women across the fire. Their gazes were flat, their expressions solemn. Ellie was not lying. She knew.

They all knew.

"How?" Graeson asked.

"Graeson!" Dani hissed, slapping him in the side.

Graeson ignored her, his attention on the Tetrians. If they knew, there was no point in pretending.

"You have your secrets, and we have ours," Medenia said, her voice quiet, but an eeriness coated her usually sweet tone.

"How many?" he asked.

"How many know?" Medenia asked, and Graeson nodded. "Only those who need to. Your secret has been safe with the royal family and their closest advisors for centuries. It will not come out now."

Graeson nodded and threw another log in the fire.

Before he knew it, Armen was dragging Graeson to his feet and away from the fire.

Graeson threw Armen's arm off and shoved him in the chest. Armen stumbled backward, face flush with anger.

"Armen, what the—"

"That's it?" Armen asked. "You're just going to take their word for it?"

Graeson blinked. "Yes, yes, I am."

"You are breaking our code!" Armen spat.

"Our *code?*"

"Yes! Our entire kingdom's safety is at risk right now!" Armen hissed.

Graeson sneered. "And what do you expect me to do?"

Armen's gaze flicked to the fire behind Graeson. His jaw flexed. "We need to kill them."

Graeson snorted. "Now *that's* fucking ridiculous."

"Is it?"

"This conversation is *over*, Armen. They are our *allies.*"

"But—"

"No," Graeson growled.

"Domitius may have been wrong about many things, but he was right about others."

Graeson stepped forward. "What is that supposed to mean?"

Armen's lip curled as he tipped his chin up.

"Armen," Terin said, having joined them. "Go cool off. We will deal with this later."

Gaze flicking between Terin and Graeson, Armen finally stormed away with an annoyed huff.

Dani joined them as Armen disappeared into one of the tents.

"This isn't going to be a problem, right?" Graeson asked his friends.

He said what he needed to say to Armen, but a part of Graeson hesitated to give the Tetrians his complete trust. The last time he had trusted a woman, she had stabbed him in the back.

Terin was quiet for a moment, then he said, "It was going to come up at some point. I believe them when they say that only a few know."

Dani nodded. "Perhaps we can use this to our advantage. It was going to get more than complicated if they didn't know. Now, we don't have to worry about that."

Graeson brushed a hand through his hair, nodding. It did simplify some things, at least.

The three of them returned to the fire. Then, without telling the Tetrians every little detail, Graeson revealed the basics of their plan. Starting with how Emmett would mask their identities to get them inside the castle without being spotted and ending with taking Kalisandre back.

"You do know that if you are successful," Ellie said, "you will be the reason war will break out. While we are on your side, the other kingdoms will not look kindly upon Pontia."

"If we take Kalisandre, whatever plans Domitius had that require her will be thwarted. For some reason, she is essential to his plans. If we separate her from him, we can get ahead of this." Graeson shrugged. "Because, as I said, war is already coming. No matter what happens."

"We need to send word to the others," Sylvia piped up beside Moris.

"You're right," Medenia said, nodding. "My mother needs to hear about this. Sooner rather than later."

"As does mine," Terin added in agreement. "She has already expressed her hesitancy. Maybe this is the push she needs. We need to get ahead of this while we still can."

They all looked around the circle, exchanging glances.

"What?" Graeson asked when all of their stares fell on him.

"Who are you sending?" Dani asked.

"This is my decision?"

"This is your mission," Terin said. "It is your choice."

His gaze swept over the group sitting in front of him. In total, there were three Tetrians and seven Pontians. Ten people who all had something to add, who had their own strengths and weaknesses. Graeson didn't know who he could lose. His entire team served a purpose. They wouldn't be here otherwise. His gaze bounced between Moris and Sylvia. If Armen didn't have insider knowledge about Domtius, the choice would have been easy. If Emmett, who was currently snoring in his tent, hadn't been gifted with the ability to conceal their identities, he would have been a viable option as well. But one: Graeson didn't trust him to get home without straying from the designated path. And two: the man's gift was too valuable. He could—

"I'll go," Ophelia said, straightening.

"But—" Ellie began.

"It's fine," Medenia said, cutting Ellie off. "I will be fine."

Ophelia looked at Medenia, and the Tetrian warrior grabbed the princess' hand. Medenia squeezed it, giving her a gentle nod. Over the fire, Graeson saw the sadness filling the princess' eyes. Ophelia stood, hand still in Medenia's.

Graeson opened his mouth to object, but Ophelia shook her head before he could. "I have seen how important this mission is to you." Ophelia's gaze was steady as she looked at Graeson, then the others. "*All* of you. If it were Medenia in your Kalisandre's shoes, I would do anything to get her back. This is not up for debate."

Graeson regarded the three Tetrians. While sorrow filled their eyes, determination was painted across their countenances. Ophelia was right; there was no debating this.

"Very well," Graeson said. "We will guard Medenia with our lives."

"I would expect nothing less." Ophelia tipped her head in silent gratitude. Ophelia glanced down at the princess, a smile splitting her face. "Although do not underestimate her. She may wear a crown, but Medenia is a warrior at heart. The fiercest warrior."

Medenia blushed. "Not as fierce as you, my love."

Ophelia straightened, her chest puffing out.

When the warrior looked at Graeson, her expression hardened, gaze frigid despite the flames flickering in them. "But if any harm does come to her, you will have earned a second enemy."

Graeson did not flinch but nodded in mutual agreement. He did not doubt that Ophelia and the rest of the Tetrian warriors would come for his head if their beloved princess met the same fate as Fynn. Medenia was safe with them. Graeson would not let her see the same fate as Fynn.

"I'll head out in the morning," Ophelia said.

Medenia stood, and hand-in-hand, the two women walked to the tent. In the faint light of the flame, Medenia pulled Ophelia close, kissing her before they headed into their tent.

Graeson hated that he was splitting the two women up. Over the past several days, Graeson saw how close they were. Inseparable, really. Quickly, he realized that this trip was one of the few times the women had to spend uninterrupted time together. In Tetria, they both had their duties that required their attention. But there was no other choice. Graeson needed the others at his side to accomplish what they set out to do. While this trip may have provided Ophelia and Medenia time together, it was Graeson's duty.

Ellie poked the fire with a stick, her brows drawn together in thought.

"What are you thinking now, Ellie?" Terin asked.

"What happens if you can't convince her to fight for our side?"

"*Our* side?" Graeson asked.

"You are not the only ones who detest the bull king," Ellie said, smirking. "But what will you do if Kalisandre doesn't go willingly?"

Graeson bit down on his tongue. "Whatever means necessary."

"Good," Ellie said. "But do not forget, the gods may have granted your people various abilities, but we all know who truly are the gifted warriors in Vaneria," she added with a wink.

"We will see about that, Ellie," Dani said, knocking her knee into Ellie's leg.

Ellie pushed back. "I'll take the first watch."

"Suit yourself," Dani said, standing up and heading toward one of the tents.

Graeson turned to Terin. "Ready?"

Terin sighed. Exhaustion filled his face, but they had one more thing to do before they could sleep.

"Ready as I'll ever be."

CHAPTER 30
KALLIE

KALLIE TOSSED AND TURNED IN THE BED THAT WAS TOO BIG IN A ROOM THAT was too empty.

Huffing, she threw her head back against the silk pillow. When the restlessness continued to stir beneath her flesh, she turned onto her side with a disgruntled huff.

"Have you always been this restless, Princess?"

Kallie's eyes flew open. Her breath hitched in her throat, the air cold in her lungs.

She was imagining things. She had drunk too much wine at dinner. There was no other explanation. The exhaustion, the alcohol, and the sugar were making her hear things. She needed more sleep and less wine. Kallie squeezed her eyes shut.

There was no way he was here. He couldn't be.

"Stumbling again, are we, little mouse?"

His breath was a soft tickle against her throat, but Kallie refused to move.

It was only the wine making her thoughts grow wild. The gods were playing tricks on her mind. Nothing more.

Why, then, did Kallie refuse to turn? Was she afraid to be proven right?

Or was it that she was scared to be proven wrong? She didn't know. She didn't want to know because knowing would only make her believe the worst.

"Look at me, Kal."

She inhaled, the crisp air sharp in her lungs. As a finger brushed across her chin and turned her face to the side, she squeezed her eyes closer together.

"Won't you open those sweet blues for me?"

It was as if the command ran through her veins and tugged on her muscles. His words called to her, slithering their way into her blood and into her mind, shaping her will, bending it to his.

It wasn't just her mind playing tricks on her. It was her eyes, too. Because when she opened them, bright silver irises stared down at her.

When she spoke, his name was no more than a breath on her lips. "Graeson?"

Graeson was in her room.

In her bed.

In Frenzia.

"What are you doing here?" *Kallie's gaze narrowed as warning signals spiked through her nervous system.* "How . . ."

"How what?" *Graeson asked.*

The corner of his lip flicked up, his eyes alit with mischief. The moon's beams bounced against his midnight black hair, shiny and wild. His fingers dug into his hair, his hand propping him up on his side. Graeson looked the same as the night when the world was shut out, when their identities were hidden behind masks, secrets, and lies. When everything was simple.

And before everything had crumbled to ash in her hands.

"How are you here?" *Kallie asked, her gaze dancing across his face. There could only be one reason. One reason he would be here.*

She swept a hand beneath her pillow, and her heart pounded against her chest as she felt nothing beneath it. Nothing but silk sheets beneath her palm.

Her dagger was gone.

"Looking for this, little mouse?" *Dangling between Graeson's fingers, her dagger swung in the air like a pendulum, rocking back and forth.*

"Give it back," she growled, reaching for it.

But Graeson was faster than her. He rolled her over, forcing Kallie onto her back with a quick maneuver of his legs. With one hand, he locked her wrists above her head. "I don't think so."

"Plan to kill me with my own blade?" Kallie wiggled beneath his body weight. "I didn't think that was your style, Gray."

His grip on her wrists tightened. His thighs pressed against hers, his legs wrapping around hers, keeping her in place and preventing her from kicking him off.

"Is that what you think?" Graeson asked, staring at her, brows drawn together. "That I'm here to kill you?"

"Of course!" Kallie shrieked. She tried to twist her hands out of his hold, but Graeson's grip remained steady. "Why else would you be here?"

"You tell me, Princess." He smirked down at her, his hair falling down his face. His features were cast in darkness, yet his silver eyes beamed. "It's your dream."

Kallie froze. "This isn't real?"

The corner of his mouth quipped upward. "Would my answer change your reaction?"

Kallie scanned his face, searching for an answer that wasn't there. Per usual, Graeson kept everything hidden behind a calm demeanor. Even in her dreams, it seemed.

Kallie looked away, biting the inside of her cheek. The pain of the bite spiraled through her body. She used that pain as a focal point, pushing away the memory she had tried and failed to keep at arm's length the past few weeks.

"Kalisandre, look at me." Graeson's fingers brushed her chin, tipping her head up. "It does not matter if this is real or not. I do not care if this moment is a figment of our imaginations. I do not even care if we will forget about it come morning like the rest of our dreams." His thumb slid across her chin. "What matters is that you are safe. What matters is that you are happy."

Beneath Graeson's earnest gaze, Kallie remained silent, unable to say anything. She couldn't admit the truth. She didn't even know what the truth was.

"Are you happy, Kalisandre?"

She huffed.

"Do not dismiss your happiness, Princess."

Even in her dreams, Kallie could not think of a lie, so she shut her eyes and shut him out, refusing to say anything. Because, real or not, she didn't want to lie to him. Not again.

Graeson clicked his tongue. "See, now that just won't do, little mouse." *His thumb brushed across her cheek. A cold wetness spread in its path from the tear she hadn't known had fallen.* "Tell me, what will make you happy?"

Graeson's voice was so . . . earnest, gentle. She wanted to fall into it. And maybe right now, she could.

She forced herself to look at him.

The places where he touched her heated. A burning, insatiable fire. The same fire she had felt whenever he had touched her in the past. Yet Kallie knew that his touch could not be real. As he said, this moment was only a figment of her imagination. But maybe . . . maybe that wasn't a bad thing.

Her gaze dipped down to his lips.

Graeson stared down at her as if he could sense the change in her emotions. He chuckled, a noise too short-lived. "Come on now. That won't fix things."

Kallie lifted her gaze from his lips, a task harder in this dream state than it usually would have been. Maybe it was because she knew this moment wasn't real or because she wanted to wipe away the other kiss from her lips. Or perhaps it was something else entirely. Either way, Kallie lifted her head, inching closer to him—as much as she could, anyway, with her hands still locked beneath his palm.

"Kalisandre," Graeson warned.

"See, Graeson. That is how I know this isn't real," Kallie said.

"And why is that?" Graeson asked, brow arching.

"Because," Kallie leaned closer, her cheek brushing against the scruff on his jaw, her lips near his ear. *"If this were real, you would already know full well the effect that my name on your tongue has on me."*

"Is that so?" Graeson asked, his eyes darkening, his voice growing huskier, deeper. *"Then why don't you explain exactly what effect it has on you, Kalisandre?"*

Kallie chuckled. "Explain? Oh no." Kallie's hand slid down his arm, cold prickles following in its wake. "I think you will understand better if I showed you."

A sinful smile slipped over Graeson's face, and the bottom of her core heated. Her gift hummed within her veins. And Kallie allowed herself to fall into the dream, head first.

THUNDER STIRRED KALLIE AWAKE. Lightning flashed, and shadows scattered along the walls.

Her nails dug into the sheets as she sat up. Her skin was sticky with sweat, and her heart pounded against her chest.

She had been dreaming. She knew it in the way her heart beat against her ribcage. For once, however, it wasn't from fear. For once, her throat didn't ache from screams.

But something else ached low in her gut.

And it was at that moment, as she sat in a cold, stone room, she realized that the dream with Graeson was far worse than any nightmare she had ever had. This dream was a reminder of what could have been and what almost was. What she could have had in another life if things had gone differently.

But it was only a dream. A dream and nothing more.

Yet, when Kallie laid back down, she could have sworn the faint scent of cedar lingered on her skin.

CHAPTER 31
GRAESON

"Weapons?" one of the guards checking their luggage asked, holding out a hand.

They had made it to the castle with one day to spare and without any other issues. Although, Ophelia's absence was apparent. Medenia had grown quieter, more withdrawn. She had tried to play it off, but Graeson saw through her fake smiles. All that was left was to pass through the guard's check at the gate.

Dani cleared her throat, and Graeson pulled out his scimitars and handed them to the guard. As the guard inspected the scimitars, Graeson forced his features to remain neutral and unbothered. He was not worried about the man or anything of note on the blades. Any distinguishable marks on the hilts had been covered with fresh leather.

However, the beast inside of Graeson growled as the Frenzian surveyed the blades, running a finger along the metal.

Mine, the beast shouted.

Jaw tense, Graeson shoved the voice back.

The guard held it out, hilt to Graeson. "Fine blade."

"It does the job," Graeson said, struggling to pull back the venom on his tongue.

Graeson returned his scimitars to their holsters on his back as the guard finished his inspection of their belongings.

Graeson was keenly aware of the fact that the man's gaze didn't linger on his scar. Emmett, it seemed, was already proving useful.

Handing Dani her throwing knives, the guard turned to them. "By the king's orders, weapons are not permitted on the castle's premises outside your designated guest house."

"But Princess Medenia—" Ellie began.

"No exceptions," the guard said, interrupting her.

Medenia stepped forward, hands clasped in front of her stomach and a sweet smile plastered on her face. "As to be expected. After all, this is a joyous occasion, is it not? Let us hope there is no need for anyone to draw a weapon for all of our benefits."

The guard bowed. When he rose, he cast a hand out. "If you will follow me, Princess, I will take you and your party to your accommodations."

Medenia smiled, and they all followed.

Graeson and Dani picked up the tail of their group. As they made their way around other guests that had arrived, Dani leaned toward Graeson and mumbled, "Like I need a weapon to snap someone's neck."

Graeson snorted.

The silence between them resumed as they followed the Frenzian guard to a nearby guest house on the outskirts of the castle's property.

That night, they went through the plan one more time. However, no amount of planning could have predicted the dominoes that would fall the next day.

CHAPTER 32
KALLIE

KALLIE STRAIGHTENED THE DAINTY SILVER CROWN ATOP HER HEAD. IT was the one piece she wore today that was Ardentolian made.

Even her dress had been stripped of its Ardentolian style today. For as long as Kallie could remember, she had always been dressed in blues and whites, the colors of the Ardentolian mountains. The only other time she hadn't dawned on those colors of Ardentol was when she was masquerading as someone she wasn't in Pontia.

For years, Kallie had been happy to represent her kingdom, to be the king's diamond. But as she looked at herself in the mirror with the red satin dress slinking over her faint curves, Kallie couldn't help but feel that those colors never belonged on her skin in the first place. She had been draped in fabrics of cerulean and snow-white to seem moldable. Appeasable. Painted to be the king's daughter. Someone no one would suspect. Someone who could be controlled. The pearls and diamonds sewn into her Ardentolian dresses were meant to hide what lay beneath: the monster that resided within her. The manipulator and the seductress. Everything King Domitius had raised her to be, everything he had taught her to nurture while simultaneously keeping that side of her hidden beneath the facade of a naive princess. Until the moment she could shed her skin and reveal her true identity.

With the red fabric dripping down her body, for once, the outside matched the monster within.

The winning piece of the ensemble was the intricate piece hanging off her shoulders. An expertly crafted piece by the Frenzian jeweler that clasped around her shoulders. Strings of black diamonds dripped from the metal wiring that molded around her shoulders in the shape of armor.

By the end of the week, she would no longer be the Princess of Ardentol. She would be the Queen of Frenzia.

What would her father think if he was here tonight? Would he be proud of her?

"Ready, Kals?" Myra asked.

Dragging her gaze from the mirror, Kallie looked toward the entourage behind her and nodded.

The diamonds on her shoulders swung as she walked, hitting one another like rain falling onto a tin roof. With the flock of handmaidens and guards behind her, Kallie headed out of the queen's rooms and toward the grand hall.

Kallie nodded to the various guards as she passed. Over the past few weeks, she had learned most of their names: Sansil, Syrus, Flinch, Rowland, and so many others. After the recent attack on the outskirts of Frenzia's borders, the king and his advisors were taking no risks when it came to the castle's safety. Every day, there were new guards, new names to memorize, and new faces to learn as the wedding approached. Armed men now stood guard around the clock as more and more guests arrived.

If only the guards could protect her from her dreams.

Remnants of last night's dream were a flickering flame in the back of her mind. She tried to forget the feeling of Graeson's touch against her cheek. She tried to snuff the flame out, but it kept coming back to life. Imaginary or not.

Kallie took a steadying breath, counting to ten as she neared the doors to the balcony. She glanced over her shoulder and surveyed the handmaidens at her back.

Myra gave her an encouraging nod, and Kallie offered her a soft smile in return before facing the doors again.

The chatter on the other side seeped through the wooden door. For many in the crowd, this would be their first introduction to Kallie. For others, it would be the first time they saw her since the suitors offered their hand in marriage and vowed to honor and protect her choice. Unlike that ceremony in Ardentol, no guard would accompany her, no father would guide her, no king would hold on to her as she made these first steps. Kallie would do this alone.

A smoky voice echoed in her mind: *What will make you happy?*

She steadied her shaking hand, folding her hands in front of her lap, the gold ring cold against her skin.

This was still the dream she wished for, she reminded herself. Behind those doors, her future awaited. No matter how alone she might feel, this was what she had been fighting for her entire life.

Kallie nodded at the guards.

As the doors creaked open, Kallie stepped forward, and the room fell silent.

CHAPTER 33
GRAESON

They had a plan, but they were not prepared for their plan to fall apart before the day had even begun.

The morning of the welcome dinner, Dani had fallen ill. Unable to keep anything down and barely able to walk without the nausea returning, there was no way Dani would make it through the dinner. Gifted or not, some things could not be superseded.

Forced to change tactics, Terin, Moris, and Sylvia opted to stay back with Dani, leaving Graeson, Emmett, Armen, and the Tetrians to handle the welcome dinner.

While Graeson had to admit that six people were easier to maneuver than ten, walking into the castle without Dani and Terin felt strange.

Even stranger, though, was the presence of Emmett's gift. While Graeson had visited the Cavern of Catius many times, he would never get used to its presence. Emmett's gift was like a light layer of oil on Graeson's skin, barely noticeable, but he could still feel the sticky film that didn't seep into his skin comfortably. Like with Fynn's mind reading or Kalisandre's manipulations, Graeson could always sense the presence of something *other* trying to infiltrate his mind or body. Graeson actively had to allow another's gift to perpetrate his senses, or it would slide right off him. Usually, this was a blessing, but it was more of a hindrance when it came to Emmett's gift. He couldn't afford Kalisandre or anyone else to recognize him before it was time.

The six of them had been directed to a table near the front of the room. Sitting at the nearby tables were other noteworthy members of Vaneria. Graeson noted Lucien's attendance, one of the princes of West Borgania. It was unsurprising to Graeson that the Western half of Borgania was represented at the wedding while the Eastern half remained forgotten. Since the Great War, the kingdom of Borgania had been divided. Lucien and his brothers were known for their impressive hunting skills, but the Pontians knew the truth. They were savage and cruel, tearing apart animals in brutal, unforgivable ways.

Graeson scanned the rest of the tables. Everywhere Graeson looked, enemies surrounded them.

A gold crown caught his attention and dragged it toward the front of the room. Like the rest of the people in the room, the king wore all black. A flash of color twinkled on the cuffs and buttons of his suit jacket. Brilliant red gemstones glittered in the candlelight as if a small fire breathed and danced inside each ruby. Even in the abysmal lighting, Graeson noted that the young king took after his mother more than his late father. However, unlike the king's mother standing beside him, Rian's naivety was blatantly obvious. His eyes sparkled with hope. Graeson knew that look well, for he had often seen Fynn wear it. It was the belief that he could change the world—that he *would* change the world. But Graeson knew that traditions were so engrained into the Frenzians' way of life that those dreams would quickly be squandered.

An older man at the table said something unintelligible, and the rest of the table roared in laughter at his joke. The woman beside him and the former queen of Frenzia shook their heads at the man with restrained amusement.

Armen leaned over and whispered in Graeson's ear, "Those are the king's maternal grandparents. King Rian's mother comes from an old, wealthy line of Frenzian lords and ladies."

Graeson nodded but said nothing else about it, for he didn't care about the king's family history. He continued scanning the room.

All around Graeson, the faces of the guests were shrouded in darkness. Not even the faint glow of the thousands of candles on the tables could provide enough light to shine onto them. Yet even with the looming darkness, Graeson knew without a doubt that one face was absent from the buzzing crowd.

"Do you see him?" Graeson asked Armen.

Armen shook his head, and Graeson narrowed his gaze. Domitius' absence should have settled the nerves pulsing in Graeson's stomach, but for some reason, it didn't.

"Maybe he's late," Armen whispered.

Graeson raised a brow. "When have you ever known Domitius to be late?"

Armen scratched the back of his head, brows drawing together as he looked around the room.

A bell rang at the bottom of the balcony stairs, and the crowd grew silent. Once those who were standing took their seats, the musicians at the back of the room began to play. The balcony doors creaked open, and suddenly, the darkness in the room no longer mattered.

When Kalisandre stepped through the dark oak doors and into the moonlight pouring down from the skylights, Graeson's breath caught in his throat. Red fabric dripped down her body, and the moon's light bounced off the diamonds that hung from her shoulders. And Kalisandre became the light in the room, the chandelier that sparkled above them all. As she strolled toward the top of the stone staircase, Graeson couldn't look away from her.

Kalisandre scanned the crowd, searching, and Graeson couldn't help it. He straightened in his seat, his muscles growing taut.

Then she smiled, and Graeson deflated.

Kalisandre wasn't looking for him. She didn't even know Graeson stood in the same room. Even if she saw him, it wouldn't be *him* whom she saw, but the masked version cast by Emmett.

That vision Terin had helped him weave did not matter to her. Not like it did for him.

No, that wide, toothy smile accompanied by a soft blush that rose to her cheeks wasn't because of Graeson.

It was because of *him*.

Chairs scratched against the stone floor, plates rattled on the tables as guests bumped into each other as they stood for the King of Frenzia. Even though their eyes were on Kalisandre, their movements followed the crown's command. Because when the king stood, the rest of the room followed.

Graeson bit back his annoyance but forced himself to stand with the rest of the crowd nevertheless—if only not to have his view obstructed.

He wondered if Kalisandre was also annoyed with how the people reacted to the king's presence. If this was the sort of power she craved? If this was the price of her loyalty?

Did she not know who she was? What she could do? She could manipulate anyone she wanted. Wasn't this just a flashy, frivolous display of that kind of power?

As Rian weaved through the standing crowd, a few faces turned toward him, but the rest remained on Kalisandre. The strangers in the room wanted to know who she was. They craved to know who would be the next Queen of Frenzia.

On the balcony, Kalisandre's hand floated down to the railing, and she began her descent down the stairs, her gait set at a leisurely pace. Her heels snapped against the steps, and smoke trailed after her, its tendrils wrapping around her ankles. The light of the moon and the flames of the candles bounced off the diamonds around Kalisandre's shoulders and crown. Tiny, broken shards of light flickered across the wall as she descended the stairs. It was as if she was the light that the people in the room had been searching for, and she was finally giving it to them, dispersing the darkness that blanketed them.

For him, Kalisandre had always been the light in the sea of darkness.

Still, as Graeson watched her, he was not ignorant of what he saw. He saw the manipulator at work. When they were traveling together before, he hadn't noticed the intricate dance of emotions Kalisandre had displayed at all times. The performance she had put on. Now, it was impossible to miss.

She timed her arrival at the bottom of the staircase perfectly so that Rian had to wait for her, for she wanted the people to see the king waiting for her and not the other way around.

The king extended his hand to her. When Kalisandre placed her hand atop his, a clap thundered in the room, ricocheting off the walls. Light erupted in the stone castle. Fire burst to life atop the torches in the hands of the servants scattered around the room. An aisle of flames lit the royals' paths as they weaved their way through the crowd hand-in-hand. And in the flicker of the fire, Graeson caught the flash of the gold ring Kalisandre still wore.

Her finger twitched, and Graeson smirked.

She felt it, too. The hum of the metal, the connection that still existed between them.

Yet she continued walking, and his smirk fell.

The guests bowed and curtsied when the two royals passed them. The king either tipped his head in their direction in acknowledgment or, on occasion, stopped and said some greeting that the music prevented others from hearing. There was a sense of familiarity in his actions, while Kalisandre, on the other hand, only offered small, soft smiles to the strangers.

Then they approached Medenia. When Kalisandre observed the rest of the people at the table and looked at Graeson, he stopped breathing. He exchanged a quick, sideways glance with Emmett, hoping he had a lock on their identities, and Emmett nodded ever-so-slightly. Still, Graeson did not relax.

"Princess Medenia, so glad you could make it," King Rian said.

Medenia smiled. "I wouldn't miss it for the world, Your Majesty."

Graeson barely heard the rest of their conversation, his attention too focused on Kalisandre standing beside the king and smiling politely. Up close, Graeson was struck by how much Kalisandre had changed since he had last seen her. Her skin had lost the sun's sheen. Her cheeks seemed more hollow, although the rouge on her cheeks attempted to mask it. It was almost as if the life inside of her had washed away when she sailed away on that ship. The Kalisandre he knew and cared for was withering away.

When Kalisandre narrowed her eyes slightly at him, Graeson snapped his gaze up, looking beyond her as if something behind her was more intriguing. Even if his identity was hidden, he should not have stared at Kalisandre so carelessly. What if she saw through it?

Although a part of him—a very foolish and stupid part of him—hoped that Kalisandre would recognize him. That she would see through the facade. That she would recognize his presence instinctively.

A foolish hope.

As the king tugged on her hand, Kalisandre turned her back on Graeson. In the back of his mind, the beast roared as Graeson watched her walk away.

The exchange wasn't even a minute long, yet Graeson craved more.

CHAPTER 34
KALLIE

It hadn't dawned on Kallie until her fingers were wrapped around Rian's hand that she was once again being handed to another man. Given to another king to parade around a room as if she were a prized heifer being shown to its bidders.

In her mind, today was meant to prove to the world that Kalisandre Helene Domitius was no longer the Princess of Ardentol, that she was stepping into her new role as a future queen. When, in fact, tonight's display only showed that Kallie was Rian's queen. Because Kallie, in her red satin dress with diamonds draped over her shoulders, was simply another ruby in Rian's vast collection.

But Kallie wasn't a diamond, nor was she a ruby. She was the fire that forged them.

Kallie lifted her chin.

Rian would be the last man she would let guide her, the last man to treat her like a piece of jewelry to be worn and shown off whenever it suited him.

Frenzian lords and ladies, whom Phaia had often pointed out on their morning strolls, greeted them as Kallie and Rian passed. While Kallie recognized their faces, she knew nothing about them. She did not know what made them smile or their aspirations. And they knew nothing of hers. Because as familiar as their faces were, they were strangers.

They did not know who she was or what she could do.

"Is something funny, Princess?" Rian whispered as they neared their seats.

"My King?" Kallie asked.

Rian pulled out a chair and signaled for her to sit. "You laughed as if something was funny."

A flush of red rose to her cheeks, her legs freezing. She hadn't even realized she had laughed aloud.

Kallie cleared her throat. "Oh, it's nothing."

He leaned down as he pushed her chair in, his words a light brush against the side of her cheek. "Perhaps once we become more acquainted, you will share your moments of laughter with me."

To the guests standing in the room, it must have looked like the king was whispering sweet nothings into his bride's ear. Secrets between two lovers being shared. And while his words were sweet, they were just that: *sweet*. Kallie and Rian would never be lovers who shared secrets or whispered sweet nothings into each other's ear. Nor would they ever be two people who gave secret touches beneath the table or exchanged flirtatious glances as they sipped their wine.

Perhaps they could have been in another life. But not in this one. Neither friends nor lovers manipulated each other. And Kallie had been manipulating Rian from the first day they met. From here on out, the manipulation would only continue.

Until that is, Kallie got what she wanted. After that, Rian would serve no purpose, and there was no room for loose threads in Domitius' plans.

Beside her, Rian offered a kind smile, and she almost regretted those plans. Almost regretted the violation of his mind, the manipulation of his friendship and his heart. But she didn't regret it enough to stop. Because at the end of the day, Kallie could not change what she had already done. She could only continue marching forward, like the weapon she was. One swing at a time.

When Rian signaled for the crowd to sit, chairs scraped across the floor as the guests took their seats, and the music halted.

"I am thrilled to see so many familiar faces today, many of whom my family and I saw only a few months ago," Rian began. He cleared his throat, shaking the rising sorrow from his voice. "Today, we gather for a more joyous occasion. And for that, I am grateful. Because today, we celebrate life and all the joys that it can bring. Today, and for the rest of the week, we celebrate our marriage." He laid a gentle hand on Kallie's shoulder, and Kallie placed a hand over his as she smiled up at him. "And we shall continue celebrating our union for the rest of our lives. Please, raise your glasses to my beautiful bride, Kalisandre Helene Domitius, Princess of Ardentol and Future Queen of Frenzia!"

"And to you, Your Majesty," Kallie said with a soft smile as she raised her glass.

Rian smiled down at her and sipped on his wine. "Now, please," Rian said, gracefully waving his hand to the tables before them, "eat. There will be plenty of time later for long speeches."

Light laughter filled the space as the musicians began to play again.

When Rian sat down, the people turned their attention to the feast before them.

Kallie sank back into her chair. She could have been marrying someone much worse. Someone like Sebastian. Her attention flicked to the king's brother, who was sitting only a few chairs down beside Tessa, and to Kallie's dismay, the captain was staring at her.

Sebastian only looked away at last when a servant asked to refill his glass.

Still, she sensed the ghost of someone's gaze lingering over her skin. She couldn't explain it. All she knew was that there was a tug pulling her toward the crowd.

Heartbeat racing, her gaze darted across the room. Sweat moistened the back of her neck. But as she scanned the room, she couldn't decipher friend from foe in a room filled with strangers.

Instead, Kallie focused on Rian, trying to shake the feeling.

He smiled as he sipped his wine. However, when his lips touched the glass, his smile faltered. Rian's complexion was even worse than before he left with Sebastian. Even the powder he wore on his face couldn't mask the exhaustion that plagued him.

Beside her, Laurince dove for the food on his plate as though the king's guard had not eaten in days. His gaze caught on her. Slipping the fork out of his mouth, he swallowed and straightened in his seat as he set his fork down.

"Do not stop on my account, Sir Laurince," Kallie said, tipping her head before biting a slightly smaller portion of potatoes.

Laurince's shoulders relaxed. Chuckling, he looked past Kallie and at Rian. "Have I mentioned I like her, My King?"

Rian cocked his head, amusement licking his lips. "You might have mentioned that once or twice." Rian leaned toward Kallie. "He might have also mentioned something about you being pretty, Princess Kalisandre."

"Is that so?" Kallie asked, smirking at Laurince.

"I—" Laurince pointed his fork at Rian. "Do not lie. It was only in agreement with *your* comment, My King."

Kallie turned to Rian, a single brow raised as the king's cheeks turned red, matching his hair.

Rian coughed and focused driving his knife through the venison on his plate. "I cannot possibly recall everything I say."

The knife dragged along the plate, producing a high-pitched screeching noise, and his cheeks reddened even more.

Beneath the table, Kallie placed a gentle hand on Rian's. She leaned closer to him and whispered, "I don't find you too bad to look at either, My King."

The little bump in the center of his throat bobbed.

Kallie sat back in her chair, pleased with the king's reaction. Yet when she looked at her plate, the assortment of food looked unappetizing. And the sensation of someone watching her still hadn't disappeared.

WITH DINNER HAVING COME and gone, Kallie now stood in the center of the room.

Rian nodded to her once with a small, polite grin. There was no heat behind his gaze, no concern. Nothing but order and control lay beneath those brown eyes. Without another word, the king abandoned her and returned to his seat.

Kallie knotted her fingers together in an attempt to steady them. She should have been more relaxed than she was. Her father was not here to add unnecessary stress, yet her gut still twisted.

Hands behind her back, Kallie swept her gaze across the room as chairs scratched against the floor. Lystrata had prepared Kallie for tonight's event, yet it was strange seeing the group of men circle her. The coveted Last Dance was the final chance for a man to demand a dance from the bride before she bound herself to one partner for the rest of her life. A Frenzian tradition, Lystrata had explained. According to the Frenzian ancestors, dancing was an intimate act. To follow your partner's footsteps and anticipate their movements, one must be intimately familiar with their partner. When two people danced, breaths were exchanged, rhythms synced, and bodies read. Centuries ago, if a married woman were to dance with a man who was not her husband, the woman would have been questioned. To the Frenzians, your dance partner was your life partner.

Although Kallie disagreed with the tradition's history, she would let the so-called Last Dance commence. But she would do so with a grimace hidden beneath the smile plastered on her face. This tradition wasn't just to remind the bride to be faithful but to remind her of where her position was. Because as she stood in the center of a circle of seven men, she was a deer in the middle of a pack of wolves.

Among the men in the circle was a representative from each kingdom of Vaneria, except Pontia, of course. The Frenzians had put forth two men in exchange for a Pontian representative. Laurince stood with a welcoming smile. In contrast, Sebastian stood beside him, his head tilted up and a slimy smirk on his face. Sebastian's gaze slithered over her. His gaze was a little too eager, too excited as he stood in the circle of men.

Kallie dragged her attention away from him.

Representing Kadia in the circle was Trenton, the cousin of King Valrys, who could not participate himself since he was already spoken for. Then there was one of the Borganian princes, Lucien. Next to him was Jaxcyn, an Ardentolian lord whom Kallie became acquainted with after one of her father's assignments to settle a dispute over some land. The second to last man in the circle was a stranger.

The man arched a brow when Kallie's gaze met his. Based on the Ragolian crest on the man's chest next to him, Kallie quickly deduced that this man was from Tetria. She vaguely recalled him standing at the table with the Tetrian princess.

Kallie tilted her head in question. She had always been told that women made up the majority of the Tetrian guard. Were the princess' personal guards an exception, Kallie wondered.

The man's features were unremarkable. Everything about him was average: his hair, his jaw, his height. Although she gave the man some credit for confidence dripped off him. Even as princes, high lords, and a highly decorated king's guard stood around him, the Tetrian man, who wore no badges of honor on his chest, kept his chin high.

Across the dance floor, Rian raised his glass to her, then tipped his head at the musicians.

The band started playing, the song's introduction slow. It was Kallie's signal. Because even though this tradition was an opportunity for the men to have their last chance to dance with her, it was Kallie's dance to start. One thing she was thankful for.

Kallie smirked, her hips swaying in the air. She sauntered around the inner edge of the circle, her dress sweeping across the floor. Dancing was the closest thing to fighting a princess could publicly partake in without ridicule. Like sword fighting, dancing was a battle between bodies.

Her old instructor's words echoed in the back of her mind: *You must read your partner's movements and anticipate their next move, lest you wish to ruin the magic of the performance.*

Kallie approached the first dance partner of her choosing: Laurince.

Laurince bowed before stepping out of the circle and taking her hand. "Lady Kalisandre."

"Sir Laurince," Kallie said, smiling.

He held her hand high in the air as he paraded her around the circle, easing his way back to the center. The instruments picked up, and then they danced. Laurince spun her around, his palms light on her ribcage and a smile on his face.

"You're enjoying this, aren't you, Sir Laurince?" Kallie asked, grinning.

"A chance to dance with my future queen and make my best friend jealous?" He spun her around, laughing. "I am having the time of my life, Princess."

Kallie couldn't help but chuckle along with him.

When the spinning stopped, he pulled her closer. His hand was on the center of her back, his face shielded by hers. "And to be chosen first? Before Sebastian? Oh, he is never going to let me live this down."

The song increased in volume.

Kallie arched a brow. "Is there something I should know about him, Laurince?"

Throat bobbing, Laurince leaned forward, preventing anyone from reading his lips. "May I speak openly, Your Highness?"

"Always, Laurince."

"Sebastian has always been . . ." Laurince hesitated, his voice barely even a whisper now. "Jealous. He believes his title as second son and captain is enough to have anything he wants." Laurince gave her a pointed look. "Besides, of course, when his brother gets to it first."

"Why are you telling me this?" Kallie asked. The Captain of Rian's guard had barely said more than a few words to her since she had arrived in Frenzia. For him to give her this insight into the king's brother without her even using her gift on him? Something was amiss.

"Rian's a good man, but he often ignores what is right in front of him." Laurince spun her away and quickly reeled her back in. "Be careful, Princess. Sebastian is not one to be taken lightly."

Kallie offered a small smile. "I think I can handle myself, Laurince."

"I do not doubt it, Your Highness." Then his gaze turned serious. "Even still. While he respects his brother's title, it hasn't always stopped him from pursuing his desires."

Laurince spun her away from him, and Kallie's hand slipped from his and into someone else's before she could respond. Her conversation with the king's guard disappeared into the air as Trenton appeared before her.

The Kadian smiled and spun her around. As the song picked up, Kallie spun from one man's hand to another. Her dress glided through the air as she was swept across the floor, the diamonds on her shoulders rattling against each other.

The lord from Ragolo grabbed her hand and immediately twirled her. Once, twice, three times. In the blur, the whisper of a grin graced her face. Laughing echoed around her. Soon enough, she couldn't even identify the men's faces, their time with her blurring past her faster than she could recognize them.

How many men had she danced with already? Four? Five? She had lost count. She was swept into the music and the motions of the dance. The chaos of jumping from partner to partner intoxicating.

First, the room was spinning. Then, the room was upside down as Lucien dipped Kallie low. She giggled, her smile wide.

She couldn't remember the last time her cheeks hurt this much. Her disinterest in the dance before it started was a distant memory. How could she have disliked this?

At least, that was what she thought before she was thrust back up and into the hands of the next dance partner. Her body knew who it was before she did, and the joy washed away as the air shifted. Her smile faded.

When she looked at the man in front of her, Kallie wanted to run as the smell of smoke overtook her senses. Sebastian's green gaze bore into her skin. Unlike the other men who kept a respectable distance between themselves and Kallie, Sebastian used the momentum of pulling Kallie up from the dip to pull her closer to him. The places where their bodies connected burned, and Laurince's warning echoed in her mind as the music thrummed louder. Sebastian's closeness made her want to break the connection before his flesh melted into hers. Because the way Sebastian stared at her, the way he held her gaze, and his left hand kept inching lower and lower down her back, gave her the impression that Sebastian wished to own her. Control her.

This was not how a man should dance with a woman about to

marry another man. Especially not one who would soon be said woman's future brother-in-law. But that fact did not appear to be a concern for Sebastian.

He pulled Kallie closer.

Kallie searched for a helping hand, her gaze landing on Rian sitting at the head table. However, the king was not looking at her. No, instead of watching his betrothed like the rest of the crowd, he was listening to his mother, who had since claimed Kallie's unoccupied seat.

Then, as if he felt Kallie's eyes on him, Rian glanced at her, and Sebastian's hand lowered even further. An emotion flickered across Rian's features but disappeared almost as fast as it came. The king returned his attention to his mother.

Did Rian not see how his brother's gaze bore into Kallie's flesh? How Kallie's body had gone rigid the moment her hand fell onto Sebastian's palm? Was Rian that oblivious? Or did he not care? Was this the whole purpose behind this wretched tradition? For the other men to see what they could not have—to tease and taunt them?

And in that second, Kallie knew then who Rian would be in their relationship if Kallie didn't take control—if she didn't continue to manipulate him. She would become the crown's shadow, never truly seen but always there.

Rian might have been *good*, but he would never be her savior. He would never interfere in traditions, never make a stand to protect her. He would ride the line in between, never steering too far off the path to avoid disturbing the natural order of things.

Rian was a traditionalist, while Kallie, on the other hand, wanted to tear apart those traditions. And that was why they would never work. A kind man or not.

She forced space between herself and Sebastian.

Thrown off, Sebastian twirled Kallie in an attempt to hide her pushing him away. As Sebastian went to pull her back into his arms, another man stole her outstretched hand from his grasp.

"There you are, Princess." The Tetrian guard pulled her toward him, a coy smirk tugging at his lips.

Masking the sickening feeling that had grown in her stomach from dancing with Sebastian, Kallie forced a light giggle. "Have you been looking for me?"

The man chuckled, the noise quiet yet boisterous. He held her hand high, spinning her toward him as his other hand slid across her back to her hip. His footsteps were light, gentler than she expected for a guard of his stature.

Then her muscles tensed as Sebastian approached her again.

Before Sebastian could steal her back, the Tetrian guard twirled her away. He picked up the pace, matching the music as it hit the song's bridge.

Still, Sebastian followed, relentless. He weaved through the other men as they hopped and clapped to the beat. A pang of hunger flashed in the prince's eyes, and Kallie's heart rate picked up, momentarily transported back to the ship.

As Sebastian made chase, the Tetrian managed to cut him off. Kallie's lips parted in shock as the guard winked at her and smoothly guided them across the floor with graceful maneuvers.

It wasn't just a coincidence that the man kept pulling her away at the right moment. He was intentionally helping her stay out of Sebastian's reach.

Was she that obvious?

The Tetrian led them backward with quick, graceful steps, but there was no way the guard could hold off Sebastian forever. And before she knew it, Sebastian was cutting in, forcing the man to let go of her or ruin the dance.

Kallie concentrated on the music—on anything but Sebastian's hand in hers, the sliminess coating his very skin.

Sebastian pulled her closer. As his scent overwhelmed her, the words slipped out of her mouth before she could pull them back, the command on her tongue. "You will not touch me."

Like the low fog atop the grass in the early morning hours, the haze coated Sebastian's eyes, dulling the sickly green color of his irises. Within a second of the command, Sebastian pushed her away from him as if her touch had physically burned him.

Kallie, light on her feet, twirled, hiding the interaction from the watching crowd.

Her back hit one of the men, but the Tetrian effortlessly slid one arm across her back and dipped her low. Her leg slipped through the slit in the red fabric as she pointed her foot out, the tip of her crown nearly touching the ground.

The man's head hung over her, and long dark strands of hair floated in his face as he looked down at her, wrinkles forming in the corners. As her gaze bounced across his face, the song ended, and clapping erupted across the room. She inhaled, and her eyes widened as the air stuck in her throat. The skin at the back of her neck prickled. A thin layer of sweat coated her skin.

"Princess?" The Tetrian man's brows furrowed. "Are you all right?"

"Mhm." Her voice was caught in her lungs. Her heart spun in her chest as cedar and citrus filled the air. And before she could think twice about it, Kallie ran.

CHAPTER 35
KALLIE

Kallie raced out of the grand hall, slipping down a side hall. With small smiles, she rushed past guests, their faces a blur as the oxygen caught in her throat. She couldn't breathe; she couldn't speak. Her vision spun.

Once she found a hall void of guests, she pressed her back against the wall and counted.

One.

She inhaled, closing her eyes.

Two.

Her heart threatened to burst through her throat.

Three.

Kallie could feel each pump, each beat, echo in her throat. It throbbed. It screamed.

Four.

She tried to exhale, but the air was shaky in her throat.

She swore she had noted cedar and citrus in the air. It was faint, but it was there. *Somewhere* in that ballroom. Was it just because of her recent dreams? Kallie didn't think so, and yet . . .

She lost track of her count, her breaths becoming more labored.

Breathe, Kallie. Breathe.

Her nails bit into her palms. She was imagining things. She had to be. It was the pressure of the week. The stress was getting to her head.

Graeson wasn't here. He couldn't be.

But if he was . . .

Footsteps echoed in the main hallway, and her eyes snapped open. Her nostrils flared.

There it was again: the faint scent of cedar.

If he was here, it only meant one thing.

Kallie reached underneath her dress. With shaky fingers, she unlatched the dagger that was strapped around her lower thigh, hidden by the layers of fabric.

The music was only a faint whisper this far from the grand hall.

Kallie shouldn't have been following the trail. She knew she shouldn't have been, yet she needed to see the truth. She needed to know if her imagination had gotten the best of her or if she was going crazy.

As she stormed down the hallway, her hands shook at her side, and her legs trembled.

She had to be crazy.

She had to be insane.

Because even though she did not see him, even though she did not hear his voice, she *knew* he was here. He had to be. Graeson's presence was unmistakable. In a crowded room full of strangers and chaos, her body would know he was there. She didn't understand why, but she could feel it in the pit of her stomach in the same spot where her gift lay. She didn't understand it, but Kallie somehow knew she would find the Pontian here. Even when she shouldn't, even when her mind should be on another man—on her betrothed, on the key to her power.

But Rian . . . Rian was a means to an end.

Kallie swallowed the lump in her throat.

Rian wasn't Graeson though.

When she rounded the corner, her fingers grabbed the edge of the oak table in the hallway.

What was she doing? *Rian* was the one who had the power. Graeson was a wishful thought, only a possibility in her dreams. She had chosen Rian. She was *choosing* the King of Frenzia. Now, today, and tomorrow. She didn't love Rian, but she didn't need to. It wasn't as if she loved Graeson either. They had only spent a couple of months together, most of which was spent under pretenses. So why did the thought of him being here shake her so?

Her chest rose fast and hard. Strands of hair were loose in front of her face. Her knuckles grew white around the wood as her fingers gripped the edge.

Jaw flexing, she exhaled.

Kallie wasn't one of them. The Pontians hadn't chosen her, and Kallie was done putting herself last. She was done letting men think they could storm into her life and change the trajectory of it.

Her power, her *freedom*, needed to be her priority.

And she would make sure Graeson knew that. Because as she lifted her gaze from the table, she saw him leaning against the wall at the end of the hallway. His palms were pressed against the stone, his head slunk, eyes on the ground, hair falling in front of his face. He looked just the same as the last night she had seen him: black sleeves rolled up to his elbows, paired with clean black trousers and brightly polished shoes. Yet everything was different now that the truth was out.

Peeling her fingers from the wood, she tipped her chin up and rolled her shoulders back.

This would end here. The thoughts, the dreams, the past. All of it.

Her future couldn't begin if the ghost of her past lived on. If the what-ifs, the should-haves, and the could-have-if-onlys continued to haunt her mind, Kallie would never move forward if she didn't put it all behind her.

Dagger in hand, she stormed forward.

CHAPTER 36
GRAESON

GRAESON SLAMMED HIS FIST AGAINST THE WALL.

He was stupid, so incredibly stupid. He should have made Emmett dance with Kalisandre. He should have known it would have been too much. But when one of the king's advisors told their table they needed to send a representative for that idiotic dance, Graeson jumped at the opportunity to get close to Kalisandre.

If Dani had been here instead of at the guesthouse, she would have stopped Graeson. There was no doubt about it.

But Dani wasn't here, and now Graeson had nearly ruined their entire plan.

However, what was he supposed to do when fear flashed across her features? Kalisandre didn't want to dance with her fiancé's brother. Graeson could see that as clearly as the Red Sea. He didn't know what had happened between them, but the look in her eyes had stirred Graeson into action.

When his hand had touched hers, when he smelled the mint and lavender in her hair, he saw nothing but her. Heard nothing but the song that sang between their gifts.

Then the prince pounced, and Graeson had almost ruined everything in order to keep her out of his grasp.

When the song ended, Kalisandre had disappeared right after. As the guests rushed toward the dance floor, Graeson had lost her in the swarm. Without a word to the others, he had chased after her even though he knew they would yell at him later.

But fuck the plan. Graeson needed to find her, to make sure she was okay.

However, when he had entered the hall, she was nowhere to be found.

Until she appeared behind him, a blade pressed against his throat. He couldn't see her, but he didn't need to. Even if he hadn't seen the dagger's hilt, he would know who it was. Because when she was near, his entire being came to life. Graeson's lips twitched.

He raised his hands in surrender as the cold metal kissed his skin. "I think you may have misplaced your blade, Princess."

"What are you doing here?" Kalisandre asked through clenched teeth.

"Just catching my breath."

"No," Kalisandre said, the hilt of the dagger pushing against his throat. "What. Are. *You*. Doing. *Here*."

Graeson tipped his chin up. "I was just dancing—"

"*Graeson*," she hissed.

"Excuse me?"

She shouldn't . . . how did she . . .

"Cut the act, Graeson."

His stomach dropped, for Graeson could no longer feel the oily presence of Emmett's gift on his skin. There must have been some sort of limitation on Emmett's reach that he wasn't aware of. He tried to turn around, but Kalisandre shook the blade.

"Don't. Move," she bit out.

Graeson frozen. "All right. Just take it easy."

She shook him, growling. "Shut up and answer my question."

He couldn't help it. A chuckle escaped. "Well, what is it? Do you want me to shut up, or do you want me to answer? Because I cannot do both, little mouse."

The music was only a soft hum this far away.

"Right now," Kalisandre said through clenched teeth, "you are doing neither. So I would suggest you choose one."

"Ah, like you did when you chose to betray us?"

At her silence, Graeson tried to peer down at her, but even in heels, she was still too short to see in his peripheral vision. When they had traveled together, though, he had spent many days studying her reactions. He could almost picture her now. A slight twitch at her left nostril as her lips pursed while she sucked on the inside of her cheek, trying to bite back the rising frustration.

Somewhere, sets of footsteps echoed in a nearby hall, followed by echoes of giggles. At the sound, Kalisandre stopped breathing behind him.

Graeson acted then. One hand grabbing her wrist, he turned the doorknob behind him and pulled her inside the room with him. He pressed her back against his chest and shut the door behind them, locking it.

Graeson pressed his ear to the door. The footsteps and giggling grew louder as the people turned down the hall Graeson and Kalisandre had just occupied.

Beneath his arm, Kalisandre's chest rose, fast. "Let me—"

Graeson covered Kalisandre's mouth with a hand. "Shush."

Kalisandre jerked against him, but he held her firm with his arm wrapping around her arms and torso.

"Unless you want someone to find you in a dark room with a man who is not your betrothed," he hissed against her ear, "I suggest you bite your tongue."

Kalisandre stopped fighting.

The giggling was just outside the door now.

As they waited for the people to pass, Graeson took in his surroundings. Fortunately, the room they were hiding in was empty of any other occupants. It was a simple sitting room with only a few pieces of furniture. A table sat behind a stiff burgundy couch. In the far corner, coals hissed in the hearth. Someone had been here at one point today, but they hadn't visited for at least a few hours.

With his back pressed against the one entry point of the room, He could feel every rise and fall of Kalisandre's chest as much as he tried not to think about her body pressing against his. But he was only a man. If she were any other woman, he would have been stronger. He wouldn't have let it cloud his thoughts. But it wasn't anyone else. It was Kalisandre. She would always be his weak point.

Soon, the voices in the hallways faded, and Kalisandre bit down.

"Ow!" Graeson jerked his hand away.

"I said, let me go." Kalisandre pushed forward, breaking through his hold, her distraction having loosened Graeson's grip on her. She spun, blade in hand.

Graeson sighed. He was already tired of this game, but Kalisandre, it seemed, wasn't.

CHAPTER 37
KALLIE

"Put the dagger to my throat, little mouse. I beg you." Graeson lifted his chin, granting her full access.

With the fire roaring in her gaze, Kallie raised her hand and pressed the cold metal against his neck, just like he told her to.

His eyes darkened as he looked down at her with a cocky smirk pushing at the corner of his lips. "That's a good girl."

Kallie snarled. Yet, even though she bared her teeth, her hand shook. She begged it to stop, but her body betrayed her and leaned into him instead. Her chest pressed against his. His thigh between her legs. Heat licked her skin as her recent dream resurfaced, daring her to find out what would have happened if the thunder hadn't woken her up.

She tossed the image aside and forced her chin up. Quirking a brow, she ignored the heat that rose in the pit of her stomach.

"Oh, come on. More pressure, don't you think?"

His fingers wrapped around hers, applying more pressure on the blade. His leg shifted, and Kallie froze.

"What's wrong, Kalisandre? Cat got your tongue?" he murmured against her ear. The vibrations of his deep voice cascaded down her chest, doing little to soothe the fire.

All Kallie had to do was slide the knife across his throat. Make Graeson bleed red, make him shed his soul from his body like Kallie already had. All it would take was one move, one swipe, one twitch of a hand.

It *should* be easy.

It was one small movement. Nothing more than slicing through the dummies her father had made Kallie use during her training.

If she hadn't drawn her blade first, she would have been the one pressed against the wall. She knew that fact like she knew the night sky. If Graeson had gotten to her first, he would not hesitate. He hadn't hesitated to kill the Ardentolian soldiers when they were fleeing through the woods months ago. And Kallie was better than him. She *had* to be better than him. She had to prove to her father that her heart wasn't some fragile thing, that *she* wasn't the weak woman he thought she was.

Kallie dropped her gaze.

If she kept looking at that stubborn glint in Graeson's moon-gray eyes, she would never be able to do it. However, she regretted her choice instantly. Heat flushed her cheeks as his tongue swiped across his teeth, and she mentally cursed herself.

It was just her body's reaction. Graeson was without a doubt attractive, and they had a history—a short, complicated history, but a history nonetheless. She knew what those lips felt like on hers.

Focus, Kallie.

She directed her attention back to the dagger. A pebble of red bubbled where the tip of the blade had pierced Graeson's skin.

"Don't tell me you're scared of a little blood?" Graeson asked. "If that's the case, then perhaps this wasn't the right form of attack for you. A slice through the throat, while fairly quick if done right, does produce a lot of blood. It's not for the faint, I'm afraid."

Kallie huffed. Afraid of blood? Ridiculous.

Her hand tightened around the dagger.

His fingers, which were still on top of hers, flexed as he whispered, "That's right. Just like that."

"You talk too much," she gritted out,

"Hm. Never been told that before," Graeson said as if they were having a friendly conversation—as if her blade wasn't piercing his skin, as if it hadn't already drawn blood. "Maybe the problem is that you don't talk enough. Tell me, Kalisandre, what other secrets lie in that pretty head of yours?"

"Wouldn't you like to know?" Kallie asked, infusing more venom onto her tongue and ignoring how her stomach twisted at the sound of her name.

Graeson cocked a brow. "Yes, actually I would."

Kallie narrowed her eyes and snapped her mouth shut.

His gray eyes were storm clouds in the darkness as he stared down at her. His chest rose beneath her arm at a steady rate. Graeson wasn't nervous; he wasn't even shaken by the dagger Kallie held against his throat. He was eerily calm. As she continued to observe him, the corner of his mouth twitched, amusement sparking in his heated gaze.

He was provoking her, and she had fallen for it. She was never this sloppy. *Never.*

Unless it was with him.

"I'm going to ask you one more time, Graeson." Kallie forced her hand to remain steady as she kept the blade pressed against his neck. "Why are you *here?*"

With a face of stone, Graeson said, "I'm here for you."

Kallie cackled. "And what was your plan? Were you going to run after me and stab me in the back?"

"What?" Graeson's features contorted in confusion. "Kalisandre, I'm not here to *kill* you. If there is one thing you should be certain of, it is that."

Kallie's gaze bounced across his face, but there was no twitch of the nose, no wandering eyes. Graeson stared her down, unmoving.

But how could that be? What other reason did he have to be here besides to kill her? He had been there in the hallway of the Cavern of Catius when her shields had finally cracked, when Fynn finally could read her thoughts. As much as she wanted to blame Sebastian for driving the blade through Fynn's heart, Kallie was the one who had put it there. She was the one who had led Fynn onto the ship unintentionally. She was the one who had orchestrated the entire raid months before with her father.

Her eyelids burned; her throat ached. But Kallie would not cry here. Not in front of *him.*

"Do you think me a fool?" Kallie spat, clenching her teeth. Her voice shook, her throat raw and burning. "I am no fool, Graeson."

His grip around her wrist tightened. "Kalisandre, you are not to blame." His words were no more than a whisper.

But it wouldn't have mattered if he screamed them, for they were still a lie.

"You know nothing, Graeson."

"I know enough," he growled.

"Why do you even care what I think?"

His gaze bounced across her face, his brows knitting together. "Have you let that man twist your mind so much that you don't even care about your own worth? I care what you think because it matters. Because *you* matter."

Her laugh came out strangled.

"Do not dismiss me when I say that you matter. You have surrounded yourself with men who do not respect you, who do not believe you are capable of great things. Rian only cares about your title. Domitius only cares about your—"

"Do not speak about my father." Kallie tugged at her arm, but his calloused fingers remained firm around her smooth skin, his grip unshakable.

"Have you forgotten what he did to you? What he did to Pontia? What he did to your birth father and your brother?"

"I—" The words became a knot stuck in her throat, and no matter how much she tried, she could not untangle them.

"He's using you."

"He *needs* me."

"If he needs you, why are you letting him sell you off to the highest bidder?"

Kallie snarled. "I *chose* to come here. But that still does not explain why you are here."

For once, Graeson didn't have an answer ready. He stumbled. "Do you not see what you are doing to me? What you have done to me? You are all I think about. For years, for decades, I have fought for you. My thoughts, my goals—"

"Then perhaps," she hissed, interrupting, for she had heard enough, "it is time you acquire a new goal, *Gray*."

Graeson tipped his head down an inch, glowering. "That is not possible, and you know that."

"Do I?" Kallie ripped her arm from his grasp, rage fueling her. Screw the throat, she'd just stab him in the heart. "And what possible reason could that be? Because from my perspective, the only person here who stands to gain something from this conversation is you."

Pain spiked her jaw, but she didn't dare show it. Graeson had not earned her pain, nor had he earned her truth.

He once said love was worth the fight, worth the risk. But why? No one ever fought for anything if they didn't stand to gain something.

Kallie had always felt like something was off, as if something was missing. Her entire life, she had strived for more. More power, more control, more freedom. The reason she even stood in this ghost of a castle was because she sought the Frenzian crown. Kallie knew her own motives but was still ignorant of Graeson's.

"What's in it for you?"

Graeson's mouth parted then closed. Once, twice. And that look—his head tilting to the side, deep wrinkles forming in the center of his forehead, silver eyes darkening as confusion then realization formed—was answer enough.

Kallie turned on her heel, but Graeson's hand found her wrist yet again.

She sucked in a breath, his coarse fingers reminding her of a different time. But she wiped the memory from her mind when she faced him again. "Either let go of me," Kallie whispered, the words cold on her tongue, "or tell me the truth."

A moment passed. It was a moment that seemed to span time. A moment that suggested that Kallie was wasting her time waiting for an answer from Graeson. Because when had the Pontian ever been upfront with her? Ever since she had known him, he had evaded the truth.

They were too similar in that way, she supposed. They avoided the truth as if it were quicksand, one wrong word, and they would sink.

"You don't get it at all," Graeson said. "You *consume* me, Kalisandre. Heart and soul. You could carve my heart out, and I would let you."

Kallie looked up at the ceiling, her nails biting into her palm. She should force him aside. She should scream for help. But instead, she asked, "But *why*, Graeson?"

"What do you mean 'why?'"

Kallie stepped forward and instantly regretted the movement when the faint note of citrus hidden behind the woodsy odor became more prominent. She would not retreat, not now.

The left side of her lip curled, her gaze sliding up his body as two of her fingers scaled his chest. As her nails scraped against his skin, right where the purple vein throbbed, Graeson inhaled.

"Don't say it," Graeson whispered.

The inside of her cheek was raw, and she let it loose. Unclenching her jaw, she dropped her shoulders, trying to release the tension permeating her bones. "It'll never be enough."

His hands wrapped around each of her wrists, gentle and loose yet present. When Graeson spoke, his words were barely above a whisper. "Why can't this be enough?"

Kallie sighed and looked away. "This could never work."

"See? Does my reason even matter when your reason not to trumps that? You want power; you crave it. You feel as though you cannot live without it." Graeson tugged on her hand. "Look at me."

Kallie gritted her teeth, but she refused to look at him. She kept her gaze on the wall beside him.

Graeson tugged again. "*Look* at me, Kalisandre."

Kallie's gaze snapped to him like a rubber band that had been stretched out too far and then was released.

"Why are *you* here?" Graeson asked.

"Because it is my duty to protect—" Kallie began but shut her mouth as Graeson spun them around. Kallie's back hit the cement wall, not enough to cause any actual pain, but enough to force the air out of her lungs from the shock.

"Why are you *here*," Graeson repeated, his words sharpening, eyes glowing, grip tightening.

Kallie dropped her gaze to her wrist. Graeson, having noticed where her gaze had gone, uncurled his fingers.

"Because it is where I am meant to be," she said at last.

His fist smacked against the wall a foot away from her head.

He hung his head, black strands of hair falling in front of his face. "You cannot mean that!"

Graeson was standing so close that when she inhaled, her chest rose and brushed against his. In the small space between them, the air was hot.

He was too close.

Yet, not close enough, a small part of her whispered in the back of her mind.

In her peripheral, his arm flexed, the veins pulsing as he clenched and unclenched his fist that was still pressed against the wall.

Without thinking, Kallie's hand rose. Her fingers wrapped around his bicep. The muscle tensed at her touch, and his head lifted. Her attention dropped to his lips. Even months after, Kallie could recall the taste of butter on his lips from that first night in Pontia and the sweet taste of spring from the second time.

But how would they taste now? she wondered.

One kiss wouldn't hurt. One last taste.

"Didn't I tell you what would happen if you did that again?" Graeson asked, his voice hoarser, darker, lower than before. The anger from moments ago disintegrating into the air, a raw tension left behind in its place.

"Hmm?" Kallie hummed.

This was not the time to be getting distracted, yet what did she have to lose? Her morality was already gone.

Fabric shifted. The space between them vanished. His thumb scraped her bottom lip and pulled at it. The back of his finger slid across her neck, his nail scraping against her skin. His thumb lay across the center of her throat, his palm on her collarbone.

Kallie swallowed. But that slight movement of her throat only made her more aware of his skin on hers.

Heat formed in the tiny space that existed between their flesh. She tried to focus on that space rather than the points where they connected. But whenever she thought of the distance between them, Kallie only wanted to eliminate it.

Perhaps she was going at this the wrong way. Maybe to rid her mind of him once and for all, she needed to give her body what it thought it wanted. Then she would prove that it was the farthest thing from what she needed.

Her hand slipped to the back of his neck, pulling him closer, and Kallie claimed him for the last time.

The whole purpose of this ridiculous night was to show the men what they had missed out on, what they had given up. What would no longer be theirs to have.

This was the last time.

This was their goodbye.

Their last dance.

CHAPTER 38
GRAESON

GRAESON HAD MEANT WHAT HE SAID. HIS HEART WAS HERS. KALISANDRE could carve it out, and he would do nothing to stop her.

Gods, Graeson would even give Kalisandre the knife.

In truth, he had already given it to her a long time ago. Since Esmeray had told him about his mother's vision when he was a child, Graeson had believed that Kalisandre was his, a woman promised to him. A woman fated to him. A woman so intrinsically tied up with who Graeson was that Kalisandre could not be torn from him.

But this kiss . . . No, this entire trip was proving to him how wrong he had been, how foolish he was being. And how right everyone else had been from the beginning. Because Graeson would sacrifice anything to save the woman before him.

His honor.

His kingdom.

His friends.

Graeson would do anything if it meant that Kalisandre was his. That she was his as much as he was hers. He would do anything if it meant that these lips only ever tasted of him. That another man never touched her again, never kissed her skin, never felt her breath caress his ear.

And maybe that was why Graeson refused to let go. Why his body leaned forward, why it pressed against hers. He wanted to remove any remnant of the Frenzian royals that lingered on her clothes, on her skin, on her hair.

Graeson's hand swept up her neck, caressing the side of her head, the spot right behind her ear. Her body arched into him, arched for him, arched *because* of him.

Mine, the voice in the back of his head growled.

A feral noise slipped his lips. Graeson wasn't sure if the sound was his or the beast within, but it didn't matter. Not when it only made Kalisandre press against him more.

Beneath his palm, goosebumps scattered across her arm, and his lips curled against her mouth.

He inhaled, but Kalisandre scraped her teeth on his bottom lip before he could say anything.

She pulled it.

She looked at him through long, dark eyelashes, and a deep hunger stirred in the sea of blue. "For once, Graeson, shut up," Kalisandre said, her breathing heavy, her voice husky.

Graeson narrowed his eyes, but then he smirked. "Fine."

Kalisandre reached for him, but he pulled his head back. "Ah. Always so eager, little mouse. First things first." He snatched the dagger from her hand and then tossed it into the corner of the room.

Kalisandre arched a brow.

Graeson craved to kiss the curve that formed. But instead, he shrugged. "As much as I like that dagger of yours, best we keep it far away."

Kallie grabbed his collar, pulling him closer. "Are you sure it's the dagger you should be concerned about?"

"You tell me, Princess."

Kalisandre smirked and then dragged him further into the room.

Even though Graeson could have easily outmaneuvered her and controlled the situation, he let her guide him. He didn't care if Kalisandre looked at him as if he was prey. He didn't care if she was using him. He didn't care if they still hadn't discussed everything. He was starving for her touch. And right now, he knew that what Kalisandre needed—what she *craved*—was control. So, he would let her carve him out piece by piece until she had her fill.

Because if this moment was any indication, Graeson knew all too well that one day he would get his chance.

When Kalisandre pulled him closer, Graeson gave in to her. His fingers weaved into the soft curls of her hair at the back of her neck. Still, it wasn't enough. He wanted more of her, wanted all of her.

What he wanted most, however, was to take her away from here and run. Run until they were outside of the castle walls. Run until they had surpassed the city limits. Run until their legs broke and their fears were behind them.

It was a lofty wish, a disillusioned desire. Even if they could outrun their enemies, wherever they went, their enemies would follow. Wherever they went, their enemies would find them.

And as if hearing his thoughts, Kalisandre stepped back, and his heart sank again. Because Kalisandre didn't need a dagger to stab him in the heart. All she needed was one word.

"Stop."

CHAPTER 39
KALLIE

Cedar had always been her favorite scent, for it had always felt like home. But now, it smelled of regret.

Because even though nothing had changed, so much had.

Graeson was not her home. He had never been and never would be. Frenzia was her home now.

Kallie bunched Graeson's shirt within her fist.

Graeson's breath mingled with hers, his scent consuming her. His fingers brushed across her chin. "Kal, just let me give you what you deserve."

The pit of her core hummed, but she would not listen to it. She would not let Graeson sway her.

"Graeson," Kallie began, but the words were cut off as he took a half step closer. The muscles in her body grew taught, her skin cold. The old coals now turned to ash.

"If you wanted to walk out of this room, you could have a long time ago. You've had several chances." He tipped her chin up, forcing her to meet his gaze. "But before you do, can I say one thing?"

Unable to say anything else, Kallie nodded.

"You are deserving of love." His eyes bounced between hers.

"Whether it is mine or someone else's. But by the gods and the sea, if you let me, I will do whatever it takes to prove to you that you are worthy of love."

Kallie's hands acted of their own accord. Her fingers knotted in his shirt, pulling him toward her. Her lips found his. And she kissed him. She kissed him before he could take those words back and see the truth. Before he could realize she was undeserving of his attention—undeserving of his forgiveness.

She refused to call whatever existed between them love. She refused to admit what she knew in her heart. Because if she admitted that truth to herself, she would fall to pieces. Because whatever it was that they had, it couldn't happen.

She kissed him because she wanted to. She kissed him because this was her last chance to have a glimpse of the fire that breathed between them.

This was it. A goodbye hidden in the shadows.

He pulled back, then laid his forehead against hers. "Kalisandre." Her name was a growl on his tongue, vibrating against her neck.

Even though she knew she needed to, her body wouldn't let her pull back. Her body craved his touch. She wished his lips were once again on hers, wished they had never left. But she couldn't allow that to happen. Someone would come looking for her soon enough.

Then, without thinking, the command slipped out.

CHAPTER 40
GRAESON

"Let me go."

Graeson blinked as the command poked at his mind. It knocked on the walls, trying to find a crack in the marble.

Had she meant to command him? Kalisandre knew she couldn't manipulate his mind, that her manipulations didn't work on him. Yet he had felt the command coating her voice. He had sensed it trying to infiltrate his mind.

He took a step back, and Kalisandre refused to look at him. He tipped her chin up with a finger, but she only closed her eyes. "Whatever is going on, you can tell me."

She shook her head, and she sensed a tear forming. It hung on her eyelashes for a brief moment before rolling down her cheek. Graeson wiped it away with his thumb.

"We shouldn't be doing this," she whispered. "Nothing has changed, Graeson."

"Nothing?" He searched her countenance for an explanation, for something that would explain what had happened. For a moment, the old Kalisandre had been back, but now she was gone once more. "Everything has changed, Kalisandre. Don't you see that?"

An amused, noncommittal sound escaped her lips, sending spikes crawling up the back of his neck. An eerie cold slithered over his skin, but there was no breeze inside of the room, no window allowing the cold to sweep in. Only an icy look in her eyes as her gaze fell upon him.

"Perhaps for you, but not for me." Kalisandre turned around, her back to him as she approached the door.

What are you doing? Stop her! the beast shouted in the back of his mind.

Graeson grabbed her wrist and pulled her back. "What is that supposed to mean?"

Kalisandre shook her head. "Graeson, you believe me to be the girl I was. I am not that girl anymore. I haven't been in a long time."

"But—"

"Listen to me," she hissed. "My goals have not changed. My desires have not changed. My *life* has not changed simply because you have walked back into it for a moment. I told you before that my word means something to me." She stepped forward, frustration coloring her cheeks. "Does it mean nothing to you?"

Graeson's lips fell open, yet no words came out. How could he explain it to her to make her understand? How could he tell her what he knew?

Kallie shook her head, lips drawn in a straight line. She pressed the heels of her palms against her temple. "Of course not. They never have, have they?"

"That's not true," he said, sneering.

She huffed. "If it were true, Graeson, you wouldn't be here."

Red coated the edges of his vision, but he pushed the beast back down. He would handle this himself. "I'm here *because* of you, Kalisandre. I promised you I would never stop fighting for you. I told you once that your safety and happiness mattered."

"Yet you're still not listening to me! Do you even hear yourself?" Her hands fell to her side in fists. "I could *never* be happy with you."

Graeson shook his head in dismay. How could she know that if she didn't even give him a chance? She had been fighting the pull that called them together from the beginning. Was Domitius' hold so strong that it prevented her from hearing it?

Graeson reached for her hand, but Kalisandre snapped it away.

She exhaled exasperatedly. "*They* will never forgive me, Graeson."

She didn't need to say who *they* were, but Graeson knew her mother and brother better than she did. Kalisandre never had the chance to learn their souls, to understand how much her disappearance had affected them. When Kalisandre discovered the truth about her family, she had already concocted an image of who they were: people who seemingly didn't care about her. But the fact of the matter was that they cared too much. Too much to risk her life and put her in even more danger.

Without thinking, his fingers wrapped around her arms. Beneath his hold, a slight tremble rocked her entire body. She was carrying too much, holding too much back. He already saw what that had done to her appearance. How much would she let the guilt cost her?

"Fynn's death is not your fault, Kalisandre."

She finally looked at him, her faded blue eyes bouncing between his as though she was looking for the lies hidden within them. Kalisandre would find no such thing in his. His friend's death was not her fault. Domitius was the one who brought the ship to his kingdom's shores. Domitius had brought the unruly Frenzians soldiers. He had taken Kalisandre from them years ago. He had been the one who had raised Kalisandre to view Pontia as the enemy. He was the one who had turned her into a weapon.

She wasn't meant to be used. To be misguided and misdirected. She wasn't meant to be commanded.

Kalisandre wasn't a king's weapon. She was meant to command, to wield. To be the one guiding the shots she threw. She was meant to push the blade, not have someone else guide it for her.

Graeson needed to tell her.

"Kalisandre, you need to know the truth. Fynn and I—"

"I don't want to hear your excuses! I don't need to hear your elaborate reasons for coming here. I don't need to hear your false promises."

His frustrations were rising to the surface. He couldn't help it. Her anger, her ire, awoke the beast within him. Graeson could only be made a fool for so long.

Before he knew it, the beast slipped out.

Red saturated his vision as he pushed her against the wall. His fingers dug into her biceps. Whatever hold Domitius had on her was too strong, too intertwined with everything she believed.

"I do not speak of excuses or faulty promises, little mouse. Have you forgotten that Domitius is *not* your true father?"

Kalisandre tried to shake his hands off, but his grip remained firm.

"Blood only means so much when it forgets about you—when it doesn't fight for you," she spat. "Blood is blood, and that is all it is at the end of the day. Actions are for more telling of one's true nature."

"And Domitius? What has he done to prove that he is worthy of your love, of your loyalty? He *kidnapped* you! He manipulated you!"

Kalisandre snarled. "So did you."

The red in his vision spread further as Graeson stared down at her. "*He* killed your brother."

Kalisandre spat in his face.

The beast inside of him growled, and ice coated his veins.

Kalisandre, however, didn't back down. "My father did not kill Fynn."

"Then who did?"

"Sebastian."

Graeson huffed, looking away. She was gravely mistaken if she thought that the princely captain held the reins here. "Tell me, Kalisandre—and for once, do me the justice of being honest with me—did you know about us before we rescued you?"

"You mean *kidnapped*?" she spat back.

"Semantics, Kalisandre," he hissed.

"The truth?"

"Please," Graeson gritted out. He could see her debating on what and *how much* she should reveal. Kalisandre knew more than she had made them believe when they all had been traveling together only months ago. She had hidden her secrets well, nearly was impenetrable to Fynn's efforts when he had tried to read her mind. If Graeson was going to convince the others that she was worthy of saving, he needed proof. Evidence. Even in this state, when the monster had control over half of him, Graeson knew that much.

"I knew that a group of Pontians was going to attack my carriage."

"*How* did you know?" The red hue spread. He was on the verge of losing complete control.

Kalisandre saw his control slipping, too, yet she did not waver. She raised her chin, meeting his stare with the same fervor. "My father had been warned about the attack by one of his men."

A traitor was in their mix then, but who? As far as Graeson knew, no one had raised Fynn's suspicions when they were planning their attack or afterward.

"And what did *Daddy* tell you about us?" Graeson asked. The beast was at the edge of his mind now.

Kalisandre snarled, her nose twitching, and Graeson forced the beast back.

"Nothing besides that you were all like me. He thought you would know how to help me strengthen my gift."

"So he did not tell you who we were? Our identities or the twins' relation to you?"

Kalisandre directed her stare at the ceiling, the veins in her forehead pulsing. He had her now. The mental walls she had built were breaking. The truth seeping out.

"No."

Domitius had intentionally misinformed her. He had people everywhere, an endless well of knowledge at his disposal. If he had known the Pontians would attack, he would have known who Fynn and Terin were.

He bit back the snarl pushing at his lips and tried to remain calm. "And why do you think that is, Kalisandre?"

The muscles in her jaw ticked. The little vein in her forehead growing more prominent. "He didn't—"

Graeson cut her off. "Do not fool yourself. He *knew*. How would a king with unlimited resources, people, and knowledge at his fingertips *not* know that not one but *two* princes of another kingdom entered his kingdom? You truly believe that Domitius did not know?"

Kalisandre swallowed hard. "It wasn't important," she whispered.

Graeson huffed. "Come on, Kalisandre. You're smarter than that."

She wiggled against his grip, but Graeson kept his hold around her arms. She wasn't going to run from this. Kalisandre needed to face the truth for once in her life. Graeson's gaze swept across her face. "He's manipulating you. Do you not see that?"

Her gaze grew cold. "I don't know what you're talking about."

"Yes, you do. Or else you wouldn't still be here with me."

When Kalisandre shook against his hold again, Graeson let go.

"I'm here because I was going to kill you."

"And how is that working out, Princess?"

"I said 'was,' didn't I?"

"But you're not now?" He couldn't help but smirk.

"Leave, Graeson."

Graeson took a step forward as he reached for her. "Kal—"

She turned away from him, and his hand fell.

"Just leave," she whispered.

The beast slipped back inside its cage, the fire that burned inside him dwindling. The red clearing. "If that is truly what you want . . ." Graeson said, hesitating to turn away from her.

He had come all this way. Was he going to give up that easily? But if Kalisandre didn't want him here . . .

"Leave!"

His mouth pressed into a thin line, but he relented and turned to the door.

Kalisandre spoke from further away now. "If you know what's good for you, Graeson, you won't come back. I'm not worth it."

"No." His knuckles turned white as he gripped the doorknob. "You are worth everything."

She may have chosen Rian, but that didn't mean Graeson would give up on her. He made a promise. He would set her mind free. He would break whatever hold Domitius had on her. That was his mission here, not to capture her, not to kidnap her and force her to go with them, but to set her free.

It didn't matter if Kalisandre was not his. He was hers. And he would do anything to protect her. Graeson would rip the man's throat out and feed it to the kraken that prowled beneath the Red Sea if he had to. He didn't care if the man was a prince, a general, or a king. Titles meant nothing to him.

Gods did not bow down to kings.

CHAPTER 41
GRAESON

Graeson's back hit the wall as soon as he stepped inside the guest house.

"You chasing your girlfriend was *not* a part of the plan," Ellie spat, driving a sharp nail into his chest.

The pictures shook against the wall. Dani, Terin, Moris, and Sylvia snapped their gazes up from the table littered with maps of the Frenzian castle and kingdom.

"*Euralys,*" Medenia hissed.

The Tetrian warrior ignored her, her finger only digging deeper into Graeson's chest. Ellie's deep black eyes sliced through him as if she believed that she could force out an explanation by looking at him.

When Graeson had left Kalisandre, he had ducked back into the grand hall to find the others. Without an explanation, he ordered them to leave. At the command, Ellie and Medenia had exchanged silent glances.

"Not here," Graeson had said at the time. He would only admit his failure once and would not do it in this castle where prying ears could overhear.

Without further questioning, the four of them hurried out of the grand hall, Emmett tossing back the remains of the wine into his mouth as they weaved between the guests.

On the way back, guards patrolled the streets leading to the guest house, so they walked in silence. Their confusion and anger guiding them. Graeson knew it was only a matter of time before the questions came, and he dreaded the conversation they were bound to have. He didn't want to be told he was wrong or foolish for believing it would be easy to convince Kalisandre of the truth. He already knew he was an idiot. He didn't need someone else to remind him.

Graeson shoved Ellie's hand off his shoulders, saying, "She's *not* my girlfriend."

Across from them, Armen leaned against the back of the couch, ankles crossed as he watched with a smug look. Graeson contemplated smacking it right off Armen's pretty little face, for Kalisandre had wound him so much that the tension in his body was too tight. He needed some release, and punching Armen might do the trick.

"What's going on?" Terin asked, rubbing his temple.

Graeson bit down, pain spiking through his jaw.

Ellie groaned, her features reddening. "I don't care what she is to you. What I do care about, however, is that your behavior endangers Medenia. If I cannot trust you, Graeson, we're out. We're done."

"My behaviors?" Graeson shouted, pointing a finger at himself.

"What happened?"

Graeson barely looked at Dani, for he could only handle one angry woman right now.

"Yes," Ellie said. Her hands sat on her hips, the tips of her ears red and stark against her white hair. "Do not play dumb with me, Mr. I-Can-Do-What-I-Want-Because-I-Think-I'm-A-Big- Shot."

With a huff, Graeson rubbed his chest in the spot where Ellie's long, pointed black nail had nearly pierced him, and for a split second, he wondered if she had drawn blood.

"*What. Happened*," Dani repeated, this time with more bite filling each word.

Graeson scoffed, "No one was ever in danger."

"Really?" Ellie tipped her chin up, cocking a brow. "Are you sure about that?"

"Yes," he hissed. "She doesn't know any of you are involved."

"Graeson, what did you—"

Terin's words were cut off when Sylvia interrupted, asking, "Kalisandre recognized you, didn't she?"

Graeson opened his mouth but snapped it shut only a second later, the lie unable to come out.

"Did they just say—" Moris began.

Dani cut him off with a sigh, saying, "Graeson, you didn't."

Graeson rubbed his jaw, the muscles growing sore from clenching it for so long. He looked at the others as they all stared at him, waiting for an answer.

His gaze fell upon the men resting against the front door. This wasn't his fault. At least, not entirely.

With a laissez-faire expression, Emmett stood with his hands in his pockets and his head against the door.

Graeson's lip curled. "She wouldn't have recognized me if Emmett hadn't failed at his job."

Emmett's eyes sprung open.

"What do you mean?" Terin asked, now standing with his arms crossed beside Dani. With his hair now past his ears, it was jarring how much he looked like Fynn.

Graeson straightened and tipped his head in Emmett's direction. "Ask him."

Emmett held up his hands in defense. "Hey, now! Don't go blaming me," he said as he pushed himself off the door with his foot.

He pointed a wandering finger at Graeson. "*You* were the one who ran off."

"Of course he did," Dani spat.

Graeson ignored her. "That shouldn't have mattered. You can hide hundreds of identities back at the cavern, yet you failed to hide *three* tonight!"

Armen scratched the back of his head. "I mean . . . my identity was—"

"Shut up, Armen!" Graeson shouted.

Armen threw his hands up. "Fine. Whatever. If you don't want my opinion, fine. I'm going to bed. Just try to keep it down, will you? Some of us like to sleep."

Sylvia stood to follow, mumbling something about not wanting to be involved in whatever mess they had created.

Ignoring Armen, Graeson returned his attention to Emmett, who was trying to sneak away. "We're not done here," Graeson said as he reached out to grab him.

Emmett ducked, slithering away from Graeson's reach. He rubbed his palms against his face, exasperated. "I already told you. It's a delicate business."

Graeson crept forward, but Dani and Ellie's arms simultaneously smacked him in the chest. He grunted.

"Three people, Emmett!" Graeson growled. "How is *that* a 'delicate business?'"

Emmett shook his head. Shoving his hands into his pockets, he meandered toward the couch, his lengthy body hunched over. Nearing the sofa, he spun around and began walking backward. He held up a finger. "First, the environment matters. I am at the cavern almost daily. Most of the people who come there are very familiar to me. Their identities, who they are—their general aurora, if you will—are easily recognizable. It's like seeing an old friend. Familiar, welcome, *easy*."

Graeson stared at Emmett, the incredulity plain across his face. "Again, you've hidden my identity before, Emmett."

The back of Emmett's legs hit the back of the couch. He shrugged, then plopped onto the dark red couch, rolling over the top of it and onto the cushions on the other side. He waved a hand in the air dismissively and threw up two fingers. "Second, the cavern is practically my home. I know it well. This—" he waved his hands in a circle in the air, "is completely foreign to me. Your identity would have been safely secure *if* you hadn't run off. Those walls . . . I don't know what it is, but there's something about them. They're thick, *mushy*."

"That doesn't even make sense," Graeson argued.

If he claimed that the castle walls were blocking his ability, they had bigger issues. Tonight was only supposed to be surveillance. Graeson wasn't even supposed to talk to Kalisandre. No one was. While she didn't know Graeson was working with the Tetrians, there would no doubt be an influx of guards. If Kalisandre revealed their presence to the king, their situation would become more complicated than it already was. Add Emmett's inability to keep their presence a secret, and it was almost impossible.

Emmett popped his head up and peered at Graeson over the couch, squinting in the flickering light from the lamp. "I never said it made sense. I'm just telling you how I see it." Emmett picked his teeth with his nail. "Like I said, if you hadn't run off or if you had asked me to go with you when you went gallivanting after your girlfriend, this wouldn't have happened."

Graeson's hands rolled into fists at his side as Ellie held him back.

"She is your *princess*, Emmett. Act like it," Graeson said, snarling.

Dani walked over to the couch. Leaning down, she stared at Emmett, then sniffed.

"What's she doing?" Medenia mumbled to Terin.

Terin shrugged, scratching the back of his head. "Your guess is as good as mine."

Unfazed by Dani's intrusion into his personal space, Emmett twirled his hands in the air and reached toward Dani. When Dani jerked back, something akin to a whine escaped Emmett's lips as he laid back down.

Turning around to face the rest of them, Dani leaned her hip against the couch and pointed her thumb over her shoulder. "The walls aren't *mushy* or whatever he claims. The bastard's drunk."

"Goddess above! You all are complete imbeciles!" Ellie shouted, throwing her hands into the air. She turned to the Tetrian princess. "Medenia, I do not care if they are our friends. We are going home. We are going home now before they kill us all!"

Medenia shook her head. "No, we are not."

"What do you mean we're not? We're *doomed*, Medenia! This whole plan of theirs was idiotic, to begin with, but now? They can't even keep it together for one night. And tonight was supposed to be easy, *simple*. We have this love-sick puppy over here—" Ellie pointed at Graeson, "and this other buffoon who can't even hold his liquor. Dani can barely stand straight. I mean, look at her; she's growing green already."

"Wine, actually," Emmett said, holding up a finger.

Ellie stared at him, dumbfounded. "Excuse me?"

"You said that I can't hold my liquor. I had no liquor," Emmett explained, popping his head up.

"Then why are you—"

"Wine, ladies. Sweet, delicious Frenzian wine." Emmett smiled a wide, toothy grin that wrinkled the corner of his eyes. How they hadn't noticed he was drunk in the first place was beyond Graeson. The man was utterly wasted.

"Dead." Ellie's head fell into her palms as she began to trace circles into the ground with her steps. "We're all dead."

Terin shifted on his feet, his gaze falling to the ground.

This was it then. The game was up. Graeson had failed yet again. Even if the Tetrian women didn't back out, Kalisandre didn't believe him. He could see that as clearly as the Glaciers in the Northeast. He exhaled, the breath long and shaky as he attempted to regain the little control he had maintained since his encounter with Kalisandre.

We will not leave her. She is ours.

At the sound of the god's voice, Graeson's jaw flexed.

Kalisandre is not something that can be claimed, Graeson spat back.

Graeson would not force her to listen to him. Because when she had been given the choice, she had chosen power over him. A crown over him. A title.

What is a title? A title is nothing when—

Enough, Graeson shouted.

The god within him growled. *Is it her choice when that bullheaded king has wrapped her mind around his little finger?*

Graeson tightened the locks on the mental door, but the god within him was right. Graeson would give up everything he had to save Kalisandre from Domitius. Even as foolish as it may have seemed to the others.

Perhaps it would have changed things if he had told Kalisandre the entire truth. But that wasn't what he wanted. Graeson didn't want her to choose him because of *what* he was but rather *who* he was. And this rescue mission was greater than his mother's vision. His feelings about Kalisandre aside, they could not let Domitius have her. If she became as strong as he believed her to be, there would be no hope for the coming war. Her manipulations thus far had been simple party tricks. There was more that she could do. Graeson felt it when her gift knocked on the door to his mind.

But he couldn't do that if his anger won.

He needed a distraction. He needed space.

The last thing he wanted to do was talk this out with the others. Inside the guest house, Graeson felt trapped. There were too many of them sharing this three-bedroom house. There was no privacy, not even a dark corner he could slink into and hide among the shadows.

Pushing himself from the wall, he grabbed his cloak from a nearby chair and threw it on.

"Where are you going?" Moris asked, concern bunching his brows together.

"Out," Graeson gritted out.

"Out?" Dani asked, pushing away from the couch, her hands falling to the side. "Are you serious right now?"

"Mhm," Graeson mumbled.

Dani rushed forward, slamming a hand against the door. "And where are you going to go, Graeson?"

Graeson brushed his hand through his hair, tugging at the strands. "I don't know, and I don't care."

Dani shoved him in the chest. "If you do something stupid—"

He tossed her arm off him. "I'm not going to see her. You can calm down."

"Then why—"

"Rescuing Kalisandre is not some foolish, lovesick mission of mine. Think about what will happen if she remains in Domitius' hold. Terin, think about what your great-grandmother did to Vaneria, her reach. Do we really want Kalisandre to get that powerful and be in the enemy's hands?"

Dani, Terin, Medenia, Ellie, and Moris stared at him, but they said nothing.

Graeson shook his head, huffing. He swung the door open, not bothering to wait for a response. If they wanted to doom the rest of the seven kingdoms, that was on them. He slammed the door shut behind him, but he didn't hear it crash against the frame.

"Go away," he growled.

"I don't think so, grumpy," Ellie said, catching up to him.

From the corner of his eye, Graeson peered at Ellie. He didn't want the company, but while many things about the Tetrian warrior had changed over the past three years, he knew one thing hadn't. Ellie would always do what she wanted.

THE EMPTY JUG slammed against the tabletop.

"Another?" the barkeeper asked.

"Yes, but this is the last one," Ellie said, a devilish smirk across her face. A few thin braids framed her face, the rest of her white hair wild.

"We will see about that," the barkeeper said, winking.

Graeson snarled beneath the hood of his cloak and watched the barkeeper walk back to the bar.

The walk to the tavern from the guest house was short. The night was still early enough for plenty of people to be out, their stomachs filled with piss-poor ale and wine. The last time Graeson had visited a tavern was before Kalisandre's choosing ceremony with Dani and Moris. The three of them were so full of hope that night. They hadn't known Kalisandre would be there that night, but when Graeson saw her, he recognized her immediately. He would recognize those blue eyes anywhere.

What he would do to have even half of that hope back.

"Oh, enough of that, you grump. He's just flirting. No harm in that," Ellie said, slapping him on the arm and bringing him back to the present. Then, Ellie gasped. "That's why you're all wound up."

"What?" His nose twitched, and he dropped his gaze, taking a slug of the ale.

Ellie gave him a knowing smile and wiggled her brows. "You were gone a long time, Gray. Your hair was a mess." She took a long sip of her ale. "As if someone was running their hands through it. Your neck has a new knick on it."

Graeson brushed a hand across his neck. He scratched at a bead of dried blood.

"What? Did you two have a little argument?" Ellie leaned over the table. "Did you at least make up afterward?"

Graeson snarled.

Ellie sat back in her chair, laughing. She took a swig and wiped the dribble of ale from her mouth with the back of her hand. "Of course not, because you wouldn't be here with me if you had."

Graeson was about to respond, but the barkeep approached with a jug of ale. Ellie reached for it, but the man pulled it back, just out of her reach. "What do I get for it?"

"If you're lucky, a copper." Ellie twirled the butter knife between two fingers and cocked her head. "But if you're unlucky . . ."

The man raised his hands in defense. "By the gods, lady. Can't a man have some fun?" he said, setting the jug on the table. He nudged Graeson in the shoulder with his elbow. "No wonder you're in a shit mood. Not all beauties are worth it, pal. Take it from me."

A feral noise vibrated in Graeson's throat, the edges of his vision turning red as he glared at the man from the edge of the cloak.

"If I were you," Ellie said with a saccharine smile, "I would walk away. If you think he's in a bad mood now, you don't want to see him in a minute if you touch him again."

The man's gaze flicked back and forth between them. "One fight breaks out in my tavern, and the both of you are out of here."

As the barkeep turned on his heel, he mumbled under his breath, "Weddings make people fucking crazy, I'll tell ya. Freakin' out-of-towners, no doubt."

The music swept across the tavern as a fiddler, a lutist, and a drummer played song after song upon the small raised platform. Loud chatter and dancing surrounded them.

"I told you this once already," Ellie said, leaning forward. "You need to be prepared for her to deny you."

Graeson grunted.

Ellie shoved the ale at him, the jug hitting Graeson's forearm. "Enough of the grunting and groaning already. You have barely said anything since we left the house."

"Hmm, maybe that's why I left in the first place," Graeson whispered.

"Ha! Nine words," Ellie said with a satisfied smile as she leaned back in her chair. "Come on, talk."

Graeson cracked his jaw. While the blood-red splotches had vanished from his vision, he knew the god inside of him was watching, waiting.

"So, what will you do if she says she doesn't want to come with us?"

He twisted the jug between his hands. "I've already told you. She doesn't have control of her mind."

"And that's for you to decide?"

Graeson squeezed his eyes shut.

Ellie placed a hand over his. "Look, I know you mean well. I know you only want to do right by her, but you must be prepared when she does not see it that way."

"We've been through this already," Graeson said, pulling his hand out from under hers and folding his arms over his chest as he leaned back in his chair.

"Apparently not enough." Ellie scooted her chair closer to him. "You practically ran out of there tonight."

"And?"

"And you have less than a week to convince her to leave with you. The chances of her going willingly are—"

"I know the chances," he spat.

"What will you do if she would rather stay?"

Graeson tightened his fist. "If that were truly what she wanted, then that would be that. But the fact of the matter is she does not know truth from fiction right now."

Ellie chewed on her lip. "Fine, but what happens when you can't fix her? What if . . ." Ellie sighed. "What if you're wrong?"

"I'm not wrong," Graeson snapped.

"And if she believes she was happier before? If she was happy here?"

"She's not."

"How can you know that?"

"Did you not see her tonight?" Graeson's fist smacked against the table, and the nearby patrons sent him wary looks. He ignored them and whispered, "She's withering away. They are *letting* her wither away into nothing. She is not meant to be some prized jewel, some pawn to be pranced around a ballroom. She is not happy there. If she stays there, she will never be happy. Her happiness does not matter to her."

"Then what does?"

Ice coated his veins, his muscles tightening. The music grew louder, and laughter filled the air. But all Graeson could hear was the fear in Ellie's voice, the incredulity.

"Her father's approval. That's all she cares about. She deserves to put herself first for once. That man—he does not care for her."

Ellie gnawed on the bottom of her lip, her brows drawing together. "Graeson—"

Graeson snapped his gaze away from hers because, at that moment, as his silver eyes stared into the pitch darkness of hers, he saw everything. His present, his past. Everything he didn't want to admit right now.

This was not the time for regret or worries. Kalisandre needed him first.

He stood. "We're not talking about this anymore."

"Maybe not here, but we will. There's more to this story."

CHAPTER 42
KALLIE

He's manipulating you.

They were the words Kallie had fallen asleep to, the words she had woken up to, and the words that repeated in her mind as the group of women babbled about tomorrow's hunt. She should have been focusing on conversing with the women of Frenzia, making friends and allies in her new kingdom. However, Kallie was too fixed on her encounter with the man she wished she could forget.

Had Graeson gone completely mad? She was the one who manipulated minds. *She* was the one who could distort reality and make demands of whomever she wished. Domitius couldn't do that.

Her father manipulating her? A preposterous claim.

Had Domitius tested her? Yes, but only to see where her loyalties lay. Had her father pushed her limits? Of course. How else would he have discovered Kallie's weaknesses and fixed them? Everything Domitius did was for the betterment of Vaneria. Everything he put her through was to make sure Kallie was ready for anything that came her way, to make sure she was prepared to rule.

Because that's what fathers did. They pushed, they challenged.

They did not manipulate.

Her nose twitched.

Clink. Clink.

Kallie's nails dug into her palm at the incessant, high-pitched noise of Tessa's spoon hitting the porcelain cup as she stirred her tea. Every minute, Tessa would follow the same pattern while she listened to the prattles of the other women: *stir, clink, slurp.* Only to pick up the golden spoon not even a minute later and repeat the cycle.

Clink. Slurp. Tink.

Kallie ground her teeth together, her head pounding from the pressure. While the men prepared for the hunt, sharpening their arrows and polishing their boots, Kallie was forced to sip tea, eat pastries, and gossip on the patio. Hearing the seamstress' voice in the back of her mind, Kallie took a small bite of the cinnamon pastry on her plate. It disintegrated to ash in her mouth.

"Princess Kalisandre?"

Shaking the intrusive thought of smashing the porcelain cup onto the floor, Kallie dragged her attention to the woman sitting across from her at the table.

As one of the prominent ladies of Frenzia and a seemingly close confidant of Tessa, Resenia visited the castle often. Her brilliant gold jewelry on her neck and wrists brought out the warmth in her brown skin and complimented her magenta dress.

"I beg your pardon?" Kallie asked.

Resenia cocked her head to the side and raised a brow in question. The thin, gold-rimmed glasses on the tip of her nose rose at the movement. "I asked if you were looking forward to tomorrow's hunt?"

Kallie smiled. "Of course. I cannot wait to see what the men bring home for us all."

One of the young ladies—Jocelin, Kallie recalled—coughed, spewing her tea onto the table. In her haste to grab a napkin, Jocelin knocked over the creamer, and the two women beside her jumped back in their seats, shaking the table.

Kallie cocked a brow, and the young woman's eyes widened.

"My apologies, Your Highness," Jocelin said, patting her lips with a napkin, her cheeks reddening. "I meant no offense."

Kallie took a sip of her tea. "Is there something I should be offended by, Jocelin?"

"Oh, uhm." The young woman looked around the table with a wary gaze. She began patting her dress with the napkin frantically. "It's just—" Jocelin cleared her throat, "has anyone told you about the hunt, Your Highness?"

"What do you mean?"

The woman opened her mouth, but Tessa interrupted, "Jocelin, perhaps you should go clean yourself up instead of talking Kalisandre's ear off?"

The tips of Jocelin's ear reddened as she winced. Standing, her knees banged against the table, and her teacup tipped over.

"Oh!" she shouted as tea soaked the tablecloth, the white fabric darkening as the liquid stained it.

"*Jocelin*," Tessa hissed.

Cheeks aflame, Jocelin mumbled, "Yes, Your Highness. My apologies, Princess." With her head down, she skittered out of the room.

An older woman who had been sitting beside Jocelin stood and turned to Kallie and Tessa. "Please excuse my daughter's clumsiness, Your Highnesses."

"Of course, Lucinda," Tessa said with a toss of a hand and a grimace.

After curtsying, Lucinda hurried after her daughter.

Before Kallie could ask for clarification about what Jocelin had meant about the hunt, Tessa returned her attention to Resenia. "I heard your daughter is opening a shop in the village?"

"Ah, yes." Resenia pushed the glasses up the bridge of her nose as she straightened in her seat. "Torince and I are very proud of her. Ryla is very excited." She sighed, the corner of her mouth pushing into a sad half-smile. "It is nice to see her excited." Resenia paused and fidgeted with the handle of the gold-rimmed tea cup. "Since the passing of her husband, we weren't sure if she was going to follow through with the plans, yet here we are."

Tessa reached a hand forward, nodding. "Yes, my sincerest condolences. It has been a hard year for many of us."

"That indeed. But at least my son-in-law's endeavors were not for naught. After all, you are here now, Princess Kalisandre, safe and sound."

About to take a bite of the pastry, Kallie froze, her brows knitting together as she stared at Resenia. "I'm sorry, Resenia, but do you mean to suggest—"

"Ryla's husband was one of the many soldiers who died during the fight to save you," Tessa said, interrupting Kallie. With her teacup hovering in front of her mouth, Tessa arched a brow. Kallie could practically hear the unsaid words on her lips: *he died because of you.*

Another person to add to Kallie's growing list of people who had sacrificed their lives because of her decisions.

Resenia shook her head. "So many of our young men died that day. War has not graced our lands for over a century, and now look at where we are." Her lip curled around the teacup as she took a sip.

Kallie's hand fell back onto her lap, lifeless and heavy. Everywhere Kallie went, death followed her.

"It truly is despicable," Tessa said in agreement.

"The Pontians have always been crude people," Resenia said. "What gives them the right to think they can just waltz into our lands and kidnap someone? It's preposterous!"

The other women hummed in agreement.

To the world, the Pontians were the villains in Vaneria's long history. Once, Kallie believed the same, but now her opinion of the island kingdom was skewed.

Tessa clicked her tongue as she picked up the porcelain cup with long, slim fingers. "It was only a matter of time."

"A matter of time for what?" Kallie asked, twisting the ring around her finger.

Tessa pulled the teacup away from her lips, swallowing. "Well, for another war, my dear."

"I heard"—Resenia leaned forward—"that one of their villages was utterly destroyed."

Tessa nodded. "Nearly."

Another woman, Gilliana, leaned forward, suddenly interested in their conversation. "I also heard that the Pontians were trying to commandeer the Prince's ship."

Kallie straightened in her seat.

"Oh! I believe I heard that too, Gilly." Resenia dipped a cookie in her tea. She took a bite, and crumbs fell onto her plate. "Didn't ten of those miscreants jump aboard before the ship left?"

"Ten? I heard *dozens* had," another woman countered, leaning back in her chair to join the conversation.

Beneath the table, Kallie's nails bit into her palm, the pain piercing.

Lies. They were all lies. There weren't dozens of Pontians that night. Only one. Kallie, however, did not say that. Instead, she did her best to refrain from shaking her head as everyone grew more and more interested in the conversation. Eager eyes bounced from woman to woman as they provided new tidbits of gossip and tried to piece together the story.

"Princess, you were there, weren't you? How many was it?" Resenia asked, leaning toward Kallie.

"How many?" Kallie asked, brows raised.

Resenia nodded. "Mhm. Put the rumors to rest, won't you, dear?"

She waved her cup in the air. "How many Pontians did our valiant soldiers have to fight off on the ship before you all could depart?"

Avoiding the women's stares, Kallie's gaze dropped to her cup. Raising it to her lips, she mumbled, "One."

Gilliana tipped her head to the side. "Excuse me?"

"Did she say *one*?" one woman whispered to another.

Kallie's heart rate increased. Her palms grew sweaty, and heat flushed her neck.

"Your Highness?" Resenia asked, eyebrows drawn together. "Are you sure? The soldiers said it nearly took all of them to get rid of them."

"Poor girl was probably too traumatized to remember," another woman whispered at one of the nearby tables. However, she did a poor job of keeping her voice quiet. "I heard she had fainted on her way out of the castle and had to be carried back to the ship. She must not know."

Tessa shifted beside her, raising her chin and pursing her lips.

An ice-cold shiver ran through Kallie's body. Her blood vibrated beneath her flesh. "I am not mistaken. There was only one Pontian aboard."

Clink. Metal hit porcelain, and a snarl sat upon Tessa's face.

"One? Are you sure?" Resenia asked, just as Tessa scoffed and said, "Impossible."

Ignoring Tessa's remark, Kallie cocked a brow and met Resenia's gaze. "Yes. I'm sure."

"Who could have possibly required that many people?" Gilliana asked.

Kallie took a deep breath and relaxed the muscles in her jaw before answering. "The Prince of Pontia."

Some of the women inhaled, the conversation coming to a halt. The clatter of dishes stopped. The only sounds that permeated the silence were the birds chirping in the nearby rose bushes.

"The heir?" Resenia asked after a moment.

Kallie nodded, swallowing the lump in her throat.

A few of the women gave Kallie odd glances. She saw the questions of why the Pontian heir would have risked his life for her flash across their features.

If only they knew.

"Don't worry, ladies. The prince got what was due to him." Tessa smiled, smoothing down her dress. "Sebastian made sure of that."

Kallie gripped the napkin, her nails testing its durability as they bit into the fabric.

Hurried footsteps sounded behind her.

"Pardon the interruption, Your Highnesses," Myra said.

Kallie's shoulders sagged slightly at the welcomed interference. She turned to face her handmaiden with a relieved smile. "Yes, Myra?"

"Your presence has been requested, Princess." Myra's voice was calm and polite, but her hazel eyes sparked with an intensity Kallie was all too familiar with.

Kallie's smile faltered. Her chair scratched against the brick pavement as she stood from the table. "Ladies, it has been a delight," she said to the women with a saccharine smile. Tossing her napkin on the table, she spun on her heel.

Myra's interruption was well-timed. Kallie had listened to enough gossip for one day. The women could say what they wanted about the Pontians, but she would not sit there and listen to them defile her brother's name.

Still, as convenient as the interruption was, Kallie did not look forward to the next conversation awaiting her presence.

"He's arrived, hasn't he?" Kallie asked as they strolled past the guards.

Myra nodded. "The king is waiting for you in your room."

Kallie forced the tears back that threatened to spill from the emotions the conversation with the women had stirred up. But no matter the mask she wore, the truth lingered beneath it.

Because of her, Fynn's death had been misconstrued and twisted. Somewhere nearby, Graeson and, no doubt, the others were waiting. For what? She did not know. She had not told anyone she had seen the Pontian. She still did not know what to make of his presence or their conversation. All Kallie knew was that she needed to hold on for a little longer. She couldn't let her guard down now, not with her father finally having arrived.

As the doors closed behind them, Tessa's voice floated on the breeze. "Please excuse Princess Kalisandre. She's still adjusting. You know . . . the *trauma*."

Myra wrapped her hand around Kallie's, and Kallie straightened.

"And they believed it?" King Domitius asked.

"Yes," Kallie said.

As Myra had predicted, Domitius was already waiting for Kallie in the queen's quarters. Instead of staying in the castle, however, her father led her out of the castle. He was silent the entire walk until they neared the castle's fence line. Now, the two of them walked along the edge of the castle's property with Myra and Lundril, the Captain of Domitius' personal guard, following in their wake. The others followed far enough behind to not hear their quiet conversation.

"Let us hope so," King Domitius said with hands folded behind his back.

The fog had still not let up. The Frenzian sky was dark and dreary today like it was every day. Kallie didn't think she would ever get used to the muted colors cast across the land. Even the influx of people in the castle halls and around the grounds did little to lighten the mood. Instead, the bright fabrics representing the kingdoms across Vaneria clashed against the dismal background. The icy blue of Ragolo, the forest greens and autumnal oranges of Borgania, and the sage green of Tetria were a stark contrast against the normal shades of red and black of the castle. It was as if the guests were trying to force life back into the kingdom, but the landscape was fighting against their efforts.

"Now, for your next task," Domitius said.

Kallie's gaze snapped to him. "Next task?"

He cocked a brow as he plucked a piece of lint from his collar. "Kalisandre, you are no longer in training. Everything you do must be calculated. Everything you say must serve a purpose." He jerked to a stop, staring at her with a cold expression. "We are building our future. If you are not ready to do that, then speak now."

Kallie wrung her hands behind her back. Taking in a deep breath, she rolled her shoulders back. "What do you need me to do?"

"That's better." He nodded and continued walking. "Now, before I tell you what I need you to do next, how are things developing with the young king?"

"Nicely," Kallie said. For the most part, it wasn't a lie either. Thus far, Rian had been receptive to her manipulations. Was he the man she wanted to spend the rest of her life with? No, but her father wasn't asking how her chemistry was with the Frenzian King, for that wasn't the purpose of the arrangement.

"What have you gathered about the knowledge they keep?"

Kallie swallowed the lump in her throat and inhaled. "The king spends a lot of his time researching."

"Researching *what* exactly?" Domitius asked, stopping once again.

Kallie spun the ring around her finger behind her back as she shifted on her feet. "Myths, legends, old histories of the kingdom."

"Like?" Domitius pressed, and enough irritation filled that single word that Kallie couldn't help but stumble when she spoke.

"He, uhm—Rian's been focusing heavily on the Frenzian histories. Many of the, uhm, texts are written in an old language that I do not know."

Domitius said nothing, only raised a brow.

"There was a dragon though in one of the books."

"A *dragon?*" Domitius asked, incredulous.

"Mhm." Kallie nodded. "He seems to be searching for the reason behind their disappearance. I think . . . I think Rian believes they still exist."

Domitius squinted up at the sky. Then with a huff, he continued walking. "So, the young king is interested in fairytales. Perhaps you and him are a perfect match after all. You also have been obsessed with those kinds of books since you were a child."

Hurrying after him, Kallie blinked as her jaw dropped, but she snapped it shut before he noticed.

"*Dragons,*" her father chuckled. "How ridiculous. I suppose it is a good thing that we are getting rid of him in due time. Now, if it had been his brother who sat on the throne instead, perhaps we could have worked with him." He flicked his hand in the air. "Sebastian is more . . . focused; his goals clear. He does not bother wasting his time with petty tales." He brushed two fingers across his beard.

Then, a slow smile spread across his face, and the blood rushed from Kallie's face, her stomach dropping. That look never meant anything good—not for her, at least.

"I suppose if once the king does fall ill, there is always the option of handing you off to Sebastian. We could spin a tale of how he helped you grieve your husband's death, and in that comfort, you found solace, companionship, love." He nodded, rubbing his chin. The smile grew wider, his brown eyes alit with satisfaction. "Yes, that indeed would work. Much less messy than killing Sebastian off as well—which you would no doubt have to do in order to protect your claim to the title. Unless that is, you were to get pregnant *before* the young king's passing."

Kallie's body grew cold, and a gasp escaped her lips. She had to have misheard him. Neither remarrying nor bearing a child had ever been a part of their plan.

"I'm sorry?" she asked.

But her father did not hear the faint words on her lips. He did not notice the way her skin had gone pale, nor did he detect that she had stopped walking.

Domitius marched forward, his plan taking shape on his tongue. "Yes. You will bear Rian a child, *then* you will get rid of him. If the people still question your claim after, the brother will be a solid backup plan. Don't you agree, Kalisandre?" He looked down at his side at last, and his brows quivered.

He looked around him, searching for her until they finally landed on where Kallie stood a few feet behind him, paralyzed.

Killing the king was one thing. Kallie had been prepared to do that. It would not have been easy, but she could have made it quick, painless even. But bearing Rian's *child*? The throne was supposed to be *hers*, not passed off to a child once they were of age.

Kallie didn't even know if she wanted children. Many people were more than grateful to have the opportunity to bear a child, to give someone life. But Kallie? Kallie did not know the first thing about raising a child. She was raised without a mother in her life. She knew nothing about being one. She had been trained to fight, to seduce, to manipulate. She had not been trained to raise a child, to care for another being. For years, she had been taking a tonic with her teas in order to prevent pregnancies.

Her teeth ground together, the pressure stinging.

"Kalisandre, keep up now, will you? We must discuss what I need you to do next." Domitius demanded, turning back around. He didn't wait for her to move but rather expected her to follow along—like she always had.

Kallie knotted her hands together behind her back, her feet immobile, rooted to the ground.

When she still hadn't moved after a moment, a gentle hand wrapped around hers, and the soothing scent of lavender filled the air.

"Kals," Myra whispered, squeezing Kallie's hands.

Despite everything inside of Kallie screaming at her to tell her father no, that she had not agreed to marry Sebastian or bear anyone's children, Kallie's mouth stayed sealed.

She shook the familiar voice that began to creep into the back of her mind. A whispered lie.

Her father was only making alternative plans, Kallie reasoned. They were simply options. He could not force Kallie to bear a child. He could not force her to marry Sebastian after Rian died.

With Myra's gentle hand guiding her forward, Kallie followed after him.

Together. They would deal with this together.

CHAPTER 43
KALLIE

"The hunt has been a long-standing tradition in Frenzia," Jacquin, the king's treasurer and eldest advisor, said to the large crowd standing before him.

An intoxicating energy buzzed in the open field as everyone awaited the start of the hunt. On the raised platform, a step behind Rian and her father, Kallie watched with a flat expression as a crowd of women and men wearing various shades of black listened with bated breath.

Early that morning, Myra asked Kallie if anyone had taken the time to explain what the hunt entailed. At the time, Kallie had brushed her off, saying, "It's a hunt. What is there to tell?"

Now, Kallie had wished she had entertained Myra's question more. If this were an ordinary hunt, the crowd would not have been nearly as excited as they were. Nor would the women have been wearing belts and straps around their garments. When Kallie was getting dressed, she had questioned the choice in apparel. But that, too, Kallie had dismissed with a shrug.

On the stage, Kallie stood clad in a black bodice. Light, sturdy plating had been sewn between the layers of leather. Atop the bodice was a unique piece of armor that Kallie had admired when she put it on. The Frenzian seamstress had collaborated with the most renowned blacksmith in Frenzia to create a custom piece for Kallie that showed off Frenzia's wealth and military stature. Having grown up in a castle, armor was not a foreign sight to Kallie—but armor crafted for a woman's body? Now, that was a sight to behold. The piece Marsinia and the blacksmith created wasn't as clunky as the Ardentolian soldiers' armor but instead moved with Kallie's body. It was a true piece of art.

Even in her training sessions with her father, Kallie never had the opportunity to wear any armor. Her father had dozens of weapons made for her—weapons that she hid beneath her skirts, in pockets that had been sewn into the inside of her jackets, nestled into intricate hairstyles. Armor specifically crafted for her, though? Definitely not. According to her father, women didn't wear armor, so there was no point in Kallie getting used to wearing it. While it was important for Kallie to be skilled in wielding a weapon, in King Domitius' mind, her true strength was her gift. The close-combat training had only been necessary to help Kallie get close enough to manipulate her opponents if required.

"A proper queen does not wear armor," he had said.

Which made Kallie wonder what her father thought of her now as he stood beside her.

They hadn't spoken since the other afternoon when Domitius arrived, but his plans laid heavily on her shoulders.

The two brothers stood before her, the two men who held the answers she sought.

Rian stood tall, his back straight, his hands neatly folded behind his back. Beside him, Sebastian held his head high. He, like Rian, was wearing all black. Unlike his brother, his stance exuded an arrogance that dared to be squashed.

A slight smirk slipped onto Kallie's countenance as she thought of how Graeson had bested him during the Last Dance and outmaneuvered the prince. But the smirk was wiped clean when she thought of the threat her father held over her. Kallie needed to prove to her father that the young Frenzian king was more valuable than his brother, that Rian wasn't just obsessed with fairy tales. With Rian alive and serving as her mouthpiece, she would use him to command the kingdom. The people would remain loyal to him and Kallie. There would be no need for heirs or second marriages.

She only hoped that Rian and whatever knowledge he held would be enough to sedate her father's thirst.

Domitius would get what he wanted, and so would she.

Kallie still had yet to inform anyone about the Pontian sighting, but it was of no consequence. There were dozens of guards out tonight. Graeson would have been foolish to try anything. If he were smart, he would be on his way back to Pontia.

At the front of the stage, Jacquin continued, "It is both a celebration of life and death. When two people take part in the marital rites, their old lives are set to the wayside as they embark on a new journey together. However, before two people marry, they must decide to choose one another. They must entice the other, charm the other, and form an everlasting bond with their chosen partner. The hunt represents the patience it takes to create these bonds, the cunningness to sway the heart, and, most importantly, the strength to keep those bonds strong." Jacquin glanced over his shoulder, and shadows slipped over his face as he turned away from the torches and looked toward the line of royals behind him. "King Rian has already captured the heart of the princess. She has chosen him. But the question remains: can she capture him? Can she tell him apart from the others?"

Kallie held back a snort, the resulting sound a mix between a cough and a gurgle. Her father peered down at her, annoyed.

"Ladies, please step forward."

Kallie's brows furrowed as she watched three dozen women step forward, most of whom were around Kallie's age, give or take a few years. Some of the women Kallie had seen around the castle, strolling through the gardens or lounging in one of the gathering halls. Others she had just met a day or two at the dinner or during the ladies' tea. She recognized a few women from the other kingdoms.

Rian cleared his throat, and Kallie glanced at him from the corner of her eye. He tipped his chin forward. Kallie scanned the crowd again, her brows knitting together.

In front of her, Jacquin held out a hand. "Princess, will you please join the women?"

Kallie stood momentarily frozen as she pieced everything together.

The woman's question at the tea, Myra's small interrogation, Jacquin's words—this was indeed not a normal hunt as Kallie once thought. What had Jacquin said? Something about Kallie being able to capture Rian? This hunt was not some extravagant display of raw masculinity but rather some frivolous test of a woman's loyalty and faithfulness. Yet the people in the crowd, women and men alike, all cheered, their excitement echoing in the forest behind them.

Her father raised an impatient brow at her.

"Of course," Kallie said with a small smile as she stepped forward and headed for the steps.

As she passed, the women gave Kallie a wide berth before they dipped into curtsies. Both pleasant smiles and jealous glares greeted her. And although Kallie now stood alongside the women, she wasn't one of them. She didn't belong among the Frenzian women, nor did she quite belong with the foreigners. Here, she was the future queen, not a lady of the court, guest, or hostess. She was something in between, something beyond yet further away.

Wasn't this the life she had chosen, though?

Once Kallie was settled, Jacquin moved on. "Now, the men—please gather here to the right."

A hoard of men separated from the crowd, grouping in the spot Jacquin had directed. Rian followed after them, tipping his head to his mother.

It was strange seeing Rian in the middle of the other men. He, like Kallie, had always been forced apart from the other people his age. He had been raised separate from his counterparts, always standing out, always something more. Yet, as Laurince whispered something into Rian's ear and nudged him in his side, laughter spilled from the king's lips. The smile hid the exhaustion that plagued his mind. It was sweet, innocent, joyful. A smile fitting for his face, a smile that made it appear as if he belonged among the crowd of young men.

Even more, it was an expression that reminded Kallie just how young the king was—how young *both* of them were. Neither of them was older than five and twenty. Yet here they stood: rulers of kingdoms—or nearly, in Kallie's case.

All the rulers Kallie had grown up around were older and more mature. They were serious and stern. She had learned to follow that path—to be cold and disinterested. It had become second nature when she was around her father or his advisors in Ardentol. Kallie had been led to believe that if one showed a trace of humor or enjoyment, they were not a serious leader and, as a result, could not be taken seriously.

So, Kallie had long ago shaved away those pieces of her. Hid them away when she was in the presence of rulers, staff, or citizens of her kingdom until she didn't even recognize those parts of herself when they snuck out. Kallie had become the version of herself they wanted to see: the meek, innocent princess who listened attentively, who held her tongue. Someone who could be trusted to remain in line.

Kallie once believed that to lead her own people, she would have to forgo the laughter, the jokes, the fun. But here Rian was, smiling and joking with his friends. When his laughter soared through the air, the thick noise reminded her of Fynn. It was a laugh that infected those around him, forced smiles on everyone's faces, and made everyone feel welcome and a part of some secret group.

Kallie bit down on her tongue to the point where water threatened to gather behind her eyes.

She was not them. She was not her brother or Rian. She could not afford slips in her demeanor. She had not been handed a crown. She had been raised to take one.

CHAPTER 44
KALLIE

A LAYER OF SWEAT COATED HER PALMS AS THE LIGHT FROM THE TORCHES licked the dark black metal in Rian's hands. The Frenzian men put on the helmets sitting on the table. Spikes lined the comb of the helmet and spanned to the front, where a dragon's head had been carved into the metal. Even from afar, Kallie could see the flames flickering across the scales carved across the dragon's metal form as its head and neck wrapped around the helmet. The nose and top jaw of the steel dragon formed the visor of the helmet. Within its mouth, sharp onyx teeth pointed down, protecting the men's faces while simultaneously swallowing them whole. The light bounced off the metal teeth as if the dragon were alive, preparing to spit fire. When Rian turned, Kallie's attention caught on a glittering blood-red ruby embedded into the dragon's eye that twinkled beneath the moonlight.

There was no doubt that the helmet was beautifully crafted. In truth, it was extravagant and fierce. Yet all the same, it made Kallie's stomach turn as the image of her father's bull helmet and the night that had haunted her dreams for over a decade surfaced. It had been weeks since Kallie had thought about that night, but now the memory was like a torrent inside her mind.

Suddenly, the armor felt too tight around Kallie's ribcage, squeezing the air from her lungs.

Laurince tipped his head back. The dragon's mouth pointed to the sky, and he shouted an animalistic howl into the night air. The other Frenzian men echoed his call, Rian included. The noise echoed in the air and sent the birds sleeping in the trees scattering.

Kallie's legs wobbled underneath the faux skirt, but she had nothing and no one to lean on in the sea of women.

Then, the men charged into the forest.

All but one, anyway.

With his helmet propped on his hip beneath his arm, Sebastian remained behind as the rest of the men disappeared into the shadows of the forest. Dozens of servants holding torches moved to flank Sebastian, creating a wall between the woman and the disappearing men.

Around Kallie, the women grew restless. They bounced on their toes, giggling to one another as they waited to charge into the forest after the howling men.

Sebastian's gaze scanned over the woman, and when it landed on Kallie, a slimy smirk slithered its way onto his face. The tick of his mouth sent an unwanted chill spiraling across the back of Kallie's neck.

"Ladies, I am sure you are nervous about walking into a forest alone at night. But please, rest assured. Our guards have monitored and searched these woods for the past week. The most dangerous thing you will come across in there," Sebastian said, cocking a brow, "will be us. But don't worry, if and when you meet one of us, we promise not to bite." He looked at Kallie and winked. "Too badly, anyway."

First, Kallie wanted to hurl; then, she wanted to stab him.

Kallie, however, was not the only one disgusted by the prince's words, for a woman beside her muttered, "Goddess above! I feel unfortunate for whoever happens upon him."

Kallie snorted, then instantly cleared her throat to cover it up, for she was keenly aware of her father watching her.

The woman inhaled sharply. "Did I just say that out loud?"

Sebastian continued talking, but his words slipped past Kallie unheard.

Kallie mumbled, "Mhm." Kallie glanced at the woman from the corner of her eye and recognized the Tetrian princess immediately. The top half of Medenia's pitch-black hair had been sectioned into three braids joined at the crown of her head and held together by a thin black rope. A white feather had been tied around a single braid beside her ear. She wore a black fur shrug connected by a leather strap around her shoulders.

Tetria was the only Vanerian territory where a queen had ruled since its existence. The only true matriarchy. When Kallie inquired about the queendom, her father had always found some reason to dismiss her questions. He had described Queen Cetia as a wild woman without morals, for she and the other Tetrians favored the goddess of femininity and motherhood, Nerva. Domitius had described their traditions and customs as being wild, untamed, and uncouth. He had described their castle as a mutilated thing infested with tree roots and pests. That alone was reason enough for her father, who thrived in his marble castle, to dismiss the queendom.

"My apologies, I had not meant—" Medenia began, but Kallie cut her off.

"No need to apologize. He is not *my* brother." If anything, Kallie was glad to know that at least one other woman in the crowd was not fawning over the Frenzian prince.

"Not yet, I suppose."

Kallie's stomach turned sour. Before she could respond, a pair of servants handed Kallie and Medenia a light wooden bow. Taking it, they inspected the weapon. While a bow and arrow was never her weapon of choice, Kallie did know how to handle one, even one this light and flimsy.

Meanwhile, Sebastian continued his speech as the rest of the women were handed bows, "Do not worry about hurting us either. We are not giving you real arrows. Giving an untrained person an actual weapon would be foolish. Our weapon's master has designed the arrows you will receive before you head into the forest only to stick to our armor rather than pierce it." Sebastian knocked a fist against his chest. "Now, ladies, I believe it is your turn to hunt. Good luck." Sebastian winked.

Somewhere nearby, a couple young women giggled, but Kallie's flesh crawled as Sebastian smirked at her. Kallie tore her gaze away from him as he donned the helmet and jogged into the forest.

Jacquin stepped into the space Sebastian had evacuated at the front of the platform. Clapping his hands together, he directed the women to form a line. Before the men had run off, Jacquin had informed them that the women would enter the forest one at a time after the men had ample time to hide in the woods. As the bride, Kallie would be the last to enter the forest to make it more challenging for her to find her betrothed.

Standing in front of Kallie in the line, Medenia glanced back over her shoulder and whispered, "A strange tradition, no?"

Kallie chuckled softly. Even though Kallie didn't know the Tetrian princess well, her aura was sweet and warm, comfortable somehow. Perhaps their shared titles connected them, the familiarity of bearing a kingdom's name on one's shoulders.

"If we're being honest," Medenia whispered as she shifted on her feet, "I would much rather go hunting for real, and I do not even eat meat. This fur isn't even real."

"Then why participate at all? You're a guest. Surely you could have opted out," Kallie asked, brows furrowed.

Medenia huffed, taking another step forward as the line continued to dwindle. "I would think you, of all people, would understand."

"Understand what?"

"One's responsibility to their kingdom and their parents. I am here representing my entire kingdom. I cannot simply bow out."

"Of course, but there should always be a choice."

Medenia tipped her head to the side. "Have you always had a choice, Kalisandre?"

Kallie knew what she *should* say—what her father would want her to say, yet the lie would not come out. She had been fighting to have a choice for her entire life. Up until now, she had lived under her father's rule in his kingdom. But was she not abiding by his rule even now? Obeying his every request? While she did not want to have Rian's children or marry Sebastian after Rian's death, would she be able to disobey her father?

When would she draw the line in the sand? When would she stand up for herself and choose her own path?

Her stomach twisted.

"We are led to believe that power, Princess Kalisandre, will grant us the ability to choose. But with power comes sacrifice, be it small or large."

Kallie pursed her lips. "So what have you sacrificed by participating in this hunt?"

Medenia tsked. "My humility, certainly."

"I, at least, am glad you are here. If only so I am not the only one who feels a sort of embarrassment from this trivial pursuit. However, . . ." Kallie grew silent, the question she wanted to ask hanging on the tip of her tongue as the women continued walking forward in the line.

Past the forest line, darkness soaked the earth. Giggles sounded from within as leaves rustled and twigs cracked.

Medenia's brows quirked up, creasing her forehead slightly, and her freckles scattered across her nose shifted. "However?" Medenia prompted.

Kallie cleared her throat. "However, if I am being honest, I did not expect you to be here at all."

Ahead of Kallie, Medenia shrugged, briefly looking over her shoulder. "It was a last-minute change in plans. I heard it would be an event of the century. I would be a fool to miss that." The corner of Medenia's mouth turned upward.

Kallie hummed in response.

Ahead of them, only one other woman remained in line, the rest having already run into the forest.

Medenia said, "I am truly grateful to bear witness to this week's events that will surely be remembered for lifetimes to come." Medenia stepped toward Jacquin and the servant.

As the princess waited for Jacquin to signal for her to head into the forest, she looked back at Kallie. Adjusting the fur shrug on her shoulders, Medenia said, "May you find who you are looking for, Kalisandre."

The Princess of Tetria winked, then strolled into the forest with the grace of a gazelle, the wind sweeping Medenia's hair back.

Stepping forward, Phaia held out the bundle of arrows to Kallie, but Kallie hesitated as she stared at the entrance to the forest.

"Princess," Jacquin said, ushering her forward. "May the gods guide you in your search for your king."

Kallie inhaled, shaking away her thoughts and taking the arrows from Phaia with a nod of appreciation. Then, she headed into the forest.

DARKNESS SURROUNDED HER. Twigs snapped in the nearby distance as the other women made their way through the woods, searching for their prey.

Kallie weaved a path through the dark forest and made a silent blessing to the gods for gracing them with a full moon. The dim light shone through the foliage above, lighting her path and preventing her from tripping over the fallen logs. As she held the flimsy bow and fake arrow, Kallie felt silly. A curved rubber piece had been attached to the tip of the arrows so that they could stick to the men's armor. And although the hunt was a farce, Kallie couldn't shake the sensation that something lurked within the forest.

Since she had seen Graeson, she had been on edge. Her father's backup plans only made it worse. Too much rode on this week. She needed to find Rian and prove to the rest of the world that their relationship was strong.

While Kallie did not believe Graeson would be so foolish as to come here tonight, she was not taking any risks. She kept her dagger strapped around her thigh. This time, if she saw him, she would not hesitate.

A scream from the left startled her, making Kallie jump. She crept closer, using the trees as cover. She didn't care if Sebastian said the guards had cleared the forest of dangerous animals. Kallie didn't trust a word the prince said. And she wasn't afraid of running into a deer. Far worse things lurked in the shadows of the forest tonight.

She peeked past the trunk and spotted a woman throwing her hands up, her bow discarded on the ground. She jumped and repeated the screeching sound that had initially startled Kallie.

Kallie's shoulders dropped.

A few feet away from the woman, a man stood with an arrow sticking to the bottom of his armor. He removed the arrow from his greave and tossed it on the ground before reaching up and taking off his helmet.

A wide, amused smile split across Laurince's face. "We're going to have to work on your aim, my lady."

The woman strolled up to him and smacked him in the chest. "Oh, hush, Laurince," the woman said. "I'm just glad I found you instead of some other bloke. Could you imagine if I had struck Sebastian instead? It was a good thing we planned ahead."

Laurince had never mentioned he was courting someone. Kallie assumed he was not since he had participated in the Last Dance. Then again, why would he confide in her? They rarely talked.

The woman threw her hands around Laurince's neck, and Laurince looked down at the woman. With a smirk, he murmured, "Oh, I'm a bloke now? Tell me how you really feel, Ferencia." Laurince wrapped his arms around the woman's waist.

"Make me," the woman said.

Laurince tightened his grip around her as he lifted her up, forcing a giggle out of the woman. Laurince gripped the back of the woman's thighs.

The heat in their locked gazes forced Kallie to turn away.

As Kallie continued the trek through the forest, the woman's statement rang in Kallie's ears. Why hadn't she and Rian planned a meeting spot? That would have been the smart thing to do, the logical thing. Instead, Rian kept the whole charade a secret, not even bothering to mention that she would participate. What good was hiding the truth when Kallie was supposed to find him among the rest of the men? How was she supposed to differentiate Rian from the others? The Frenzians wore the same helmets and armor, the same simple black trousers and shirts that faded into the night.

It was ludicrous. Madness, really.

She kicked a rock as she walked, sending it skittering into a nearby bush.

Walking deeper into the forest, more giggles bounced between the oak trees. Through the brush, Kallie spotted a man weaving between the trunks with a hurried pace. She tightened her grip on the bow. But as she continued to observe him, she knew his shoulders were too narrow to belong to Rian and loosened her grasp once more.

Not a minute later, a woman came sprinting from the direction the man had fled, shouting, "Stay still, you buffoon!"

The man shouted over his shoulder, laughter filling his words, "You have to be quicker than that to catch me, Draekina!"

Twigs snapped in his wake as he ran deeper into the woods. With a disgruntled groan, the woman picked up her pace and followed after him, a renewed sense of determination propelling her forward.

Kallie shook her head. She supposed the men still held some power in their hands, the ability to decide whether they wanted to be caught. Kallie only hoped Rian wouldn't want to drag this out longer than necessary like that man.

But where would Rian be?

She looked up at the treetops. A small spot among the leaves and branches was empty, revealing a crack in the starry night sky. And as she stared at the twinkling stars, she recalled a conversation she had with him one day in the library a couple of weeks back.

RIAN FLIPPED his book onto his lap, saving his page, and looked up at the skylight. "When I was a child and couldn't sleep, I used to come here in the middle of the night."

Kallie brought her gaze up from her book, tilting her head. "You had sleeping problems as a child?"

"Mhm," Rian nodded. "Still do."

"Me too." She didn't realize she had admitted that out loud until he looked at her, not with a look of sympathy but rather with understanding. Kallie folded her legs underneath her on the plush wine-red chaise.

Rian cleared his throat and returned his gaze to the sky. Dawn was coming, and the sky had begun to melt from dark navy to a rosy pink hue. "Losing myself in a book always helped clear my head, for the words on the page silenced the noise. Sometimes, I would get so lost in whatever fantasy I was reading that I was still here when the stars disappeared and morning arrived. While I no longer read fantasies, I still find myself wanting to chase the stars."

Kallie remained silent, unsure of what to say. In a strange sense, she understood what Rian meant. She, too, often felt like she was chasing dreams beyond her reach, beyond her control. Every time she came close to achieving one of them, something else got in the way, distracted her, and pushed the dream further from her grasp.

"Do you have a favorite constellation, Kallie?" Rian asked.

Kallie turned her head to the sky as though she could still see them through the sun's glowing rays. "Sabina's constellation is probably my favorite. I have always felt a sort of . . ."

"Connection?" Rian asked.

"I suppose," Kallie said, not wanting to say more, for she now knew the real reason for that connection. Sabina's blood, however diluted it was, ran through her veins, granting her the gift that made Kallie who she was. Clearing her throat, she tucked her folded legs tighter to her body. "What about you? Do you have a favorite, Rian?"

He was silent for a moment, making Kallie think he would not give her this one piece of information about him as though it was a closely kept secret. Then, at last, he said, "It is not as well-known as the constellations of the gods, but the Draconian constellation is my favorite. There's a story about my ancestors that perhaps one day I can tell you that draws connections to Draconian. So maybe that's why I have always found myself drawn to it. As a child, I often followed it to see where it would take me. It's to the right of Ryla's constellation and points to the east. Whenever I'm lost, I still feel myself following it."

The recollection of their conversation had Kallie catching her breath. Could it be that Rian had given her a hint? That he could be just as cryptic as she? Or was that wishful thinking?

Either way, right or wrong, she found herself heading east.

When she came across the large cluster of sequoias among the thin pine trees, she followed.

In the center stood the largest one, and the back of her neck prickled. It must have been the oldest tree in the forest, based on how wide the trunk was. The base was as wide as the main cobblestone street that cut through the village near the castle in Ardentol. Perhaps even wider. Her gaze ran up its trunk, where thousands of thick branches sprung. Walking along the edge of the trunk, she was careful to step over its wide roots. The bark was rough against her skin as she ran her hand across it and circled the tree. Then, halfway around the trunk, a hole the size of a tall child had been carved out of the tree. Kallie ran her palm across the edge of the hole. The edges were smooth, as if they had been there for decades. Had Rian found this place? Had he been the one to cut the hole?

When she peered inside, she found a set of stairs leading beneath the ground. A warm glow pulsed wherever the stairs ended.

Kallie chuckled. Of course, Rian would go somewhere to hide so that none of the other ladies could find him before she did.

Somewhere deep in the woods behind her, a crack of a twig sounded.

Better now than never, she thought as a victorious smile graced her lips.

After taking a deep breath, she ducked under the small entrance and descended the steps.

CHAPTER 45
GRAESON

Graeson's breath caught in his throat, his brows scrunched together as he leaned against one of the enormous sequoias.

Despite Graeson's outburst a couple of nights ago, the Tetrians had decided to stay. Medenia, with a strong chin and fierce stare, said they did not turn their backs on their friends. To which Ellie had added, "Even if they are stupid fools who are being led with their dicks instead of their brains."

Graeson had ignored her. This wasn't about that. It never was. Kalisandre would get her freedom.

So now Armen, Moris, and Graeson were in the woods, hidden among the shadows as women with flimsy bows and arrows chased after men like a fox would chase a rabbit. Graeson had been trailing after Kalisandre for a while. Finding her was easy. It was convincing her to leave that would be the challenge.

He hadn't expected Kalisandre to participate in such a ridiculous event willingly. But then again, if it meant she was one step closer to getting the power she wanted, Graeson supposed she would do anything.

But he definitely hadn't expected her to walk inside of a tree.

He pinched the bridge of his nose, praying to the gods that Kalisandre would turn around, that he wouldn't have to go after her. That he wouldn't have to follow her. Graeson, however, had not been in the good graces of the high gods for a while, had he?

With a long exhale, he pushed himself from the tree and headed toward the sequoia. Upon approaching, he eyed the small entrance in disgust and swallowed the lump in his throat. Graeson didn't fear much. To most, Graeson appeared fearless. His ability to close off his emotions helped him fight without restraint and mercy. While he did not enjoy the act of killing, the ability to separate his emotions prevented him from being paralyzed by indecision. Of course, it did not stop the onslaught of regret that followed. The need to act, however, was often more pressing than the need to think.

Sometimes, anyway.

Either way, shutting off his emotions never eliminated his fear of small spaces. He supposed there were some things he couldn't stop from feeling. And perhaps his claustrophobia never went away because the god within him hated small spaces, too. Perhaps, when Graeson was in a confined space, the monster within was reminded that he was limited to this human body, to this mortal world.

Still, Graeson reached inward and cracked open the door where he kept the god locked up. A sheet of ice enveloped him as a slim strand of the god slithered out. Graeson did not care for the sensation, but he called upon it, nevertheless. Inch by inch, the god crawled out as a part of Graeson was pulled into the god's cage. This was the price Graeson had to pay. A piece for a piece.

And for Kalisandre, he was willing to do anything.

He crawled through the hole in the sequoia.

THE SPACE WAS EVEN MORE cramped than Graeson had expected. Standing straight wasn't an option, so he crouched, awkwardly climbing down the steps. Whoever had carved this place out of the tree had not intended it to be a place for adults to access. It was as if a child had found the tree long ago and carved their way through the bark, creating a place to hide from others.

Little humans do like to hide, don't they? the god whispered in the part of Graeson's mind that they now shared.

Graeson, still conscious, groaned. His mind was crowded as the god fought for more control. When he shared the space during a fight, Graeson was distracted by the activity, but now there was nothing but a narrow walk space to occupy his mind. He hadn't lost complete control since he was a child, and he would not do so. Not when so much was at stake. As long as Graeson remained level-headed, the god could not slither its way out.

A light flickered at the bottom of the stairs, and Graeson could make out Kalisandre's shadow that was thrown along the floor at the base of the stairs.

He stopped walking and inhaled. When he exhaled, regret filled his senses as the air bounced back off the carved-out walls and warmed his face. His muscles strained as he tried to regain control of his limbs. The stairwell was too narrow, too cramped. Too warm.

The darkness had never scared him, not now or as a child. He thrived in the dark. In the dark, his ghosts disappeared. Under the cloak of darkness, he could release the demons he held within himself. Among the shadows, Graeson could breathe.

Graeson gritted his teeth and took tiny, slow breaths to prevent the air from suffocating him. The sweat on his back began to soak through his shirt. The air was growing thicker by the minute.

A cackle reverberated through his body as the god watched Graeson suffer, but Graeson saw through it.

A crash sounded from the bottom of the tunnel, followed by a screech.

Now, *human*, the god barked.

Teeth clenched, Graeson hastened down the steps.

The anger reverberated throughout his body as Graeson's tether to him loosened. A sickening feeling formed in the pit of his stomach. He picked up his pace. His heart pounded, his blood turned ice-cold.

Graeson prayed to the gods that his gut was wrong.

Do not pray to them. I am your god, the beast yelled from inside Graeson's mind.

When Graeson reached the end of the staircase, the last thing he heard was the god growl *mine* before his vision went stark white. And then the god burst through the cage, locking Graeson inside.

CHAPTER 46

KALLIE

Kallie should have known better. She should have known by his laissez-faire posture that he wasn't the king. She should have known when the room's aura had shifted the moment she entered. When the sweat beaded at the nape of her neck and tiny prickles spread across her skin.

The little voice inside her head told her to run. That if she turned around, safety would greet her. But Kallie hadn't listened. The hum in her chest had distracted her, thrown her off, and had her stumbling into the room.

When she had turned the corner at the bottom of the narrow staircase beneath the tree, a man wearing a dragon helmet greeted her. A man whom Kallie had believed to be Rian. He sat in the single wooden chair in the tiny room much too small for his body, his legs spread and a weathered book in one hand while he tossed a ball in the other.

She should have known then, but she hadn't. She hadn't suspected even when the man stood up from the chair with that stupid, egregious helmet still on.

She should have questioned him when he stalked toward her and shoved her against the wall with such brute force that was so uncharacteristic of the kind, quiet king she had come to know.

She should have done something, *anything*.

Instead, she stood there, mouth agape. Because Kallie had been wrong about so many people in her life, she could have been wrong about who the king was, too, when there were no witnesses.

At the very least, she should have known the moment he had spoken that the man before her was not Rian. His voice was all wrong, too sharp, too hungry. But Kallie had been distracted by the strange feeling coating her skin.

The realization hadn't struck until he had removed the helmet. The smug smirk on his face was too menacing, his eyes too green, the shade of red hair too bright. And by then, it was too late.

Sebastian's leg pressed against hers, his torso crushing her chest. The cage he created with his body inhibited Kallie from slipping out of his grasp, from fleeing as the iron helmet crashed onto the floor.

His hand hovered over her face a hair's breadth away, and a savage hunger darkened his irises. "Have you ever come so close to something—so close that it's right at your fingertips—yet you can't grasp it, Kalisandre?"

Sebastian's hand danced across her face without touching her and with a look of curiosity painted across his hazy gaze.

Kallie's brows furrowed. "Sebastian, what are you—" Kallie gasped.

He couldn't *touch* her. The command she had given him during the Last Dance still lived on in his mind.

She smiled, her head cocking to the side. "What's the matter, Sebastian?" Her voice cracked, but she pushed through it. "It's just the two of us. Now's your chance, isn't it?"

He ran his tongue across his teeth. "You see, that's just it." He wiggled a finger in the air as he leaned in, his breath smelling of whiskey. "There seems to be . . ." He paused. Confusion contorted his countenance as he thought of an explanation for why he couldn't lay a hand on her.

He shook his head. "It does not matter."

He pressed his leg harder against hers, and Kallie's grin dropped.

If her command was still working, how could he keep her restrained?

Her nails bit into her flesh. The command Kallie had made when they were dancing had been made in haste. Her intent had not been clear enough to be all-encompassing. The parts of him covered with clothing could still press against her. Only his flesh could not touch her.

Kallie's blood stirred, the gift rising. She opened her mouth. "You—"

He shoved the ball in her mouth, her jaw cracking as he forced her arms behind her back and used her body to keep them locked behind her.

"Ah-ah," Sebastian hummed against her ear. "Here's the thing, Princess. I find that I like you better when you're not talking."

Kallie struggled against his grasp. Saliva built in the back of her throat, but she couldn't swallow. She couldn't speak. When she tried, the ball vibrated in her mouth and only a strangled hum escaped.

His eyes darkened as they soaked her in. His teeth scraped over his bottom lip as tears began to pool in her eyes.

"Yes, just like that. See? You're perfect when you're quiet. When you *listen*." He cocked his head, tracking the tear falling from her eye. "My brother never was good at appreciating what fell in his lap. Ever since birth, everything has been handed to him: the crown, the favor of our parents, and now, you." He inched closer, the light scruff on his jaw scratching against her cheek, burning, as he brought his lips near her ear and whispered, "But he doesn't have you yet, does he?"

Kallie jerked forward, but Sebastian pressed his forearm against her throat, forcing her head to the wall and restricting her airflow even further. "That's right, fight me. I don't like it when they're too eager, too . . . *easy*."

Kallie glared at him behind a water-filled stare as she tried to figure a way out of his grasp.

With the fabric between them granting him a loophole to her command, his other hand fell to her waist and ran up her side, bunching up the fabric of the skirt.

"It would go against my vow to the *king* if I didn't inspect the goods before he was handed them." Sebastian's breath was warm against her throat, suffocating. "What do you think, Princess? Shall we see just how perfect my brother claims you to be?"

The blood in Kallie's veins buzzed with anger. She hated this man. With every fiber in her body, she hated him. Her gift rose like a tidal wave, and Kallie pulled at it, tugged, begged for it to rise. It flowed through her body as though it was eager to be used, as though it had sensed the danger she was in and yearned to protect.

Kallie tried to speak around the gag again, but Sebastian pressed his forearm against her throat. Harder, rougher. Without the ability to speak, she couldn't command him. She couldn't manipulate him. More tears threatened to slip. Yet despite everything else, she was thankful for two things at that moment: the first being that Domitius had taught her how to fight *without* her ability, and the second being that Sebastian had too large of an ego to think a woman could best him.

Popping her shoulder out of its socket with no more than a grimace, Kallie slipped her hand out from behind her back and reached for the opening in the fabric at her waist. Her fingers brushed against the leather strap, and she unclasped the hidden dagger.

Obscenities poured from Sebastian's mouth as she drove her dagger into his thigh.

Once Sebastian released her, Kallie removed the gag with shaking hands, keeling over as she inhaled. She struggled to regain control over her breath. But as Sebastian bent over to pull the dagger out, adrenaline soared through her body, and she charged forward.

She grabbed him by his shoulders and kneed him in the groin. He groaned, folding over again. He tried to recover, but Kallie didn't give him the chance and struck, her fist smashing into his jaw. He spat blood onto the floor, and anger colored his face.

With the back of his hand, he wiped his mouth. "So the princess can pack a punch, huh? Now, what will my brother say about that?"

"The king's opinion on the subject does not matter," Kallie sneered, her voice as coarse as sandpaper.

"No? But what happens when he finds out you're not the person he thinks you are?" He stepped forward, blood smeared across the back of his hand. "You see, if it were me, I would welcome the challenge, the fight. But my brother, ha." Sebastian laughed and reached for the dagger again.

Kallie balled her hand into a fist and steadied her stance. But as she went to strike, Sebastian hit the floor before she even moved. Her mouth fell open, gasping. Kallie didn't need to see his face to know who was now sprawled on top of Sebastian. She would recognize him anywhere.

"Graeson?" Kallie gasped. Swallowing, she touched her throat, which was still swollen and dry. "What are you—"

The words escaped her as Graeson looked over his shoulder. His eyes were the brightest shade of silver she had ever seen, nearly white. His ordinarily calm demeanor had vanished, and a feral snarl was plastered across his face. The Graeson Kallie knew was nowhere to be seen.

Sebastian wiggled beneath Graeson's hold. "Get off me, you bastard!"

Kallie stood paralyzed as Graeson forced his focus back on Sebastian. He lifted Sebastian off the floor by Sebastian's shirt.

Graeson hovered near the Prince's ear. Kallie, however, couldn't hear what he said, the words too quiet.

Sebastian released a mangled laugh. With an amused grin, he said, "She belongs to Frenzia now."

Graeson chuckled, the noise feral and animalistic. The sound alone should have made Kallie turn away or at least should have sent a shiver of terror zipping down her spine, but it didn't. And that was more nerve-racking than anything.

"You do *not* touch her," Graeson spat, throwing Sebastian back against the floorboards. Then, he struck, hard and fast, his fist smacking into Sebastian's jaw.

At the ferocity with which Graeson attacked, Kallie didn't know what she was more afraid of, the strength Graeson was emitting, her father losing his mind if the captain died here today, or her creeping desire to watch and sit through until the very end.

One thing was for sure: she needed her dagger back.

However, when she looked at Sebastian's thigh, the dagger was gone. Her hand fell from her neck, limp. Had Graeson grabbed it after he forced Sebastian to the ground? She couldn't recall. Everything had happened so fast.

Sebastian coughed, spitting a combination of saliva and blood onto the floor. The prince tried to fight back. He tried to force Graeson off him, but he was quickly weakening. He was losing this fight. He knew it, Graeson knew it, Kallie knew it.

Then, the light from the torch hanging on the wall bounced off a piece of metal near Sebastian's hand, and Kallie didn't think. She tumbled across the floor and reached for Sebastian's wrist, twisting his arm.

A sharp *pop* sounded. Bone snapped, and the dagger slipped from Sebastian's grasp. It clattered onto the floor as Sebastian hissed from the pain shooting up his arm.

Meanwhile, Graeson continued to throw punch after punch. With each strike, Kallie's heart rate increased as her father's words cycled in her mind. And she hated to admit it, but she needed Sebastian alive.

She crawled forward and knelt beside Graeson. Sebastian's gaze was unfocused, lazy. His eyelids fluttered as he tried to keep them open, but he was losing consciousness. And quickly.

"Graeson," Kallie said.

Graeson, however, made no move to stop.

"*Graeson,*" she repeated. She touched his shoulder, and he flinched. Kallie bit down on the inside of her cheek and steadied herself, forcing the strength back into her voice. "*Enough,* Graeson."

With his fist in the air, ready to strike, Graeson froze. As he looked over his shoulder at her, his eyes narrowed as if he didn't quite trust her. And he shouldn't. He never should have.

Right now, *he* was not her concern, though. The man beneath him was.

Her gift hummed as her fury rose inside of her. "He's *mine* to deal with," Kallie said through clenched teeth, her fist pressing into the ground.

Graeson looked her up and down, and his lip curled. "So be it, little mouse."

He leaned back, but his legs remained atop Sebastian, holding him down. Kallie knew Graeson's efforts were pointless, for Sebastian was going nowhere with his body limp and battered.

Still, the prince was alive, and that was what mattered. His breathing was shaky, but he still breathed. He would not die, not today. Kallie had made sure of that.

Death would be too easy for him anyway, too quick of an end for everything he had done. For the way his gaze always lingered too long on her body, for the way his hands roamed too freely when they were dancing.

Now, she only had one other thing to do. She reached out, fisting his ginger hair in her hand, forcing him to look at her. Her gift sang at the base of her core, hungry. Just as hungry as Sebastian was when he fought Fynn, when his thirst for blood was palpable.

Kallie tipped up her chin, quirking a bow, and released the command. "You will forget this fight. You will forget coming down here. You will forget what you tried and failed to do to me tonight."

Her voice became steadier and stronger with each pull of her gift. She was not powerless. Even when her hands were tied or her voice was taken away, she was never powerless. And as she commanded the captain of the fiercest military in Vaneria, she reveled in the power, in her gift. Kallie would never let someone take this feeling away from her. She would never let them take her voice away again.

The faint haze slithered across Sebastian's green irises just before his eyes rolled over.

As her gift flew through her, a fire within her blazed, and its flames begged to be coaxed, to be fueled with more anger. And Kallie questioned her decision to let him go. Because this? This wasn't enough. It wasn't enough to stop here and let Sebastian wake up in the morning.

Fynn never got to wake up.

Fynn hadn't been able to carry on.

Fynn was dead because of *him*.

Sebastian didn't deserve a false peace, a false victory. Fynn deserved better, and Sebastian deserved so much worse.

Her fingers wrapped around her dagger, quickly finding their natural place on the worn leather handle. The right corner of her mouth tipped upward, a malicious grin forming. Eyes blazing, the fury pushing her forward, encouraging her. She reared her hand back and—

"Kalisandre?"

CHAPTER 47
KALLIE

The dagger fell from Kallie's hand as she swallowed the curse on her tongue.

Please, gods. Tell me I'm wrong. Tell me he's not here.

But no prayers could change what she saw.

Rian's hair was a mess, dark scarlet strands going every which way with no sense of direction. The iron dragon helmet was tucked beneath the crook of his elbow, his chest rising and face flushed. Confusion and hurt contorted his features as he looked at her, then at Graeson, who still sat atop Sebastian, and at last at the dagger clattering on the ground.

In one fluid movement, Rian pulled his sword from its sheath. "Kalisandre, get behind me," Rian ordered, the authority of a king and a protector backing his words.

Kallie, however, hesitated, her gaze flicking between the two men.

The flames that had coursed through her veins only a moment ago began to shrink, a coldness replacing it. She didn't want the fire to go out. She didn't want to go back to holding back, to pretending. It felt too good to release her control over it. Too good to reign the monster that she was back inside.

Graeson exchanged glances with Kallie. The rage was still evident in his silver irises, but his face was controlled and showed no emotion otherwise. Slowly, he held up his hands, his knuckles bloody and bruised, as he stood. Sweat glistened across his palms.

As Kallie stood, she kept her hands low.

It was all over. She had ruined everything. Weeks spent building trust between her and Rian wasted. A thread that needed constant coaxing, a thread of trust that was as fragile as the glass panes covering the wall of the Ardentolian castle. Only a day and a half before the wedding and Kallie had ruined it.

The crown had been at her fingertips, but now Rian had seen too much.

Perhaps Sebastian was right. She did know about being close to something before it disappeared from her grasp.

There was only one option.

"Kalisandre," Rian warned, his voice taking on a sharp edge. "Now."

Then realization struck.

Rian thought *Kallie* was the one in danger. He thought the dagger she had held in her hand was meant for Graeson, not Sebastian. And why would he think otherwise? Why would he believe that his *brother* was the one who had put *her* in danger? Who had tried to . . .

Kallie swallowed the lump forming in her sore throat.

Rian didn't know who his brother was. Even when they trained together, he didn't recognize the hatred that fueled Sebastian's punches, that kept him from holding back. Rian didn't know the predator lurking beneath Sebastian's skin. He didn't see Sebastian's jealousy or the fact that his brother strived for more. He didn't know that Sebastian wanted the crown, the title, the power. *Her.*

Rian believed Graeson to be the monster. And while Kallie had seen the beast that resided in Graeson, she also knew that even though Graeson might hate her, might even flinch at her touch, Graeson was *not* the villain here.

Sebastian was.

She was. But never Graeson.

She saw the question in Graeson's silver gaze. Kallie could not give him the love he wanted. She *couldn't* love, for it was not written in her blood.

And Graeson was only a man, a soldier. Not a king. Although he fought with the strength of ten soldiers, he could not give her what she wanted, what she needed.

She turned to Rian, who extended a hand with a wary eye still on Graeson. But Rian was looking at the wrong enemy. He didn't even realize that he was reaching out to the person who would betray him once she had what she came for. He was too naive, too ignorant. And for a moment, Kallie felt sorry for the young king.

But only for a moment.

Kallie grabbed his hand, and Rian shoved her behind him, shielding her with his body. She gripped the back of his shirt, fisting the material in her palm as she peered around him. She met Graeson's gaze one more time, and her chest ached as if she was ripping off a piece of herself by going to Rian.

Even though she might not be able to go with Graeson, she could at least give him one thing.

A chance to escape.

"Go," she mouthed.

Without confirming he listened to her command, Kallie stood on her toes, her mouth inches below Rian's ear. Her gift was still strong, no longer weak from a single use, and she released another command.

CHAPTER 48
GRAESON

INSIDE GRAESON, A BATTLE RAGED ON. EVERY PART OF HIM WAS ON fire, burning him from the inside out as the god tried to regain his control. Graeson was barely holding on, and that single word that left Kalisandre's lips did nothing to help the situation.

Didn't Kalisandre understand that he didn't need saving from a king who could barely hold a blade?

What he really needed saving from was the thread of fate that was now disintegrating before him.

The blood running in his veins urged him to stop her, to beg her to choose him. It ached for her as the invisible threads that kept them connected unraveled from one another, inch by inch.

Did she not hear it? The tearing of their connection, the screaming of their gifts? Did she not hear the song that hummed in their very bones?

If Kalisandre did, she showed no signs of it.

Was this Domitius' control on her at work? Did it somehow block the connection? Block her ability from reaching its full potential? Graeson couldn't help but wonder if that was the case.

But when their gazes had met, when he had taken that bastard to the ground after Sebastian had dared touch her without her permission, there was something there. Kalisandre was still in there. *Somewhere.* Her mind wasn't completely lost. He knew that like he knew his soul. And yet...

Graeson slammed his eyes shut. But being unable to see Kalisandre did not prevent her words from ringing in his ears or prevent the image of her from surfacing in his mind. The look she bore, the idea of her shrinking herself for this king, was painful enough. He didn't need Kalisandre to confirm his worst nightmares out loud, too.

"You will let the man go unharmed and forget he or Sebastian was here. You found me here alone, waiting for you," Kalisandre whispered in the king's ear.

It was as if Kalisandre had driven that pretty little dagger of hers through his heart, twisted it, and then pulled it out without any care in the world about the blood that poured from his chest.

Rian's body straightened. The king's anger rushed out of his body, replaced by an eerie blankness. Graeson had seen Terin react the same way when Kalisandre had practiced her manipulations on him. But Kalisandre wasn't just commanding Rian. She was granting Graeson the safety to pass, the ability to walk away without a fight.

That was the worst part. He couldn't fight his way out of this. He couldn't release his anger through brute force. Instead, it festered in his mind. It inflated his lungs, filled his veins.

Kalisandre didn't have to walk into Rian's arms. She could have chosen Graeson and returned with him, but she didn't. She chose a crown over him.

The god's rage bubbled at the edge of the surface, and Graeson was tired of fighting it. The previous scrap with the prince had already worn him out. His internal walls were weak, the hinges on the god's cage nearly broken.

And then there was the god's whisper that slithered across his consciousness: *blow out the flame.*

Graeson inhaled, letting the oxygen fill him. Cold dirt, blood, and lavender lingered in the air, mixing around him. When he exhaled, he let go of everything.

CHAPTER 49
GRAESON

GRAESON COULDN'T FEEL HIS LIMBS OR SEE HIS HANDS IN FRONT OF HIM. *The darkness was too thick, heavy, and all-consuming.*

This . . . This can't be right, he thought as he squinted into the shadows.

His stomach twisted. He keeled over, retching, yet nothing came up. Graeson was no longer in control of his body but inside his mind, locked behind a steel door. He crawled to it, or at least, he thought he did. He couldn't tell in this state, for his body was only a figment of his imagination. Something he conjured up to make sense of the situation.

Graeson had never had his entire consciousness locked inside of his mind before. Whenever he had released the god in the past, he had always been careful not to exchange too much of himself for the god's aid. But this time, he had gone too far. This time, his entire soul had been ripped from his body and forced inside the god's cell within Graeson's mind. Now, Graeson understood the god's fear of small spaces.

On the steel door, there was a single window. When Graeson peered through it, anger surged through him and filled the small cell. He pounded his fist against the wall, watching the scene unfold through the god's vision.

It's my turn now, the god sneered.

Then Graeson was thrust back, the window slamming shut. And for once, Graeson found no solace in the darkness that surrounded him.

It was time the god had a chance to play with the mortals.

The god looked down at the woman who should have been his. He had half of a mind to rip her away from the pretend king, but then he heard the banging.

It seemed the mortal did not enjoy his new accommodations, but the change in ownership was for the best.

Fucking humans, the god thought as the human screamed inside of him.

You wish what is ours to be taken from us? So be it. He growled at the man inside of the cell. *We will leave the woman with this masquerade of a king. After all, humans do learn best when they make irreversible mistakes. So let us see how she fares. Let her see the consequences of her own actions.*

And then, the god turned his back on the woman whom the human had fought for his entire life, whom the god had been promised.

As he walked through the narrow staircase, he felt nothing. His throat didn't clench up; his skin didn't perspire. His jaw didn't ache. He felt nothing as whispers crept up from the tiny dwelling beneath the tree.

The god had spent decades inside of that mental box. The human could handle a few hours or days.

He was done playing this game of cat and mouse. The woman would be his as she was always meant to be, but he would not beg. He would not grovel at her feet like the man wished to do.

Taking her now would be too easy. This king's death was not the one the god craved. He wished for destruction, chaos. And right now, he would not get it.

The ounce of freedom the man would give the god when his assistance was required was insufficient. Those moments were nothing more than a tease, a fleeting escape from the torment of the cell that the man kept the god locked in.

It was time the mortals remembered what happened when they invoked the wrath of a god.

"You had your chance, and you blew it, Graeson. Admit it." Sitting on the dresser, the woman—Danisinia, the god recalled from his time inside the man's mind—swung her feet in the air as she gripped the edge of the dresser.

The god sighed heavily as he stood across from Danisinia in the corner of the room. She was a talented warrior, and he could have appreciated that *if* she wasn't so agitating. Especially when, in the back of his mind, the human hissed that her words were supposed to strike him in the gut. That they were supposed to make the god experience some emotion.

Guilt? Pain? Sadness? Anger? The god did not know. Nor did he care.

He was numb to it—all the mortals' screams and shouts. It was as if a blanket of darkness coated every inch of him.

It was pure bliss. He hadn't experienced this much control in years.

He peered out the window through the small gap in the curtains and scanned the area. This world was so simple. For the last five and twenty years, he had only been able to see bits and pieces of the world.

After he had left the woods, the god had taken his time returning to the guest house. He had wandered the woods for hours, enjoying the wind brushing against his cheek, the ground beneath his feet. He became a part of the darkness like he was always meant to be. The shadows of the night molded around him, called to him, beckoned him. And he welcomed them with open arms.

By the time the god had made his way through the forest and to the guest house, midnight had come and passed. Kalisandre's manipulation must have worked since none of the guards seemed to be on alert as he traveled through the shadows of the village. He was not surprised. His little mortal was capable of many things. Manipulating one man was only the beginning. If only she let her mind free, she would see all that she was capable of.

It also gave the god some satisfaction that she had not betrayed him. She had kept quiet about seeing him. She might have been in denial about the existence of the thread that connected them. But despite her tangled mind, she was still in there.

When the god finally strolled through the front door, everyone had been sitting in the foyer. Waiting. The other mortals who had accompanied the man into the forest had already returned hours ago.

The god didn't need to say anything when he walked through the doors. Once the others saw that Kalisandre was not trailing behind him, they knew that the man had been unsuccessful yet again in convincing their mortal to return with him. But that was only partly true.

When they asked what had happened, the god reluctantly explained, for he knew all too well from watching the human man that they would not stop asking questions until he explained. Once he relayed the night's events, the god leaned back against the wall, letting them take over.

"I'm sure it was more complicated than that," the sweet woman with pitch-black hair said from the couch. The black leathers she had worn earlier had already been replaced with a simple nightgown.

Part of the god felt he should ask her how it went, but that part was small, infinitesimal. A natural reaction for the human, but for him? No, he didn't have the patience.

"Prince Sebastian is a prick, after all," the white-haired one said with a shrug.

For once, the god agreed.

"Complicated or not, you failed, Graeson. That was our last chance of getting in and out without being seen. It was the easiest chance we had, and you blew it," Danisinia said as she gathered her braids together, gripping them in one hand.

He shrugged.

He didn't have time for these dramatics. Who knew when the human would force his way out and push him back into that cell? The man was exceptionally strong-willed for a human. Until that moment came, the god did not wish to waste time by talking.

"Did you not hear me? You failed."

She won't stop, the man caged within said with a sigh. The god could feel the man's exhaustion creeping in, the annoyance lacing his words.

Fine, the god grumbled back. *I will entertain them for a moment.*

The god pushed himself off the wall. "I do not recall asking for your opinion on the matter."

Not what I meant, the man said.

"Do you think I care if you asked for my opinion or not?"

The god opened his mouth, but the man started pounding on the door, his anger seeping out.

They can't know, the man shouted.

Oh, so we are keeping me a secret now, are we? The god smirked.

"You know what, Graeson? If you don't want to admit it, fine."

Danisinia crossed her arms over her chest. "What's your backup plan?"

"I do not need a backup plan."

Danisinia scoffed. "Well, you shouldn't *need* a backup plan, Graeson, but here we are." She threw her hands out.

"Have you forgotten why we came here?"

"No, but it seems you have," Danisinia said, hands on her hips.

Huffing, the god began sharpening one of the gleaming scimitars on the table. "We came here to teach them a lesson, did we not?"

Danisinia's hands fell from her hips.

"We came here partly to save Kalisandre, but that was not the only reason." He took a step toward Danisinia, who lifted her chin in challenge. "Domitius thinks he is untouchable, that he has won. We must show him that he is wrong."

"So we're moving to Plan C then?" the man with the buzz cut said as he bounced on his toes.

A malicious smile crept up on Danisinia's lips.

The prince stepped forward. "Dani, are you sure you are well enough?"

She waved Terin's question away. "Sylvia?"

The red-headed Pontian sitting in a rocking chair perked up. "Am I finally going to do what I came here for?" they asked, a mischievous glint sparking in their eye.

The god smirked. "I think it is about time, don't you?"

"Fuck yes!" Sylvia shouted, punching the air. They stood from the chair, sending it rocking back into the wall with a bang. "I'll go get my things!"

"Things? What *things*?" The white-haired woman shrieked, her head swiveling back and forth.

"Wait! Hold on," Terin said, holding out his hands, and Sylvia skirted to a stop before they rounded the corner leading to the cellar.

"What in the god's breath are you talking about? If Kalisandre isn't with you—"

"It does not matter," the god said.

"Doesn't matter?" Terin asked. "But if we go with this plan—"

The god shook his head, cutting off the prince. "No more waiting. No more hiding."

The room grew silent as Terin and the god exchanged glances. Terin's hesitation was palpable, but they both knew what had to be done. They did not come all this way to do nothing. They had seen what the Frenzians were capable of creating in the forest. The creature that was a poor recreation of the dragon's the original gods flew down on.

"Terin?" Medenia turned to the prince, breaking the silence. "Are you sure about this? Do you realize what you all will be starting?"

Terin shifted on his feet, his gaze sweeping over Danisinia and the god. Hesitation flickered in his eyes. But when Danisinia looked at him with a combination of eagerness and sorrow filling her countenance, Terin straightened. "Yes, I'm sure. Domitius has taken too much from my family to let him get away unscathed once again."

"Finally!" Sylvia groaned before running down the steps leading to the cellar.

Shortly after the door to the cellar slammed shut, banging echoed beneath the floors, and the god smirked. He could almost taste the revenge on his tongue, the havoc that would soon ensue.

Medenia sighed, but she did not shrink away. She would not abandon them, for the Tetrians had known what they were signing up for from the beginning.

"Wait," the feisty white-haired warrior said, having stepped forward. "What's that in your hands?"

The god held up the helmet. "The prince's helmet."

Euralys took the helmet, turning it in her hands as she examined it. She passed it to Medenia, and one by one, they each looked at the helmet. When Danisinia held it, her top lip curved into a snarl as she examined it.

Danisinia placed it on the table. "We have one more chance. But if we help Kallie and she decides to return to them, what then, Graeson? If you have all these plans, what is your plan when *that* happens?"

"Let me deal with her," the god said, lowering his voice.

"Yeah, because that has worked great for us so far," the blond-headed pretty boy mumbled as he sat on the couch.

The god snarled. "The past two times we have infiltrated the castle were simply to test the castle's defenses and get a lay of the land. It would have been too easy to snatch Kalisandre tonight."

"Sometimes I like easy," the blond man mumbled.

"You would," Euralys said with an irritated sigh.

"Graeson," Danisinia said as the god made to slip past her, fingers snapping around his wrist. "You need to be prepared for the worst. She is no longer the girl we used to know."

He shook her hand off him.

Dani grabbed his chin, forcing him to look at her. Her fingers smashed his cheeks together, and the tips of her nails dug slightly into his skin.

How dare she touch me.

"What is wrong with you?" Danisinia asked.

The man's anger rose inside him, and fear laced each strike against the cell's door. *If you lay a hand on her—*

Do not worry, little human. I will not harm your precious friend.

"Nothing," the god said, the syllables mushing together.

Danisinia jerked his head forward. "What did you do?"

The god blinked, and Daisinia's hand fell, her shoulders sinking.

"You didn't," she whispered. Her gaze flicked to the others in the room. To the prince who sat at the small table, sharpening his knife, to the Tetrians now huddled in the corner, to the angry blond man leaning back on the couch, yawning.

She knows, the man hissed.

The others didn't know who Graeson truly was, *what* he was. They knew he was deadly, but they didn't know how deadly he was. But the human did not have to worry. The god would keep his little secret. For now.

"The bullheaded king will die. That is all you need to know," the god said before turning his back on the group.

CHAPTER 50
KALLIE

"Stop that."

"Stop what?" Kallie asked, looking over her shoulder.

"The tapping," Myra said, pointing to the ground as she set the dress on Kallie's bed.

Kallie followed her gaze and noticed her foot tapping the chair's leg post. She uncrossed her legs and planted both feet firmly on the ground before straightening in the seat.

"Thank you," Myra said, flattening a hand down the front of her dress. "It was making me nervous."

Kallie dug the heels of her palms into her eye sockets, yet the queasiness did not go away. No matter how hard she pressed or how hard she tried to distract her body, the nausea persevered. There were no events today in order to give the bride and groom time to relax before the big day tomorrow. However, Kallie had found no comfort in the extravagant bath Myra had drawn for her that morning. Kallie hadn't even found comfort in talking to Myra and dismissed her friend before she disrobed and bathed herself. No amount of oils or kind words could soothe the strain in her muscles today. And sometimes, she could still feel Sebastian's hand wrapped around her throat.

Myra had returned to assist Kallie with her hair, so now Kallie was stuck staring at Myra at a reflection of herself she did not recognize.

After grabbing the brush off the vanity, Myra came to stand behind Kallie at the vanity. "I understand you're nervous about the wedding, but—"

"It's not the wedding," Kallie blurted and snatched the brush from Myra's hand. "I can brush my own hair."

"Then what is it?"

Kallie's mouth fell open, but she snapped it shut. She didn't know how to explain everything that had happened last night to Myra, for it would require Kallie to be honest with her friend about several things she had been keeping secret. It was one thing for Myra to know that Kallie was still grieving, but it was another for Myra to know that Kallie had let Graeson go. *Twice.*

But Kallie needed her best friend. She needed the walls to stop closing in around her.

Outside, rain tapped on the windows. The Frenzian fog that hung over the city finally had its fill.

"It's going to be all right, Kals," Myra said after the silence loomed too long, squeezing Kallie's shoulders.

Kallie flinched at the touch, and her gaze fell to the items atop the vanity. "Myra . . . there's a lot you do not know."

"Whatever it is, you can tell me." Myra reached out a hand, and as Kallie made to dodge her hand, her hair fell off her shoulders.

Myra gasped, her hand flying to her mouth. "Kals! What—what happened?"

Kallie's eyes widened, and she snapped her gaze to her reflection in the mirror. Bright green and purple bruises marked her pale neck. Kallie quickly brushed her hair forward, covering the bruises.

"Nothing," she mumbled. "I fell."

"You fell?" Myra stepped closer and pushed the hair away. "On your neck?"

Kallie bit down on her tongue. It was a bad lie. She knew it when she said it, but what was she supposed to say instead? Where was she supposed to begin?

The rain crashed harder against the glass window pane.

How could she tell her friend that she was beginning to question her father's choices? She was still the Princess of Ardentol. To speak out against the king's plans was to commit treason.

But if marrying a king wasn't enough for him, what would be? Her father wouldn't need a backup plan if he trusted her and her gift. He wouldn't have even thought to make Sebastian one of them. Sebastian, whom Kallie had saved from Graeson's wrath. Sebastian, who believed he owned her. She could not marry that man. She could not look into the eyes of the man who had killed her brother without a hint of remorse. Even if that marriage was only a possibility, Sebastian was still Rian's brother, one of his advisors. She couldn't look in those eyes every day and not see that night flash in his green irises. Not see Sebastian try to force himself on her.

She hated Sebastian. She hated him with every ounce of her body.

But at that moment, she hated herself more. Because if it weren't for her, if she hadn't given that command to the soldier, maybe Fynn would still be alive.

Myra peeled the brush out of Kallie's hand, setting it on the vanity. Then she pulled Kallie into her arms.

Kallie leaned into Myra's embrace and inhaled. The bath oils swept over Kallie, a calming scent that, for a second, made Kallie want to forget everything she had done. But she couldn't live in silence anymore. Kallie had been quiet for too long. She could no longer keep everything locked up inside of her. For if she did, it would tear her apart. She needed to tell someone. Even if doing so meant changing Myra's entire opinion of her.

"I stabbed Sebastian," Kallie mumbled into Myra's hair.

Myra's hand froze on her back. She pulled back, her gaze fixed on Kallie's. "You did what? When?"

"Last night."

"Last night?" Myra repeated as her attention dropped to Kallie's neck, her brows furrowing. "Is that how . . . ?"

Kallie bit her lip. "I think . . . I think we should sit."

Myra nodded once. "Okay." She nodded again, her head bobbing as she pushed back a loose strand of long blonde hair. "Yes, we should sit."

Kallie joined Myra on the plush couch and fixed her gaze on her shaking hands. She rubbed her thumb against the dainty gold ring. "Perhaps I should start from the beginning."

"The beginning is always a good place to start," Myra whispered, twiddling her fingers.

Biting her tongue, Kallie nodded.

It is okay to lean on a friend, Kallie reminded herself.

She took a deep breath, and then Kallie told Myra everything that transpired last night—well, everything she could. She told Myra how she had wandered the woods looking for Rian like she was supposed to. How she had found the giant sequoia in the center of the patch of trees and discovered an alcove carved out of it. How she had ventured down the dark stairs believing the king to be down there waiting for her, but Rian, of course, hadn't been down there.

Bile filled her throat at the memory of what happened next, and the words became too thick to say out loud. Living it was one thing, replaying the memory was one thing—but speaking it aloud? That was entirely different.

Myra grabbed Kallie's hand. With that single touch, the heavy weight on her shoulders lifted an inch. Kallie no longer felt alone.

She latched onto that feeling and pushed through.

When Kallie finished telling Myra what had happened between her and Sebastian, she brushed her hair to her back, revealing the bruises on her neck. Pain laced Myra's countenance.

"Myra, I can't—if something were to happen to Rian, my father wishes that—" Kallie choked on her words. "How am I supposed to marry Sebastian after that? After what he tried to do? I—I can't. I *won't*."

Soft fingers wrapped around Kallie's wrist. Myra pulled Kallie's hands away from her face and scooted closer. "Breathe, Kals. Rian is still alive and well. There is no need to make yourself sick with worry. We can tell King Rian. We can—"

"No!"

"No?" Myra asked.

"I will deal with this how I wish to, Myra. We will not involve the king. If Rian knew I was with his brother alone..."

Myra gnawed on her lip, reluctance tainting her gaze. Her shoulders sagged. "Very well."

Kallie nodded, inhaling for four seconds, holding for two, then out for three. Slowly, her body stilled, the shaking ceasing.

Myra squeezed Kallie's hand. "Did Sebastian...?"

Kallie's gaze hardened, and she shook her head. "No, he didn't get the chance."

Myra's attention dropped to the bruises. "We can cover these up. I know of a trick we can use with powder and paint."

"All right," Kallie whispered.

Myra grew quiet, her gaze dropping to the floor as if searching for something. "How?"

Kallie tilted her head, deep wrinkles forming in the center of her forehead. "What do you mean?"

"How did you escape?"

"I—" Kallie's eyes flitted back and forth between Myra's, and she hesitated. And because of that hesitation, because the fabricated story wasn't already at the tip of her tongue, Kallie told Myra the truth. "Graeson stopped him."

Myra jerked back, and Kallie's hands fell onto her lap. "*Graeson* is here? Are you sure?"

Kallie nodded before taking a deep breath. When she exhaled, she said, "He's been here for a few days."

"A few *days?*" Myra shrieked. Casting a wary glance at the door, she cleared her throat, speaking quieter this time. "So, this was not the first time you saw him since . . ." Myra's words fell off.

Kallie looked away, and that was answer enough.

"When?" Myra asked.

Kallie watched the rain splatter against the window, the sky a murky gray. "I saw him the first time in the hallway after the Last Dance."

"In the *castle?*" Myra hissed.

Kallie nodded again. "He must be working with someone. How else could he have gotten in the castle?"

Myra gnawed on her lip. "What did he want?"

Kallie shrugged. "Me, I guess."

"Why?"

Graeson's words echoed in her mind: *He's manipulating you.*

She trusted Myra, but Kallie didn't know if she could trust her with those words. Yet if they were false, why couldn't she bring herself to speak them out loud?

"I—I don't know, Mys."

Myra ran her finger across the edge of her sleeve. "Do you think he's alone? Or . . ."

Kallie swallowed. She didn't want to know if anyone had joined him, for she still hadn't seen Terin or Dani. Graeson was already more than enough to shake her. She couldn't face them, too.

"It would only make sense if the other two were with him."

Myra nodded. "But I still don't understand why. Do you think . . . Do you think they've come for you again?"

Kallie scoffed, shaking her head. She didn't care what Graeson had said. There was only one logical option here. After what she did, she wasn't worth saving. "If they did, it's to kill me."

"Why would they want to kill you?"

Kallie laughed and stood from the couch. "Why? Because to them, *I* am to blame for Fynn's death." Kallie's nails bit into her palms, but the burn didn't make the pain of her brother's death disappear. "Even if I could explain to them that he was not supposed to die, it wouldn't matter. It doesn't matter that I mourn his death, too."

"But you're . . ." Myra fell silent.

Kallie scoffed. "I'm what, Myra? Their daughter, their sister? It doesn't matter! Fynn is *dead* because of me." Kallie gripped the back of the chair, her knuckles blanching. "The fact that I share blood with him does not matter."

Myra shook her head. "If that was truly the case, why wouldn't Graeson have killed you last night? From what you told me, he had the opportunity. He could have taken it."

"I don't know, Myra!" Kallie threw her hands in the air and turned away. She scraped a hand over her face as if to wash away the rising emotion, but nothing she did settled the turning in her stomach. The blood in her veins vibrated, the anger pushing at her gift. Kallie slammed it back down.

Myra crossed her arms over her chest. "But you let him go."

It was not a question but rather a statement—an accusation.

Why had Kallie said anything? If anyone overheard their conversation, if word got to her father . . .

Myra was loyal to Kallie, though. Kallie had seen the way she eluded his attention. She would not willingly seek it out.

Kallie sighed and nodded. When Myra quirked a brow, Kallie

already knew the question of *why* was on the tip of Myra's tongue, so Kallie saved her the breath. "His life is of no consequence to me."

"But is his *presence* of no consequence?"

Kallie shrugged a shoulder, hoping the indifference she offered was plain across her face.

"Are you sure about that?" Myra asked, not bothering to hide her disbelief.

"What other reason would I have, Myra?" Kallie asked, her tone taking on a sharp edge. Plopping back on the couch with a huff, she tucked her feet underneath her.

"Fine. If you don't want to say it, that's fine." Myra shook her head. "But we both know why you truly let him go. Keep in mind, tomorrow you are to be married."

Kallie stared at the fireplace, the coals having long gone cold. There was no going back. She already knew that. She had made her choice last night. "I know."

"But, Kallie," Myra grabbed Kallie's wrist, "I have to ask . . . who else knows?"

"No one, Mys."

Myra drew her head back. "We need to tell someone. The guards—the king. King Rian should know. If we don't tell him, he will—"

Myra tried to stand, but Kallie panicked and snatched Myra's hand, keeping her friend in place. "Myra, you *cannot* tell anyone."

Kallie's gift hummed beneath her flesh. There was an easy way to handle this, a way to ensure Myra would keep quiet. But Kallie had made a promise to herself a long time ago. Her jaw popped as she ground her teeth together.

Lightning struck, and the window flashed white.

Myra's gaze flicked toward the door, fear lacing her gaze. "But—"

Kallie squeezed her hand. The air stilled, and the humidity of the storm filled the room. The temperature in the room grew too hot as Myra gnawed on her bottom lip. Kallie's eyes darted across her friend's face. Her breaths became too short. Her palm grew damp atop Myra's.

Kallie *wanted* to trust Myra. Of all people, Myra was the one person who had never let Kallie down, who had always been there for her. But when Myra's sweet, worried hazel eyes flicked to the door again, her face pale, the words slipped out of Kallie's mouth before she could stop them. "You will *not* tell the king."

Kallie slapped a hand over her mouth, but it was too late. The command had already slipped free. The familiar heat of her gift coated her blood even though she hadn't reached for it. It had come rushing out in a torrent when the fear of the unknown consumed her.

It was a simple command, but a command nevertheless. And with it, Kallie had betrayed her friend for the first time. Kallie had promised herself that she would never manipulate the people she loved. But now, even if Myra didn't know it, Kallie had crossed that invisible line.

Water prickled at the back of her eyes, and she dropped Myra's hand.

CHAPTER 51
GRAESON

"Is this the smartest thing to be doing right now?" the woman with the endless black eyes asked.

The god snorted, and the sound was so human that he mentally checked the lock on the door of the man's cell. He found the man still locked up.

"I mean," Euralys continued, "aren't you worried?"

"And what do I possibly have to worry about?" He asked as they slid past a group of pedestrians walking around the streets beyond the castle. Even at this late hour, there were still several people out. The god and the woman had been chosen to collect supplies for the arsonist. When the god had attempted to ignore Danisinia's request as she spewed the morning's breakfast into a bucket, the human man had forced his thoughts through the door. An image of the mortal promised, her blue eyes shining. Sticking to the plan was the only way they would get Kalisandre back. So, they searched for flint, sulfur, and oil in the middle of the night.

The woman glanced over her shoulder. "Of being recognized."

"Why would I worry about that?"

She grabbed his arm, tugging him to a stop and pulling him into an alcove.

In the shadows, she stepped closer, squinting at him. "I am not so impudent that I cannot recognize a god when I see one."

"And yet," the god said, tilting his chin up as his lip curled, "you dare touch me?"

"If you wanted to kill me, you would have done so already."

The god's nose twitched. This woman . . . she was not like the others. Her eyes alone had that cursed look within them.

"Are you so sure about that, Euralys?"

At the sound of her formal name, the woman flinched. She tried to cover it with a laugh as she tossed his arm off her, but the god saw through it.

"All of you are the same," she spat. "You think you are so smart, so unique, but you are not the first god to walk among humans." Cocking her head, she took a steady step forward. "The only question is, what have you done with Graeson?"

"Nothing." His gaze flicked to the crowd behind her.

It was the night before the royal wedding, and some civilians seemed to have decided to celebrate the union early. But if the god had anything to do with it, there would be no union to celebrate tomorrow. This would be the Frenzians' last night of peace.

Euralys' smirked. "He's fighting you, isn't he?"

He noted the way the muscles in her face flexed, her calm demeanor. She thought she knew what was happening, but she knew nothing. "These other gods you have come across, what have they led you to believe?"

"They have not led me to believe anything. You all come down here, borrow human bodies, and bend them to your will."

The god laughed. In the reflection of her pitch-black eyes, he could see that his eyes now glowed as silver as the moon. "And that is where you are wrong, little witch."

Her brows furrowed, lines creasing her foreheads as she studied him. She was trying to read him like she did the man. But she was not a mind reader, not like the dead prince.

"Then where—"

"He is still here," the god said, pointing to his head. When her lips parted, he cut off her words. "Ah-ah. Your arrogance, little witch, will get you killed. You think you know everything, that your people's connection to Nerva has granted you some access to knowledge that the others do not have. But you do not know everything. Not even close."

The woman narrowed her eyes. "Just tell me what you did to Graeson."

The god stepped forward. "He would not want anyone to know the truth about his nature. Even he is afraid to admit that truth himself." The god paused, contemplating. Perhaps if the truth were spoken, the man would have no reason to deny it. "You think I took this body? I was born into this body. This body is mine just as much as it is his. Because here is the thing, little witch, him and I? We are one and the same."

The muscles in her face twitched as she tried to piece together the information.

"It is only because he is in denial that I *am* him that he splits us apart. Deep down, he believes that if he admits the truth, he will have to admit that this power, that everything I do when he shuts down and closes himself off to the world, is his true soul acting. Not some other being. Not some wild *thing*. But him."

The woman took a step back. "But how can that be?"

"I thought you knew everything, Euralys?" The god cackled, the sound rough and low. "How does one acquire their gifts to begin with?"

Euralys' black eyes dashed across his face. "Because of the god's blood that runs in your veins."

"Mhm," the god hummed.

"But if you're—" she gasped, halting her thought. "Gods cannot die, though."

"And?"

"Graeson said his mother died when he was born."

The muscles in his jaw tensed.

Her face paled. "Who is Graeson's father?"

Behind the caged door, the man was silent as the god whispered the name of the father who had abandoned him.

CHAPTER 52
KALLIE

It was tradition that the bride dine with only her family the night before the wedding to represent the last night the bride's family needed to take care of her. Which meant Kallie dined with her father alone. Even if the staff had been dismissed from the room until Domitius rang for them

Knives scraped porcelain, the sound screeching in the surrounding silence. The pressure of tomorrow was heavy in the space between them.

When Kallie passed the royal dining room earlier, she heard the loud chatter from Rian's family. Here, in the secondary dining room in the castle, the large table was set for two. Kallie on one end, Domitius on the other. Kallie couldn't help but look at the empty chairs and think of the faces missing. The faces that would have been there if her life had turned out differently.

She straightened in her seat.

Kallie had bathed twice already, yet she still couldn't get the feeling of Sebastian's fingers off her, his stench. With Myra's help before the other handmaidens had arrived, the bruises along Kallie's throat had been meticulously covered up with paint and powder. No matter how much powder Myra dabbed on her flesh to cover the green and purple coloring, the ghost of Sebastian's fingers still crawled across her skin. Thankfully, her father barely glanced at her long enough to notice the layer of makeup or the heavy curls pushed over her shoulders. The only comment Domitius had made was about her tired gaze, saying it was unbecoming of a queen.

Across from Kallie, Domitius twirled his glass of whiskey. "The other kingdoms have been talking nonstop about how impressed they are with the festivities. This wedding has already done wonders in forming stronger connections with them. It's splendid," Domitius said in between sips, "truly splendid. Can you imagine the alliances that will form once the two of you are married? Borgania has always been a tricky kingdom to deal with since its internal battle during the Great War. The rulers of the western half seem to like the young king well enough, so we will need to ensure we nurture that relationship moving forward."

Kallie tried to smile, but the corners of her lips only twitched, unable to form anything but a ghost of a grin.

Her father was proud of her, but at what cost? What was the price of earning his approval, of earning his respect? Kallie had been fighting for his respect and love for years. And to achieve the small remnant of it that she was receiving now, she had to be grabbed and gagged by Sebastian. What more must she do to earn her father's full respect?

Love was supposed to be unconditional. But this? The happiness that sparkled in her father's expression? It was earned on the condition that Kallie sacrificed her body, name, and self-worth. Was that really what she wanted? Was power worth that sacrifice?

Growing up, she had always believed it was worth everything and anything.

A tang of guilt slid over her tongue, and a small voice in her head whispered that she was doing this for them, for their future.

Power came with sacrifice. Wasn't that what Medenia had said? Didn't Tessa say that, too? The former queen had forgone her name being written down in the history books in order to put her kingdom first rather than achieve glory for herself. Was that what Kallie had to look forward to as queen? Sacrificing bits and pieces of herself? What happened when she had nothing left to give? When the people, the advisors, and her husband took too much? What happened when her father demanded too much of her? When she withered away?

That morning, Kallie had barely recognized herself in the mirror. Her neck swollen and bruised, her face sunken and pale. The fire in her eyes had gone out as if someone had doused it with water. And all of this only after two months.

What would she look like in a year, in five?

Who would she be when everything she thought she was became merely a memory?

Domitius picked up his glass of whiskey and took a sip. "It's quite cute, actually."

"Cute?" she asked, her voice hoarse, shaky. Kallie swallowed, but it did little to soothe the burn at the back of her throat.

Domitius nodded. "How enamored Rian is with you. It's cute. Comical, really. He doesn't even know who he is marrying, yet he looks upon you as if you are the answer he's been searching for his entire life."

Kallie stabbed a carrot with her fork.

Rian was a means to an end, but he was a better path than the alternative. For that, Kallie was thankful. She would manipulate him as much as it required if it meant she was safe, if her body was still hers. She would be the perfect bride for Rian while she manipulated him in private, in the whispers that they passed one another at dinner, in the quick touches they exchanged beneath tables. She could be that person. For the kingdoms and for her father.

She exhaled softly. She could do that.

"We will give it one year."

Kallie glanced up. "A year?"

With a wave of his glass, he said, "A year for you to provide an heir. Come on now, keep up."

The carrot lodged itself into her throat, and she pounded on her chest with a fist, coughing. The corners of her eyes filled with water.

When she finally spat out the carrot in a napkin, Domitius shook his head. "Smaller bites tomorrow, yes? You'll be less likely to embarrass us."

Kallie's lips parted, but she snapped them shut before her jaw dropped completely. Straightening in her seat, she smoothed out the fabric of her dress as if she could settle the rising anger in the same movement.

Domitius grabbed the decanter and poured a second glass of whiskey. He swiped a lemon peel across the rim. "Here," he said as he slid the glass to her.

Kallie grabbed the whiskey and stared at the amber liquid. She hadn't touched the alcohol all night, for she hadn't had the stomach for it. She reached out, the glass cold against her fingertips, and sipped. The liquid burned her already sore throat as if she had poured fire down it.

"Better?"

Kallie cleared her throat. "Much. Thank you, Father," she said with a tight smile. For once, she didn't wish to drown her worries with alcohol. It had done nothing for her over the past couple of months besides give her blistering headaches and a sour stomach.

He nodded, then turned his attention back to his plate. "As I was saying, I do not think it will be hard to convince the brother to—"

"No." The glass banged against the table before Kallie could think better of it.

"Excuse me?" Domitius questioned, setting his fork back on the table.

When Kallie looked up, the blood rushed from her face, but she couldn't stop. She had already denied him; she could not go back on her word now. She needed to show him that she could stand on her own, that she had her own desires and wishes. Her own mind. "I said *no*."

His voice was ice cold as he asked, "What do you mean 'no?' This is the plan we discussed."

"No, Father, it is the plan *you* discussed. This is *my* life, and I get a say in it." Kallie was standing now. Her weight leaning onto her fists as they pushed against the wood. Pain pierced her skin, but she didn't care. Let her knuckles bleed. Let them scar.

Her father could marry her off to Rian. He could have her report to him about the happenings of the kingdom, but he would *not* control her body. That is where she drew the line.

King Domitius' lip curled, and a light chuckle seeped from his throat. "Oh, Kalisandre. Do you think that you have actual power now because you are one step away from the Frenzian crown and have won over the rosy king's heart?" He leaned back in his chair. And even though he peered up at her, his glare made her feel small.

Kallie sneered. She didn't know if what Graeson had said was true or not. She didn't know who she trusted. She could barely even trust herself. But one thing was for certain: she always had power. She did not need a crown to be powerful. She did not need a title to have control. Power was in her blood. It ran through her veins.

And as Kallie stared down at her father—the man whom she had grown up respecting, whom she had loved, cared for, and sacrificed for—Sabina's blood buzzed beneath her flesh. It rushed through her body, the anger blazing through her, fueling her. For the second time that week, Kallie broke her vow. "You will not—"

Kallie choked on her words before she could finish the command, and a flood of emotions overtook her. Warning bells sounded in her ears. Or was the bell on the table ringing?

She couldn't move, she couldn't speak. Her limbs grew numb as she stood grappling for the words. Her body swayed. Notes of lavender and cinnamon filled the air. A heavy pair of hands landed on her shoulders, metal clinking.

Her father stood and strolled around the table as she was led back into the chair. "My darling Kalisandre, you have such potential."

Domitius lifted her chin. When he peered at the covered-up bruises on her neck, heat flushed Kallie's face, but she couldn't move away. She couldn't do anything.

"If only you listened," he hissed.

Kallie gawked. In the reflection of her father's eyes, she saw something move, and panic rang throughout her entire body. She tried to get up. She tried to reach for her dagger, but when she moved, the person behind her held her down, forcing her to remain seated.

The world spun as they jostled her. Her vision blurred. Her father's face became distorted as if she had been submerged underwater and was now looking up at the surface.

"Did you think I would not learn about your little stunt?"

"What are you—"

"Do you think I am daft, Kalisandre? I told you I have spies everywhere, yet you still try to lie to me?"

Kallie's tongue grew heavy in her mouth.

"You are lucky Rian and Tessa fell for it, but that wasn't the point." Domitius stared down at her, his brown eyes blazing. A curl fell from his perfectly styled hair. "The loophole you found was smart. And perhaps I could have forgiven you for finding a way around killing the servant yourself. But that is not the only secret you have been keeping from me."

Kallie's chest rose, her heart racing as she grappled for air. The walls were closing in on her.

"You still care about them, don't you?" He crouched down, his hands gripping the arms of the chair.

Her mouth fell open, her brows quivered, and the question slipped out, "Who?"

"The Pontians," he hissed.

Kallie panicked. "No, no, I don't."

Her head swung, and her cheek burned from the sting of his slap.

"Do not lie to me!" Domitius looked past Kallie, his voice muffled, "Squander it."

Behind her, someone said, "Of course, My King."

The melodic voice was familiar, but Kallie's senses were scrambled. The sensation was all too familiar. It was just like when Terin had forced her unconscious. But that—that was a darkness that had consumed her, a sense of peace that had awaited her on the other side. This? This was the exact opposite. This was control being ripped from her. This was her veins swelling, her blood heating, sweat slicking her skin. This did not have the remnants of Terin's gentle touch. This was something far worse.

Fear swallowed her.

The whiskey. The woody caramel scent had been flavored with something else. Something . . . floral?

But her father wouldn't—he couldn't—

"All you had to do was *listen*, Kalisandre. Was that truly so hard?"

Kallie's body was on fire as she tried to straighten out her vision, as she tried to clear the fog from her mind. She tried to call upon her gift, but it was heavy in her stomach as if whatever Domitius had put in the whiskey dulled it, paralyzed it. She tried to fight it, but no matter how much she struggled against it, she couldn't get her gift to even budge. Whatever he had put in the whiskey was overtaking her, numbing her body and mind.

The pad of her father's thumb ran over her cheek. "Have I ever told you that you have your mother's eyes? Such pretty blues. As blue as the sea." Domitius jerked her chin up, squeezing it. "But here's the thing about the sea: the tide can turn at any moment. If you become lost in its beauty, in its vastness, in the hope of it all, it will drown you before you even see the wave coming. And you, my darling Kalisandre, are too full of hope."

He released her chin and looked at the person behind Kallie. "Now," he commanded before turning to the fire.

The sound of paper ripping split the air and rang in Kallie's ears. She couldn't see what it was, her attention fixed on the woman before her.

Domitius looked back at Kallie. "Don't worry, my darling, you will be back to normal just in time for the wedding tomorrow. We just need to do a little ... recalibrating, don't we?"

But Kallie barely heard him as she stared at her friend. "Myra?" Kallie wheezed, the name heavy on her tongue.

Myra's brows quivered, her fingers twisting together in front of her lap.

"Myra, please," Kallie whispered. She tried to reach out, to grab her friend's hand, but the man's grip remained firm on her shoulders. "Help me."

The handmaiden didn't meet Kallie's gaze. Myra bit her bottom lip, and Kallie was speechless as she stared at her best friend. The one person who she had counted on to be loyal to her. But loyalty always came at a price, didn't it?

"The least you can do"—Kallie gasped, her breathing becoming more labored as the poison weaved its way through her system—"is look at me when you stab me in the back."

Somewhere, someone chuckled.

"We do not have all day, Myra."

"Yes, My King," Myra said at last. She took a step forward, reaching out a hand. Kallie stared at it, brows furrowed. "It's going to be all right, Kals. I promise."

Kallie's eyes burned, her vision blurring. She wiggled against the arms holding her back as Myra's hand touched her cheek, but Kallie was too weak. She tried to speak a command, to will her gift to fuel her words, but the honeyed warmth was gone. Her energy depleted, her gift drained.

Domitius' footsteps were heavy on the wooden floorboards as he stepped toward the fireplace. "Oh, and be sure to clean this mess up before the other servants see. He'll help you with her, for I have more important matters to take care of."

"Of course, My King," Myra said as the man behind Kallie said, "Yes, My King."

And his voice was familiar yet distant. She could almost picture his face but couldn't quite place him. One of Rian's guards? Her father's?

In the corner of Kallie's vision, she saw Domitius toss something into the fire before walking out of the room. Kallie squinted, trying to identify the paper he had thrown into the fire, but the unshed tears blurred her vision.

Then, at the sound of the door closing and the latch clicking into place, two soft hands touched Kallie's neck. Their fingers cold and nimble. And at their touch, a sense of calm poured over Kallie, drenching her in golden sunshine and honey.

The last thing Kallie felt before the white haze consumed her were the cold, wet tears rolling down her face as the smell of lavender and cinnamon blanketed her, and the ripped family portrait curled in the flames.

CHAPTER 53
GRAESON

Having returned with the supplies for the arsonist, the god watched over the sad prince. Terin's features were contorted as he sat on the floor. Sweat dripped from his forehead, rolling over the deep wrinkles.

"I can't reach her," Terin said at last.

"What do you mean you cannot reach her?" the god asked.

For the past few weeks, Terin had been infiltrating Kalisandre's dreams, conjuring up different scenes, both imaginary and old memories. A couple of times, Terin had been able to connect Kalisandre's dreams with the man's. But with the mortal still fighting his connection to his godly side, the god had not been privy to those dreams.

The prince stared at his hands, his shoulders sinking as he glanced up. Deep creases marked the center of his forehead, his brows bunching together. "I don't know—it's like she's—she's—"

The god grabbed Terin by the collar and pulled him up and off his knees. He shoved Terin against the wall. "She is *not* dead," he spat. "I would know if she was dead."

Terin grabbed the god's wrist, tugging it away. "That's not what I meant, Graeson. Calm the fuck down."

"Then be clearer next time lest you wish for your heart to be torn from your chest," he growled.

The god walked to the other side of the room and leaned against the wall across from Terin. The prince stared at him, with different emotions flashing across his face far too quickly for the god to decipher. Human emotions were always erratic, so chaotic and temperamental.

"What the fuck is wrong with you, Gray?"

You've done it now, the man inside said.

The god's nose twitched. "Nothing."

Terin snorted. "Well, that's the lie of the century. I've known you since we were children, Gray." The prince squinted at him. "You're acting weird. Weirder than usual, anyway."

The god scoffed.

Then, in the back of his mind, he heard the small voice say, *He's going to figure it out. You're a bigger fool than I first thought if you think you can trick them all. Terin may not be Fynn, but that does not make him any less observant.*

It is not I who am ashamed of myself, human, the god said back to the man trapped inside the cell. *It is of no consequence to me if they discover the truth.*

Terin and Dani are one thing, but if the others find out? There will be questions. Are you prepared for that?

The god scoffed, both internally and outwardly.

Terin stepped forward, and his mouth fell open. "You didn't."

Told you, the man said.

"I thought you had control over it."

The god grinned, a mischievous glint sparkling in his eye. "I *do* have control."

Terin snorted again. "Obviously not." He waved a hand in the god's direction, pointing. "If that was the case, this—"

The god kicked off the wall and stalked forward. "I would be careful what you say next, princeling."

Terin pursed his lips. Unlike his former twin, Terin was not as outspoken as the other. He was more reserved, careful of his words. Fynneares would have talked back, would have pushed. It had made him reckless. It was probably what killed him in the end, the god thought to himself.

The human banged his fist against the mental door of his cell, his anger rising as the thought traveled through their mind.

It is true, is it not? the god asked.

The man snarled back. *It does not matter if it is true or not. Do not disrespect the dead.*

As if the god of the dead could do anything to me.

Do not be so ignorant. You are not untouchable.

The god slammed a second door in front of the cell, shutting the human out. It did not do well to dwell on this topic, not right now. There would be a time and place for that. And now was not it.

"We're forgetting the point here," the god said, crossing his arms.

Terin raised a brow and crossed his arms over his chest, mocking the god as he stood his ground. "This is important, Graeson."

The god stared at him, his voice even. "Not as important as Kalisandre."

Terin tapped his foot on the floor as he looked out the window. In the distance, the spires of the Frenzian castle could be seen piercing the clouds in the sky. Somewhere inside was Kalisandre.

Terin looked back at him, the muscles in his jaw ticking. "Fine," he spat.

"Tell me why you cannot reach her."

Terin ran his fingers through his hair. Since they had been traveling, his hair had gotten even longer. A thick beard now covered his jawline. He was looking more and more like his brother every day.

But the exhaustion he wore like a weapon, the unruliness of his hair made him look wild, untamed. It did not make him look like the future king of Pontia.

"I'm not sure exactly," he said. "It's like something is blocking me out. I've never had this happen before unless the person is—"

The god growled.

Terin cleared his throat, and his gaze fell to the floor as he began to pace around the bedroom. "I can feel her presence, but it's like the door has been locked, and I no longer have the key."

"What does that even mean?"

"I don't know," Terin stopped pacing, his brown eyes stricken with fear when he met the god's gaze. "But whatever it is, it's not good, Gray."

CHAPTER 54
GRAESON

For two days, Graeson had been locked inside his mind.

For two days, he had watched from the small window and banged at the door. He shouted. He screamed. Yet the god did not let him out. Graeson knew that the god could hear him and that his thoughts were still impacting the god's actions, yet he remained caged.

The only thing keeping him sane was that Graeson knew the god would not do anything to harm Kalisandre. As much as Graeson despised the monster within him, their goals did align.

While the others acted as staff members or guests, the god elected to be one of the guards. And now Graeson was not only forced to watch through the small window inside his cage but also through the tiny slits in the stolen helmet. But despite his distorted vision, Graeson couldn't help but smile when the god seethed with anger as his breath smacked him in the face, bouncing off the metal helmet.

Serves you right, you arrogant bastard.

I can hear you, *the god retorted.*

Good.

The god snarled back.

In front of the line of soldiers, Sebastian stood beside the general of the Frenzian army, surveying them.

Two nights ago, Graeson was only half aware of what was happening around him when he was first locked away. Now, the memory returned in flashes as if Esmeray was showing him bits and pieces of the night.

He recalled the way Sebastian's hand crawled over the fabric of Kalisandre's shirt, the moment terror flooded her ocean-blue eyes as she was gagged and choked.

Then he remembered nothing, nothing but a red-hot fury.

Graeson couldn't shake the rage building within him. He couldn't hide behind it. He couldn't smother it. Not in the confinements of this cell. It spilled from him.

And for the first time, Graeson was thankful that he was trapped inside his mind. Because if he weren't, he would not be able to promise that the king's brother would go unscathed. Sebastian was the one who had come to Ardentol asking for Kalisandre's hand on behalf of his brother, the one who had come to Pontia and killed Fynn. And Graeson wanted to cut off the man's head right where he stood.

In due time, human, the god whispered.

BENEATH THE HELMET, the god's lip curled as the general beside the smug prince shouted commands and instructions for the ceremony.

The Frenzian man would not die, not yet. The god was too close to achieving everything he desired. Too close to getting what he had come here for. By the end of the day, Kalisandre would be his, and destruction would fall upon Frenzia. As it always should have been.

He would not ruin that now, not because of this mortal before him.

So, the god remained in line with the humans. He would not

attract attention to himself. Even if every time the red-headed man looked down his nose at the soldiers, the god's skin itched, burned.

Unlike the rest of the men, Sebastian wore no helmet. Not that the captain had one to wear, for his helmet sat firmly on the god's head. Sebastian had not addressed the missing helmet, only tipped his chin up in indifference when the soldiers looked at him.

From the little of what the god knew about the prince, the man seemed to relish any attention he could get. Even if the prince had his helmet, he would not have worn it, for how would he receive what he sought after if he was covered from head to toe in armor? If he was undistinguishable to anyone who looked upon him? No, Sebastian preferred to stand out from his men.

The man huffed in his cell, and his thoughts floated out. *If it were Dani, she would have put her soldiers first. This man is no leader.*

Now *that* they could agree on. Sebastian was nothing short of a selfish, arrogant mortal.

Only easier to pick out from the crowd, the god said.

Sebastian sauntered down the line of men, occasionally stopping and stepping up to different soldiers. Sometimes, he commented on their scratched armor; sometimes, he said nothing. It was as if the man got off on seeing the men stand just an inch straighter when he approached.

The god sneered beneath the helmet.

As if that kind of power meant something.

The metal heel of Sebastian's polished black boots clapped against the stone floors. Each step echoed in the exterior hall of the temple.

The god would have to wear this odious thing for two more hours. For two hours, he would have to wait in lines, stand at attention, and listen to the silly commands of the mortal.

Swallowing the groan inching in his throat, the god kept his gaze forward as Sebastian continued to make his way down the line.

A few paces away from the god, Sebastian stepped toward a

soldier. He tugged on the armor covering the man's shoulder, the metal clanking as the joints knocked into each other. The prince huffed, then continued.

When Sebastian stopped in front of the god, the god met the prince's gaze through the slits. As Sebastian scanned the helmet, the god remained steady despite the panic rising in the back of his mind. The god quickly shoved the man's thoughts aside, closing the window of the cell. He did not need any of the man's worries seeping out.

Sebastian squinted at the metal helmet. They had checked for any unique markings on the black metal, but nothing seemed unique about it. No name or jewels marked it. Unlike the king's helmet that night, there were no rubies in the dragon's eyes. It was the same as every other soldier's helmet in the line. Was there some marking on the helmet that Danisinia had missed when she had examined it? Did the Frenzian know it belonged to him?

Sebastian's gaze continued to sweep over Graeson. It was a look meant to strike fear in his subordinates, yet the god remained steadfast. The god had no reason to fear him, for victory was at his fingertips.

And the blood of this mortal man was even closer. He could almost taste the prince's death.

As the god stared back, he couldn't help but smirk, satisfied with what he saw.

The prince couldn't even wear his bruises and scars with honor. He had to hide them away and cover them up with powder.

From the encounter with Sebastian, only the god's knuckles brandished a visible sign of the fight where the skin was slightly discolored. The bruises would fade in a few days. The memory, however, would not. The man inside might have thought he was a monster, but at least he owned every scar on his body. No matter how faded or fresh, each scar was a reminder of what he had done.

Dampness coated the back of the god's neck as Sebastian

continued to stare at him, although not from fear. The sun beat down on him, heating the metal armor and practically cooking him from the inside. Yesterday's storm did little to diminish the humidity.

Sebastian raised a hand, bringing it to the helmet, and the god bit back the snarl rising to the surface. He flicked the metal. "Clean your helmet, soldier, before you are in the king's presence."

King. What are kings to gods? he thought.

He doesn't know who you are, the man inside said.

Internally, the god snorted. *Who* we *are, little human.*

I am not *you,* the man spat.

Yet.

When Sebastian raised a brow, the god swallowed his pride with an eye roll and mumbled, "Yes, *sir.*"

Sebastian crossed his arms over his chest, then flicked his hand in the air. "*Now*, soldier."

The god lifted the helmet off his head.

Emmett better not fail us again, the god heard the man whisper.

But the man did not have to worry. The god could still feel Emmett's gift blanket his skin like a sticky residue that wouldn't go away.

Nearby, Emmett swept the entrance of the temple's doors, his broom brushing over the same spot ever since Sebastian had neared. Although this time, the man wasn't drunk, and Graeson would not be running off to places he shouldn't be, not with the god in control. An intense focus shined across his features as he swept slower.

When the god removed the helmet, he inhaled. The unobstructed air was a small blessing. He turned the helmet in his hand, looking for the spot of dirt Sebastian had pointed out. On the front of the helmet, beneath the dragon's eye, a splotch of dark red was smeared across the metal. Blood.

Sebastian's blood, no doubt.

With his gloved hand, the god took his time cleaning it. His amusement rising as Sebastian shuffled on his feet.

Once the helmet was spotless, the god finally met Sebastian's stare. The bruises on Sebastian's face were even more evident without the helmet obstructing his view. The faint remnant of some emotion flickered in the back of his mind, but the god stomped it down without a second thought.

Sebastian cocked his head. "Are you one of the recent recruits, soldier?"

"Yes, *sir*." The god swallowed the bile that ran up his throat every time the address left his lips.

Sebastian clicked his tongue. "Our training must lack discipline if they do not teach you to keep your gear clean."

"My apologies, sir."

"And you lot are supposedly the best of the best." Sebastian's lip curled into a grimace. "Consider my forgiveness a gift on this most *gracious* day."

The god's lips pressed into a fine line, but he nodded in feigned gratitude.

Sebastian shook his head before he continued down the line, with the general following behind him.

The god held back the eye roll until the helmet was in place. Then, he imagined his blade going through the prince's body a dozen different ways. The question was never *if* Sebastian would die, but how?

CHAPTER 55
GRAESON

Even from his vantage point at the right of the podium, the god found it hard to keep an eye on everyone in the room. The group had spread out as much as possible to ensure they could keep their sights on everything.

Emmett, having discarded the broom once guests had started to arrive, now stood at the back of the room with a few other staff members.

The Tetrian women sat closer to the front, so the god didn't have to search for them for long, especially with Euralys' unamused grimace acting as a beacon. After their conversation two nights ago, the Tetrian warrior was still upset with him. But she had yet to confide in the others about the battle raging inside of Graeson's body. The message was clear: no harm would come to him as long as the god stayed on the path.

The god laughed internally.

As if the little witch could hurt him.

It took the god a moment to spot Danisinia, Terin, Armen, and Moris. They sat among the other guests in the middle of the crowd, visible but hidden among the common men and women in attendance. The sickness Danisinia had been suffering the past few days seemed to have dwindled at least, for her complexion had returned to its typical golden hue.

In hushed whispers this morning, the god had overheard Terin trying to convince Danisinia to assist the arsonist, to be their eyes on the outside in case things went south. However, Danisinia had not budged. Her skills were needed inside, she had claimed.

The god, however, knew the truth. Dani wanted to be in the room so that she could kill the bullheaded king. The god also knew that if she weren't careful, this desire would blind her. It would cloud her vision and prevent her from sticking to the goal.

Danisinia would have one chance. If she failed, the god would take matters into his own hands without hesitation. If the king were manipulating Kalisandre and making her less than who she truly was, the god would drive his blade through the bullheaded king before the man could utter a word.

To the side of the podium, the quartet began playing. Hearing the music start, those who were standing sat down, and the god straightened. It was time.

FROM THE SMALL WINDOW, *Graeson watched the temple doors open. If he weren't some incorporeal being right now, his heart would be thundering in his chest. Instead, the god's heart barely reacted as the iron doors peeled open while the quartet played a slow, ethereal tune.*

A man wearing an elaborate embroidery robe stepped into the room. Gold embroidery decorated the velvet fabric. Embroidered flames bedazzled with red and gold gemstones danced across the front panels of the robe. The priest's hair that showed through the tall burgundy hat was as white as parchment. Leaning his weight on the staff in his left hand, the priest strolled down the center of the black aisle. Atop the golden staff was a dragon with its tail wrapped around the pole. It was as if the dragon was climbing the staff, its claws wrapping around it. The dragon's head tilted to the sky, its mouth slightly agape as if breathing fire.

In the priest's wake, dozens of acolytes followed. The young boys all wore white ensembles consisting of gaudy white tops, slick white trousers, and little capes that tied around their necks. In their hands were similar, albeit smaller, golden dragon-topped staffs. Their steps were synchronized as they followed the priest, their faces void of any expression.

Nearing the dais, the acolytes formed two neat rows. Their heels clicking together as they turned to face each other.

The music picked up as the Frenzian king stood before the temple's doors. Rian wore a sleek, black jacket with black diamonds and brilliant rubies glittering across it in the likeness of dragon scales. At the shoulders, tiny spikes protruded out of the fabric like the spine of a dragon. In comparison, his trousers were simple, with small black gems sprinkled lightly across them. The gold crown sparkled atop his wine-red hair as the light from the candelabra hit it.

Rian held his arm out, and his mother joined him. The Queen Mother wore a deep-red, almost black dress. Clasped around her neck was a long red cape made of chiffon and decorated with red and black lace at the shoulders. It dragged behind her as they walked down the aisle. Her dark auburn hair was tied up in neat twists at the back of her head, with the front slicked back.

As they made their way down the aisle, the guests tipped their heads down as the king and his mother passed. Rian stopped at the first row, gently kissing his mother's cheeks before taking his place by the priest at the center of his dais.

Behind them followed the king's advisors and close relatives. Graeson recalled Armen saying the older couple who followed were the former queen's parents. They were dressed in a similar fashion, extravagant fabrics draping their bodies.

A hum echoed through his physical form and in all corners of his mind. Graeson watched with bated breath.

Kalisandre was close.

The god's amusement, stained with a lust for blood, seeped beneath the locked door, catching Graeson's attention. Faint whispers breezed across the room as Sebastian walked down the aisle, his gaze sweeping across the crowd. Graeson didn't need to see his face up close to know what caused the whispers. He had seen the bruises earlier, and while the makeup hid them from afar, the paint did nothing to conceal the coloring from the guest sitting closest to the aisle. Sebastian tipped his chin, folding his hands behind his back. However, as much as the prince tried to hide that he was not bothered by the whispers, the twitch of his nose gave him away.

Perhaps he will now know not to touch what does not belong to him, *the god said.*

Graeson, however, knew it was wishful thinking. Men like him never learned.

Sebastian stood a few steps below his brother, and Graeson smirked at the prince's irritation.

The humming grew louder, and the air shifted in the room. Graeson could sense his body growing rigid as a mix of emotions flooded his system at the sight of the two figures. The bullheaded king stood before the room wearing a white suit with gold and navy detailing. But Graeson did not care to look at him, for his attention was solely on the woman beside him.

When Graeson took Kalisandre in, his heart stopped.

The dress she wore, Graeson admitted, was beautiful and fit her bodice perfectly. The skirt was large and blossomed from her hips, but it did not overwhelm her short physique. The sweetheart bodice with intricate beading and lace enhanced her curves and drew attention to her collar bone, where four gold chains swept across her neck and chest, connected by a single chain that slid in between her breasts. She wore a sparkling white cape attached to white leather in the form of armor with capped sleeves, which were decorated with the same lace and beading as the bodice. The white leather rose to her throat, wrapping around it. Loose curls framed Kalisandre's face while the rest of her hair cascaded down her back in a loose, thick, intricate braid with little diamonds sparkling throughout.

Kalisandre was more than breathtaking, but not because of the dress.

Because as beautiful as the dress was, it wasn't her. She was not meant to be covered in gems, tulle, and leather. She wasn't meant to wear chains around her neck. She wasn't meant to force a smile on her face that didn't quite reach her eyes as she held Domitius' raised hand. Nor was she meant to be looking fondly at her Frenzian groom at the other end of the aisle.

It was as if she had forgotten what had happened two nights ago.

As she floated down the aisle and the doors closed behind her, Graeson could feel his heartbeat picking up, echoing throughout his body.

When she was only a few yards from Graeson's position near the dais, Domitius and Kalisandre stopped. Domitius embraced his false daughter. From Graeson's vantage point, he saw Domitius' lips move, but he couldn't quite make out the words. Whatever the bullheaded king said, it made Kalisandre straighten. She gave a slight nod, then curtsied the moment Domitius released her.

With a satisfied grin, Domitius took his place in the front row beside the captain of his guard. The king's gaze as he looked upon Kalisandre was not that of a loving or caring father. It was the gaze of a man selling his daughter off to the highest bidder. A man boastful of his accomplishments.

This moment was not for Kalisandre. It was for him. A celebration of what he had made happen.

Then, as Kalisandre turned and reached for Rian's hand, Graeson could feel the god strain to remain still. At the onslaught of anger rising, Graeson narrowed his gaze as he peered through the window, searching for what awakened the god's wrath.

The leather around her throat had hidden the bruises well, but not well enough. The fabric had begun to rub off the powder and paint, the white material now stained salmon. Purple skin peeked through the paint.

Graeson growled.

He would kill them.

He would kill them all.

Soon, *the god hissed.*

When Rian grabbed Kalisandre's hand and turned to face the priest, the priest slammed the staff against the ground. Fire erupted from the dragons' mouths, and fierce flames roared down the aisle, lighting the path to the king and his bride.

The priest's voice boomed across the room as he spoke, "Today, we gather to unite two families, two kingdoms."

Through the window within his mind, Graeson looked toward the iron doors. Squinting, he saw a thin layer of smoke snake beneath the door.

It's time, *the god said, smirking beneath the helmet.*

CHAPTER 56
KALLIE

Kallie straightened as the familiar smell of smoke weaved its way down the aisle.

The priest's nose twitched, and he scanned for the source. His eyes settled on the staff in the acolytes' hands, and his shoulders relaxed. But Kallie knew better. The smell was too distinct to be from the flickering flames of the torches.

The Pontians had come. There was no other explanation.

Her father had warned her that morning that the Pontians were savages. That they were cruel and unrelenting. They didn't care about her. They only cared about destroying everything she had.

And he was right.

In her peripheral, Kallie saw her father arch a brow at her, looking at her expectantly. Not at the smoke or the people in the back of the room who waved their pamphlets near their faces as the room heated. He stared at her, for the power was in her hands.

Soon, the people would become restless. Once the smoke scratched their throats and filled their lungs, their concern would grow exponentially. Their panic uncontrollable.

Kallie needed to hurry the ceremony along. She needed to finish this, for an overwhelming need to appease her father shot through her body. Kallie would not let him down again.

Holding Rian's hands, she reached for her gift. At first, it was reluctant to answer her call, but then it filled her veins.

With a sweet smile, she looked to the priest and whispered so no one else could hear, "Move onto the vows, Priest Havering."

The priest stuttered, stumbling over his words as the command swept through his mind.

Having heard the command, Rian tugged on Kallie's hands, but Kallie's grip remained firm around his fingers.

"Kalisandre," Rian whispered as he leaned toward her. "What are you doing?"

Kallie offered him a sweet smile. "Only eager to marry you, Your Majesty."

Rian's brows furrowed, but he remained silent.

Priest Havering cleared his throat. "Let us get on to the vows, for we are all eager to see our king and his bride unified. Princess, repeat after me, 'I, Kalisandre Helene Domitius.'"

"I, Kalisandre Helene Domitius." When her name left her lips, Kallie's brows quivered.

Was Domitius her real last name, or was it Nadarean? Did it matter if the last name she spoke was not truly her own but one that was instead thrust upon her? Would the marriage even hold if her name was a lie?

She gnawed on her lip, the fear of failure coating her throat.

She took a deep breath. To the people, she was the Princess of Ardentol, daughter of the King of Ardentol. It did not matter where she came from or how she got here.

She continued to repeat after the priest. "Promise to protect the Frenzian kingdom, to put the kingdom's safety first. Promise to protect the king of Frenzia, serve him, and obey him as his wife and servant to the kingdom."

The smell of smoke was more prominent now, the people in the back growing more restless. Whispers hissed throughout the temple. Rian looked out to the crowd, and Kallie bit down on her cheek as she watched her chance slip away. The smoke began its slow descent down the aisle, and the people started shifting in their seats. Whispers filled the room.

Kallie almost had everything she wanted. The marriage alliance was almost sealed and finalized. Kallie was almost Rian's wife. Almost the Queen of Frenzia.

But *almost* wasn't good enough.

Her gaze slipped to her father.

Now! King Domitius' glare beckoned.

Ignoring the sweat coating her skin, Kallie snatched up the king's hands.

Rian stared at her, brows furrowing. "Is that smoke?" he whispered.

With a deadly grip on his hands, Kallie released another command, "You will stay here. You will command the crowd to sit, that it is only something burning in the kitchens, and we will finish the vows."

The words tasted like burned charcoal on her tongue, dry and numbing. But this had to be done. She would not disappoint her father. Not again.

With a strand of smoke running across his irises, Rian addressed the crowd, his hand still in hers, "Please, everyone, remain calm. It is only a little smoke from the dinner. The staff must have gotten too carried away with the pig roast. Please sit and let us continue. It is an old temple with an old ventilation system. We shall be quick, as we are as eager as you to be married." Rian turned to the priest. "Please, proceed, Priest Havering."

The guests quieted, the words of their king soothing their anxiety, and the tension in Kallie's shoulders fell away. However, some guests, Kallie noticed, remained tense in their seats, their bodies not quite touching the back of the benches as if they were ready to run at a moment's notice.

The priest pulled at his collar but continued. "Please repeat after me: I, King Rian Lochan Lothian Dronias."

"I, King Rian Lochan Lothian Dronias," Rian said, and where his palms touched hers, sweat coated their skin.

"Promise to continue to serve Frenzia as its king, to protect it, to act in the name of Frenzia," Priest Havering started, and Rian repeated the words as the air grew coarser, hotter.

The temperature in the room increased. Beneath the many layers of fabric, Kallie's thighs became slick with sweat. Fits of coughs echoed across the temple.

The priest looked at the king with concern, but Rian merely stood there, Kallie's command forcing him to remain. Clearing his throat, the priest continued, "I welcome Princess Kalisandre Helene Domitius into my home, into my heart, and into my kingdom."

"I—" Rian cleared his throat and restarted, "I—"

The smoke had reached them and filled Rian's lungs, preventing him from finishing the vow as he keeled over. It had crept up the aisle, and now the air was thick with its ashy stench.

Kallie's heart rate increased as her knuckles grew white around Rian's hands. Kallie tried to slow her breathing, inhaling only a small amount of air to lessen the scratch that now coated the inside of her throat.

Eyes bloodshot, Rian looked from the priest to Kallie.

"Rian," Kallie whispered, "finish the vows."

The king did not look at her as his hands slipped from hers. He clenched his fist in front of his mouth and coughed louder. He held up a finger with the other hand. More coughing fits filled the temple as the smoke wrapped its tendrils around the guests. As the vows grew increasingly delayed, the whispers increased.

In between wheezes, the king managed to say, "I apologize, but I cannot. This—smoke. We need"—more wheezing—"Bash!"

Sebastian moved to the center of the podium and shouted, "Guards, open the doors!"

One of the guards sprinted toward the iron doors. When he reached for the handles, the hiss that left his lips echoed in the grand hall as he shook his hand at his side.

The door was metal. If there were a fire on the outside of it, it would be too hot to touch. The ghost of an old memory flitted to the surface at the image of the guard shaking his hand, and she fought back the tremors that begged to come out.

Wrong, wrong, wrong, a voice inside her head repeated.

More guards hurried forward, their metal armor screeching as the joints rubbed together.

All around, shouting erupted. The crowd rose, panic forcing them onto their feet.

Kallie's heart pounded. Fear stabbed her in the gut. She grappled for her gift, pulling at its heavy weight. "Stop!" she shouted. "Stop!"

But the command rose and fell within her.

Tears streamed down her face, burning as the smoke wrapped around her. She searched the crowd, looking for her father and Myra.

Where are they?

Bodies rushed around, blurring in Kallie's vision. Nearby, a flick of burgundy fabric fluttered, a tapestry on a wall waved in the air. A crash sounded from above. The glass ceiling shattered.

The torches fell to the ground as the acolytes shielded themselves. Kallie threw her arms over her head to shield herself as her knees hit the ground and glass fell. Sharp shards pierced her skin as they poured from the sky. She hissed in pain but did not dare move as tiny pieces continued to fall atop her. Glass rained throughout the temple, screams and cries ricocheted off the walls as the pieces *tinked* across metal and wood. It poured and poured. An endless spout of glass, tears, and screams filled the temple hall with no end in sight.

CHAOS. Pure chaos filled the temple.

Somewhere above her, Rian shouted, "Guards!"

When Kallie unfolded her arms and pried her eyes open, she saw Rian sprinting down the narrow path toward the iron doors. He covered his mouth with his arm as he ran past the small fires spurred to life from the fallen torches. Guards charged forward, joining their king. Others tried to put out the flames bursting to life across the aisle.

Speckles of blood freckled Kallie's skin, pieces of glass embedded into her arms. She pulled out a chunk of glass, hissing out in pain as blood oozed from her arm. She ripped a strip of fabric from the bottom of the dress and tied it around the wound.

Standing, Kallie looked around as mayhem swallowed the room. Fathers and mothers unfolded themselves around their small children, their skin marked with dozens of tiny red slashes from the sharp glass. Cries echoed in the hall, both infant and adult. Guests hurried toward the door, frantically trying to escape through the door, which the guards still struggled to pry open.

Kallie jerked her attention to the front row. She searched and searched, but her father was nowhere to be seen. She spun around, her dress swishing across the floor. Pain surged through her chest, an ache she couldn't dull.

Was her father okay? Was he hurt?

The other royals previously sitting in the front seats were also missing, including Tessa, Rian's grandparents, Jacquin, and the other advisors.

And the realization of what must have transgressed when the glass poured from the ceiling was as sudden as an arrow piercing her chest.

They had all abandoned her.

Even her own father.

No. Kallie thought, mentally slapping away the traitorous thought. *No, that can't be right. Father wouldn't abandon me. He* needed *me.*

Kallie's mind spiraled as she thought of the alternative options.

Perhaps the others had dragged her father with them, and he had no choice but to go. Maybe he had tried to reach Kallie, but there was no time.

Yes, that had to be the reason. There was no other explanation—not one she was willing to entertain anyway.

Kallie bit down on her lip. She needed to find him. She needed to get out of here. She would not be stuck in here, she told herself. This would not be her fate. She had survived too many fires to burn down in this one.

There had to be another way out. There was never only one entrance to a building, especially one this large. There had to be another room, somewhere the priest—

Kallie spun around, but the priest had already disappeared. She tried to recall what she had seen before chaos ensued. Priest Havering was right next to her when the ceiling shattered. At least, she thought he had been.

She sprinted past the podium, past the grand piano. She searched the walls. There had to be something. Some door, some tunnel.

Something.

Her hands scraped across the bricks.

"Fuck!" Kallie smashed her fist against the wall.

The priest had run. He had abandoned them. His king, his people. He had left them to burn.

Kallie squinted at the shattered ceiling, the sun blaring straight down at high noon. It was too high to climb. But Kallie could have sworn she saw someone up there.

Then, a head popped out and tossed something down. Then another and another. Smoke spiraled around the objects as they fell. One landed in front of her, and an explosion of air kicked her back.

Heat soaked the air, and her body shook from the impact. Or was that the ground? Kallie wasn't quite sure. She wasn't sure of anything anymore.

Her head ached, and she peeled herself off the floor. As her vision cleared, she saw a Frenzian guard racing toward her.

The guard grabbed her hand and pulled her up.

Kallie winced as her head spun, but she ignored the pain. She needed to find her father. She grabbed onto a piece of his armor, shaking it. "Where? Where is the other exit? We have to get out of here!"

"You need to calm down, Kalisandre,"

And it wasn't the words the man said, but rather how her name rolled off his tongue as if it belonged there, that made Kallie stumble backward.

She bundled up her heavy skirts. Unlatching her dagger, she brandished her blade. While the helmet may have hidden his face, she would recognize him anyway.

"Graeson," she hissed. She was quickly growing tired of meeting him like this.

Flames danced across the metal, illuminating the scales of the dragon. Behind them, the fire was growing wild in the center of the temple, forcing the guests to the sides. The benches closest to the aisle disintegrated into ash as the fire consumed them. People squeezed themselves against the walls, jumping over the benches that the flames hadn't yet touched. Screams filled the heat-soaked air.

"Don't you look ravishing, little mouse," Graeson said, his voice a haunting echo inside the helmet.

Kallie sneered as she ripped the bottom of her dress, cutting off the extra fabric. She swung, the shredded material falling to the ground as she aimed for an opened joint in the armor.

"Now that was just rude, Kalisandre," he said as he dodged her attack. Shifting several spaces back, he pulled the helmet off, and it rolled across the floor. His irises were as bright as the full moon, nearly glowing, and his intense gaze sent a shiver down her spine as he ran his tongue across his teeth. "I wanted the task of ruining that pretty little dress of yours."

Heat flushed her cheeks, but she ignored it and aimed for her new target: those stupidly bright, searing eyes.

Graeson, however, was quick, evading her attack in one smooth movement. Kallie thrust the blade again, aiming for the joint at the hips, but Graeson, yet again, slipped out of her reach. He spun, putting the table overflowing with roses between them.

"Is that all you got, Princess?" Graeson smiled, eyelids lowering in challenge.

Snarling, Kallie charged. She thrust her body weight against the table, and the thorns dug into her skin as she pressed into them. It was a stupid move, but she didn't have time to chase him. The smoke was thicker now, and she had no time to waste. She swung her blade, and Graeson shifted, sliding over the table.

Kallie flipped over and pushed herself up. She threw her hand up and aimed for Graeson's neck as she spun back around to face him. Graeson snatched her hand in the air and threw her against the table, the edge of the oak slamming into her back.

"Ah, so the little mouse has teeth, does she?"

Her brows knitted together as his gaze danced over her.

Something was off about that bright silver gaze. Something was missing.

Graeson quirked a brow when she did not attack immediately. "Oh, is the fun already over?" He clicked his tongue. "What a pity."

Kallie's nose twitched. Then, she kneed him in the groin, and Graeson folded over as he groaned out in pain. Men's armor always seemed to keep their most fragile parts exposed. Still, he recovered quicker than she would have liked. She acted fast, swinging her blade. Once, twice, three times.

Graeson slipped her attack each time, ducking and weaving around every strike. On the fourth swing, Graeson dropped low, and Kallie fell flat onto her back, tripping over his leg. The room spun, and the dagger was knocked out of her hand.

Her vision was slow to stabilize, but before he could put his body weight over her, she bent her legs inwards and locked them around his neck, choking him.

A vein in Graeson's forehead pulsed as he used his hand to pry her legs apart. She pulled him as close as the dress permitted and punched him in the face. He jolted back.

Graeson cracked his jaw back into place and smirked. "There she is."

Kallie rolled over and snatched up her dagger. She stood, readying herself. She took in a deep breath and then—

Panic. Smoke filled her lungs. Her legs grew weak. Her vision became blurry. Her head became lighter.

Beyond Graeson, golden brown eyes stared at her.

She gasped. "Fynn?"

She blinked, and Fynn morphed into Terin. Terin's mouth moved, but she didn't hear what he said.

Kallie tried to remain standing, tried to fight the sweet music of Terin's gift, but her mind became heavy. Her limbs grew weak. She was too late, too slow, too weak.

Her father would never forgive her for this.

As she fell back, she reached out, extending a hand, trying to grab onto anyone, anything. But there was nothing there to hold onto. No one to—

"I got you, little mouse."

Her breathing stopped as the air whooshed past her ears. As her vision distorted, one thing was abundantly clear: Graeson hadn't once tried to attack her.

CHAPTER 57
GRAESON

GRAESON SPRINTED FORWARD AND DROVE HIS SHOULDER INTO THE DOOR.

The door shook.

Not enough, he growled.

He threw himself at the door again.

And again.

And again.

The side of his ribcage burned, yet he continued ramming his body into the door.

Wasn't it enough that Kalisandre was fighting him? Didn't he already have more than enough to deal with? Did he really need to be fighting with himself on top of that?

Despite the god's desire for Kalisandre, the god did not take well to someone fighting back. Each time Kalisandre came at him, it took everything Graeson had to fight against the god's control, to force his body to dodge instead of bite back.

The hinges on the metal cage were bending, weakening.

What are you doing? the god shouted at him.

What I should have done days ago, Graeson said as he sprinted forward one final time.

THE CROWN'S SHADOW

G**RAESON FELL TO HIS KNEES**, catching Kalisandre in his arms before she hit the ground. Everything came rushing over him as if he had come up for air after having been submerged underwater for a dangerous amount of time. All the emotions he had blocked out came crashing into him in a torrent.

Kalisandre lay in his arms, the mark of Terin's ability softening her expression as she fell into a deep sleep. Graeson's hand hovered over the red scratches that marked her skin. Pieces of glass protruded out of her skin. Her dress was torn, covered in freckles of blood. He brushed her hair back from her face, cradling her head. The makeup around her neck had rubbed off, making the bruises more prominent. As he stared at the discolored skin, warmth spread across his hand. His brows furrowed, and he shifted. He peeled his hand away from her head, and his breath caught in his throat as he stared at the blood covering his shaking palm.

When Sylvia had dropped the smoke bombs from the roof, Kalisandre had been knocked down onto the ground. She must have landed on something and nicked her head. At least Graeson hoped it was only a knick. Since Terin had knocked Kalisandre unconscious, Graeson couldn't be sure.

He snatched the ripped fabric from her dress and tied it around her head. It wasn't perfect, but it would do for now. He brushed away a strand of hair that had fallen in front of Kalisandre's face, and her features softened. Or maybe he imagined it.

Guilt coated the inside of his stomach. He hated that they had to do it this way, that they had to kidnap her against her will yet again to save her. But there was no other way to free her from Domitius' hold.

All Kalisandre wanted was a choice, but how was Graeson supposed to leave her here when Domitius was manipulating her? Kalisandre's choice had been stripped away from her years ago. None of the decisions Kalisandre had thought she made in the name of justice had been wholly hers, for Domitius had been pulling the strings all along. He had shaped her, morphed her, manipulated her into something she wasn't until she became completely unrecognizable.

When Kalisandre woke up, she would hate Graeson, but it was a price he was willing to pay to free her mind and give her back her agency.

The bullheaded king couldn't even take his supposed daughter with him when he disappeared as the ceiling shattered. Domitius had vanished and abandoned her. He didn't care about her. He only cared about what he stood to gain.

It was clear that the man knew when he was losing the battle. And if he wanted to win the war, Domitius had to run. So he did.

He was not a bull but a cockroach, doing whatever he could to survive.

Terin's hand fell on Graeson's shoulder and squeezed. "Graeson, we need to find Armen and Moris and get out of here. I saw Dani and the others followed after Domitius."

Graeson nodded and picked up Kalisandre, scanning the room as he stood. Chaos continued to rain around him. The flames rose higher, dividing the dais from the rest of the crowd. Sylvia had gotten carried away. He should have listened to their warning that the smoke, once alive, was bound to get out of their control. Sylvia had crafted some device, a bomb of sorts. When the smoke seeped through the doors, those sitting in the pew had released the bombs Sylvia had given them.

They hadn't accounted for the torches, though. And once the chemicals in the bombs interacted with the flames of the torches, the air became thick, the fire wild.

The god had known the risk when he saw the torches ignite, but the god had too much faith in his ability. He knew he would get out alive. But the people? To the god, they were a needed sacrifice. Graeson, however, would not sacrifice his own people.

He squinted into the smoke.

"There!" Graeson said before running forward with Kalisandre clutched against his chest.

All around him, people screamed, shouting at each other, at nothing, at the thick smoke and flames filling the room. The Frenzian guards were piled against the door as they tried to force it open. Behind them, babies cried in their mothers' arms as fear filled the room. Children held onto their father's legs, trying not to get trampled as other, more careless guests ran forward.

On the other side of the dais, Armen and Moris struggled against a flurry of guards. A circle of bodies stood paralyzed as Moris held out his arms. Moris, Graeson knew, could only keep so many people under his paralysis for so long. Moris' face was already paling. The well inside him was emptying.

Graeson picked up his pace, charging forward, but he was so fixed on Armen and Moris that he didn't see the man before he ran into him.

The man groaned. "Either my brother has neglected his duties as captain, or you are not where you belong, soldier."

Graeson skirted to a stop as the King of Frenzia stood before him. His gold crown sat crooked on his head. Rian, having abandoned his guards at the door, dropped his gaze to the woman draped over Graeson's arms. "Give me Kalisandre, soldier."

But Kalisandre wasn't Rian's to take. The vows were incomplete. Kalisandre would never be the queen Rian wanted, the one who stayed in the shadows. She was born to bring the shadows to life.

"That was an order, soldier." Rian's fingers flexed over the hilt of his sword.

This man thought he could command me?

Graeson didn't know if the thought belonged to him or the god, but either way, Graeson couldn't help but laugh.

His attention flicked to Moris and Armen. They would need to hold out a little longer.

"That's where you are mistaken," Graeson said, handing Kalisandre to Terin. "No king commands me."

Rian's knuckles turned white, his face reddening as people nearby turned to look at the soldier who disobeyed the king's order. But Rian was not Graeson's king.

Graeson drew his sword, and with a swift turn, he swung. "Go!" Graeson shouted, and Terin ran.

Blades collided.

When Rian pushed back, Graeson spun, thrusting the king's sword back and away from him.

Metal clashed against metal. Nearby, people screamed, and the smoke continued to filter in through the cracks.

When the king breathed, he wheezed, his throat raw from the smoke. Graeson had seen Rian run off to pry the doors open, but instead of making any progress, he only weakened his body.

Graeson struck, hard and fast, the blade swiping through the air.

Rian's stance wavered, his lungs betraying him as he keeled over, coughing.

Graeson did not hesitate. When their blades met again, Graeson kicked Rian in the chest. The king flew back into the crowd with a grunt.

His crown fell from his head, and his hand flew to his side as he hissed out in pain. When he peeled his hand up, blood stained it.

"Brother, we need to get you to a healer."

At the sound of Sebastian's voice, the blood in Graeson's veins turned into an icy river. Rage colored his vision as he imagined Sebastian's hands on Kalisandre, the fear perspiring across her skin, the helplessness in her water-stained eyes.

Graeson took a step forward, his knuckles blanching as his grip tightened around the hilt of his sword.

"Sebastian," Rian grabbed his brother's wrist, "Kallie . . . they have her. *Please*," he begged.

Before Sebastian could get up, Graeson ran.

CHAPTER 58
GRAESON

Graeson pushed past the people in the crowd, shrugging them as they shoved him. His sight was locked onto the woman laying unconscious on the floor.

Terin had since joined the fight, assisting Armen and Moris as they fought off the Frenzians. The three men fought in front of Kalisandre, providing a protective circle around her. But Graeson didn't know if it would be enough to stop the rush of guards.

This is your fault, the god spat. *She would not be in danger if you didn't hand her to him.*

Graeson gritted his teeth. Part of him believed the god. He had vowed the night of the fire that he would never leave Kalisandre again. But he had already made his choice, and he couldn't go back on it now.

With each step, Graeson's heart beat faster in his chest. He battled through the sea of people rushing toward the main door, past the flames. Over the crowd, Graeson could see Armen continue to strike down the Frenzian guards, but the enemy's reinforcements were coming too fast.

Shouts echoed off the walls.

He thought there was the faint sound of wood cracking as guards continued to pound against the door. It was faintly there, in the back of his mind, but Graeson was only vaguely aware of everything happening around him.

Then a trio of Frenzian soldiers intercepted Graeson, forcing him to a stop. Graeson didn't give them a chance to raise their blades.

One quick slice. One quick flick of his sword was all it took for one soldier to fall and for Graeson to jump over his shaking body and strike down the other two.

As Sebastian crept up on Graeson's heels, shouting at anyone who would listen to stop him, Graeson unleashed his wrath. The god's rage slipped out, and Graeson's blade met the hearts of anyone who stepped in his way.

He told Kalisandre once that he would not be merciful if someone tried to take her away from him again. He had not been exaggerating. But despite the number of soldiers he knocked out along the way, more followed.

His rage fueled him, empowered him. With their goals aligned, Graeson welcomed the god's assistance as a trail of bodies followed in his wake. Red seeped into the edges of his vision, but Graeson did not fear the god's anger. He embraced it.

Graeson broke through the crowd. With a breath, he lined up his targets. When he exhaled, two daggers flew through the air. He didn't wait for his targets to crumble to the ground as he knew they would. Finding his next victim, he thrust his sword through the man's back. Blood spurted from the man's mouth, and his body fell to the ground alongside his comrades.

Pulling his sword free from the Frenzian's body, Graeson grabbed the man's weapon. He flipped the blades in his hands. They weren't his scimitars, but they would do.

Graeson drove a sword through the next Frenzian with a grunt, the god's rage propelling his blade forward. It was as if Graeson and the god had reached a symbiosis. When he swiped the blade through the air and fought to reach Kalisandre, his body worked in tandem with his mind. There was no fighting, no snide remarks from the god, nothing but pure euphoria.

When Graeson finally joined the others on the dais, Graeson could have sworn he saw relief flicker in Armen's gaze. But the glimmer of relief vanished as Sebastian pounced.

"Go help Terin!" Graeson spat and didn't bother waiting to see if Armen, who had moved closer, listened. He spun and kicked Sebastian in the chest, forcing him back.

"Gray, you need to go! Get her and the prince out of here!" Moris shouted over the chaos, his words clipped.

Sebastian swung his sword, cutting off Graeson's response. The hunger for blood was a storm in Sebastian's demonic stare as he sliced the air with his blade. Graeson dodged the attack.

Then as a Frenzian aimed for Armen's head, Graeson pulled Armen back and drove his blade through the Frenzian's ribcage.

"Are you crazy?" Graeson hissed as he blocked Sebastian's next strike. Someone's blade clashed against his armor.

"No—yes," Moris said with a groan on the other side of Terin. "It doesn't matter! *They* are what matter right now. Armen and I can hold them off."

Sebastian delivered a low blow, forcing Graeson to jump. All around him, metal clanged metal as the four of them fought off the Frenzians.

He stumbled against Armen, and Armen leaned his back against Graeson, throwing his stance off. He shoved Armen back with a growl and braced his sword against Sebastian's.

When Graeson found an opening and thrust his sword forward, a soldier dove, pushing Sebastian out of the way. Graeson's blade bounced off the soldier's armor. Growling, Graeson snatched the

Frenzian by the collar, yanking him back to his chest. With one movement, Graeson sliced his blade across his neck.

"Graeson!" A shout from above cut through the noise.

Dropping the soldier's body, Graeson spared a look up, and Sylvia waved frantically at him through the broken glass, then pointed. Graeson followed their direction as he struck another soldier down. The fire had spread, and it now crawled up the walls.

They were running out of time.

Sebastian stared wide-eyed, his gaze bouncing between the dead bodies on the ground and the fire spreading.

Then, a crash sounded, and the iron door fell. A cloud of heavy black smoke billowed into the temple as the familiar stench of the Frenzians' foreign weapon filled the air. Momentarily paralyzed, the Frenzians and the Pontians watched as the crowd stormed through the new opening, pushing past each other, climbing over each other. It didn't matter if it was a woman, an elder, or a child—the people were ravaged, knocking down whoever lay in their path of survival. The sea of bodies only forced the opening closed again, blocking it.

Sebastian's free hand fell to his side, where a golden crown hung from his belt. "Kill them!" Sebastian ordered.

The guards charged forward, and Sebastian and Armen got lost in the crowd as the temple became a slaughterhouse once more.

Graeson and the god worked in tandem as Graeson swiped his blades and knocked the soldiers down one by one as Moris paralyzed them. But no matter how many men they slew, more followed.

Graeson drove his sword through the Frenzian before him, then twisted the blade. He felt the soldier's life leave him as he held onto him by the shoulder.

"Go, Armen and I—" Moris words were cut off. "That fucking coward!"

Graeson looked toward the crowd. Pushing past the crowd of

guards and using his sword to shield himself, Armen ran toward the door, abandoning them.

Sweat dripped down Moris' forehead. "It'll take some time for the ones unconscious to wake. I can hold them off."

"There are too many," Graeson spat back.

Moris shook his head.

"But—"

"I can't hold them for much longer!" Terin shouted from behind Graeson. "Not without releasing my hold on Kallie."

Moris's hair was soaked, his face was red, but he continued to hold on. "I saw Dani slip behind the tapestry behind the dais. She's gone after him."

Graeson glanced at his friend. Terin's fists drove into the ground as sweat dripped from his face. He was losing the fight. His strength was waning.

"This is bigger than me, Gray," Moris said, his voice strained. "Go."

If he were Fynn, he wouldn't abandon his people. Graeson, however, wasn't a prince. He was a monster.

Graeson swallowed and nodded. He hurried to Kalisandre, throwing her over his shoulder. "Can you walk, Ter?"

"I'll manage," Terin said as he stood, his legs trembling beneath his weight.

"Go!" Moris shouted.

Without delaying the inevitable any further, Graeson put an arm beneath Terin's armpit and rushed forward. They slipped behind the swarm of guests much quicker than before as the people clawed their way through the main exit.

Reaching the wall, Graeson lifted the corner of the tapestry, ushering Terin forward. As Terin pushed through the hidden door, Graeson took one last glance back.

The soldiers Terin had rendered unconscious were slowly rising, Terin's hold on them now waning. Moris' body swayed.

A soldier's hand twitched. A soldier broke free from Moris' paralysis. Then another.

Snatching his swords from his side, Moris released his hold on the men. As they came forward, he blocked their strikes. Switching back and forth between paralyzing his opponents and slicing them down at an unparalleled speed, Moris was depleting his strength rapidly.

As a soldier came from behind, Graeson shouted to warn Moris as the soldier moved, but he was too far away. The Frenzian ran his blade through Moris' back. Blood spilled from his mouth, and he folded over, his hand grabbing onto the blade. As Moris' knees hit the ground, all the Frenzian soldiers stirred back into action and stormed forward.

"Gray! We have to go!" Terin shouted from the hidden hallway. Sweat dripped down his face, and his olive skin drained of its warm hue.

There was no helping Moris, Graeson knew that. This was how he wanted to go—fighting for his kingdom, for his people, for the future. Graeson would not let his death be in vain.

And he would find Armen and make him regret abandoning them.

Screams echoed in the hidden hallway.

He knew those screams.

This time, though, the screams were not consumed by grief or denial; instead, they were drenched in pain, anger, and rage. Dani had found the source of her revenge.

CHAPTER 59
KALLIE

A COMFORTING WARMTH BLANKETED KALLIE AS THE SUN'S HEAT POUNDED *down on her, hugging her. She wiggled her fingers, and coarse sand rubbed against her palms. Burying the tips of her fingers in it, Kallie let herself fall into the sand. When she inhaled, she did not choke on smoke. Instead, moss and bergamot lingered in the air as rushing water filled Kallie's ears. Gone were the screams, the shattering glass, the pounding feet.*

The last thing she remembered was the smoke and screams filling the temple. She didn't know how she got here—wherever here *was. She didn't care. All she cared about was—*

Kallie gasped as the faint note of lavender wafted toward her.

Father.

Her eyes sprung open, and the sun blared into them, blinding her vision. She tried to get up, but her body ached, her head spun, and she sunk back into the ground. She had to find him. She needed to know if he was safe, if he was all right. She needed to—

"Kalisandre," a gentle, melodic voice said.

That voice . . . it was familiar, but there was a strange tone to it. She raised a hand, shielding her eyes from the sun. As her vision adjusted, she realized the color of the sky wasn't quite right. Something was . . . off. It was too perfect, too bright, too blue.

"Kallie."

She forced herself up and onto her elbows. When she spotted the ghost before her, her heart skipped. "Fynn? But you're—"

"Dead?"

The smirk on Fynn's face was filled with all the boyish charm he had possessed in real life that Kallie questioned if he truly had died on that ship. In this version, however, Fynn's eyes sparkled a little brighter, a little more golden. His chestnut brown waves were too soft, too smooth.

"Always the observant one, sister," *he said with a wink.*

She stared at him, unsure what to do or what to say. "Why—how are you here?"

"Which is it?" *Fynn asked, extending a hand.*

Blinking, Kallie grabbed it, and he pulled her up.

"What?" *she asked.*

The wind breezed by, and the petrichor tickled her nose and whispered in her ear. Kallie, however, did not want to hear what the wind had to say. Because despite the tranquility that surrounded her, her heart was tearing itself apart.

Fynn quirked a brow. "Do you wish to know *why* or *how* I am here? Because those are two vastly different questions."

"I—" *Kallie stumbled. She couldn't formulate the proper words, for she was still shocked that Fynn was here. Not covered in blood, not screaming or stabbing her in the heart. How many nightmares had she had where he had threatened to push a dagger through her chest? How many nightmares had she had where she had to watch him die over and over again?*

But this . . . this wasn't one of those nightmares. The colors were more vibrant, and the air was too rich. In her nightmares, her heart pounded against her chest, and her insides screamed at her. But right now? Her heart beat at a chaotic rhythm for an entirely different reason.

Although she supposed there was still time for this dream to go sideways, too. A dagger could still end up in her heart.

Fynn cocked a brow, and Kallie blushed. Could he hear her thoughts even now? As if to answer, Fynn chuckled.

Kallie squinted at him and their surroundings. The Whispering Springs sat behind Fynn. It was all so reminiscent of a dream she had once months ago. A dream she could barely remember, but the feeling of it was the same. However, in that dream, the man who had greeted her was faceless. She recalled having that dream when she was on the ship to Pontia after she had let—

Kallie gasped. "Terin—he's doing this, isn't he?"

Fynn nodded with a small smile. "Our brother has always been too humble about his gift. When asked, he tells people that he can force people unconscious."

"But that's not the only thing he can do, is it?" Kallie asked, even though she already knew the answer.

Fynn sighed and turned toward the waterfall. The water was crystal clear, and there were no clouds in sight.

"The mind is a strange place, Kalisandre. We do not know everything about it or why certain things are possible. And dreams?" he huffed. "Dreams are even more confusing. Terin's ability extends far beyond knocking his victims out cold. He can manipulate dreams. Once he has a hold of someone's mind, he can create imaginary scenes or make them recall different memories as they sleep."

Kallie's brows furrowed. "Is that why . . . ?"

Fynn looked at her from the corner of his eyes with a knowing glance. "Is that why you've been having such vivid dreams lately?"

Kallie nodded.

"Yes, it is. And if I had to guess, knowing my brother and our friend, those dreams tended to be focused around Graeson?"

Kallie's mouth fell open. Against her will, a blush rose to her cheeks, and Fynn chuckled.

Recalling one dream in particular, Kallie gasped. "Wait. Can Terin see the dreams?"

"While I don't think that is the most pressing matter to discuss—no, not always." Fynn scratched the back of his head. "That would be exhausting, wouldn't it? If he had to be awake in our world and see the dreams of his victims? Can you imagine the headaches and confusion that would transpire?"

Kallie sighed in relief, and the embarrassment slowly faded from her complexion.

Fynn rubbed his finger against the scruff on his chin. "I suppose it would explain why he was always so tired. For a man who can force others to sleep, he sure does have problems sleeping himself." *Fynn arched a brow.* "What is it that you wished he didn't see?"

The heat returned to her cheeks. Desperate to change the subject, Kallie cleared her throat and asked, "Are you just a figment of Terin's imagination?"

"Not quite. It's more complicated than that, but I don't have much time. In simple terms, the wall between the dead and the living is thinner in the dreamscape, so Terin has created a small opening to connect us."

Kallie's heart rattled at the new information. "Does Dani know?"

"No, she doesn't, and I hope she never does."

"Why? I'm sure she misses you," *Kallie said, brows knitting together. If Terin could create a connection between the living and dead, shouldn't Fynn be happy that he would still be able to see his wife? They could still be together.*

"That's exactly why I never wish for her to know." *Fynn stared at the glistening lake, the amusement long gone from his face. As the sun's rays bounced off the water, sparkles glided across the surface. He folded his hands behind his back.* "I do not wish for Dani to live in the past. I care about her too much to have her waste her life away in dreams. She deserves to live. She deserves to love again."

"Then why—" *Kallie swallowed the words, afraid of the answer.*

Fynn looked at her and smiled, but the twitch of his lips was sad, his countenance full of sorrow. "I came today because of you—because you need to listen to what I have to say. Because if you do not, you will not be able to live your life the way you're meant to either."

A cold breeze swept by, and Kallie shivered. She rubbed her shoulders, but it did little to soothe the chill crawling up her skin. "What is it?"

Fynn dug a hand through his waves, his gaze wary.

"Fynn?"

He took a step forward. "You need to listen to me carefully, Kalisandre." *He gripped her arms. Her skin pinched beneath his hold, and fear crept up her throat.* "Your life depends on it."

CHAPTER 60
GRAESON

With a metal torch, they locked the door. It wouldn't hold the Frenzians off forever, but it would at least slow them down.

The small hallway behind the tapestry split off into two directions: one way veered to the right, which, by Graeson's guess, would lead them to the priest's back room and hopefully an alternative exit; the second led down into a dark, musty hallway.

Terin picked up a black feather that had been in Ellie's hair. He started to go down the path on the right, the safe-looking option, but then Dani screamed.

They both stared at the path that led down the narrow steps. The walls were wet with moisture, stinking of mildew and iron.

Graeson took a deep breath. There was only one path for him to go down. And, of course, it was the narrow one.

"You go that way, I'll go this way," he said.

"No." Terin shook his head. "Every time we have separated, bad things have happened. Ellie, Medenia, and Emmett must have escaped that way. They know where to go. We will find them. Right now, we need to stick together."

Graeson's grip on Kalisandre tightened. Her breathing had

thankfully returned to normal, but the wrapping around her head was already stained red. "But—"

Terin stepped forward. "No buts. If I take Kalisandre, you'll be distracted worrying about her well-being. You should know that better than anyone. The best option—" Terin shook his head. "No, the *only* option is for us to go with you."

Graeson was about to fight him, but another scream echoed from the hallway beneath the temple. Dani needed him. As fierce as a warrior as Dani was, Domitius had escaped them once before.

"Fine." Graeson gritted out at last. Maneuvering Kalisandre to lay over his shoulder, he hurried down the steps. "But at the first sign of trouble, you take her and run. We cannot lose either of you. Esmeray would have my head if anything happened to one of you."

Their feet clapped against the floor. The air was musty and cold as they descended the steps, but Graeson could not let himself focus on the narrow path. He swallowed the bile rising in his throat.

"She just might when we return," Terin mumbled.

Graeson huffed. "But at least both of her children will be safe."

She cannot lose another, which is what Graeson actually thought but refused to say aloud.

Graeson jogged down the steps, almost sideways, as he shuffled down two at a time. He focused on the small flame that flickered at the bottom of the stairs. If Domitius was down here, there was another way out. He was not stuck down here.

He kept his mind off the small space, the closed-in walls. Instead, he allowed the darkness to sweep in as they followed Dani's screams down the steps. Their footsteps echoed, bouncing off the empty stone walls.

When they reached the base of the steps, there was one straight hallway, and the torches were few and far between. Patches of darkness filled the space. Where the walls met the rocky ceiling, thick cobwebs existed. A few of them hung in the hall as if someone had rushed by them.

Behind Graeson, Terin shuffled, his hand scraping the wall.

"Terin, if you need to—"

"No," Terin said, interrupting. "There's no going back now, only forward."

Biting down on his tongue, Graeson only nodded.

As they continued their trek through the tunnel beneath the temple, the sound of clashing metal bounced off the walls. Grunts and shouts darted down the hallway. He couldn't tell if they were getting closer or falling behind. Sometimes, it sounded as if Dani were hundreds of yards away. Other times, it seemed as if Dani was right beside him. But then, when Graeson turned, all he saw was solid stone.

They quickened their pace.

Until, that is, they saw the cells built into the walls.

The first cells were empty. Just old, untouched dirt inside. Then, the bones started to appear. At first, Graeson couldn't identify them in the surrounding darkness. But when one of the torches illuminated one of the cells, Graeson spotted a deer skull with antlers still attached in one of the cell's corners. Bones of other animals appeared as well. Having observed Dani countless times when she would track animals through the woods, Graeson quickly identified the other bones belonging to wolves, alligators, and eagles.

"What is this place?" Terin whispered behind him.

"A dungeon?" Graeson suggested.

"But why the animal bones?" Terin whispered in the darkness. "If it were human bones, that would make sense. But these have all been —" Terin stopped talking, crouching at one of the cells, and Graeson peered over him.

A human skeleton lay slumped against the wall. They scanned the cell, trying to find anything to help explain what they were seeing. Was this Frenzia's prison? If so, why was it under the temple?

A growl further up the path had both men straightening.

Terin looked up, face pale. "What in the god's breath is *that?*"

The hissing snaked down the hall, and their steps became more hesitant as they traversed it. Graeson couldn't see it in the darkness, but he could hear the inhuman breathing that was unlike any animal he had heard before.

An animal charged at the cell, and Terin fell to the ground, shuffling back and cursing. Its teeth gnawed on the metal, spit spewing out as it growled. It scratched and clawed at the iron railings.

Graeson's arms tightened around Kalisandre, pressing her body closer to his. "Are you all right, Ter?"

Terin nodded. "Let's just find Dani and get out of here."

Graeson nodded. They hurried down the hallway. Dozens of questions ran through Graeson's mind, but he would not find any answers here. Animals of all sorts thrashed at the cells as they passed. Limbs slipped through the iron bars as the animals tried to dig their claws into Graeson and Terin. The animals were rabid, hungry, and angry. It pained Graeson to leave them that way, but what choice did he have? If he freed them, the feral animals, with their dilated pupils and rancid breath, would attack. They had no choice but to continue forward.

The shouts were becoming fewer and farther between.

Then, a torch lit one of the cages. And Graeson inhaled, jerking to a stop again. A creature Graeson had never seen before was slumped against the back wall of its cage. It was skeletal, its bone nearly popping out of its thin, translucent skin. It reminded him of the dragon-wolf they had seen in the forest, but this creature had neither fur nor muscle. As Graeson approached, it barely could even lift its head.

Graeson's heart hurt. He felt helpless. He wished he could release it or put it out of its misery. He had no keys, no way to unlock the cell. When he scanned the bars, he couldn't even find where the lock was. He didn't even have a bow and arrow, only his sword and Kalisandre's dagger. And if he missed or the blade didn't pierce deep enough, the animal would only be worse off.

"They're experimenting on animals, Ter."

"Not just on animals."

"What do you—" Graeson stopped short, the words escaping him as he turned around and stared at a human child. Or whatever was left of the young boy whom the Frenzians had mutilated.

The boy was folded over in the corner of the cage. Scales crept up his neck. His fingers and toes had been morphed into claws. His ears were pointed and flat against his head. It was a vision from a child's nightmare; the creatures that crept into the shadows of the darkest parts of a child's imagination come to life.

The child groaned. He peeked over his arm, and a dark red eye landed on Graeson. In a flash, the child was at the front of the cage, with large wings spanning from his back as his hands flew past the bars.

Graeson scurried back, bumping into Terin.

"Shit," Terin spat.

The child thrashed and thrashed. Pain sparking in his blood-red eyes. Pain and something else.

Hunger.

Desperation.

Graeson sat Kalisandre on the ground away from the cell and grabbed his sword. Then, with a quick prayer to the gods asking for forgiveness, he grabbed the child's hands in one of his. The child tried to squeeze his head through the space between the iron bars.

Graeson thrust his sword into the child's chest, and the child released a deadly screech. An inhuman, piercing sound echoed in the stone hallway.

Graeson released the child, and he slumped against the iron bars, limp and lifeless.

With a pain throbbing in his chest, Graeson picked up Kalisandre. "Let's get Dani and get out of here."

"You don't have to tell me twice," Terin whispered.

The two of them ran down the hall, ignoring the rattling noises in the cells they passed. They had wasted enough time. In a full sprint, Graeson rounded the corner at the end of the hall and skidded to a stop with a sharp inhale.

"Fuck, Gray," Terin said as he ran into Graeson. "Give a guy a—warning." The last word landed in a near whisper as the two men took in the sight before them.

Domitius thrust his blade forward as Dani hunched over, sweat dripping from her face. Graeson didn't think. He didn't worry if he got hurt. He transferred Kalisandre to Terin and then dove.

CHAPTER 61
GRAESON

THE BLADE KISSED GRAESON'S ARMOR AS HE GRABBED DANI AND shoved her out of the way.

Dani landed on her side with a thump. Blood oozed from a deep cut on her left bicep. The bottom of her dress had been slashed, a jagged piece of fabric now loosely hanging from the bottom as if she had narrowly missed a jab at the ankles.

"Are you all right?" Graeson asked, attempting to pull her arm away to inspect the wound.

"I'm fine," she growled, snatching her arm.

There was no blood or wound Graeson could see, yet her hand trembled as it lay atop her stomach. His lips parted, the question on his tongue.

Dani shook her head and squeezed her eyes shut, pushing a tear out. "I'm *fine*," she repeated.

Graeson pursed his lips, but he kept the question unspoken.

"Gray," Terin whispered beside him.

When Graeson looked up, he found Domitius holding a blade against a woman's throat. In Graeson's haste, he hadn't even seen the petite blonde handmaiden standing there, but now he couldn't help but stare at Myra. She stood paralyzed with water filling her eyes.

Graeson shifted, readying to strike. But when Domitius tightened his grip around his sword and nicked the woman's throat, drawing blood, Graeson froze.

"Ah, not so fast. Move, and she dies," Domitius threatened, and the color rushed from Myra's face.

What are you doing? the god yelled. *Do not listen to him. She is nothing.*

She is an innocent woman, Graeson said back.

An innocent woman? The god laughed. *As if that holds any meaning. How many men did you just kill? How many of those soldiers were just following orders?*

Graeson's lip curled. The rising anger spread throughout his body like an icy torrent.

If I kill her, Kalisandre will never forgive me.

The god grew silent at that, for they both knew how much Kalisandre cared about her handmaiden. She was the one constant in Kalisandre's life. If Graeson killed her, she would be devastated. There would be no turning back after that.

Domitius cocked his head to the side. "And which one would you be? Surely not the one who knocks people unconscious, because if that was the case . . ." He chuckled, waving the blade in the air. "I would already be on the floor, wouldn't I?" Domitius studied Terin, who held Kalisandre tightly to his chest. Domitius smirked. "No, that would be *you*. The brother, right? You must take after your father. A pity, really. He always seemed to be more brawn than brain, in my opinion."

"Do not talk about my father," Terin spat.

"Ah, hit a soft spot, did I?" Domitius' eyes lit with malice. "I suppose I'm standing here still because you're drained, correct? Weak. All of you." Disgust twisted his face.

Graeson's hands fisted into tight balls at his side, his nails biting into his flesh.

"Our little Kalisandre here told me *all* about you. The quiet one, the timid one. Your brother . . . now he's the fighter." He tilted his head. "Oh, my apologies. Did I say *is*? I meant *was*. So much for his ability to read minds proving to be of any use."

"You fucking—" Dani jerked forward, snarling.

"Dani! Don't." Graeson said as he pulled Dani back, his arms wrapping around her and locking her in place.

Domitius shook his head as he drew the blade across the woman's throat, and a mangled sob escaped Myra's lips. "What is it about women who don't *listen*? Honestly, it's exhausting."

Then Myra screamed.

The shriek echoed in the hall, bouncing off the walls as Domitius sliced her arm. Ravenous screeches from the animals in the cells mixed with Myra's cry.

"You hear that? Now, *that* is what happens when you listen. Progress." Domitius smiled and then jerked Myra against him. "Next time, the blade goes through her heart."

Domitius squeezed Myra's face, and she stifled her screams. Her body shook as the terror consumed her. Tears streamed down her face, but she didn't make another sound.

Enough, the god roared. *You let this man command you?*

No one commands me, Graeson said.

Then prove it.

"Terin, Dani, get out of here," Graeson ordered.

"I don't think so," Domitius said as he lifted a finger off the hilt and wiggled it in the air.

They all froze.

"What did I say? One move, and she dies," Domitius snarled, tightening his hold around Myra. He pressed the bloody dagger against the handmaiden's throat, smearing the blood across her flesh.

"Kill her then. What is she to us?" Graeson asked, bluffing. Maybe if he could get Domitius talking, he could find an opening. Dani's throwing knife was within reach. If Myra shifted over...

Domitius smirked, cocking a brow. "You might not care, but *she* would." Domitius' gaze fell upon Kalisandre, and Graeson clenched his teeth.

"If the girl is remotely important to Kalisandre, you won't kill her."

"And why wouldn't I?" Domitius asked.

"Because Kalisandre matters to you. If you kill her handmaiden, Kalisandre will hate you."

Domitius shrugs. "A means to an end."

"You don't mean that." Graeson scoffed. "You need her."

Domitius huffed, his face contorting into feigned indifference, and it was an expression that Graeson had seen Kalisandre wear one too many times.

With a snide chuckle, Domitius said, "I don't *need* her. I already *have* her. Take Kalisandre if you wish, but a word of advice? Don't get too comfortable. She *will* crawl back to me."

"She won't," Graeson spat. "Not this time."

Domitius clicked his tongue. "Oh, don't tell me, you think you can *save* her?"

Graeson fell silent.

Domitius laughed, his eyes wild. The careful mask of the perfect king disintegrating, and in its place was that of the bull-headed king. "Son, she's not yours to save."

"She's not *yours* either. Kalisandre belongs to no one." Graeson slowly reached for the blade beside him.

"Oh, but that is where you are wrong." Domitius tightened his hold around Myra. "Isn't that right?"

Graeson froze. The back of Graeson's neck prickled as Myra stared at him.

Terin, voice weak, asked, "What does Myra have to do with any of this?"

Then, Graeson felt something rush over his mind as if someone was prodding it, poking it. Knocking on its door. He searched for the source.

Domitius wore a victorious smile on his face. Graeson's brows drew together in question. Esmeray never mentioned Domitius having a gift, but what other explanation was there? That prodding sensation only happened when someone tried to infiltrate Graeson's mind. Was that how he was controlling Kalisandre? If he killed Domitius, then Kalisandre would be free.

"Should I tell him, or do you want to?" Domitius asked, shaking Myra.

Myra released a strangled weep. Her chest rose in quick, rapid breaths as she looked at each of them. Her lips parted, but the handmaiden said nothing.

Domitius shook his head, and a menacing laughter poured from his lips. "Oh. You are all so naive, just like her." He looked at Kalisandre and clicked his tongue. Domitius grabbed Myra by the chin, his fingers indenting into her flesh. "*She* is the real reason your prince is dead."

"Myra, what is he talking about?" Terin asked, his voice shaking.

When Myra opened her eyes and peered at Terin, regret filled her watery gaze.

Pressing his cheek against Myra's, he whispered, "Should *I* be the one to tell them then about how you betrayed your friend? Should I tell them what you've been doing to our little manipulator?" Domitius rubbed his thumb across her face.

Myra struggled against his hold. He put his lips against her ear, but Graeson couldn't hear the king's words. Whatever it was, Myra stopped struggling. She swallowed, closing her eyes, and a stream of tears rolled down the contours of her soft face.

"You see, Myra here has been playing our little Kalisandre this entire time." He snatched her chin. "Haven't you?"

"Myra wouldn't do that. Kallie trusts her." Terin looked between Graeson and then back to the handmaiden. "Right, Myra?"

But Myra squeezed her lips shut, and her tears spilled, rolling over the king's hand. The cut on her shoulder had stopped bleeding, but now, a long drip of blood covered her arm.

"Awe. Would you look at that? They fell for your tricks, too, didn't they?" Domitius grinned and rubbed his thumb across her chin. "You've done better than I thought you would."

"Myra?" Graeson asked, calling her attention to him.

Myra's hazel eyes bore into him, and her silence was the only answer they needed. For in the silence, she admitted her compliance, and it was a punch to the gut.

Domitius shook her head, his nails digging into her skin. "Come on, Myra. Don't be shy now. Tell them. *Tell* them how you changed her emotions, how you infiltrated her mind, how you have been manipulating the manipulator this entire time."

Myra struggled against the king, but Domitius' hold remained firm.

"You see, the handmaiden is like all of you," Domitius said, pointing the tip of his blade toward Graeson and the others. He flicked his sword in a circle. "She, too, has what you all call *gifts*. Let's see. Kalisandre here can command people, manipulate their very will." Domitius pointed at Terin. "We've already established what you can do. A neat little party trick, I suppose, when you have the strength anyway." Domitius shrugged.

A feral growl vibrated in Graeson's chest, but he didn't move.

"And you," he continued, pointing to Dani, "are the huntress, I assume? Is that really the best the gods could have given you? The ability to find things and people? I suppose it would be handy if you were stranded somewhere. It would have made my life easier once upon a time, but I digress."

Domitius tapped the blade against Myra's cheek as he stared at Graeson. "And then there is you." Domitius tilted his head to the side. "What is your name again? Graeson? No, that's not right." Blood smeared across Myra's cheek as he continued to tap. Then he smiled, his brown eyes darkening. "*Graeson.* According to the handmaiden, Kalisandre has a sweet spot for you. The one she hid from me, the one who has been sneaking around the castle, right?"

Graeson's veins turned ice-cold, his fury a sheet of ice now, vibrating within him.

"It's cute, really. Kalisandre thought she had kept her little infatuation a secret from me. But everything has a way of coming out, and Myra here has helped deal with that little problem."

"Graeson," Dani hissed, squeezing his arm when his fingers found the blade on the floor.

Domitius cackled at the interaction. "But anyway, according to Kalisandre, *you* are somewhat of an enigma. Your mind cannot be read, nor can you be manipulated. A useful gift indeed." He tilted his head to the side, studying Graeson. "You see, some might say I'm a collector of useful things, and you would be a valuable piece in my collection. What do you think, Myra? Shall we bring him back with us? Call it a trade, perhaps? The girl for him? It's only fair."

Fear covered Myra's countenance, and her body went rigid.

"You wouldn't be able to get within three feet of me," Graeson said, his grip tightening around the hilt of the throwing knife despite Dani's warning.

Domitius raised a brow. "No?"

"What's your point?" Dani spat.

Domitius smirked. "Myra here can change emotions, *feelings*. She's had her little hands on Kalisandre's mind—for what? Seven? Ten years? Who knows at this point? Either way, even if you take

Kalisandre, she'll kill you. She'll betray you just like she did last time." Domitius chuckled and arched a boastful brow. "The Kalisandre you all knew once upon a time is long gone."

"No, she's not," Graeson spat.

"You actually think you can free her, don't you?" Domitius laughed. His gaze darkened in challenge. "Go ahead and try. You'll see." Domitius reached inside his jacket and pulled something out, his fingers wrapping around it.

Graeson's fingers twitched.

No! the god shouted.

Graeon's hand froze. *No? You just said her life did not matter! She betrayed Kalisandre. She betrayed all of us. We can end this now.*

I said no, the god hissed. *We do not know how her manipulation works. If the handmaiden dies, Kalisandre could be lost forever.*

But—

No! She must live.

Domitius turned his attention to Terin. "Do say hello to your mother for me, won't you? If you survive the crash, that is."

"The crash?" Terin whispered.

But Graeson was already moving as Domitius shifted. As he reached for Myra, a black iron ball hit the ground, and an explosion erupted, shaking the ground and forcing Graeson onto his back.

Someone screamed as black smoke filled the room and rocks fell, the ceiling crashing down around them. Then, Graeson was knocked out, darkness sweeping over him as everything fell apart around him.

KEEP READING FOR A SNEAK PEEK
OF BOOK THREE IN

OF FIRE AND LIES

CHAPTER 1
MYRA

Myra tried to melt into the wall of the dark, cold room beneath the Ardentolian castle. In the damp cells, the shadows loomed large. Melancholy coated the walls and oozed from the stone, making the air thick with agony and misery.

Since Myra was a child, she had struggled to contain her ability. Many thought their abilities were gifts from the gods, but Myra's could only be described as a curse. Bearing one's own emotions was already a burden enough for many, but to experience the emotions of every person you touched? It was a torment Myra would never wish on anyone.

Humans were not the only emotions she could sense either. Buildings, too, thrust their emotions at her. If Myra was lucky, some buildings had a warm and inviting aura. When she visited homes filled with laughter and love, it was reminiscent of the sun shining down on a field of freshly bloomed daisies in late spring.

Myra was rarely lucky. These days, those kinds of places were few and far between.

The places Myra had to frequent often reeked of death and dread. And this humid dungeon beneath in the Ardentolian castle was the

CHAPTER 1

worst of them all. The air beneath the castle was sticky with agony, torment, and rage. The stone walls were soaked with the cries of the victims who had been tortured in the cell. The ground had been watered with the tears and blood of the dying, so much so that Myra could barely remain standing. The call for death was too strong here, and it tugged on her limbs.

Unlike the emotions of humans or animals, Myra could not manipulate the emotions of the walls or floors. Those emotions were etched in the very stone. Permanent and unbendable. The very infrastructure of a building would have to crumble for the stories melted into the concrete or the memories buried inside the walls to disappear. Even if the building was demolished, there was always the chance that the earth remembered.

An emotion's effect was always worse when Myra's memories were tied to the place. And here, in the dungeons, grief wrapped around Myra's lungs, agony twisted around her limbs, and rage coated her throat.

However, Myra wasn't the one bound to the wall this time. This time, she stood behind the king, her hands trembling, while an unfamiliar woman sat chained to the cement floor.

Myra wondered what the stranger had done to be chained beneath the castle. Although perhaps the better question was *why* Myra was bearing witness to it. This was the first time in years she had been dragged down to the cells, and the last time . . .

Myra swallowed the memory, forcing it back down her throat.

Domitius crouched before the woman. Her black hair hung in thick, grease-coated strands down her face. Her skin was nearly transparent as if she hadn't seen the sun in years. She wore a ragged dress, stained and worn thin with holes throughout the fabric.

Domitius snatched her chin with his hand, jerking her face upward and squeezing her sunken cheeks together. "You said the fates were aligned," he hissed.

CHAPTER 1

Though frail, the woman wrenched her chin from his grip. As lifeless as she may have looked, there was still some fight left in her.

"How many times must I tell you?" The woman pulled at the chains. "The fates change."

"What is the point of having a seer if you cannot tell me the truth? You *said* it would work, that my plans would come to fruition if I had the girl."

Myra's eyes widened in fear. *A seer? But if she's a seer, how did she end up here?*

The woman rolled her eyes, and something about the woman's features felt familiar, but Myra couldn't place them. This room—the memories and feelings that dripped from the walls—clouded her judgment. Here, she always saw the ghosts of her past.

"Time is an illusion. Things shift," the woman hissed. She sank against the wall, exasperated, as if her current circumstance of being chained to a cell was not her primary concern but rather a simple annoyance. "My visions can only be so accurate—as I have told you many times."

Domitius pulled on one side of the chain, the links tightening around the women's limbs. "Then make them more accurate."

Myra forced herself to remain still despite the screaming desire to run away. There was no running from the bull-king, though. She learned that a long time ago.

The woman tipped her chin up, snarling. "It doesn't work like that. My visions are not meant to be forced out as you so often seem to forget, *Kage*."

Domitius pulled at the chain.

"My *King*," she spat.

He tossed the chain onto the ground, and the metal links clattered against the stone floor as he pushed himself up into a standing position. Turning around, he began pacing in the small cell.

CHAPTER 1

His feet wore a line in the dust-covered ground—Myra on one side, the woman on the other.

Myra couldn't help but find the similarities despite the line between them. They were both the king's prisoners. Only the woman wore chains, while Myra did not. However, Myra wondered if it would have been easier to have rotten inside of a cell rather than given a false sense of freedom. Freedom that was frail, fickle, and false. A privilege she knew could be taken from her at any minute. A privilege that had resulted in Myra betraying her best friend.

The choice, however, had never been hers to make. Once Domitius discovered what Myra could do, her path was set.

As Domitius paced back and forth, the woman lifted her head, and her eyes locked onto Myra. She cocked her head to the side. Her eyelids fluttered, her head swayed. Then, she abruptly straightened, and an eerie chill crept over Myra's skin as the corner of the woman's lip twitched.

When she turned her gaze to Domitius, her eyes narrowed. "You still don't get it, do you?"

"Get *what*, woman?"

The woman grinned, her teeth yellowed and rotten. A rancorous sound that made Myra wonder how long the woman had been in Domitius' captivity poured out of her mouth. "You'll never win. The fates may appear to be in your favor one minute, but *they* have one thing that you lack."

Domitius lunged forward, brandishing a blade to her throat. "What could they possibly have that I do not?"

There was that laugh again. Then, a deafening silence filled the room as the woman quirked a brow.

The woman raised her chin as if to dare Domitius to kill her. The king was not that merciful, though.

"Love," she whispered.

Domitius huffed. *"Love?"*

CHAPTER 1

"Mhm."

"How does that have to do with anything? Love is nothing. Love is—"

"*Everything*," the woman spat, interrupting the king. "Why do you think the fates have changed?" When Domitius didn't respond, she continued, "It is because, despite everything that has happened, the Pontians still have love in their hearts for that girl. You have manipulated your false daughter's mind and her emotions countless times, but the one thing you cannot manipulate—the one thing you cannot falsify—is love. You thought making Kalisandre fear love was the answer, but that is far from the truth. It is because Kalisandre craves to love and be loved in return that you will never win. Despite everything you have done, she still has love in her heart for them, for *her*."

Myra pressed her back against the wall, wishing she could disappear as the woman stared at her. But she was stuck in here. The door was locked, and Domitius was the only one with the key.

Domitius looked over his shoulder at Myra, then back at the woman. "What are you talking about?"

"The future is not a straight line, but rather it is like the knotted roots of a tree, and we seers stand at the base of it. There is always more than one path to choose from, and while we can sometimes predict which route a soul will take based on past decisions, the future is never certain. It branches and splits out in different directions. As relationships change, so too do our paths. The fates are ever-changing for this reason. A tangle of choices waiting to be unraveled. You never know what you'll get until you pull, until you tug. Until you *choose*."

"Enough of the riddles. Speak sense, seer," Domitius hissed.

She shook her head. "The handmaiden cares for your false daughter. Up until now, her love for her family has been leading her decisions, but something has changed." The woman paused, her

CHAPTER 1

nearly white eyes staring at Myra thoughtfully. Her lip twitched. "Multiple forces now guide her."

Myra's body grew rigid, and before she knew it, Domitius was pressing the heel of his palm against her throat.

"So, this is your fault!" he shouted, his voice ringing in the cell.

Myra never wanted Kallie to get hurt. Despite betraying her trust since she entered the princess' employment, Myra had grown to care for her. Kallie was troubled, her emotions twisted and torn. But Myra saw what lay beneath the tangled mess. She knew Kallie's heart. Even so, she did not know what the seer meant. As much as Myra hated that Domitius forced her to manipulate Kallie's emotions, she had no choice but to obey.

"I—I don't know—" Myra choked on her words as he squeezed her throat. Her eyes watered as her lungs begged for air. She tried to focus on the king and bite back the fear bubbling to the surface, but her vision was clouding. Black splotches pulsed in her blurry gaze as he tightened his grip.

Anger painted the king's face when he stared down at her. He had lost. He had lost, and the Pontians had won. They had taken Kallie and escaped.

And now Myra was forced to reap the consequences of his failure. She couldn't defend herself. She couldn't explain, for Domitius wasn't here for answers.

He wasn't here for an explanation.

He was here for an outlet for his anger, for a release.

The spots in her vision grew, and before she knew what she was doing, she pulled from the pit of her stomach. She instinctively followed the iridescent string that floated in the air, invisible to all but her. She tugged on it, grabbed it, tried to bend it to her will. She tried to coax it, soothe it. Snuff out the fire that coated its strands. But as she sent the emotion down the string that ran from the fingers

CHAPTER 1

wrapped around her throat to the nerves in his mind, Domitius' nose twitched.

His fingers dropped from her throat, and Myra wheezed, gasping for air.

The oxygen struck her lungs in an icy and painful burst. Sharp and bitter. Before Myra could catch her breath, she was thrown across the room, and the wind was knocked out of her as she hit the wall.

Domitius' mouth was moving, but Myra couldn't make out the words as everything spun around her. The back of her head throbbed. Pain shot down her spine, and her vision pulsed. She couldn't breathe. Her body had gone stiff as pain erupted all over her.

The door creaked open behind the king. Two figures entered the cell, but her vision was still too fuzzy to make them out. One of the figures shoved the other forward, and the second, shorter figure fell to their knees.

Myra inhaled, but her body couldn't process the intake of oxygen. It stopped short, lodging itself in the middle of her throat, choking her.

She tried to move.

She tried to crawl, but her limbs were too weak, and they folded beneath her weight. She slipped, her face smacking against the floor.

Still, she tried.

Even as the tears blurred her vision and drowned her voice. Even as a sharp pain seared through her body, even as a burst of poisonous laughter echoed in the cell, Myra crawled.

She needed to touch him. She needed to make sure he was real. She needed proof that this wasn't an illusion Domitius somehow concocted.

But the man on the ground didn't look at her, his tired gaze fixed on the floor.

Still, Myra reached out to him. "Mynhos?" Myra whispered, the

CHAPTER 1

single word scratching her vocal cords. It was a name she hadn't said aloud in over a decade, a name she called out for in her dreams.

Her brother was alive.

Alive and in front of her.

But *why* was he here?

Her fingers brushed his shoulder, and he flinched.

Domitius stepped forward, blade in hand. "Perhaps you need to be reminded about what you are *truly* fighting for."

The king snatched Mynhos' hand, and her brother at last looked at her with anguish swimming in his hazel eyes. Domitius pressed Mynhos' hand flat against the stone floor.

In his ear, Domitius whispered, "Don't bleed on my floor."

He struck.

And all Myra could hear was her brother's screams echoing in the small, stone room as he bled. Mynhos hurried to bury the severed limb in his clothes as he rushed to fulfill Domitius' command. Myra reached for him, but she was being dragged back by her braid.

She tried to fight it. She tried to wiggle out of Domitius' hold but couldn't.

She couldn't fight him.

She couldn't grab hold of anything.

The door shut behind them, the locks clicking into place. Mynhos' screams rang in her mind on repeat as she was dragged down the hall with tears streaming down her face.

She couldn't save Mynhos' hand, just like she couldn't save her parents all those years ago. Myra had barely even saved herself.

But saving herself had come with a price.

BEFORE THERE WAS TRAGEDY, THERE WAS THE DEAL.

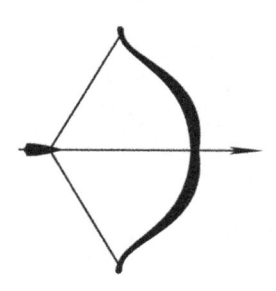

DANI & FYNN'S STORY COMING SOON

Author's Note

Thank you for reading *The Crown's Shadow*, the second book in the Of Fire and Lies series! I hope you enjoyed reading it as much as I did writing it (even if that experience included yelling at Kallie for some of the things she does in this part of her journey).

If you enjoyed this book, please consider leaving a review on Amazon or Goodreads. Reviews are so important to authors and help readers find books that are a good fit for them!

I knew writing a sequel would be challenging, but this story challenged me in more ways than I thought it would. From questioning how morally grey a female character can be without facing "too much" ridicule to the grief the characters experience throughout the story during a time when I, too, was grieving. There were many times when I questioned the route the story was taking. But in the end, I know this is the story that it needed to be.

While an outsider can see the many red flags popping up around her, Kallie cannot. As a result, writing Kallie's chapters became extremely frustrating at times. At her heart, Kallie is a fiery-spirited individual. She is intelligent, cunning, and loyal. However, like many of us, she makes bad choices and ignores things she shouldn't. But when we love someone, we often overlook the red flags that may seem glaringly obvious in retrospect. Especially when they are the people closest to us, like our parents. Suffice to say, Kallie still has much to learn.

All I can say is that Kallie's (and Graeson's) story is not done yet, not even close.

ACKNOWLEDGMENTS

What started as a fun little New Year's Resolution in 2022 has become something much bigger than I could have imagined. While I always wanted to be an author, I thought it was one of those lofty dreams that were nice to have. When I published *The King's Weapon*, I was unsure if I would even find my readership or anyone who understood Kallie and her internal turmoil. But now, this is the second acknowledgments page I have written, and it feels surreal. There are several people to whom I would like to give a special thank you for constantly encouraging and supporting me even when the words fought against me.

First, my husband, Nathan. Your support truly knows no bounds. When I talk to you about my dreams, you push me to dream bigger. When I shy away from celebrating my accomplishments, you shout them out loud enough for both of us. But more than anything, you keep me grounded. I will forever be thankful for your patience when I am in writing or editing mode.

Gabby, thank you for always being willing to read the bad drafts when I need a reader's honest opinion. Your constant positivity and encouragement mean so much to me. Here's to Scotland.

Jess, thank you for your enthusiasm and advice. I am forever grateful to be able to bounce ideas off each other. Seeing you embrace your creativity again has been wonderful to witness. I cannot wait to see where your adventure takes you in the future and continue to cheer you on.

Heather, thank you for your honest reactions and for helping me push Kallie to be the character she needed to be.

Mom and George, thank you for always supporting me and cheering me on. I am so lucky to have been raised by two people whose support is unrelenting.

Thank you to my family, from my siblings to my grandparents to my aunts and uncles to my extended family and in-laws. I honestly did not expect the overwhelming support I have received since publishing *The King's Weapon* from you all. I am so thankful to call you family.

Thank you to my friends who continue to cheer me on from near and far. I am lucky to be surrounded by so many amazing people whose friendship knows no bounds.

Thank you to the entire writing community I found on TikTok and Instagram. Each one of you inspires me every day. Thank you for always lending a helping hand and providing encouragement.

Thank you to my editor, Emma Jane, for continuing to help push my writing.

Thank you to my cover designer, Bianca, for making my visions come to life, yet again.

Lastly, to you, the reader. Thank you for continuing to give this series a chance, even after that brutal death in the first book. Your messages and support bring me so much joy (even when you're yelling at me for the plot twists and cliffhangers. Please don't ever stop!). These stories, which once lived solely in my head, now live in so many of you, too. That is something I will never get over.

With love,
Neena

About the Author

Neena Laskowski lives in Michigan with her husband and their two pets. She earned her master's in Secondary Education and bachelor's in English and Classical Studies from the University of Michigan. When she is not reading or writing about morally grey characters, you can find her camping, painting, or spending time with her family and friends.

For upcoming ARC opportunities and to be among the first to see cover reveals, character art, and more, be sure to join Neena Laskowski's newsletter, found on neenalaskowski.com, or follow Neena on social media.

Made in the USA
Monee, IL
27 December 2023